# THE ROWAN TREE

Manon Jenkins has had a cherished childhood in the sleepy village of Five Saints in the heart of Wales, but when her beloved father dies, she is left homeless and alone. The handsome blacksmith, Morgan Lewis, cares deeply for her, but she cannot make herself marry a man she doesn't love. She longs for Caradoc Jones, son of a famous Welsh cattle drover and, in desperation, she accepts a job as chaperone to Caradoc's spoilt sister Georgina and joins the drovers on the road to Smithfield market in London. She plans to seek her fortune as a herbalist, preparing medicines for sale to both the rich and the poor. Life on the trail is hard, and Non struggles to be accepted by the other women on the journey, as they walk long miles over rugged terrain. One heady, star-filled night Caradoc finally becomes her lover, but she is devastated when he refuses to marry her. She is determined to survive without him in London, but when she realises she is pregnant, she finds that it's not easy to escape the clutches of the Jones family . . .

# THE ROWAN TREE

## Iris Gower

**WINDSOR**
**PARAGON**

First published 2003
by
Bantam Press
This Large Print edition published 2003
by
BBC Audiobooks Ltd
by arrangement with
Transworld Publishers Limited

ISBN 0 7540 8720 4 (Windsor Hardcover)
ISBN 0 7540 9382 4 (Paragon Softcover)

All the characters in this book are fictitious, and
any resemblance to actual persons, living or dead,
is purely coincidental.

British Library Cataloguing in Publication Data available

Printed and bound in Great Britain by
Antony Rowe Ltd., Chippenham, Wiltshire

Dedicated to the memory
of my beloved husband
Tudor

# CHAPTER ONE

The sun was shining on the brightly coloured market stalls garlanded with cheerful bouquets of flowers. Flags billowed in the breeze and large notices declared the day a special holiday in honour of the Mayor of Swansea's birthday.

Manon Jenkins felt part of Swansea now, even though she'd only moved there with her father in the spring of the year of Our Lord 1831. She did sometimes miss the sleepy village of Five Saints where she'd been born, and yet the thriving township of Swansea with its busy streets and regular markets stirred her blood. She stood behind her stall, her sleeves rolled up, struggling with a pestle and mortar and a stubborn root of dandelion; she heard her name mentioned and lifted her head to listen.

'Stuff and nonsense if you ask me! It's not right, Miss Jenkins dabbling in witchcraft.'

Manon tilted her head to hear more clearly above the babble of market sounds. Her bonnet fell onto her shoulders and the breeze lifted her chestnut curls, but Non didn't notice, straining to see who was talking about her.

'And her the daughter of our vicar! It's a disgrace, the way the Reverend lets his daughter carry on.'

Non felt her colour rise; no one was going to criticize her father and get away with it. The crowd parted and Non saw the face of the speaker, red with heat and anger.

'If it's me you're talking about, Doris Preece,

1

then I'd watch out if I were you.' Non spoke with deceptive mildness, gently restrained, as befitted the daughter of the Reverend Jenkins.

'And why should I watch out, pray? It's not me that's playing with the devil.' Doris jerked her shawl around her shoulders as she pushed her way through the crowd standing in front of her stall, her meaty fists pressing into her generous hips.

'Well,' Non smiled, 'if I'm as friendly with the devil as you seem to think, you'd better watch I don't put a spell on you.'

Doris Preece blanched, and stepped back a pace as though expecting Non to spring out at her. 'I'll plant a rowan tree in my garden—they're supposed to keep witches away.' Recovering her nerve, she straightened her shoulders. 'But what does the vicar think of all this rubbish you're selling?' She waved her hand over the small brown medicine bottles and the boxes of dried flowers and roots. 'See these things here,' she gingerly touched the dandelion roots, 'what good will they do any soul, I ask you?'

'Hang on a minute now, Mrs Preece.' An old man shuffled closer to the stall; his face was streaked with flour and even the grey of his hair was tinged with white. 'This little girl by here helped me out with some dandelion medicine when I couldn't pee,' he touched his hat, ' 'scuse me being so blunt, like.'

Doris's bosom rose beneath her dress as she sucked in a deep breath. 'Well, Dai the bread, I won't be buying any of your loaves in the future, not if you believe in this nonsense.'

He opened his mouth to answer her, but his voice was drowned out by the babble of voices as

2

folk in the crowd began to argue among themselves. Non shook her head, there were some people who lived in the past. They readily took useless pills made up by the apothecaries who stood behind polished counters in proper shops, but wouldn't touch the natural remedies put into the ground by the Good Lord himself.

The appearance of Non's father, a man big in character if not in stature, silenced the crowd. Doris bowed her head; she had a superstitious respect for the Church in general and the Reverend Jenkins in particular.

'I see some of you are partaking of my daughter's God-given medicines.' He smiled benignly at the people surrounding him. 'They are all recommended by Mr Culpeper himself, who claims that herbs are the natural way to preserve life. Herbs and roots and plants are as good for us as the corn we cut for bread, wouldn't you agree, Dai, you being a baker?'

'I would, Reverend,' Dai clutched his hat to his thin chest. 'Jest saying so, I was, sir.'

'Good man, good man.' The Reverend turned to Non. 'Well, daughter, I think it's going to rain—you'd better start to pack up your stall. Come along, my dear, I'll help you load everything onto the pony and trap.'

Non glanced up. Her father was right, clouds were moving swiftly across the sky, beginning to obscure the sun. She packed away her remedies quickly, storing the bottles in the correctly labelled compartments in the large box made for her by Morgan Lewis. Non smiled. Morgan was a smithy, but he'd turned his hand to woodcraft for her sake, because Morgan was in love with her. She paused a moment, her hand hovering over the last few bottles of medicine; Morgan was a handsome enough man, but she was not ready to settle down with anyone just yet. She was young; she had a lot of living and a great deal of learning to do before she was ready for marriage.

'Come along, child,' her father's voice cut into her thoughts, 'we'll be soaked if you don't hurry!'

She finished her packing and stacked her wares neatly in the body of the cart. 'Is that quick enough for you, Father?' She smiled at him, loving him so much that it almost hurt. She climbed into the seat beside him and planted a kiss on his cheek. 'You're all right as fathers go, do you know that, Reverend Jenkins?'

'Now then, none of your nonsense! I've only done what any other father on God's earth would have done, and that's to bring my only child up in the knowledge of right and wrong.'

He might be dismissive of her words, but her father was a man deserving of praise. After her mother died in childbirth, her father had taken care of her. The only times he'd left her with a nurse were when he was about his parish duties, or on Sundays when he was preaching his sermons. Sermons, she later came to learn, that were delivered with a wit and humour that endeared him to his congregation.

As her father negotiated the busy road leading away from the market, an elegant coach pulled alongside. Glancing up, Non saw that the other driver was Caradoc Jones, as handsome and debonair as always. Sitting beside him was his sister Georgina, looking through Non as though she didn't exist. But Caradoc smiled at her and lifted

4

his hat and Non felt herself flushing.

'Good evening, Reverend, and evenin' to you too, Miss Jenkins.' Caradoc's voice was deep and resonant and his eyes meeting hers were full of laughter. She looked away quickly, fanning her face with her hand as if it was the heat of the day causing her to blush and not the handsome devil-may-care son of the wealthy George Jones, bank owner and cattle drover.

'Evening to you, Caradoc,' the Reverend said. 'How's that old reprobate of a father of yours?'

'He's well, and as strong as the beasts he used to drive to market.' Caradoc spoke with the confidence of the privileged; he didn't need to count the pennies the way most country folk did.

Caradoc held out his hand. 'Please, Reverend, you go first—the gate is too narrow for both of us to navigate at the same time.'

Non saw her father shake his head. 'Yours is the faster vehicle, Caradoc, and I am quite content to let my old mare amble along the road at her own pace, so I would only hold you up.'

'As you please.' Caradoc lifted his hat, and Non allowed herself another look at him. He was so handsome, so strong and manly, and he had such an elegant bearing, it was no wonder every girl for miles around the village of Five Saints, where he lived, had set their cap at him.

But not her, Non told herself sternly. Perhaps she would never marry—instead she would care for her father in his old age as he had cared for her in her infancy. In any case, Caradoc would not look at the daughter of a poor country parson. He would want a bride who could bring him riches and distinction.

'Why are you so flustered, Manon?' Her father spoke gently. 'Not getting ideas above your station, are you, child?'

'I don't know what you mean, Father!' She spoke more sharply than she'd intended and her father sighed.

'I thought as much. You've taken a liking to that young man.' He glanced at the retreating back of Caradoc Jones. 'He's not for you, my dear, he'll marry into a family as rich as his own.'

'I'm not thinking of marriage, Father,' Non spoke more quietly. 'I'm never going to get married and leave you alone.'

'Nonsense!' He glanced at her with affection. 'You'll have a husband and a brood of children before you're much older, I'll warrant. I know that Morgan is very fond of you, and he might be only a smithy but he brings in a good living all the same.'

'Let's not talk about marriage,' Non said quickly. 'The very thought of leaving you fills me with misgivings. I know you wouldn't eat right and you'd be careless of your appearance if I wasn't around to look after you.'

Her father patted her hand. 'Well, that's as maybe, but bear in mind what I've said. Some folks are not meant to be together.'

Non was glad when she saw the tall chimneys of the vicarage on the horizon. She sighed contentedly. She'd had a good day at the market and now she was nearly home, where the lamps would cast a warming light on the gardens, the supper would be underway and the old house would be filled with smells of baking and beeswax polish. Mrs Miles, who used to be her nurse and now cooked for them, would be bustling about in

6

the kitchen, anxious for their return, and Flora would be laying up the table in the dining room in preparation for the evening meal.

Non realized quite suddenly that although not rich like the Joneses, her own life was cushioned and comfortable. She had few household duties to attend to, and so her time was free to study Mr Culpeper's herbal remedies, a task which she loved, though it was not to everyone's liking.

She made a wry face as she thought of Doris Preece, who thought her a witch because she made perfectly good remedies from herbs and flowers. Non had tinctures for everything from a fever to a bee sting. Even the humble dandelion had its place in her medicine box.

The Reverend Jenkins drew the horse to a stop outside the arched front door of the vicarage, and the stable boy hurried forward to take the reins.

'Give old Bess a good rub down, Dennis, she's tired and hungry and could do with a feed.'

'Right you are, Reverend, I'll see to it straight away.'

Non called after Dennis as he led the animal round the back to the stables. 'Bring my box in the house for me, will you, please?' She smiled. 'And watch you don't break anything, mind.'

Non followed her father into the hallway, where the diffuse lights from a large candelabra threw flicking shadows against the carpet. Mrs Miles bustled forward, her hands rubbing imaginary creases from her spotless apron. Behind her was Flora, the new young maid, who had no intention of allowing Mrs Miles to take over her duties.

'*Duw*, Reverend,' Mrs Miles said, 'I thought you was never coming home! You're that late the

7

supper was almost spoiled.'

'Mrs Miles, like most women you worry too much.'

'Well, who else would worry about you, Reverend, if I didn't? Tell me that now.' Her voice was pettish but there was a smile in her eyes. She was in love with the Reverend Jenkins, everyone knew it, including him, but no one was ever impolite enough to mention it.

Flora dipped a curtsey before taking Non's coat and bonnet, and stood waiting patiently for the Reverend to slip out of his topcoat. Non glanced at her father and saw a strained expression cross his face.

'What's wrong, Father?' she asked anxiously.

'Nothing at all, my dear, it's just indigestion. I think I overindulged in Dai the bread's meat pies at dinner time.'

'I'll find you a remedy, Father, you just wait a minute. I don't expect Dennis has had time to unload the trap yet, I'll go round to the stables and fetch my box myself.'

Outside, the rain clouds had passed and the sun was setting over the fields; ribbons of red and gold light brushed the trees with warm colour and for a moment Non was blinded by it. Then she became aware of a figure standing against the backdrop of the sunset and shielded her eyes, trying to see the man standing before her.

'Good evening, Manon. It's me, Morgan, I hope I didn't startle you.' He shifted his position and then Non saw him clearly. He stood against the light—a tall man with the well-developed shoulders of a blacksmith. His head was held proudly, as though he was a rich copper baron instead of a humble working man, and Non's heart ached with fondness for him. He was like the brother she'd never had.

'Was it a good day at the fair, Manon?' Morgan asked, and Non smiled up at him more warmly than she intended. He blinked as though startled and moved a shade closer to her.

'Yes, fairly good,' she said quickly, 'though I did get a bit of a telling-off from Doris Preece.' She shrugged her shoulders. 'She thinks I'm a witch because of the potions I make out of plants. The silly woman hasn't even tried any of my remedies, that's what gets my dander up.'

Morgan chuckled. 'I don't suppose you let the old woman get away with anything though, did you Manon?'

'Are you making fun of me, Morgan Lewis?'

He held his hands out before him. 'No indeed, I wouldn't make fun of you.' He paused. 'After all, you might put a spell on me.'

'Oh, you!' Non turned away from him. 'Anyway, I've got to get round to the stables and collect my things.' She began to walk towards the back of the house, knowing that Morgan would follow her. He did, and she smiled to herself, secretly pleased. She might not wish to marry him, but he was a good-looking, upstanding man and his attention was flattering.

Non blinked a little at the dimness of the stable compared to the light outside. Dennis was just lifting her box from the cart, and before she could move Morgan had taken it from the stable boy.

'I'll carry this indoors for you, Non, you're only a little bit of a thing and the box is too heavy for you.'

Non hid a smile. She had carried the box many

times and managed it quite easily, but she knew
Morgan had been looking for an excuse to come
into the house and now he'd found one.

'If you'll take it through to the kitchen that will
do nicely, thank you.' Non pushed the door open
and the smell of roasting lamb permeated the
room. Mrs Miles had returned to her task of rolling
out pastry and smiled when she saw Morgan Lewis
carrying Non's box for her.

'Well, there's nice to see a handsome young man
in my kitchen,' she said, blushing like a girl. 'I hope
you'll be staying for supper—there's plenty of food
to go round.'

Non frowned and shook her head, but she was
too late. Morgan had put the box on the table and
was planting a kiss on Mrs Miles's weathered
cheek. 'I'd love to share the food you've cooked, if
Miss Jenkins agrees.'

'Yes, of course you must stay,' Non said quickly,
'Mrs Miles always cooks too much food anyway.
Now I'd better sort out a remedy for my father's
indigestion.'

She looked among her medicines, her slim
fingers busy as she lifted one bottle after another.
'Ah, here we are, some burnet,' she held up the
bottle, 'this usually works.'

Morgan looked interested. 'What does it do,
exactly?'

'To be blunt, it gets him belching and that
relieves his indigestion,' she laughed. 'It's a useful
herb; if the leaves are mixed with a little claret it
lightens the spirits, and more than that, it's good
for the heart and the liver.'

Morgan watched as Non added wine and a
spoonful of honey to the drink, and when it was

ready, she nodded to him. 'Come through to the drawing room and say hello to my father. I know he'll be happy to have a man to talk to, I feel he's bored sometimes with my chatter.'

Morgan shook his head. 'I don't believe that for one minute, Manon Jenkins, you are one of the most intelligent young ladies I know.'

'And do you know many?' she smiled. 'Young ladies, I mean.'

Morgan's eyebrows lifted. 'Oh, yes, I know a few.'

Non was laughing as she led the way into the drawing room, but her laughter vanished like the sun behind a cloud as she saw her father spread out face-down on the carpet.

'Oh, dear heaven!' She put down the glass and knelt beside her father, trying fruitlessly to turn him over so that she could see his face. He moaned a little and Non looked up at Morgan. 'Please, help me make him comfortable.'

Morgan lifted the older man with ease and lay him down on the scroll-back sofa. The Reverend was blue around the mouth, his breathing was laboured and sweat beaded his forehead.

'I'll fetch the doctor,' Morgan said. 'There's something badly wrong.'

'It's his heart,' Non said quietly. 'I know the symptoms. I've seen them before.'

Morgan hesitated for a moment at the door, and Non waved her hand. 'Fetch the doctor, please, and in the meantime I'll do what I can.'

Non removed her father's clerical collar and then held his head in her arms. 'Father, try to drink this,' she held the glass to his lips. 'It's just a mixture of herbs in a little claret. It won't do you

11

any harm and it might do some good.'

Her father swallowed the drink a drop at a time, and as she watched him fight for breath, Non's heart beat rapidly with fear. For the first time, she doubted her medicines—if her father's heart was failing, what good could a little burnet do?

'Oh, God help us!' She cradled her father's head against her breast, smoothing the white wispy hair from his brow. 'Please, God, don't let my father die.'

She smoothed his cheek, talking calmly to him, until at last his breathing began to ease and a little colour came back into his cheeks. He lifted his hand and covered hers.

'It's all right, I'm feeling better already. Just give me a little more of that medicine and I'll be fine.'

By the time Morgan returned with the doctor, the Reverend Jenkins was sitting up in a chair, his colour returned to normal, his breathing even and regular.

'Thank you for coming, Doctor Saunders,' Non said. 'My father seems much better, but I'd like you to look at him all the same.'

'I'll step outside,' Morgan said, 'but if there's anything you need, just call me.'

Non hardly heard him, so intent was she on watching the doctor examine her father.

'It's your heart, Reverend,' Doctor Saunders said at last. 'The beat is irregular, but I don't think you're going to meet your Maker just yet. What's this?' He picked up the empty glass and sniffed it. 'Claret, if I'm not mistaken.'

'It was a potion I made up from herbs,' Non said. 'It's just a little burnet mixed with some wine.'

The doctor was packing his bag. 'I don't hold

with such rubbish, and I would be obliged if you'd refrain from administering any more of the stuff while your father is under my care.'

'But . . .' Non began.

The doctor held up his hand. 'No buts. You must abide by my instructions, at least for the time being.' He looked sternly at her. 'I hope you understand me, young lady.'

'I understand,' Non said quietly. She glanced at her father, who seemed weary, and strangely vulnerable without his collar. 'I'll do anything you say, Doctor, so long as my father is all right.'

She saw Doctor Saunders to the door, and looked up as Morgan came to her side. 'Did I do the right thing, treating my father myself?'

Morgan shook his head. 'I don't know. I'm not a medical man, but you kept your father alive—surely that's the most important thing?'

'You're right,' Non said, but somehow there was no conviction in her voice or in her heart.

'Come on,' Morgan said, 'I'll help you get your father to bed and then I'll be off and leave you in peace.'

Suddenly Non was afraid. She put her hand on Morgan's arm. 'No, don't go, please don't go.'

Morgan put his arm around her shoulders. 'I'll stay for as long as you want me,' he said warmly.

She bit her lip. 'I'm thankful for all you've done tonight, Morgan, but don't read too much into it, will you?'

He smiled ruefully. 'Don't worry, I won't.'

Non smiled, suddenly ashamed of herself for throwing his help back into his face. She took his hand and, as his strong fingers curled around hers, she felt an overwhelming warmth for the big kind man at her side.

## CHAPTER TWO

Broad Oaks was a mansion built of mellow stone, with fine pillars flanking the arched doorway that led into an impressive hallway. A central staircase curved up to the spacious landing and it was here that Georgina stood, smiling as her father entered the house.

'I'm so glad you're home from the bank,' she ran lightly down the stairs and caught her father's hands in hers. 'It's time you took an afternoon off. You seem to spend most of your life in Llandeilo these days.'

Georgina kissed her father's cheek and, putting her arm through his, led him into the elegant drawing room with floor-to-ceiling windows looking out onto rolling fields. 'You work too hard, Father. You should be taking it easy now at your time of life.'

'My dear Georgie, there's a living to be earned and I'm the daft beggar who has to do it.' George Jones disentangled himself and poured a large brandy.

'Father, don't swear, it's so vulgar,' Georgina said. She could accept that her father was what people called a 'self-made man', but she wished he'd remember his manners when he was in female company.

'I *am* vulgar, girl! I spent my green years riding with a herd of cattle. I had a sore backside at times, I can tell you, but I always got the beasts safely to

Smithfield market in London.'

'Well, you're the owner of a bank now, have been for some time, and you must act like the gentleman everyone believes you to be.'

'Gentleman, am I? Granted we're invited to grand balls and I'm welcome at the hunt because of my horsemanship, but only because I'm a wealthy man now.' He paused to take a sip of his drink. 'But you must understand, Georgie, the Bank of the Black Ox means more to me than a few silly dances and the chance to chase a poor fox all day. I built the bank by my honest sweat as a cattle drover, not as a member of the gentry—you just remember that.'

'Well, whatever happened in the past, the bank is respected throughout Wales now, Father, and indeed in many parts of England too, and we're better than the people you call the gentry, so don't be too modest.'

'And you stop grumbling about the time I put in at the work, my girl.'

'I'm not grumbling, not really,' Georgina smiled at him. 'I just like it when you're home with me.' She shrugged her slim shoulders. 'My brother is no company at all.' Her voice held a petulant note.

Her father sank into a chair and smiled at her over the rim of his glass. 'Why, what's Caradoc done now?'

'You should have seen him at the fair today, making eyes at that awful girl, you know the one— the vicar's daughter.'

'Oh, is that all? Well, Reverend Jenkins's daughter is a very pretty girl and I'm sure Caradoc meant no harm. You know what he's like for the ladies.'

Georgina sat in the chair on the opposite side of the fire and stared at her father; Caradoc followed him in his liking for the ladies, but she could hardly say so. She tried to see her father objectively; he was quite a handsome man, although he was past fifty years of age. His hair was still fair with just a hint of grey at the temples. He was well set up, with strong shoulders and a neat figure in spite of his age. And, of course, he was wealthy too, and it was that wealth which invariably attracted the wrong type of woman. Her father was a fool for predatory women and, sadly, so was Caradoc.

'I do hope that Caradoc doesn't have one of his strange whims and ask the girl to walk out with him,' Georgina said. 'She's so below him in social standing; we all know how poorly parish vicars are paid.'

Her father spluttered over his drink. 'Don't be silly, Georgina, your brother has more sense than to fool with the vicar's daughter. In any case, from what I hear, the girl is respectable, and your brother doesn't hold with the respectable sort.'

'You didn't see the way he was mooning over her, Papa, he was like a beardless boy.'

'Well, let the matter drop for now, will you, girl? I'm tired of it. In any case, Caradoc is not likely to meet up with Manon Jenkins very often, is he?'

'Well, he'll see her at church, of course.' She caught the impatience in her father's expression, but she had to make one last attempt to get him to see the danger of her brother making a fool of himself. She knew Caradoc better than her father did—if he liked a girl, he would go all out to woo her and damn the consequences. 'I just wouldn't want my brother to be trapped into a marriage that

16

is not suitable, would you, Father?'

'Of course he won't be trapped!' Her father gave vent to his irritation. 'Your imagination is getting the better of you, Georgina. Your brother will marry when the time is right, and we'll just have to trust him to choose the right girl.'

She looked down at her hands, pouting a little, and her father spoke more mildly. 'Look, little chicken, your brother will be going away come spring, so how could the pesky Jenkins girl trap him into anything?'

'She might charm him with one of those potions she makes up.' Georgina made a face. 'I know she concocted something for one of the kitchen maids, some herbal drink that made Iowerth the footman fall in love with her.'

She saw the laughter in her father's eyes and spoke again. 'It isn't funny, Father. If the vicar's daughter makes Caradoc fall under her spell, she could always say she was with child by him. It's happened before and it could happen again.'

'No, no, that sort of thing only happens to the poor uneducated folk. Reverend Jenkins's girl has been brought up to be quite a lady and a scholar.'

'Well, I think she's sinister.' Georgina folded her hands in her lap. 'She might even be dangerous, playing about with plants and things, making medicines out of herbs from the hedgerows. Why, I heard one woman today calling her a witch, and nothing would surprise me about her. She has that fey look, do you know what I mean, Father?'

'All I know is that you just don't like the girl. Now can we let the subject drop? It's too silly for words.' He lay back in his chair and closed his eyes firmly, bringing the conversation to an end.

Georgina sank in sulky silence and stared into the fire, determined to show her father she was displeased by his attitude. The sound of the front door opening and closing brought her father into an upright position; at once his face brightened.

'Caradoc's home. Good!'

Caradoc came into the room, bringing a scent of the outdoors with him. He was very much like his father in looks, and in spite of herself Georgina loved him dearly, even while she disapproved of his easy way with women.

'Hello, Georgie, got a kiss for your brother?'

She held up her face to be kissed, and then threw her arms around his neck, wishing he would sit and talk with her. But she knew what would happen now—the men would be full of the forthcoming cattle drive up to Smithfield in London. The conversation would be all about the drovers' roads and the price of cattle.

She was right. Caradoc took his father's glass and refilled it and then poured a drink for himself. Georgina sighed. She was bored before they even began to talk. Still, she had nothing better to do so she remained in her seat, determined to have her say about the vicar's daughter when the right moment arose.

'You'll be on your way soon, my boy.' George Jones leaned forward in his chair. 'I wish I could go with you. I miss the days I spent in the saddle riding through the wild countryside.' He sighed. 'Every day was an adventure then.' He glanced quickly at Georgina, who pretended not to notice. 'Every night too, my boy, eh?' He laughed wickedly. 'What I would give to be young again.'

'What, and make a fool of yourself like Caradoc

did today?' Georgina said sharply. 'You were drooling over that girl at the fair and I felt really embarrassed by your behaviour.'

'What girl?' Caradoc stared over the rim of his glass. 'Do you mean the beautiful Miss Jenkins?'

'There, you see, Father? I told you he'd paid her too much attention, didn't I?'

'Well, she really is rather lovely,' Caradoc said smoothly. 'Manon Jenkins is probably one of the best-looking women in Swansea.'

Georgina pleated the skirt of her gown in agitation. 'Don't let yourself be fooled by her, Caradoc. She's wicked—anyone can see that.'

'I can't,' Caradoc said. 'All I saw was a pretty clever young lady who isn't content to sit on her backside allowing her father to support her.'

Georgina was stung by her brother's words. 'I would work if only Father would let me!'

'Would you really? Well, that's easy to say, but what would you do?'

'I could ride the trail with you. I'm a better horsewoman than any of the girls who accompany the cattle drive.'

'You're being silly, Georgie. You don't even realize that the women walk all the way to London. As they follow the herd they even manage to knit hosiery to sell in London shops, too.'

'And don't forget the weeding the girls do while the cattle rest,' George Jones said, a smile in his voice.

'You would never make a cattle woman,' Caradoc smiled triumphantly at his sister. 'You wouldn't get from Five Saints to Swansea if you had to walk, would you?'

'Well then, what if I didn't walk? I can ride as

well as you and I can control the beasts as good as any man. Haven't I spent a lifetime living and breathing cattle? Please, Father, say you'll let me go to London with Caradoc.'

'You are not going to ride any trail.' The smile left her father's face and he spoke sternly to her. 'No daughter of mine is going to ride a horse like a man through the rough terrain of Wales and into England, so we'll hear no more talk about it.'

'But Father, please just think about it.' She pouted at her father. 'Do you think me feeble or stupid that I can't do it?'

'What you are not going to do is act like a fool! Do you realize the dangers the women face on the trail? Not least from the men who have left their wives at home and are . . . well, never mind that, but listen to this, I haven't worked my backside off to have my daughter running wild, do you understand?'

Georgina nodded, realizing that she had taken the wrong tack with her father. Of course he wouldn't let her ride the trail, it wouldn't be at all appropriate. But then what if she requested a visit to her aunt in London? She would have to be accompanied across country somehow and by someone, and who better than her older brother? Still, for now she would bide her time; her father would soon forget her foolish proposal to ride with the herd.

When her father spoke again, his tone had softened. 'You're off to the assembly rooms with Cousin William and his wife this evening, aren't you, Georgie?' He smiled. 'But you must promise to be home early—I particularly want you home for dinner. Still, it's a good thing for you to go out, it's an excuse to dress up in one of your fine gowns.'

Georgina looked at her father in surprise. He never noticed her clothes, even though she dressed every evening for dinner. And what was so special about tonight? She was about to ask him when he spoke again.

'I expect you find sitting at home boring,' he looked at her with a twinkle in his eye, 'but don't worry, we'll find a suitable husband for you, and once you have a family to take care of you'll have enough on your hands.'

'Oh Papa, you know I never want to leave you.' She knelt at his feet and laid her head in his lap. Whenever her father spoke of marrying her off she felt as though an icicle had lodged in her stomach.

'But you need a household of your own, a man of your own and children. You want children, don't you?'

Georgina wasn't sure that she did, but sensed it was not what her father wanted to hear. 'Of course I do, when the time is right, but I'm not ready for marriage, not for a long time.'

'You will have to obey Father in that, Georgina,' Caradoc spoke sharply, 'and perhaps sooner than you think.'

'What?' Georgina was alarmed. 'What do you mean by "sooner than I think"? What are you talking about?'

'Leave it, Caradoc,' George Jones shook his head at his son. 'All in good time, son.'

'Something is going on. Are you going to tell me what it is?'

'Father has someone in mind for you, Georgie,' Caradoc spoke more kindly, 'and remember this, we all love you and want what's best for you.'

21

'Who have you got in mind, Papa? Tell me his name.'

Her father looked away. 'Nothing is settled yet, so don't start making a song and dance about it.'

'You might as well tell her, Father,' Caradoc said. 'Look, Georgie, it's Harry Mapleton. He's well set up, very wealthy and a fine handsome man.'

Georgina felt a chill in her stomach. 'But he's very old, and in any case he's married. You're having a joke with me—that's it, isn't it, Papa?'

'Harry's newly widowed,' her father spoke at last, 'and he's the wealthiest man in the whole of Wales. He'd be a real catch for you.'

Georgina shivered. 'Please, Papa, I don't want to be married to Mr Mapleton. Why, he's even older than you!'

'Hey, watch your tongue, young lady.' Her father ruffled her hair in an attempt to lighten the moment. 'Yes, I agree that Harry Mapleton is rather older than I am, but he has three children by his dead wife, rest her soul, and I expect there's life enough in him to produce another three if he has a strong young woman like you as his bride.'

Georgina bowed her head as tears of anger and fear clouded her vision. 'Listen, Papa, I wouldn't marry Mr Mapleton if he was the last man on earth.'

'Now don't go trying to lay down the law with me, girl.' There was a warning note in her father's voice. 'You will marry whoever I say you'll marry— do you hear me, Georgina?'

'Yes, of course I hear you, Father, and I hope you heard me. I'll not marry that old man, however rich he is.'

Her father slammed down his drink and got to his feet. His face was red as he glared at her. 'Harry Mapleton is coming to a late dinner with us tonight, and I don't want any rudeness from you. I want the man to like you.' He handed her his glass. 'Now stop acting like a spoilt child and fetch me another drink, there's a good girl, I could do with it. Thank the Good Lord that I only have one daughter to contend with.'

Georgina felt like snapping back at her father. She longed to tell him that she would never encourage Mr Mapleton to like her. She would not marry the man and that was final.

She dutifully gave her father his drink and then sat on the floor beside him. Her temper tantrum had got her nowhere, she might as well try coaxing. 'Papa,' she began, 'you want me to be happy, don't you?'

'Of course I do, chick,' he smiled at her, 'but I want you to be obedient, too.' He took her chin in his hand and tilted her face to his. 'Look at me, Georgina. Haven't I always known what's best for you?'

'Yes, you have, but Father, I want to choose my own husband, can't you understand that?'

He laughed out loud at that. 'Oh, and who would you choose—the stable boy or the groom, or perhaps my steward Archie? Those are the only men you ever get into conversation with. Most young gentlemen of our acquaintance are merely flirting with you; they have no serious intention of marrying you. No, you must do as I say.'

'But Papa . . .' Her words trailed off as he waved his hand at her.

'Hush now and forget all about it. Go and dress

23

for this outing down at the assembly rooms and make sure you wear your finest jewellery. I want my daughter to do me proud.'

Georgina nodded. 'All right, Papa, I'll do as you say.' She hurried from the room and, lifting her skirts, took the stairs two at a time. Her heart was thumping in her breast and she felt as though she would faint from the shock of what her father had planned for her. How could he bring an old man to the house and expect her to fall in love with him? Well, he would never make her marry Mr Mapleton, never.

In her room she rang for her maid. 'Find my plainest gown, Vera,' she said dully. 'Perhaps the brown with the lace at the neck?'

'But Miss Georgina, that gown always makes you look so pale. Why not wear the blue? You know how that brings out the colour in your eyes.'

'No, the brown will do. Now help me get ready and don't talk any more, I have a lot of thinking to do.'

Patiently, she allowed Vera to help her change into a fresh gown, then she sat still as the maid brushed her hair until it shone. She looked at herself in the mirror and knew she was no beauty, not like that witch Manon Jenkins, but at least she had breeding. She was realistic enough to know that any man who asked for her hand would do so in the knowledge that there was a good dowry to go with her, but all the same she could do better than marry an old man like Mr Mapleton.

'There, you look lovely in spite of the brown.' Vera stood with her head on one side to admire her handiwork. 'You know, Miss, the colour of the gown shows off your hair a treat.'

24

'Thank you.' Georgina looked up at the maid curiously. 'Have you ever thought of getting married, Vera?'

The girl looked flustered. 'I don't know what you want me to say, Miss, I'm happy here in my situation and I got no mind to leave your service.'

'No, that's all right, Vera. It's just that my father wants me to marry and very soon.' She rubbed her eyes, trying not to cry. 'He's set on marrying me to a man I hardly know, Vera. How will I take to lying in the same bed as an old man?'

'Oh, now don't you worry about that, Miss,' Vera said. 'Once you got a ring on your finger you'll feel different. All brides fall in love with their man, haven't you seen it many times down at the church? Every girl coming out on the arm of her new husband looks bright as a gold guinea.'

Georgina sighed. 'But what about all that love nonsense? You know, babies and such.'

'Well,' Vera shrugged, 'I suppose they just comes along when the time is right.'

Georgina gave up; it was clear that Vera knew as little about the intimacies of marriage as she did. Not for the first time, Georgina regretted that her mother had died from a lung fever when she was a child. But there was Cousin Will's wife; Grace had been with Will for five years and had born him children—she must know what marriage was all about.

Taking a deep breath, Georgina got to her feet. 'Thank you, Vera, that will be all.'

She walked out onto the broad landing and stared down the length of the curving stairs. Perhaps by dinner she might have thought of a way of putting Papa off his absurd idea of marrying her

25

to Harry Mapleton. She smiled to herself. She could always get round her father; it would be no different this time, she would see to it.

Just as she was about to leave the house, a messenger arrived with a letter. Georgina hovered as her father unfolded the paper. He looked up at her, a wry smile on his face.

'Well, what a shame. Harry can't make it for supper tonight, it seems he's indisposed.'

'Yes, what a shame!' Georgina's voice was heavy with sarcasm. 'I expect you're disappointed, Papa, but I'm only relieved.'

She had no time to wait for his reply. The coach was waiting for her and she hurried out of the door before her father could reproach her. As she settled in the seat, she found she was looking forward to an evening at the assembly rooms. Perhaps she would meet some fine young man there who would offer for her in marriage. In any case, it was about time she took her future prospects into her own hands. It was high time she began to look seriously for a suitable husband.

## CHAPTER THREE

The regular Friday market was one Non would never miss. Pie-makers and butchers vied for space with fishmongers and vegetable sellers, all calling loudly in an attempt to claim the first customers of the day. To any casual onlooker it must have seemed like bedlam, but Non was used to the rough and tumble of the one day in the week when the market was guaranteed to be busy. She loved it all; the noise, the smells, the very air of hurry and bustle were like the breath of life to her.

She stood at the gateway of the market for a moment, trying to spot a place where she could spread out her wares. Near the main gate was a good site, but it was fully taken up by Dai the bread, who was already busy selling hot pies from trays fresh from the oven.

She thought of her father back home. He loved Dai's pies, but he wouldn't be sampling them today. Today her father would be taking things easy, sitting in the sunlit garden playing at writing his sermon for Sunday. His condition had greatly improved, but Non wondered if she'd been wise to leave him alone. Still, he'd insisted he was no longer an invalid, and when Mr Robinson, their neighbour, had called offering her a lift to market, the matter was settled.

Non heaved her full box higher onto her arm and shifted the folding stool to a more comfortable position under her other arm. Gingerly, she picked her way through the noisy crowd, looking for a space where she could set up her stall. Some tradesmen were fortunate enough to own large trestle tables, but Non had to content herself with the square stool Morgan had made for her and the snowy white cloth she used to cover it. The market was more crowded than usual, but at last Non found a spot near the edge of the street, where she was sheltered from the cool breeze by the branches of a chestnut tree. She quickly set out her packets of dried herbs on the snowy white cloth, aware that people were already waiting to see what she had to offer.

As well as bunches of dried herbs and roots, she

had brought several large bottles of medicine. She was proud of her new stock; she had spent a whole day making foxglove syrup for easing pain in the heart, and pulping freshly grown watercress into wine for sweetening the breath.

'Got anything for the gout, *merchi*?' An old woman pushed her way to the front of the crowd. 'Killing me, it is. I can hardly walk, my foot's so curled up with pain.'

'Oh, good morning, Mrs Preece. So I'm not a witch today, then?'

'Forget I said all that. I'm in so much pain I'd try anything, even your potions and powders.'

'Fair enough.' Non bent down and picked up a bunch of pale flowers. 'I've got some archangel, very good for the gout.'

'What in the name of all the saints is archangel?'

'It's just a fancy name for the dead-nettle flower.'

Mrs Preece looked at the bunch of flowers with suspicion. 'And what do I do with these? Do I eat them?'

'No, don't eat them, whatever you do! First the flowers need to be bruised, then add salt and vinegar, mix with hog's grease and apply the paste to the painful swelling.' She smiled encouragingly. 'And in a few days you'll see a great difference.'

'Haven't you got anything ready made up for me? I can't be doin' with all that messin' about.'

Non picked up one of the brown bottles. 'This will help. It's made from prickly asparagus. I've boiled the buds in a little white wine so it should taste nice.'

'Well, why didn't you say in the first place? I'll have that, then.' The old woman took some coins out of her pocket and handed them to Non. 'See you next week, *merchi*, no doubt to complain that your funny medicine did me no good.'

'Try it out before you think of complaining,' Non said, wishing that Mrs Preece wouldn't call her 'girl'—it made her seem inexperienced, took away some of her dignity.

Non quickly became so busy that she had no time to think of anything, not even her father. She spent the next few hours making up and selling her syrups. But at last the crowd around her thinned and she had time to sit on the soft grass, dip into her basket and bring out the bottle of water she always carried. It tasted sweeter than wine, there was nothing like good clear spring water to quench the thirst.

'Hello Non, business good?'

Non took the bottle away from her lips so suddenly that some of the water trickled down her chin. Abashed, she met the laughing eyes of Caradoc Jones.

'Oh, good day to you, Mr Jones. Yes, my little cures are selling well enough, thank you.' Why on earth couldn't she find something bright and intelligent to say, instead of sounding like a silly child?

Caradoc dropped down onto the grass beside her and leaned on one elbow. 'Do you like butter?' he asked. He picked up one of her dried buttercups and held it under her chin.

Non's heart began to beat swiftly as she looked into the deep blue of his eyes. He was so handsome, with his thick hair curling close to his head and his lips so near to hers that with only the slightest movement he would be kissing her. The thought made her breathless.

'Ah yes, you do like butter, I can see the glow of yellow underneath your neck. Such a pretty neck I'd very much like to kiss it.'

Non drew away from him, embarrassed by his forwardness.

He took her hand. 'I'll content myself with kissing your dear little fingers then.' His mouth was warm against her skin and Non stared at him, mesmerized by his charm.

'Caradoc!' The sharp voice of his sister broke the spell and Caradoc dropped Non's hand.

'Georgina, how kind of you to come looking for me.'

'Looking for you? I've been looking everywhere. I might have known I'd find you hanging round some girl from the lower orders. That sort have very low moral standards, so I've heard.'

Non took a deep breath, biting back the angry words that threatened to spill from her lips. Instead she managed a frosty smile and spoke politely, though with a firmness that was intended to put Georgina in her place. 'I'm Reverend Jenkins's daughter and I can assure you that my morals are as sound as your own.'

Caradoc, still lying at her side, laughed. 'That's not saying much, Non. Our Georgina is renowned for her tendency to flirt with any half-decent-looking beau who comes into her company.'

'Oh, do stop teasing!' Georgina stamped her foot on the grass, to little avail. 'I want to go home.'

'Well, you go ahead—I'll come along later.' Caradoc didn't move. He looked at his sister with raised eyebrows, and she tried another tack.

'Please, Caradoc,' Georgina's voice softened.

30

'Please take me home. I've quite a bad headache coming on.'

'Then you should take one of Miss Jenkins's remedies. I hear they are most efficacious.'

Georgina shook her head without replying, but the look of scorn on her face said more than words ever could.

'*Please*, Caradoc, I really do need to get out of this awful crowd—the noise, not to mention the smell of all these people is making me ill.'

Caradoc rose to his feet in one easy, cat-like movement, and he stood for a moment looking down at Non. 'I'll see you again, Miss Jenkins, you can count on it.'

Non watched as Caradoc disappeared into the crowd. He was so handsome and charming, but a known philanderer; she would do well to put him out of her mind. She watched until Caradoc disappeared from sight and then, realizing she had another customer, turned her thoughts to the business of selling her products.

\*       \*       \*

'I don't know why you have to carry on with all these girls, Caradoc,' Georgina looked up into her brother's face. 'You know full well you're expected to marry Elizabeth Pugh one of these fine days.'

'Ah well, flirting is one thing, marriage another. Now climb aboard the carriage. You nagged enough to go home, so let's get started, shall we? I've got things to do here in Swansea, so once I've taken you home I'll have to come back again later on and you, my dear sister, are being a pesky nuisance.'

31

Georgina settled herself in the carriage and watched as her brother effortlessly swung himself up into the driving seat. He met her glance.

'I wish you'd keep your nose out of my business, Georgina. I'm a grown man, not a callow boy.'

'But Caradoc, the girls you carry on with are foolish enough to believe you're in love with them. Just look at the trouble the affair with Sarah Malloy brought you.'

'Don't keep on, Georgie,' Caradoc said. 'You'll take all the fun out of my life if I listen to you.'

Georgina shook her head. 'But it's not all fun, is it? In the end the piper has to be paid.'

She remembered the scandal that had surrounded the birth of Caradoc's daughter by the Malloy woman. Of course Caradoc refuted the accusation that the child was his, but their father had been obliged to hand out a great deal of money to hush up the affair.

'Well that's rich, and you a more blatant flirt than I am.' Caradoc tweaked the ribbon on her bonnet. 'I don't know how you manage to keep half the men in the county in love with you.'

'I don't allow any liberties,' Georgina said firmly. 'I flirt and that's all I do, and the men of my acquaintance respect me for it. I don't want to end up like that awful Malloy woman, with a babe in my arms and no reputation to speak of.'

'Shut up, Georgina,' Caradoc's voice held a warning note. 'I'm getting a little tired of being reminded of my one mistake.'

'I'm sorry, but you are incorrigible, Caradoc. You lead women on and the fools believe every word you say. Take that Jenkins girl, you can tell by the look in her eyes that she has a fancy for you.

For two pins she'd be lying in your bed with no care for the consequences.'

'I think you're wrong there,' Caradoc said softly. 'Manon Jenkins has more spirit than that. She's been brought up in a respectable home, remember.'

'Aye, well respectability flies out of the window when a girl is in love.'

Caradoc tweaked her hair. 'And how do you know that, little sister? I thought you were impervious to love.' He chuckled. 'You'll marry a man with money, and probably Harry Mapleton, I dare say. I can't see you throwing yourself away on a poor man, however much in love you are.'

He knew her well, but Georgina wasn't about to tell him so. Deftly, she changed the subject. 'Well, you'll be off with the cattle drove before very long, well out of harm's way.'

'Are you really that naïve, Georgina?' Caradoc asked. 'Don't you know that all the young women will be vying for my attention? The nights are hot and long on the drovers' roads and the starry nights are most conducive to romance.'

'Well, the girls who walk the roads are simple folk, daughters of poor tenant farmers, most of them. But Manon Jenkins is not like them, as you said yourself. She's been brought up to be respectable.'

'She isn't likely to join the drove, is she?' He didn't wait for an answer. 'Well then, what's your objection to me making a friend of her?' Caradoc flipped the reins, urging the horses into a canter.

'You know as well as I do she's far below you in social standing.' Georgina settled back in her seat and closed her eyes. 'And her sort would want much more than mere friendship. Now be quiet, I have to make up my mind what I'm going to wear to the assembly rooms tonight.' She was tired of discussing Caradoc and his women; it was high time she concentrated on her own life, and last time she'd gone to the assembly rooms she'd danced with a very handsome young man, now what was his name? She knew well enough, she'd heard one of his friends call him Clive—now that was a far nicer name than Harry. She sighed expectantly. Should she wear the muslin with the barley design in red, green and mauve, colours that flattered her pale skin and brown hair, or her older but more elegant dress of celestial blue broche levantine with the lovely shapely sleeves?

'You've gone very quiet all of a sudden.' Caradoc's voice broke into her thoughts and Georgina smiled.

'I told you to be quiet, I've got important things on my mind.'

And she had; she needed a set of new clothes, London-made dresses for day and for evening. And she would love some new bibi bonnets, with the tall crown and the broad brim that framed the face. She felt a sense of excitement as she imagined how fine she'd look in the latest fashions; she *must* persuade her father to let her go to London. She could easily ride along with Caradoc when he took the herd to Smithfield. Father could surely spare one of the good carriages; he owned enough of them not to miss one.

She glanced at Caradoc, wondering what he would make of her idea. Would he be willing to have her along on the trail?

'Caradoc?' She spoke cajolingly. 'Please can I

ask you a favour?'

'You can ask, I don't say I'll agree, but go on, what is it?'

Georgina touched his arm. 'Will you let me ride along with you when you take the herd of cattle up to Smithfield?'

'What? Have you along watching my every move? No fear! You wouldn't be able to wait to run home to Father with tales of my wrongdoings.'

'But Caradoc, I wouldn't say a word, I promise you that. Please say you'll let me come. I could be useful to you.'

'How? You can't cook, you certainly can't do weeding and so far as I'm aware you've never held a pair of knitting needles.'

'I don't need to knit, do I? There are other things I can do.'

'What other things? You can hardly sell stockings up in London, can you? Fine help you'd be.'

'But just think when we *get* to London—I would be an asset, we could do the social round together. A man never looks right attending functions on his own.'

'When I arrive in London, Aunt Prudence will be there to give me all the support I need, thank you.'

'But Aunt Pru is old, she's no fun and she's indiscreet, you know that she has an unbridled tongue.' She touched his arm. 'Come on, Caradoc, think about it. I need to get to London, my wardrobe is pathetically out of date.'

'Well go on the mail then, like everyone else,' Caradoc said in exasperation. 'I don't need you on the drove. In any case, it takes much longer to reach London travelling overland, don't you realize that?'

'If I went on the mail you'd have to come with me. If I accompany you on the cattle drive it's killing two birds with one stone.'

'We'll see. Now for heaven's sake shut up and let me concentrate on controlling the horses.'

Well pleased, Georgina settled back in her seat. She had Caradoc half convinced that her idea was a good one; all she needed now was her father's permission, and he could refuse her nothing.

\*       \*       \*

She'd had a good day. Non packed her box with what was left of her stock of herbs and medicines. It was gratifying that so many people had faith in her. She folded her cloth and put it in the basket, then folded up her stool and stood for a moment looking around her. The market was quiet now, the street empty of people; it was growing dark—high time she headed for home.

Her box was considerably lighter than when she'd arrived, and even the stool seemed to behave itself, with legs folded neatly instead of sticking into her sides. The purse hanging from her apron front was satisfyingly heavy; the coins clinked together and Non was well pleased with her day's work.

She turned down Salubrious Passage, making for the Mackworth Hotel, where she was to meet up with Mr Robinson for the trip back home. It was dark in the passageway; even the lamp arching over the cobbled way did little to dispel the gloom.

Non began to walk more quickly, sensing, rather

36

than hearing, footsteps behind her. Soon she would turn into Wind Street, where the lighting was good, and from there make her way to the busy High Street.

She was almost at the end of Salubrious Passage when she was caught roughly in a cruel grip and slammed against the wall of the building. She opened her mouth to scream but a blow across her face sent her sprawling onto the ground, her bottles shattering as her box crashed to the floor. The cobbles were hard and cold beneath her. Non heard the voices of two men arguing. She tried to get to her feet but another blow caught her above the eyes and she felt blood begin to run down her face. Blinded, she tried to call for help, but before she could form the words a hand was clamped over her mouth.

She felt other hands scrabbling at her waist and fear was like a thick fog in her throat. Her skirt was torn aside and it dawned on her that the men were not content with robbing her—they intended to violate her. A hand clamped on her breast, and Non grabbed it and bit on it as hard as she could. Her face was slapped hard but she held on to the man, hearing his cries of pain with a feeling of triumph. But her strength was ebbing. She knew she could not keep up the fight much longer.

She heard a shout from the far end of the passage and recognized the voice. She struggled to free her mouth and screamed as loudly as she could. 'Caradoc! Help me!'

The man crouching on the ground beside her muttered a curse and his companion grabbed him by the arm. 'Let's get out of here,' he said, and as suddenly as they had appeared, her two attackers

37

vanished into the darkness.

Non got unsteadily to her feet and rubbed her apron over her face, wiping the blood away.

Caradoc was running towards her. He caught her in his arms and held her close. 'Are you all right?' he asked.

'Yes, I'm a bit shaky and a bit bruised, but thanks to you I'm not too badly hurt.'

'Why are you heading in this direction anyway? How are you getting home?'

'Mr Robinson, one of our neighbours, is giving me a lift. I'm meeting him outside the Mackworth.' She took a deep breath. 'I'd better hurry or he'll leave without me.'

'I'll walk you to the meeting place and if your Mr Robinson isn't there I'll take you home myself.'

'Oh, I couldn't put you to the trouble.'

'Nonsense! It's no trouble, and if it wasn't for the circumstances it would be quite a pleasure.'

Non was very conscious of Caradoc's tall presence at her side. She felt dreadful, her head was aching and she knew her breast would be bruised from the rough handling her assailant had given her. The last thing she wanted was for Caradoc to see her like this. To her relief, when she arrived at the Mackworth Hotel, Mr Robinson was still waiting.

'Good heavens above, girl! Where have you been all this time? You're very lucky I didn't go without you. I don't know what my dear wife will have to say about me being so late, I'm sure.'

Caradoc smiled down at her. 'So Mr Robinson is not *your* Mr Robinson at all?'

'Of course not.'

As she came into the light from the doorway of

the Mackworth Hotel, Mr Robinson saw her face for the first time. 'Dear Lord, what's happened to you, child?' He leapt down from the driving seat and took her by the shoulders. 'You'll have a couple of shiners in the morning, but I don't suppose there are any broken bones, Manon.' He looked down at her blood-stained apron. 'Did the scoundrels do anything else to you?' he asked hesitantly.

'No, they just hit me and stole my money.' Non's voice was hoarse. 'I was lucky that Mr Jones came along before any more harm could come to me.'

'Oh, evening to you, Mr Jones, I didn't notice you by there.' He doffed his hat to Caradoc and then took Non's arm.

'Come on, *merchi*, let me get you home.' Gently he helped her up into the carriage, his voice full of concern. 'There's sorry I am that I shouted at you. I should have guessed that a good girl like you wouldn't keep me waiting for no reason.'

' 'Night, Mr Jones.'

Mr Robinson doffed his hat once again and then shook the reins of the horse so that the animal was startled into movement. The jerking of the carriage made Non aware of just how much she had been hurt. Her very bones ached and her skin was grazed and burning. Still, it could have been much worse. There was a warm feeling inside her as she thought of Caradoc coming to her rescue like a knight of old.

Non was relieved when Mr Robinson dropped her off outside her door. 'Thank you for waiting for me,' she said softly. 'I'll make sure I'm not late another time.'

She let herself into the silence of the house and

stood for a moment, listening in the hallway. She prayed her father would be asleep already, so that he wouldn't see her bruised face. He had been retiring to bed early since his heart trouble.

'That you, Manon?' The resonant sound of his voice echoed down the stairs. 'You're late, girl, I was worried about you.'

'I'm all right, Father,' Non called back. 'You go to sleep. I'm just going to get some supper and get to bed myself.'

'Good night. God bless, child,' he called, and then there was the sound of his bedroom door closing. Non sighed in relief as she went into the kitchen. The fire was still burning, the bright sparks comforting in the darkness. Non lit the candles and stood for a moment, wondering what to do. She caught sight of herself in the small mirror and gasped in horror. One of her eyes was almost closed and dried blood caked her forehead.

Sighing, Non pushed the kettle onto the fire and then fetched the enamel bowl from the cupboard. When the water was warm, she gently washed away the blood. She acknowledged that Mr Robinson was right—she would have two black eyes by morning. There was no way she could hide that from her father, but still, he would have his sleep tonight and she could tell him what had happened in the morning.

At last, Non crept into the comfort of her bed and eased her aching bones under the heavy quilt. She sighed with weariness. She had lost her medicines and had her money stolen, but at least she was alive and safe in her own home, and for that she was profoundly thankful.

# CHAPTER FOUR

The sun was shining into the small room at the back of the vicarage where Non was busy working. The room smelled pleasantly of honeysuckle—she was boiling the leaves to make a poultice to ease Mrs Preece's gout. The first medication had done little to calm the inflammation and Non had promised to find something new.

She consulted her copy of *Culpeper's Complete Herbal* and read out loud: 'Dodoneus saith the leaves and flowers of the honeysuckle are good to ease the griping pains of the gout, the herb being boiled and used in a clyster.'

'What? Talking to yourself again, Manon? I've told you about that before—it's the first sign of madness.' Her father smiled as he came into the room. 'Let me look at your poor face.' He turned her to the light. 'Ah, it's your own welfare you should be thinking about now, my child, not that of your customers.'

'I'm all right, really. The bruises are fading now and I'll soon be my old self again.'

'Well, I won't have you remaining at the market after everyone else has packed up and gone home. Stay with the crowd where you'll be safe, do you hear me? Soon I'll be able to pick you up myself and we won't have to rely on Mr Robinson's good will.'

'I hear you and I promise that I will leave the market earlier next time.'

She looked up at her father. She thought him a man who had the dignity of the Church about him.

Even now when he was wearing his ordinary suit of clothes with the white dog collar he looked every inch a vicar. She loved him so very much. But as she looked more closely at him now, she could see he was pale and sweating. He had never really recovered from the heart problem that had dogged him these past weeks.

'You're a fine one to lecture me, Father. You're not resting enough, are you? You are so involved with your parishioners that you don't think of yourself. Why not let me find you a remedy in Mr Culpeper's herbal?'

'Now Manon, you know what the doctor said about that, don't you?'

'But doctors don't know everything, really they don't. The herbal remedy recommended for heart pains by Culpeper is Our Lady's thistle. Now you couldn't have a more saintly name for a herb than that, could you?'

Her father shook his head.

Manon put her arms around him and hugged him. 'Listen, Papa, a little of the seed of the thistle in distilled water would do wonders for your heart troubles, I'm sure of it.'

Her father waved his hand dismissively. 'I'd prefer to follow the advice of the good doctor, Manon, my dear.' He smiled to soften his words. 'I dare say your herbs are all right for the wind, or even for the gout and such minor afflictions, but the heart is a delicate organ, my dear, the whole body depends upon it to function properly.'

Manon sighed in exasperation. It was no use arguing with her father. He had resolved to listen to the doctor, and whatever she said to him now, he would not change his mind.

'Have you finished in here?' her father asked.

Non looked up at him in surprise. 'Well, there's nothing urgently awaiting my attention, Father. What do you want?'

'I want you to come into the drawing room and talk to me, that's what I want. It isn't good for a young girl to shut herself away meddling with roots and seeds and herbs, not all the time.'

Non shook her head in exasperation. 'The other day you were telling my customers how good my remedies were, and now because the doctor says different you're turning your back on me and my medicines.'

'No, no, of course I'm not. Now I know your roots and herbs and things are God-given, but what you sell at the market is for minor ailments. That's all I mean, Manon.'

She sighed in resignation. 'All right, Papa. You go to the drawing room, I'll just wash my hands and I'll be with you.'

When she joined him a few minutes later, her father was sitting in the window with the Bible on his knee. He looked up with a smile and carefully marked his page before replacing the Bible on the table.

'What have I done wrong this time?' Non sat opposite her father. 'I'm only called in here when you want to lecture me about something or other.'

'It's not a lecture, Non, my dear child,' he said gravely. He seldom used the diminutive of her name, and suddenly Non was frightened.

'What's wrong, Father?'

'You seem to get along very well with young Morgan,' he said, and Non stared at him in surprise, wondering at the turn the conversation

43

was taking. 'Have you thought of him in, shall we say, romantic terms?'

'No, Father, of course I haven't! Morgan is a friend and that's all he is. Why do you ask?'

Her father took out his spotless handkerchief and mopped his brow with it. 'I'm not very good at this sort of thing, but I feel I must talk to you about your future.' He coughed and looked away from her. 'I'm getting old, Manon, and I want you to be well cared for when I'm taken to my Maker.'

'Don't talk like that!' Non put her arm around his shoulders. 'Please, Father, you're frightening me.'

Gently, he disentangled himself. 'Well, you must face it, my dear, I won't always be around to take care of you. Now I know Morgan is one of the labouring classes, but he's a good upstanding man and he cares very deeply about you.'

'Did the doctor say anything to you about your health, Father? Because if so I want to know exactly what it was.'

'No, no, it's nothing like that. But I am getting older and my health isn't what you would call robust.' He sighed. 'I just thought that if, by any chance, you were interested in Morgan, then I would gladly give my blessing to such a union.'

Non stood up and put both hands on her hips. 'Will you stop talking like a vicar and speak more like a father? Tell me, what's brought all this marriage business on?'

'It's nothing, let's forget I spoke about the subject.'

'No, Father, I won't leave it. You brought the matter up and I want to know exactly why.'

'It's just as I said, I won't always be here to take

44

care of you.'

'No, but while you are here I'm going to take care of *you*.' She shook her head at him. 'You'll have many years yet to worry about me and any marriage I might make, but right now I'm not interested in any man.'

That was not quite true, she realized, as a vision of Caradoc Jones came into her mind. Now there was a man who would make her heart sing with joy. How brave he'd been to rescue her from the hands of those ruffians who had robbed her. But then he was way out of her reach. Caradoc was the son of a wealthy man; his father was the founder of the Bank of the Black Ox and owned many acres of land. Caradoc would probably marry one of the gentry, a woman with beauty and a fortune to give him.

'Are you sure you've no young man in mind?' her father asked quietly.

Non shook her head. 'No, Father, I can't think of any young man who would make a suitable husband for me.' On an impulse, she kissed her father's balding head. 'Now stop worrying, we are going to be all right, you'll see.'

\*       \*       \*

It was a few nights later when Non was wakened by the sound of groaning coming from her father's room. She pushed aside the bedclothes and pulled on her dressing gown with trembling fingers.

'I'm coming, Father!'

She lit a candle and carried it before her as she crossed the landing. The shadows jumped out at her like weird ghosts and her heart was pounding as she opened the door of the bedroom.

'Oh, dear Lord!' Her father was lying on the floor. His hands, veined with blue in the flickering light, were clasped across his chest. 'Father, what is it?' She needn't have asked, she knew at once that it was his heart. 'I'll send for the doctor right away, just you lie still and don't worry about anything.'

'No!' He caught her hand. 'Stay with me, Non, my little girl, and hold my hand while I leave this life and go to my Maker.'

'No, Father, you're not going to die. I won't let you die, do you hear me?'

His blue lips parted. 'Listen to me. There's money—not much, but it's in my study in a bag in my desk—it's for you.'

'Don't try to talk, Father, please. Just lie still while I fetch the doctor.'

He held onto her hand. 'There's no time, it's too late for the doctor. Sit here with me a while, that's all I want now.'

Non swallowed her tears and knelt at her father's side. She knew he was speaking the truth, there was little anyone could do for him now.

'Remember what I said about Morgan. He's a good man, strong and honest, he will take care of you.'

'Don't worry about me, Father. You just save your strength. This attack might well pass off in a minute or two.'

Even as she spoke, his face contorted with pain.

'Papa!' she cried out. 'Don't die! Please don't die! How can I manage without you?'

He was past hearing. His lips were suddenly bloodless and his eyes rolled back in his head.

'Oh, Papa!' She kissed him, her tears falling onto

the wrinkled skin of his face. And then he was quite still, his eyes open, even though there was no light in them.

Non put her head on his chest. 'I love you, Papa. I love you so much.' And she prayed that somewhere in his heaven, her father heard and understood.

*　　*　　*

The Mackworth Hotel was crowded. It was ticketing day, when the copper barons made bids for the loads of ore that were brought upriver to the town of Swansea. The day had gone well and now the gentlemen were relaxing with a welcome drink.

Caradoc Jones sat in one of the plush chairs, a glass of whisky on the table before him, staring at his father as though he was a stranger. 'Will you stop telling me it's time I was married, Father. I'll make up my own mind about it, all right?'

'Well, I'm disappointed in you, Caradoc,' George Jones said. 'I thought you'd have a wife and a brood of children by now.' He paused and spoke more softly. 'You know how the women dance attendance on you. For God's sake, settle down with one of them.'

Caradoc ignored that last remark. 'I'm sorry I'm not meeting your very high standards, Father.' His voice was cold. He was a grown man and he had no intention of letting his father map out his future. 'The fact is I'm not ready to settle down with any woman just yet.'

'Well, all right, I suppose I should get Georgie married off first anyway, but say you'll think about what I've said.'

'I'll think about it,' Caradoc said flatly. 'When I come back from the next cattle drove up to London.'

'You're a stubborn fool, Caradoc. I was married by the time I was your age, a widower with three children to my credit.' He looked into his glass. 'It was a tragic loss, losing your mother and your brother to rubella, but we all have our cross to bear.'

Oh, Lord, Father was becoming maudlin. 'Well, you still have two children, Father, and both Georgina and I care for you very much. But you must understand that we have to run our own lives. You can't expect us to jump to your command—times have changed since you were young.'

Caradoc looked at his father, who was showing few signs of age. His hair was touched with grey, but for all that he was still lusty, with a willing young mistress to keep him entertained.

When Caradoc was young, he'd blamed his father for the coldness in his parents' marriage. Mother had been pretty and bright and always smelled of lavender. Caradoc had thought there was no finer lady in the land. But once he was old enough to taste the fruits of love for himself, Caradoc realized there were practices best conducted with a willing mistress than with a lady of quality like his mother.

'You're sulking now, are you, son?'

Caradoc smiled. 'No, Father, I'm not. I was just thinking about your mistress—she'll be waiting for you, anxious to see you by now, won't she?'

His father blanched. 'Caradoc! I wish you wouldn't talk so crudely. Other people might hear you.'

'All the married men in the place are up to the same game as you, Father,' Caradoc said. 'A little drink before running off to an exciting mistress, so I wouldn't worry about anyone hearing if I were you.'

His father leaned forward and spoke in a sibilant whisper. 'And what about you, son? You can hardly cast the first stone, can you?'

Caradoc stared at his father open-mouthed. 'How on earth did you know . . . ?'

'Ah, that's got you wondering, hasn't it? Not much escapes me, my boy. I've been asking myself why you accompany me to town every weekend, and the answer has to be a woman.'

He waved his hand as Caradoc opened his mouth to speak. 'Don't bother to deny it, you do right to take a woman from time to time.' He sighed heavily. 'But you really need a wife, if only to give yourself a bit of dignity and standing in the community.'

'I've said I'll think about it when I return from the cattle drove, Father.' He glanced at his watch. 'I must go, I'll see you in the morning when we ride back to Five Saints, shall I?'

'Aye, all right.' George Jones got to his feet. 'I'll bid you good night, son.' He coughed and when he spoke his voice was gruff. 'I do care about your future, you know, son. I only keep on at you because I know what's good for you.'

'That's all right,' Caradoc said gently. 'And I care about you, too. But on the subject of marriage I have to decide for myself who my bride will be.'

Caradoc watched his father leave the room; then he dropped some coins onto the table and let himself out through the plush foyer of the hotel, into the night.

*       *       *

Ffion Greenslade waited impatiently for her lover to come to her. She stood in the window of the hotel room staring out into the street below. In spite of the hour, there were many people about: carriages rolled by, and now and again the sound of drunken revelry drifted to where she was standing.

Impatiently she jerked the sash of her robe around her, wondering if Caradoc was tiring of her already. They had been lovers now for more than a month, and when he was with her he was as attentive as ever. But sometimes, even when she was safely in his arms, she felt as though he was drifting away from her.

The tapping on the door was discreet, but the sound startled her. She caught her breath, knowing it was Caradoc. Excitedly she hurried to open the door.

He swept her into his arms at once and carried her to the bed. He took her swiftly, without his usual finesse, without even allowing her to remove her robe. And then, when he rolled away from her, she felt cheated.

'You were late,' she said, and disappointment lent her voice a sour note. At once she knew she'd made a mistake. Mistresses did not criticize their lovers, it was foolish and ill advised. But somehow, once she had started to complain, she couldn't stop. 'And I do not appreciate being pounced upon like a common street girl.'

He looked at her in surprise. 'I don't know what

you mean.'

'I mean that I have feelings too. I need some consideration from you so that my own needs as well as yours are met.'

'So you're complaining about my performance, are you?' Caradoc spoke in a dangerously quiet voice.

She heard the warning note but chose to ignore it. 'Well, judging by tonight's standards, you couldn't satisfy even the most easy of women, not with such lack of skill and patience.'

He usually spent the night with her, but now he got up from the bed in one easy movement and reached for his clothes. 'In that case I might as well leave.' He didn't look at her as he finished dressing, then took some shiny coins out of his pocket.

She stared at the money. It was a large amount by anyone's standards and she knew what it meant. 'You're paying me off!' She looked at him in disbelief. 'Just because I complained this once?'

'I've lost interest in you,' he said flatly. 'Best to end it now before matters between us become even worse, don't you agree?'

'But Caradoc, I care about you. You are not just a quick coupling to me, you're far more than that.'

'Well in that case you should have held your tongue.' He moved to the door. 'Find some other man to service you, Ffion. I've finished with you.'

She followed him to the door. 'How dare you treat me like a piece of dirt?' She could hardly breathe, she was so humiliated. 'I curse you, Caradoc Jones, you and your heirs, and I hope you rot in hell.'

'I don't doubt I'll rot in hell, but it won't be with you.'

He left her then, and Ffion put her hands over her eyes as the hot tears flowed down her cheeks. She sank onto the bed, knowing he would never come back to her now. Well, she thought, brightening a little, she'd soon find another man to keep her. She'd do well to remember that love was only for fools.

## CHAPTER FIVE

Non didn't know how she got through the days leading up to the funeral. The vicarage suddenly seemed large, as if there were too many rooms, and everywhere there were reminders of her father. And now, as she stood at the graveside, she felt lost and alone.

'A lot of people have come to pay their respects, Non.' Morgan was at her side. 'Even Caradoc Jones has journeyed from Five Saints to represent his family.'

'I can't believe he's gone. I feel so alone.' Non swallowed hard, trying to hold back the tears.

'I'm here whenever you need me.' Morgan touched her arm and she looked up at him.

'I know, and I'm grateful.'

'Look, Non, have you thought about your future?'

'No, I don't suppose I have. But don't go worrying about me now, I'll be all right. Father left me a small legacy, I won't starve.'

'No, but . . . well, never mind, we can talk about it later when all this is over.'

Non sighed. There was the funeral tea to be

faced yet. The good ladies of the parish had done their vicar proud; the church hall was decorated with flowers and the tables covered with fresh white cloths. Large loaves of bread had been sliced and platters of ham and cold tongue placed at strategic intervals along the tables. It was time she went inside.

Non was about to turn away from her father's newly dug grave when she felt a light touch on her shoulder.

'Miss Jenkins,' Caradoc Jones lifted his hat, 'may I offer my condolences on your sad loss?'

'Thank you, you're very kind.' Non bowed her head, embarrassed by her tears.

'And if there is anything I can do to help, please don't hesitate to let me know.'

'Thank you.' The words were inadequate, they didn't express the feeling that was suddenly warming her heart. 'And thank you for coming. My father would have been very proud that one of the Jones family was here to pay their respects.'

He lifted his hat again and moved away, and Non found herself surrounded by neighbours and parishioners, all wanting to offer their sympathy.

She felt numb as she led the way to the church hall for the funeral tea. People were relaxing now away from the sombre atmosphere of the graveyard, but Non just wanted it all to be over so that she could sit alone by the fire and think her thoughts and sift through her memories of her father.

'Miss Jenkins, I'm so sorry about your father. It must all be very distressing for you, a young lady left alone in the world.'

'Oh, Doctor Saunders, please don't concern

yourself about me.' She managed a polite smile but she was vexed with him, he'd prevented her doing her best for her father with her own herbal remedies. But then, she was probably looking for someone or something to blame for her father's death.

She endured the next hour feeling only a sense of unreality; she had forgotten the number of people who offered their condolences, some even hugging her warmly, obviously moved by her loss, and she was grateful but she was so very tired.

At last, the hall was empty except for a few stragglers. Non set about clearing up the debris of leftover food. Morgan was at her side, helping in his clumsy manly way.

'I still can't believe he's gone.' Non spoke with a catch in her voice. 'It's as if any minute my father will come walking through the door. Oh, Morgan, what am I going to do without him?'

She sank onto one of the hard wooden chairs and rubbed her eyes as the tears started to tumble down her face. 'I miss him so much; the house seems empty and forbidding without him. My dear father, why did he have to die like that? He wasn't as old as all that, was he?'

Morgan stood looking down at her and she could see he was feeling helpless. He didn't know what to say to comfort her, and somehow she found that endearing.

'Come on,' he said at last. 'I'll walk you home and then I'll come back and finish up here. You need to get some rest.'

Non found herself meekly agreeing. 'Thank you, Morgan, for all your kindness.'

He was embarrassed by her words. 'That's what

friends are for.' His voice was gruff with emotion and Non touched his arm.

'You're a real true friend.'

She was silent then until they reached the large gates leading to the vicarage. Darkness was falling, but in the vicarage windows the candles glowed a welcome. With a catch in her throat Non realized that Mrs Miles had been at work trying to make her return from the funeral as pleasant as possible. She hadn't approved of Non going, she said a lady's place was in the house while the menfolk attended to the last rites of the dead.

'Come in, Morgan, have a cup of tea with me.' Non looked up at him as he stood silhouetted against the sunset; he was a big man with a big heart, and wasn't it a pity she couldn't fall in love with him?

'I'll come in if you really want me to, but there's no need for politeness, not where I'm concerned.'

'I'm not being polite, I really want you to come in and rest for a while before you clear up the church hall.'

'All right then, if you're sure I won't be in the way.'

Non put her hand on his arm. 'Morgan, I'm alone in the world now and I need your friendship more than I ever did.'

'You'll always have that, and a good deal more if only . . .' His voice faltered into silence as Non shook her head.

'Don't go on, Morgan, there's only so much I can stand right now.'

'Well, I'll just say I'll always be here if you should need me.'

It was warm and light in the hallway of the

vicarage, and as soon as Non handed her jacket to Flora, the young maid bowed her head and spoke in a low voice.

'I haven't said much these past days, Miss, but I—well, me and Cook, we're sorry about the Master. Me, Cook and Dennis as well, we've been talking and we all know the Reverend will be sorely missed.'

'Thank you, Flora, there's kind of you.' Non bit her lip, but after a moment she composed herself. 'Would you bring a tray of tea, Flora? My throat is so dry I feel it's full of wool.' She led the way into the drawing room and gestured for Morgan to sit down.

'Ah, it's nice to see a good fire.' Morgan spoke with forced cheeriness and Non smiled at him.

'I didn't ask you in out of politeness, so don't feel you must make polite conversation with me, Morgan. We've known each other too long to worry about the niceties. Just sit down and we'll have a cup of tea together.'

They sat in silence then on opposite sides of the fire, just like an old couple long married. At any other time Non would have found the situation amusing, but now all she felt was a deep sadness that never more would her father sit with her, his head buried in the Bible, or at the desk, pen in hand, writing his sermon for Sunday service.

'So how's your business doing now, Morgan?' she asked. 'Are there many beasts to shoe before the next cattle drove to London?'

'Aye, there's work enough for me. I can't grumble, Non.' He smiled suddenly. 'But who's the one making polite conversation now?'

'You're right. I'm sorry, there just seems nothing

real to say at a time like this.'

There was a gentle tapping on the door and Flora came into the room with a tray on her arm.

'That's all right, Flora, I'll pour the tea.' In silence the maid let herself out of the room, but not without first throwing an admiring glance in Morgan's direction. As Non handed him a cup of steaming tea, she recognized, not for the first time, what a handsome man he was. He met her gaze and smiled, and she returned his smile, wanting to hug him for his thoughtfulness.

'Now,' she said, 'tell me about your work—and I'm not just making conversation, I'm really interested.'

She sat back in her chair, her tea neglected on the table beside her, and listened to the soothing sound of Morgan's voice as he told her about 'throwing' the cattle. It was a difficult job that involved a lot of strength and a great deal of skill. Each animal had to be thrown to the ground and the legs secured in preparation for the shoeing. The shoes needed to be firm and strong in readiness for the long cattle drove into the green fields of England. But somehow, Morgan managed to make even that sound mundane.

Non began to relax. The sound of his voice was soothing, and a warm sense of gratitude filled her as she listened. Her father was right, Morgan was a good man. But what use was that if she could not fall in love with him?

\*     \*     \*

'How's she looking, Flora?' Mrs Miles sat astride her chair, her knees apart to encompass her full belly. 'Poor Miss Non, going to the funeral isn't proper for a lady, but then she 'ad no option, the Reverend having no sons to see him off.' She sighed and scratched at her bulging hips.

'She's looking very poorly,' Flora sniffled. 'Pale and peaky, not like herself at all. Poor thing's alone in the world.'

'Not quite alone, though, is she?' Mrs Miles closed one eye in a wink. 'Morgan's there with her, and him madly in love with the mistress and her too blind to see it.'

'Oh, he's a lovely man, big and handsome—I wouldn't mind getting my hands on him.' Flora clasped her hands together as if in anticipation. 'The way he looks at her an' all, it fair breaks my heart. Miss Non don't know how lucky she is to have a nice handsome man wanting to please her.'

'Well, it's not your place to talk about the Vicar's daughter that way.' Mrs Miles leaned back and her chair creaked in protest. 'Miss Manon's been brought up as a respectable young lady, she doesn't have bad thoughts about men. Not like you, Flora.'

'My thoughts aren't bad,' Flora's eyes gleamed, 'I'm just dreaming that one day a man like Morgan will fall in love with me.'

Mrs Miles shook her head. 'And what young men do you meet, tell me that? There's only young Dennis, and he hasn't grown a beard yet.' She struggled to her feet. '*Duw*, my bones are aching like a set of bad teeth tonight. You get that dough from the hearth, Flora, it should be proved enough by now.'

Flora obeyed and Mrs Miles watched her in satisfaction. The girl had a good way with the cooking and she was quite skilful with a needle as well. If only she wasn't so flighty when it came to dealings with men. Flora batted her long eyelashes at everyone from the butcher boy to the rag-and-bone merchant's son. She'd land herself in trouble if she wasn't careful.

'You, girl,' she poked Flora with a thick finger, 'my advice to you is to keep your hand on your ha'penny so you don't get into no trouble.'

Flora smiled cheekily. 'I'm sure I don't know what you mean, Cook. I don't have no ha'penny to keep my hand on.'

Mrs Miles shook her head. 'There's no talking to you young girls of today, flighty and giddy, the lot of you.'

'Not so giddy, Cook. Joe the shoes has asked me to walk out with him. Now then, what do you think of that?'

'I think you ought to heed my warning! Don't let any young boyo take away your good name. There's walking out together and then there's an honest wedding, and the two don't always go together.'

'I wouldn't let Joe take any liberties, so don't you worry now. I'm in love with another boy, his name's Thomas, but for now I want to keep all that a secret. But it'll be all right in the end, you'll see.'

'I don't like secrets, you just watch yourself.' Mrs Miles sighed and rubbed at her swollen fingers. 'My bone ache's bad tonight, I wonder if Miss Manon's got anything to ease the pain.'

'Well, you could go and ask her,' Flora said, 'and while you're gone I'll make us a nice cup of tea, shall I?'

'Oh, I don't know.' Mrs Miles smoothed her hands as though to rub away the pain. 'I can 'ardly go and interrupt when she's got a guest with her.'

'It's only Morgan the blacksmith, mind, not some high and mighty man like that Caradoc Jones.'

'I suppose you're right.' She heaved herself to her feet. 'I'll go and see the mistress, 'cos the pain is real bad and I don't think I can sleep with my hands aching like they do.'

Mrs Miles paused at the door, watching for a moment as Flora warmed the brown china teapot. 'You're not so bad, are you love?' she said. 'If you wasn't so flighty you'd have the makings of a good servant.'

*      *      *

Non was seeing Morgan into the hallway as Mrs Miles came out of the shadows, her face pale, her hands held out before her as though she was begging for alms.

'What's wrong, Mrs Miles?'

'My hands are playing me up like the devil, Miss. Have you got some medicine so that I can ease the pain a bit?'

'I've got some prickly asparagus; Mrs Preece said it's excellent for curing the bone ache.'

Mrs Miles screwed up her lips in disgust. 'Prickly asparagus—what's that when it's at home?'

'It's only a naturally grown plant, and mixed in with a drop of wine it's quite pleasant to the taste.'

Mrs Miles's face brightened at the prospect of some wine. 'Well, thank you, Miss, I suppose it don't do no harm to try it.'

'I'll get some for you when I've seen my visitor to the door.'

'You shouldn't be doing that yourself, Miss Non.

You should call Flora for seeing guests out. That's part of her duties, mind.'

'I know, Mrs Miles, but Morgan the blacksmith is a very special visitor and I wanted to see him out myself.'

Morgan smiled at her words and Non quickly opened the door, hoping she'd been friendly without being forward.

'Thank you for everything, Morgan.' She stood in the hall and watched as Morgan hovered on the step as if at a loss for conversation. 'I'll see you soon, then—probably,' she added as an afterthought.

Morgan nodded and made his way towards the gates. 'Bye, Non.' He lifted his hand to wave and Non closed the door, sighing heavily. Morgan was such a nice man, and yet all she felt for him was friendship, while he, clearly, wanted more.

'Right smitten with you is Morgan, mind.' Mrs Miles's voice echoed Non's thoughts.

'Nonsense!' Non pressed her hands together. 'Now, let's get you some medicine and a little drop of wine, see if that helps ease your pains.'

For a time, Non was occupied preparing the medicine for Mrs Miles, but later, when she sat in the drawing room alone, the feeling of loss overwhelmed her and she put her hands over her eyes and let the hot tears flow between her fingers. Her father was gone and there was not one thing she could do to change it.

# CHAPTER SIX

Georgina smiled; she knew her father was well pleased with her performance this evening. She had simpered and dimpled throughout supper at the odious Harry Mapleton, who had dined with them for the third time in a week.

'Father, now the weather's better, I'd like to go up to London to see Aunt Prudence. I think perhaps she could help me choose some fashionable clothes. I could take a coach and ride with Caradoc.'

Her father looked at her thoughtfully. 'Even if I gave my consent, I don't think your brother would be too pleased to have you with him slowing down the cattle drove.'

'I wouldn't slow anyone down, Papa. They all have to stop at night, the men and the beasts. I know they stay at inns along the way—I've heard you and Caradoc talk about it often enough.' She smiled and played her trump card. 'And if you want Mr Mapleton to think me a lady of breeding and not a country bumpkin, I'll need a whole new wardrobe.'

Her father stroked his beard thoughtfully. 'Let me think about it.' He rustled his paper and lifted it up to cover his face, but Georgina was smiling. She knew she had won the day: she would have her way and go to London, whatever Caradoc felt about it.

\*　　　\*　　　\*

Non was sitting in the drawing room leafing

through her *Culpeper's Complete Herbal* when Flora popped her head round the door to tell her there was a visitor. 'He's from the Church, Miss, the Reverend Powell. Shall I show him in?'

Non nodded. 'Yes, of course, Flora.'

The Reverend Powell came into the room and stood for a moment in the doorway. He was a thin man with a long face made longer by the greying beard that sprawled like an untended shrub onto his chest.

'Afternoon, Miss Jenkins. I've come to tell you that we've now found a new vicar, and to establish when it will be convenient for you to vacate the vicarage.'

Non felt her heart stop within her breast. 'I don't understand. Don't you realize this is my home?'

His voice became firmer. 'I'm sorry, Miss Jenkins, but you surely must have realized that the building goes with the position of vicar to this parish.' He stood before her like a bird of prey, thin of frame and round of shoulder. He continually rubbed his gloved hands together as though he felt chilly, despite the warmth of the house. Non stared at the gloves as if mesmerized, trying to take in what the man was saying. 'You *do* understand, don't you? I have no choice but to ask you to make other living arrangements as soon as possible.'

Non took a deep breath. 'I'm to be thrown out of my home, then?' She looked around her at the familiar room and out into the hallway, at the stairs, the banister newly polished by Flora, and up at the tall landing window which sent a shaft of light splashing like a golden stream across the carpet. Tears blurred her vision and the man coughed apologetically.

'I'm so sorry, but there has been a new vicar appointed in your father's place, a man with a large family, and so, regrettably, you have to move out of here as soon as it is convenient.'

Non felt as though she had been doused in cold water. How could she leave all that was familiar to her—the house that had been her home, her friends, Mrs Miles and Flora—and where would she go?

'Have you relatives living in the area?' It seemed the cleric had read her mind.

Non shook her head. 'As you know, my father was sent here from the village of Five Saints, and even there I have no one I could live with.' She swallowed hard. 'How long do I have to pack my things?'

'The most I can give you is two weeks, Miss Jenkins, but I'm sure you'll have found alternative accommodation by then.'

She straightened her shoulders. 'Very well, I'll be out of here as soon as I can find somewhere else to live.'

He gave her a long stare over the beak of his nose. 'Two weeks, Miss Jenkins.'

When he had gone, Non sank into a chair and put her hands over her eyes. What could she do, where could she go? She had a little money, but Papa had never been rich, so what inheritance he had left her wouldn't last very long. She would have to find work of some kind, but she wasn't trained for anything.

She thought of the work Mrs Miles and Flora did. Would she be able to cope with cooking or cleaning some big house? She looked at her pale hands and shook her head—as a cook or a maid she would be more of a hindrance than a help. She glanced down at the book she'd laid aside, *Culpeper's Complete Herbal*, and a small flame of hope lit in her heart. Perhaps she could work as a healer; she could set up shop and sell her medicines the way she did on market days.

But it would not be easy. She would need somewhere to live and work, and the small amount of money she possessed would not go very far. Still, there was nothing to be gained by bemoaning her fate. Tomorrow morning she would have to shake herself out of her misery and plan her future.

\*　　　\*　　　\*

A pale sun woke her the next day, and as soon as Non had eaten her breakfast she went around to the stables.

'Dennis, will you hitch up the pony and trap for me, please?'

'Where are you going, Miss? It's not market day, is it?' Dennis looked up at her, his cheery face split into a grin. 'I know you can't be off to sell your medicines, because you haven't asked me to load your boxes onto the trap.'

Non looked at the boy, and even as she tried to smile, her heart was heavy. Soon, he too would be homeless and out of work. She swallowed hard, tempted to tell him to go straight away to find a position in some other house. But no, it wouldn't be fair to Mrs Miles and Flora to hear the bad news from Dennis. She would gather them together this evening and tell them herself.

As she set off, she breathed in the morning air. It was fine, with a light breeze blowing across the undulating fields. The sky overhead was cloudless, a blue bowl of sky promising clear weather. She shook the reins and the pony began to trot obediently, head dipping and raising, mane blowing in the breeze.

As she guided the pony down the well-worn track to the town, Non looked around her at the green of the trees, the lush grass and the blue sea beyond, and knew she should be glad to be alive; but her heart was heavy—she had lost the father she loved, and now she was to lose her home, too.

The streets of Swansea were busy, with dray horses pulling carts laden with beer casks; bakery wagons jostled with milk carts, and the loud voices of the costermongers rang in her ears. Non wished herself anywhere but here in the heart of Swansea, where the stink of the copper works hung like a pall above the rooftops.

She spotted a lodging house to her right, just off the High Street, and as safely as she could she turned the pony and trap into Star Street and pulled on the reins.

'Stop, Bess,' she said softly. 'There's a good girl, just hold up there.'

She climbed down from the driving seat and looked up at the lodging house. The paint was peeling from the walls and the windows were grimed with copper dust from the works along the riverbank. But at least here she might find accommodation she could afford.

To her surprise, a smartly dressed man of middle years opened the door. His hair was faded ginger, though his beard was red and springy with curls. As his gaze moved swiftly over her, he seemed to sum her up as a respectable lady, and he stepped aside and told her to please come inside.

'I have just one room free,' he said, 'so if it's lodgings you require you had better be quick making up your mind, because there's a young gentleman arriving from Cardiff this afternoon and he wants to look the place over.' He smiled then. 'I'm Mr Albert Murphy, owner of this establishment.'

Non thought 'establishment' a grand word for a small lodging house, but she kept her thoughts to herself and followed Mr Murphy along the dark passage and into a room at the back of the building.

At once Non knew it wouldn't do. The room was pleasant enough, with a well-cleaned fireplace and a good wooden floor covered in a thin matting, but the only window looked out into a backyard with a high wall at the other side of the path.

'Do you have a room with a view of the street?' she asked politely.

Mr Murphy shook his head and his thin hair stood up like a faded halo around his face. 'This is the only one I have vacant—at least in this house— and all my other properties are fully taken.' He lifted his ginger eyebrows. 'I'm intrigued. Why do you need a room close to the street where you would have to put up with noise day and night?'

Non decided to confide in him. 'I need to make a living,' she said quietly, 'and there's only one thing I can do properly.'

'And that is?'

'I make remedies from recipes in Mr Culpeper's book.'

'Never heard of Mr Culpeper,' he said with a smile. 'Do these remedies work, or is it all a sham?'

'No, indeed it isn't a sham! The herbs I use are for curing all sorts of conditions, from gout to sore heads.'

'Well, fancy that!' Mr Murphy appeared impressed. 'I know who you are now—the vicar's daughter, Manon Jenkins, the one who sells medicines in the market every week.'

Non was pleased that he'd heard of her, and smiled up at him hopefully. 'You can help me, then?'

He made a vain attempt to smooth down his hair and looked at her thoughtfully. 'I can't offer you a suitable room, but I can make a suggestion.' He smiled at her, revealing a row of surprisingly well-kept teeth.

'And what's that?' Non asked suspiciously.

'I was talking to Mr Jones the other day—the cattle man, the one who owns the Bank of the Black Ox.' He rushed on without waiting for a reply. 'Of course, you know who I mean. I've seen his son Caradoc talking to you on market day often enough.'

Non felt the colour rise to her cheeks. 'Yes, I know who you mean. But what has all that to do with me?'

'Well,' Mr Murphy pressed his finger against his nose. 'The daughter, Georgina, is to travel up to London. Her brother is taking her along on the cattle drove in order to see her safely to her aunt's house.'

Non was silent. Her only brush with Miss Jones had been somewhat unpleasant.

'Mr Jones wants a respectable woman to accompany his daughter.' He smiled genially. 'Now do you see what I'm getting at?'

68

'I do see what you mean, but don't know if the position would suit me,' Non said slowly. 'Georgina Jones doesn't like me very much. She snubbed me quite badly at the market once.'

Mr Murphy tapped his nose again. 'But what you *don't* know is that a nurse of some sort is required, a woman who will not only chaperone Miss Georgina but will minister to the women who might fall sick on the trail. A very good man is our Mr Jones—he looks after the welfare of his workers, and you don't get many bosses doing that.'

Non was silent, wondering how she would feel travelling all the way to London with Caradoc and his high and mighty sister.

'Just think,' Mr Murphy said, 'up in London you might make your fortune. I hear the people there are all very rich and live in large houses. With your skills, if they are not a sham as you claim, you should soon make a good living for yourself.'

'Well,' Non said at last, 'thank you for telling me about it, but I don't think the job is the one for me.'

'Well, you must be the judge of that yourself, my dear. Now if you'll excuse me, I've got to see to my other prospective tenant.'

Non left the house and stood in the street for a moment, imagining the hot nights on the drove, with the moon overhead, the stars gleaming down from a velvet sky and Caradoc for company. Would he fall in love with her? How absurd! He would merely flirt and tease her, as he always did.

She climbed up into the trap and shook the reins, and the pony moved forward, head down in the roadway searching for a titbit to eat. Non stopped at a few lodging houses, but without success, and she wondered if she would ever find suitable accommodation. At last she gave up her search, and climbed for what seemed the hundredth time into the trap. It was time she headed home; she was tired and hungry and she badly needed a cup of hot tea.

*     *     *

It was later that night when Non called Mrs Miles and Flora to the drawing room. She looked at the older woman, whose hands were swollen with bone ache and whose eyesight was not all it should be. She would never find a place again. Flora was different, she was young and strong and would soon find a position for herself.

'I've got bad news,' Non said. 'Please, both of you sit down.'

'But we can't do that, Miss Manon,' Mrs Miles said at once, 'it's not respectful.'

'This is no time to stand on ceremony. I have some news that's going to affect you both.'

'Oh dear,' Mrs Miles said. 'When folk talk of "news" in that tone of voice, it's always a bad omen.'

'I've got to get out of the vicarage,' Non said quickly. 'The Reverend Powell told me there's a new vicar, along with his family, to be installed here.'

'Oh, *duw, duw*!' Mrs Miles sank into a chair. 'Oh my dear Lord, what is the world coming to when a respectable young lady is to be put out onto the streets, and by a man of the Church?'

'I'm sorry,' Non said. 'But look on the bright side: the new vicar might want to keep you on.'

Mrs Miles shook her head. 'Not me, I'm getting

older, mind, no one would want me now.'

'You don't know that for sure,' Non said, but she knew the old cook was right. 'And you, Flora, even if you're not kept on here, you'll soon find another place to work.'

Slow tears ran down Flora's cheeks. 'But I don't want to work for no one else, Miss. This is my 'ome and I loves it here.'

'And where will you go, Miss Non?' Mrs Miles said slowly. 'You'll need somewhere to stay. The Church ought to find you a new place to live—it's not Christian to just put you out of house and home.'

'I'll be all right,' Non said with forced cheerfulness. 'I've been told of a position going vacant already.'

'A position?' Mrs Miles sounded indignant.

'Well, it would be very respectable work,' Non said. 'I would simply need to chaperone a young lady on a trip up to London.'

Flora's eyes brightened. '*London!* Oh Miss, I wish I could come with you! I've heard that London's got streets of gold, and there's money falling down from the skies there.'

Non hid a smile. 'Well, it's a place with many opportunities to do well, I'm sure.'

Mrs Miles shook her head slowly. 'I heard from the butcher boy that Miss Georgina's going to London. If it's her you're going with, you'd be better off staying by here in Swansea.'

Privately, Non agreed with her, but she could hardly say so.

'Well, we'll see what happens when I approach Mr Jones. He might not want to give me the position anyway.' She sighed. 'But don't worry, I'm not going to be destitute. If I do stay in Swansea, I'll find a nice clean room to make into a shop. Now, off you go and make us all a nice hot cup of tea. I think we all need it.'

*    *    *

It was early next morning when Morgan came to call on her. He stood in the drawing room and shook his head at Non. 'I know you have to get out of this house in just two weeks, and that you spent all day yesterday looking for lodgings. Have you found anywhere suitable?'

'No, not yet.' Somehow, Non felt on the defensive. 'But I've only just started to search. I can't expect everything to fall into my lap, can I?'

Morgan looked at her and sighed. 'Non, why don't you marry me?'

His words fell into the silence of the room like a pebble splashing into a pool. 'I mean it, Non. I would be honoured to have you as my wife. I make a good living.' He paused. 'I would make you a good husband, Non, that I can promise you.'

'I'm very proud you asked me to be your wife, Morgan,' she said gently. 'But I'm not ready to settle down, not yet. But thank you for being such a good friend. You see, I have to prove to myself that I can make a living on my own.'

Morgan got to his feet, a big man with clear eyes and an honest face. 'Well, don't forget, I'm always here if you need me.'

She knew he meant it, and the thought gave her comfort. But there was a great big world out there, and Non was determined to see it.

# CHAPTER SEVEN

Non stood at the door of the large imposing house and felt her nerve fail her. She had come to ask for the job of chaperone to Miss Georgina Jones, but now she was here, outside the stately, sun-washed building, she had a mind to turn and go back the way she'd come. She even stepped back a pace, her heart in her mouth. In a rush of panic she turned to run, and found herself held by a pair of strong arms.

'Careful there, Miss Jenkins.' The voice spoke low in her ear and Non felt the rich colour flood into her face.

'Caradoc—Mr Jones—I'm sorry, sorry to bump into you like that, there's clumsy of me.'

'Well, bump into me any time you like.' Caradoc released her and Non backed away from him, embarrassed by his closeness.

'What are you doing here so far out of town, anyway?' Caradoc said, his eyes searching her face as though he could read her thoughts. 'Is there anything wrong? If so, I hope there's something I can do to help you.'

'I need a job.' Non blurted out the words. 'I'm to be turned out of my home. You see, a new vicar is to take over the parish, and so I came to ask for the job of chaperone to Miss Georgina when she takes her trip to London.'

The world seemed to fall silent as she waited for his reply. She felt ashamed, as though she was begging like a street urchin.

'You do know we'll be taking the trail over the

73

Welsh hills and into England in the company of a herd of cattle, don't you?' Caradoc's voice was gentle, and gaining heart, Non looked up at him.

'Yes, I know that it won't be easy, I don't expect it to be. But I can offer my services not only as a chaperone but also as a herbalist. I can make potions that will help cure folk when they fall sick, a useful skill to have with you when you're in the middle of nowhere.'

Caradoc looked at her thoughtfully. 'That all sounds very good, and as far as I'm concerned you can have the job. The only obstacle is Georgina herself.' He smiled ruefully. 'I rather think she's jealous of you.'

'Of me! Why?'

'Well, you are very beautiful, with all that chestnut hair and those lovely expressive blue eyes.'

Non held her breath. Was he teasing her? 'Well,' she said uncertainly, 'I wouldn't want to upset Miss Georgina, but on the other hand I really need this job.'

'Well, come inside and meet my father. He's really the one to do the hiring and firing. But I don't think you've anything to worry about—the job is virtually yours.'

Caradoc led the way along the wide driveway lined with trees to the arched front doors of the house. Non wasn't at all sure of her position. It didn't seem proper to be walking into the splendid spacious hall with its marbled floor and curving staircase. Should she be walking round the back to the servants' quarters?

Caradoc had no such concerns. 'Go into the drawing room and make yourself comfortable. I'll speak to Father.' He pushed open the tall double doors and Non found herself walking into the grandest room she'd ever seen. At the far end, huge rounded windows looked out onto a fine garden that sported a fountain surrounded by stone lions. To either side of the fountain, lush lawns gave way to deep woodland, and Non could see deer lurking in the shadows of the overhanging branches.

She took a deep breath. Caradoc lived in such splendour that she would be a fool to even think he might be attracted to a mere vicar's daughter. She turned to look at the rest of the room. It was furnished with luxurious fabrics and finest polished wood, and on the walls hung portraits of gentlemen in elegant clothes; these, no doubt, were Caradoc's forebears.

'Miss Jenkins, I understand you wish to travel to London with the cattle drove?' The voice was firm, rather gruff, and Non felt as if her tongue was cleaving to the roof of her mouth.

She spun round to face the famed Mr George Jones, the man who had changed the world of the cattle drover for ever, using his bank's notes instead of money as payment to the London landlords and dealers. As founder member of the Bank of the Black Ox Mr Jones was an important man, and she couldn't believe she was standing here in his house, having the temerity to ask him for a job.

'Oh, Mr Jones, Sir, I'm sorry to be forward, but I heard Miss Georgina needed a chaperone, and I've come to ask if I can have the position.'

'And why do you think you'd be suitable? Have you ever done any work of that kind before?'

'No Sir, but I've looked after people all my life.

And since I was a young child I've studied roots and flowers of all kinds; I can make remedies that help to make folk feel better.'

He smiled, and at once Non could see where Caradoc had his good looks from. 'I note that you do not mention the word "cure". Are you being modest or just cautious?'

'A bit of both, Sir. I do cure things like common chills and women's ailments, and when folk get bone ache I can help ease the pain.'

'And why would you want to put yourself through the rigours of a long journey up to London in the company of my rather spoilt young daughter?'

'I'm to be turned out of my home, Sir. The house is needed for the new vicar and his family. And I think I would enjoy travelling from Swansea; especially to London, where I hope I could learn more about herbal remedies.'

'Do the Londoners know more about it than we do, then?'

'Oh yes, Sir. The great Mr Culpeper himself used to work in London, and in his book, which I keep close at all times, he even tells of the places in and around the town where the herbs are to be found.'

'Mr Culpeper, I see.' It was clear Mr Jones had no idea who Culpeper was. 'Well then, I know you to be a girl gently and properly brought up, I knew your father was a good man and I'm sure you'd make a suitable chaperone for my daughter. But be warned, Georgina has a sharp tongue, she can be very difficult and in your role you'd have to put up with a great deal of her nonsense. If you understand all that then the position of chaperone is yours.'

Non could scarcely believe it. She'd come here afraid and trembling and had actually met the great Mr Jones himself. She felt elated—she had persuaded him to give her the job she needed so much.

'Thank you, Mr Jones,' she said. 'I'll do my best to take care of Miss Georgina, you may be sure of that.'

'Well, you can talk to my son about the drove.' He smiled again. 'I leave all that sort of business to him these days. He's a fine son, but another warning: Caradoc has an eye for the ladies. He has great charm and I wouldn't like a chaste young woman like yourself to have any foolish ideas about him.'

Non felt the colour rush into her cheeks. 'I assure you, Sir, I'm not a girl of easy virtue and I'm old enough and sensible enough to look after myself, however charming a young man might be.'

'Good then. You'll be paid the same as the lead drover—if that suits you then the matter is settled.' He smiled again. 'I hope you'll be happy in your new life. Good day to you now.'

He turned and left her standing in the room alone, and Non hesitated, not knowing what was expected of her. Should she just let herself out and make her way home?

Caradoc solved the problem by returning to the room and smiling down at her. 'Georgina wants to see you. I'll leave you alone to talk with her, but I won't be far away.'

Non bit her lip. This part of the interview was going to be the most difficult. She was sure that Miss Georgina would simply refuse to be chaperoned by her.

Georgina swept into the room, her fine gown of hand-embroidered lawn flowing behind her. She was frowning as she stared at Non and her eyes held nothing but hostility. 'You've got the job,' she said abruptly. 'But only because my brother insists on it; for myself, I wouldn't have you within a mile of me.' Her dark eyes seemed to bore into Non's head. 'But if there's any funny business between you and my brother, I'll get rid of you so fast that your feet won't touch the ground. Is that understood?'

'Perfectly.' Non wanted to rant and rage and tell Georgina to keep her job. But she needed to earn a decent wage and there wasn't much chance of that while she stayed in Swansea.

Georgina rang for the maid, and before she knew it Non was hustled from the room and was outside on the driveway. She took a deep breath as she looked back at the elegant house. Well, Georgina might not want her along on the trail, but perhaps, as they travelled the miles overland to London, things might change.

Her heart warmed a little as she thought of Caradoc insisting that she got the job. He was a fine man and a handsome man, but she would have to beware of him, she'd had enough warnings. With a lighter heart than she'd had since her father died, Non began to walk back home. She needed to pack her clothes and some good boots, and then, quite soon, she would be off on an adventure which might, if luck was on her side, change her life.

# CHAPTER EIGHT

Non had never in her life seen so many cattle gathered in one place. The herds had joined the drove from Haverford West, skirting the town of Carmarthen and continuing on to Five Saints, where Non had decided to wait for them. It was strange being back in the village where she'd been born. It all looked so small and ordinary compared to the rush and bustle of Swansea.

The sounds of the restless hooves drew her thoughts back to the present. The noise was deafening as hundreds of animals milled around on the dry earth. The sheer size of the herd frightened her so badly that Non almost changed her mind about travelling the drovers' roads to London. Perhaps she would never get used to the constant bellowing of the animals, the pushing and jostling and the awful smell of sun-baked hides.

A converted carriage drew up beside her; the wheels were those of a wagon, sturdy and strong, but the body of the vehicle was plush. Georgina leaned out of the window to look down at her.

'So, are you ready to walk all the way to London, then?' Seated inside the coach, Georgina was surrounded by bright calico cushions, and as she leaned against them her expression was haughty. But Non's attention was drawn to her young driver.

'Dennis! I didn't expect to see you here.'

'Oh, don't worry,' it was Georgina who spoke, 'we've got your young maid Flora with us too. I think my brother has taken pity on you all. He's always been charitable to those less fortunate than ourselves.' She paused. 'You know I wouldn't tolerate your presence if my brother hadn't put a word in with Papa, don't you?'

'I know.' Non looked up, shading her eyes from the sun. 'But I'll be useful. I have a whole bag of remedies in the provisions cart, and even you might need my help before we get to London.'

'Miss Jenkins is better than a doctor,' Dennis said proudly.

'Be quiet, boy!' Georgina snapped. 'Speak when you're spoken to, and as for you, Miss Jenkins, *I* won't be taking any of your quack medicines, believe me!'

The two girls stared at each other and it was Georgina who looked away first. 'Get going, Dennis, you're not paid to sit around gawping,' she said. 'Get up the front. I want to talk to my brother.'

Non watched the carriage drive away, and then she joined a group of women who were talking busily in Welsh. It was all so unfamiliar to her, and as she looked round at the green pastureland she longed for her room in the peaceful vicarage in Swansea.

She felt her arm being jostled. 'Miss Non, I've joined the drove too.' Flora stood at her side, eager as a young puppy. 'It was you who give me and Dennis the idea of going up to London.' She smiled wickedly. 'I might have a bit of romance on the way.'

'I doubt there'll be much romance about, Flora. The drove is about making money, not falling in love.'

'I don't know about that,' Flora smiled. 'Morgan will be with the drove some of the time, and he's a lovely man. You must have noticed he's fallen for you.'

'You've seen Morgan, then?'

'Oh yes, Miss. I saw him this morning—busy he was, cueing the animals.' She looked at Non from under her lashes. 'He's a good catch, mind. The money he made from the shoeing will see him right for the long winter nights.'

Non was about to reply when the sound of a horn echoed through the valley. The men on horseback began to call incomprehensible sounds to each other and to the animals. The drove was starting on the first leg of its journey, and Non felt a sense of excitement. She was on her way to the big noisy bustling town of London.

*         *         *

'Georgina, I want you at the back of the herd and you know it.' Caradoc shook his head at his stubborn sister. She had always been headstrong, but now she must listen to him or he would simply send her home.

Georgina shook back a stray curl that had escaped from under her bonnet. 'Why should I spend my time with all those ignorant women who do nothing but walk and knit all day? I'd be bored out of my wits.'

Caradoc took a deep breath. 'Those women are the salt of the earth. They stop to weed the land when our pace is slow and they work their passage, which is more than you're going to do.'

Georgina did not seem impressed. 'As for that awful witch Non Jenkins, I don't know why you had to bring her along. I suppose you think she'd make

81

a good fancy piece.'

'I think nothing of the kind.' Caradoc was irritated by his sister's constant carping; it would be a dreary journey if she kept on complaining. 'Now,' he spoke firmly, 'go to the back of the herd. The cattle sometimes get spooked; they're strange creatures, frightened by the least thing, even a gust of wind, and if they stampede you would be in the thick of it here. You'd be trampled to death before you could get out of their path.'

He hid a smile as Georgina digested this information. Clearly she'd not thought of danger until now.

'Very well, but I won't be having anything to do with that odious creature Manon Jenkins. She's a penniless witch, only you can't see it.'

'No, all I can see is a pretty and intelligent young woman who means to earn her living now that she's left all alone in the world. Now please go to the back and fall into line. Dennis, pull back behind the women, there's a good chap.'

Georgina sulked as the driver turned the horse and carriage, careful not to frighten the herd, and drove to the back of the crowd. Georgina wondered for the first time if she had been foolish to travel to London with Caradoc. She would have been more comfortable on the mail, after all. Ah well, she was here now, and after the fuss she'd made to ride with the drove she could hardly complain.

She settled more comfortably against the cushions and did her best to ignore the women who were chatting ceaselessly, like the gossips they were. She caught sight of Manon Jenkins: she was dipping her hand into the pouch around her waist where, presumably, she kept some of the more portable remedies. She seemed quite at home, but then she was one of these common women herself, so why shouldn't she be?

Georgina closed her eyes and waited impatiently for the carriage to pick up speed, wishing once again that she had listened to her father and taken the mail coach to London. Still, once she was there she'd stay with Aunt Prudence until Papa forgot about marrying her to an old man. She smiled to herself; she always got her own way in the end.

*     *     *

'Well, Manon Jenkins, you seem to 'ave got all we need to keep us well on the journey.' Mary Thomas looked down at the small phial in her hand. 'This'll cure my bone ache, will it?' She didn't wait for a reply, but tucked the bottle away safely in the large pocket of her apron where she kept her knitting needles and wool. 'But I hope you'll be all right. You've never walked the drovers' roads before, 'ave you?'

Non tried to smile. 'No, but I'm used to walking, and if the rest of you can do it, then I can too.'

Mary Thomas nodded towards Non's feet. 'But what about them boots you're wearing? Ruin them you will, if you walk all the way to London in them. Do as we do and hang them round your neck by the laces. Better for your boots, and your feet will get hardened—in time.'

Non looked down at her boots. The thought of walking barefoot had never occurred to her. The ground was rough and stony—her feet would be cut to ribbons if she tried to walk without shoes.

'I'll keep them on, thanks all the same.' She watched as Mary hitched up her skirts and tucked them into her underclothes so that her legs, brown and bare, and her large, stringy feet were exposed.

'Don't be shocked, love,' Mary caught her glance. 'I finds it easier to walk like this, but it's up to you what you does.'

Before her, the dust was rising from the beat of hundreds of animal hooves. Non looked around at the crouched cottages of the village and the fields beyond, and felt a sudden constriction in her throat. She was leaving it all behind: all her memories of home, of her dear father. She felt tears burn in her eyes, but she was too proud to shed them.

Beside her she heard the click, clack of knitting needles. She glanced around and saw Flora, knitting as swiftly as the others. She would soon be one of the crowd, and Non felt proud of her.

One woman began to sing out loud, her voice barely discernible above the trample of hooves. She sang a stirring song about the road rising up to meet her and the wind at her back.

'Take no notice of Tess, she's Irish and thinks she can sing like a Welsh woman,' Mary smiled. 'Now, you'd best learn to fasten your mind to some task, your herbs and medicines and plants and things, otherwise you're going to be wearied to death with the sameness of every day.'

Non nodded and took her small herbal book from the pocket of her apron. She tried to read, but the words seemed to jar up and down before her eyes. She read for a little while and then put the book away. The women were quite far ahead of her now, but she could soon catch up; after all, she had no knitting to hamper her.

She looked around her at the banks and fields beyond, trying to see what was growing along the well-trodden drovers' road. But the verges were thick with knotted grass, flattened in places by the beasts that trampled through it. She would need to look further if she wanted plants she could use for her work. Non climbed a small bank and stared across the expanse of land that led only to a tiny village, identifiable by the tall spire that pointed towards the clear sky. She found a plant that interested her: it appeared to be like a lily, and yet different. She took out her herbal and tried to identify the flower, but could find nothing like it in the descriptions of wild flowers.

'Don't fall behind, Miss Jenkins.' The rich masculine voice made her jump, and Non looked up from under her bonnet, her face flushed.

'Oh, Mr Jones, I'm sorry, I didn't mean to hold anyone up.'

'I should think not, we've only just got underway. But seriously, you must keep up with the other women; there are dangers along the road that you might not be aware of.'

'Oh?' Non frowned. 'What dangers could there be in such peaceful surroundings?'

'For a start, an animal might stray from the herd. Animals are frightened very easily once they are away from their familiar habitation. And the roads are known as rich pickings among the footpads— you might get attacked.'

Non was a little irritated by his attitude. Anyone would think he was talking to a stupid child.

'But I'm not carrying any money, or anything at all of value, am I?'

'What about your chastity?' Caradoc raised his eyebrows. 'It's not so long ago that you were the victim of two thieves who, if I hadn't come along, would have used you most cruelly.'

Non's colour deepened. She hesitated for a moment, and then met Caradoc's eyes. 'You're right, of course, and I'll not fall back behind the other women again. That's a promise.'

'And you must keep it. I can't be expected to look after you, it's bad enough having my sister aboard. Here, climb up behind me. You can ride with me until we catch up with the rest of the drove.'

Non hesitated for a moment, and then took the hand he held out to her. He swung her with ease up onto the animal's back, and, panicking a little, she put her arms around him and gripped him hard, afraid she would be unseated once the horse began to move.

However, Caradoc did not urge the animal into a gallop as she'd expected, but allowed the horse to trot gently, hooves barely seeming to touch the ground but sending up flurries of dry dust.

She became aware of the warmth of Caradoc, of the muscular strength of his back. Her cheek was pressed against him and her arms held him close, as though he were a lover, not a man who had hired her to do a day's work for a day's pay. She felt her cheeks burn. She had never been this close to a man before, not even Morgan.

'Are you all right, Miss Jenkins?' Caradoc's voice was rich with laughter and suddenly Non felt very stupid. He was not moved as she was by his nearness; to him she was simply an object of ridicule.

'Let me off before we reach the rest of the drove—please,' she added as an afterthought. 'I don't want the other women to get the wrong impression of me.'

'What impression would they have, do you think?' Caradoc asked, urging the animal to go faster, and she knew he was still laughing at her.

'That I'm a flighty piece!' She looked down at her legs, bare now with her skirts flying upwards in the wind. She wanted to cover herself, but she was afraid to let go of Caradoc's waist, afraid she would fall beneath the horse's hooves.

It looked as if he was going to ride right up to the drove in full view of everyone. But then, at last, he reined in the animal, and Non slid to the ground, aware that her legs were shaking.

'Are you all right?' He looked down at her and Non had a fleeting, impossible urge to sink into his arms.

'Of course I'm all right. This isn't the first time I've ridden a horse, you know.' Her words were brave, but the truth was she had hardly ever sat on a horse. She was more at home in the trap. 'Thanks for your help.'

As she stepped away from the horse, she lost her footing and, to her chagrin, fell flat on her back amid the grass. She had a brief glimpse of blue sky and then Caradoc was kneeling beside her, cradling her head in his arms, looking anxiously into her eyes.

'Are you hurt?' His laughter had gone now; he held her head against his breast and she could hear the solid beating of his heart. She breathed in the manly scent of him before she struggled in an effort to get to her feet.

'I'm all right, there's nothing wrong with me. It's your fault I missed my step in the first place, so let me go!'

She thought he would laugh at her again then, but he was looking down at her with a strange gleam in his eyes. She lay back in his arms and stared up at him. He leaned forward very slowly, and then his lips were close to hers.

Non held her breath for a long moment, waiting for his mouth to touch hers. She could feel his breath against her cheek and she longed to reach up and cup his face in her hands. She wanted very badly for him to kiss her. She moved slightly towards him and the small phials in her pocket clinked together, reminding her of why she was on the drove. She pushed at his arms and abruptly he drew away.

'Come along then, Miss Jenkins, make your way back to the herd. They're only just up ahead, you can see the dust thrown up by the hooves of the animals.'

Non got to her feet, pressing her skirts modestly against her legs. She was trembling so much she thought she would fall into a faint, but she lifted her head and made off in the direction of the drove without a backward glance.

\*     \*     \*

'*Duw*, where have you been, girl?' Mary Thomas looked at her shrewdly. 'You have the look of a girl who's met a lover.'

'If only I had a lover!' Non said quickly. 'I'm hardly likely to meet one out here, am I?'

Mary tapped the side of her nose. 'There's many

a strange thing happens on the drovers' roads, girl; especially when the nights are hot and the moon is hiding her face behind the clouds.'

'Well, you needn't concern yourself about me, Mary, I'll be off gathering my herbs whenever I can.'

'Aye, well listen to me and don't get caught for a babba. 'Tis innocents like you that fall for a man's charms and end up with a full belly.'

'Mary!' Non felt herself flush. 'As if I'd be so wicked! My father would turn in his grave if he could hear you now.'

'Well, I'm only saying, see? You're a nicely brought-up girl, and not rough and ready like some of the women on the drove.'

Non looked around. 'They all look respectable enough to me,' she said.

Mary's eyebrows shot up. 'Well, there you are then. You sees no evil so you won't be doing evil. Jest remember what Mary told you about the hot nights on the trail, though, and then you'll have no one to blame but yourself if you gets into trouble.'

Non was about to reply when Caradoc rode alongside the band of women. He doffed his hat to Mary. 'It looks as if we're going to make good time today, Mary. Let's hope the weather gods favour us tomorrow.'

'Yes, Sir. I think we'll have fine weather at least for a few days, but I can't say how long it will last, mind.'

Caradoc nodded. 'I know. We'll be at the Drovers' Arms by nightfall and we'll be resting up there.'

He was talking to Mary, but Non felt his words were for her. She glanced at him and felt her colour rise as she thought of the moments when she'd lain in his arms. He nodded then and clucked his tongue at his horse, and rode towards the front of the cattle drove.

Mary looked at her with her dark, shrewd eyes. 'That man's taken a fancy to you, girl.'

Non shook her head. 'Nonsense, Mary, he hardly knows me.'

'Knowing and wanting is two different things. Now don't you go falling for the boss's charms, because he's not our sort. He'll have a fine lady for a wife, someone high and mighty like his sister, Miss Georgina.'

'Oh, Mary, you're letting your imagination get the better of you! Mr Jones is not interested in me.'

Mary sniffed, but said no more, and her knitting needles clicked more swiftly than ever.

Watching Caradoc's graceful figure on the horse, Non sighed, remembering the feel of his arms around her. But she was a fool to give him a moment of her time.

'Oh, look Mary, I can see some hyssop, it's come out very early this year.' She dived from the road, and as she bent to pick the flower she felt tears well up in her eyes. She was longing for something that was quite out of her reach, and the sooner she put the silly feelings out of her head the better.


# CHAPTER NINE

The travelling was slow. The weather conditions had not been favourable; the days had been fine, but there had been rain at night, making the ground so soft that the hooves of the cattle sank in the mud. The hills of Brecon were still far away, at least another three days' walk. At this rate, which seemed incredibly slow to Non, it would be weeks before they got to Smithfield. She smiled. Weeks when she would be in Caradoc's company.

Non had no idea what would happen after the herds were delivered and sold. Perhaps Caradoc would stay with the aunt Georgina had spoken of, or perhaps he would travel home in the comfort of a coach. But for now she could revel in his company. And he seemed to enjoy hers; the thought warmed her heart.

The few nights they had spent at the drovers' halts, he had made a point of finding her and having a word with her. Perhaps he really liked her. Perhaps he fancied her for a wife. The thought made her blush; what on earth would Caradoc want her for, and she only a vicar's daughter? A quick roll in the hay, perhaps, but certainly not a respectable courtship.

Still, she must enjoy the moments when she was with him. She was growing accustomed to walking every day and she enjoyed the days when the sun shone. What she didn't enjoy was the way Georgina seemed to delight in taunting her. Every time she paused to pick a wild flower, Georgina seemed to hold back her carriage and find something unpleasant to say.

As if called by her thoughts, Georgina was suddenly beside her.

'Wasting your time on your silly medicines again, are you?' She didn't wait for an answer. 'You can't knit and you can't do an honest day's work weeding, so what use are you? I'm surprised

91

Caradoc allowed you to come on the drove at all.'

Stung, Non stared up at Georgina. 'And what do you do except loll around in that glorified wagon amongst all your cushions? I'm sure it's not usual to have a woman along who can't do anything at all but be a burden on the drove.'

Georgina looked as though she'd eaten a stinging nettle and it had got stuck in her throat. 'You impudent girl! How dare you speak to me like that?'

Non met Georgina's blazing eyes. 'You seem to bring out the worst in me, Miss. Perhaps it would be better if we didn't talk to each other at all.'

'I'll decide who I'll talk to, you hussy.'

Non shook her head, she felt there was nothing more to say. In the beginning she had tried to humour Georgina, but now she was tired of always being the one to back down, and she began to walk away.

'Don't you dare walk away from me!' There was a crack then, like a shot from a pistol; it rang out in the quiet country air like a bolt of thunder. Non halted abruptly as she felt a blow and then the tightening coil of a whip around her body. The lash of it caught her neck and face and Non cried out in pain.

She seemed to be in the grip of the whip for what seemed an eternity, but at last it slipped back, releasing her. Before Georgina could wield it again, Non was at her side. She caught the handle and dragged it from Georgina's hands. She even half raised it to strike back. Georgina sank against her seat, her face shocked. Non hesitated before throwing the whip to the ground.

Suddenly she was aware of the cattle bellowing,

then there was the noise of hooves beating against the ground. The earth seemed to tremble. Non looked up ahead—the cattle were turning in their tracks, heading back the way they'd come.

'Oh my God!' Georgina screamed. 'The cattle are stampeding! Drive on, Dennis! Drive on, for God's sake—the beasts are coming this way.'

The thunder of hooves grew nearer, striking fear into Non's heart. She stood as though mesmerized and watched the turf fly. She didn't know which way to turn. The cattle advanced towards her like a sea of horned devils.

She was dimly aware that Dennis was turning the wagon and heading up towards the hills. The women were scattering like blossoms from a cherry tree, running in all directions. Chaos seemed to reign, yet still Non looked round in fear, wondering which way to run.

She heard a cry—to the side of the stampeding herd was a rider. Non gasped in fear as she saw it was Caradoc, his hair flying, his face a mask of anger. Then the beasts were almost upon her. She smelt the rank odour of hide, and could see wildness in the creatures' eyes; she was going to be trampled to death and still she couldn't move.

Caradoc rode his horse dangerously close to the herd, until they were almost upon him. At the last moment he swerved towards Non. She could see his horse foaming at the mouth with fear. Abruptly, she was jerked upwards, the breath knocked out of her by the strong grip of Caradoc's arm as he held her tightly round the waist. Her hair was flying over her face as Caradoc headed his horse away from the drovers' road.

Non felt as if every bone in her body was

breaking under the strain as Caradoc urged his horse to the side of the track. She flopped unceremoniously against the animal's flank; she could smell the horse's sweat, feel the heat of it as the blood rushed to her head. Abruptly, she was dropped onto the grassy bank at the side of the road.

She lay for a moment, winded, and then, struggling to catch her breath, she sat up. Caradoc was riding away from her, chasing after the beasts. She took a deep breath—he'd risked his life for her. She put her hands to her face and shuddered; she would be sent home in disgrace, she was sure of it.

It took more than two hours for the men to bring the cattle to a standstill. The noise, the panic, the sheer terror of it all was almost unbearable. The beasts were wild-eyed, quivering with fear and foaming at the mouth. Non stood where Caradoc had dumped her, her legs trembling and her heart beating so fast she thought it would choke her.

At last, when all was calm, Caradoc called Non and Georgina together and stared down at them in anger. His hair was whipped over his eyes by the wind, his cheeks were red with exertion, and Non thought he had never looked so handsome.

'What the hell did you think you were doing, Georgina, cracking the whip like that? You've been around animals all your life. You might have known what would happen if the beasts were panicked.'

'It wasn't my fault,' Georgina said. 'This *hussy* attacked me. She pulled the whip from Dennis and tried to flay me with it.'

For a moment Non was speechless. How could Georgina lie so blatantly? Caradoc looked at his sister and shook his head. 'Dennis has told me that you were the first to wield the whip, so don't lie to me on top of everything else.'

'All right, but she was supposed to be chaperoning me, looking after me. Instead she was insolent, and told me I was a useless burden upon you.'

Caradoc almost smiled. 'Well, in that she's right enough. I can't nurse you, Georgina, and run a good drove at the same time. Just look at the animals—they're so wearied now we won't be able to complete today's journey. That means we shan't reach bed and board tonight, so be prepared to sleep rough and to go hungry as well.'

Georgina gaped at her brother. 'Sleep rough? How can I sleep rough? I'm not a man or a servant, to lie on the hard ground.'

'Please yourself. Sleep in the carriage or on the ground—that's all I can offer. Now I don't expect a repeat of today's tantrums, not from either of you. Is that understood?'

Non nodded, realizing how her loose tongue had put everyone in danger. 'I'm sorry, Mr Jones,' she said. 'It won't happen again because I'll learn to ignore it when Miss Georgina sees fit to poke fun at me or goad me with her sarcastic tongue.'

'Enough!' Caradoc said sternly. 'Now get out of my sight, both of you, and if anything like this happens again you'll both be heading home, with only Dennis for protection from footpads and murderers.'

Georgina cast one last hostile look in Non's direction and stalked away, her skirts swaying as she walked. Non looked at Caradoc. 'I *am* really sorry, Mr Jones. I will try to avoid antagonizing

Miss Georgina in future.'

Caradoc nodded but didn't reply, and Non, abashed more by his silence than she'd been at his words, made her way back to the other women, and before long they were preparing to bed down for the night.

'Better get yourself a shawl from the supply wagon,' Mary said briskly. 'We got to stay by here tonight because of all the nonsense between you and that flighty Miss Georgina. None of us will thank you for it, so learn your lesson well, Miss.'

'I'm sorry, Mary, I didn't know how easily the animals are frightened. It was the crack of Georgina's whip that did it.'

'Aye, there's a lot you don't know, and it's your place to be quiet and do your job, not to go arguing with the owner's daughter.'

'She used her whip on me, Mary. That whip really stung. I reacted badly and I know that, but I couldn't allow Georgina to get away with whipping me, could I?'

'I do understand. I can see where the whip's drawn blood, but still that's no excuse to argue and shout at your betters.' Mary turned away. 'Anyway, I've got better things to do other than stand by here talking. Me, I'm going to find a nice soft patch of grass to make my bed, and I'd advise you to do the same.'

Non walked over to the supply wagon and stood on tiptoe to peer inside. Dennis came up behind her and smartly removed the last remaining woollen shawl, shrugging his shoulders in resignation.

'Sorry, Miss Georgina needs more covering. She says she's very cold, her not being used to sleeping rough.'

Non sighed. 'It's not your fault, Dennis, so don't worry your head about it.' She turned away, but not before she saw Georgina smiling amongst her bed of cushions, her eyes narrowed in spite.

'I'll sleep by you, Non.' Flora came to lie beside her. 'I don't blame you for quarrelling with that awful Miss Jones. She's got her nose so far in the air it's a wonder she can see where she's going.'

Non smiled. 'I knew I could count on you to see things my way. Now try to get some sleep; it's going to be a long night, especially if it rains.'

Non closed her eyes, but she had never felt less like sleeping. The air was clear and balmy, with no hint of rain, but the memory of Caradoc's bravery, the way he'd risked his life for her, kept spinning around in her head.

The cattle didn't seem to sleep much, either. There was a constant bellowing from one or another of them as they stretched out on the grassy banks at the side of the road. It was as if they were reproaching her for the fright she'd given them. She closed her eyes, and when she did finally sleep she dreamed of Caradoc: he was holding her, kissing her, caressing her. When she woke, her cheeks were hot with shame.

Non thought she'd risen early, but Flora had already gone to prepare for the walk. The men were awake, and she saw one of the herdsmen urinate noisily without bothering to conceal himself from the women. This was the drovers' way of life, and Non couldn't expect the men to act any differently because she was with them. She wondered if Georgina had witnessed the act, but when she glanced over to the carriage she saw that the blinds were closed. Even now, on the road, the high and mighty Miss Jones was spared the harsher facts of life.

Mary came up beside her, her voice softer than it had been the previous night. 'We'll be on our way soon, and let's have no more quarrels, is it?'

'I'll keep right away from Miss Georgina, don't you worry.' Non stretched her arms above her head, unaware of how her breasts jutted and her small waist was emphasized until she saw one of the men staring at her. It was a good thing that most nights were spent in the relative comfort and privacy of a drovers' inn.

The other women, she knew, slept in a handy barn or some other outhouse. But because she was a vicar's daughter, Non was given a decent room, where she could at least wash and comb her hair and sleep in privacy. She knew she had Caradoc to thank for that.

Slowly, the herd began to move; the men on horseback called out the strange unintelligible words that encouraged the beasts and got them moving at a decent pace. Non walked quietly behind the cattle, knowing from the glances thrown her way that the other women were angry and wouldn't speak to her. It was only Flora and Mary who made the occasional remark to her. But then, after a few hours walking, Mary fell into step beside her, knitting as she talked.

'You can't blame the women for being mad with you. It's because of you that we had to spend the night in the open.'

'What about Miss High and Mighty Georgina, then? She was in the wrong. Was I supposed to take a whipping meekly?'

Mary frowned. 'They are the masters and we are only servants,' she said irritably. 'We do what they say, what they want, or we don't get a job with them ever again.'

Non remained silent. She supposed Mary was right; they were little more than servants. Still, they were paid a fair wage for a fair day's work.

'I suppose you shouldn't have come on this drove, knowing that Miss Georgina didn't like you,' Mary said.

'I need to work, like the rest of you. My father is dead, my house taken over by another family. What was I supposed to do?'

'Surely you could have found a job more suitable than this? We are walking, *walking*, mind you, hundreds of miles to London. Why couldn't you be a governess, or a lady teacher, or something like that?'

'I know the healing herbs, Mary; I want to be able to use my knowledge to help people. I don't want to live in some other woman's house or sleep at the back of a schoolhouse. I want to be able to help people.'

'That's mighty fine talk, love, but fine talk is best kept for women who are educated, not for wasting on the likes of us. Now listen to me—try to blend in, the women feel you think yourself above them as it is.'

Non bit her lip and glanced at the women, who were chatting while they walked, hands busy with needles. One of them caught her eye and glanced away quickly.

Non swallowed hard. 'I never thought myself above any of them,' she said softly. 'I'm a vicar's daughter, that's all.'

Mary shook her head. 'You can read and write, you can reckon up sums, that's more than most of us can do.'

Non kept quiet. She could point out that reading and writing wouldn't help make the cattle drove any easier for her, but she felt she'd said enough.

Mary fell silent too, and at last Non put a hand on her arm. 'Don't worry, Mary,' she said. 'I won't make any more trouble, and that's a promise.'

\*       \*       \*

After walking for what seemed hours, a halt was called and Non sat down with the other women to eat some dry cheese and a piece of bread. She wondered if Miss Georgina was dining on something tastier.

Mary caught up with her. She sighed and slipped her knitting into the pocket of her rough canvas apron. *'Bysedd fy nhraed i,'* Mary said. 'They do ache so.'

Non frowned. 'What do you mean, Mary?'

'The fingers of my feet, girl, they're bad. Can't you speak Welsh?'

'Oh, you mean your toes,' Non said. 'I haven't spoken a great deal of Welsh since I left the village of Five Saints to move to Swansea.'

'Shame on you, girl! Now, give me some advice.' Mary pointed to her feet. They were bare, the toes skinned and raw. 'What can I do to ease them a bit?'

'Wear your boots as I do.'

'My boots is round my neck, girl! I told you, didn't I? We all keep our boots for the towns, so that we look smart. We don't wear them to *walk* in.'

Non felt foolish. She'd not thought much about the women walking barefoot. 'It's no wonder your feet are bad, Mary.'

'Bless you, *merchi*, my feet are tough now from years of following the herds from Carmarthen to London. Done it more times than you've had hot dinners. So have they,' she jerked her head towards the other women. 'Except Flora, who came with you, of course.'

'I've got a nice balm to put on your toes, Mary,' Non said. 'Shall we stop for a minute?'

Mary shook her head. 'You don't stop on the drove, girl. Only to eat or to go into the bushes to do your business. If everyone stopped walking for the least thing we'd never reach London.'

'But your feet.'

'They'll do for now,' Mary said. 'We've time to make up now if we're to meet up with the herds from Cardiganshire at the Farmers' Arms.'

'Then we go on to Brecon?' Non felt ashamed of her ignorance.

'We might go through Brecon, but we didn't last drove. There's a toll gate there, see. Last time we went along the Builth road, but I don't know what Mr Jones plans for this trip.'

'Well,' Non said, 'when we stop for the night I'll see to your feet. Are any of the other women suffering?'

'Don't think so. I'm the only clumsy one, by the look of it, but then I am older than the rest of 'em.'

Non looked at her with fresh eyes. Mary was about twenty-eight years, she supposed, and perhaps that was old to be walking all the way from Wales to London.

'Don't look at me as if I've got two heads, girl!'

101

Mary's face brightened into a smile. 'There's many years of work left to me yet, if God be willing.'

Non fell silent. What would she do herself, once the drove was over? Perhaps she'd be allowed to go on the next one with the Joneses, but after offending Miss Georgina, she somehow doubted it. Perhaps she could take a permanent stall in Swansea market. She would have to work hard to keep her stock of remedies from dwindling, but she was prepared to do anything to make an honest living.

'What're you thinking?' Mary asked. 'You're so dreamy there anyone would believe you're in love.'

Non looked away. 'No, not in love, Mary. Just wondering what I'm going to do when we get back home.'

'Why, that's a long way off, girl. You got to see London yet. The markets are always so good, lots of animals sold there—thousands, would you believe?' She paused. 'Oh, and Barnet fair, you got to go to that, it's something you won't see the likes of in Swansea.' Mary adjusted her knitting needles. 'Got to cast off now, that's another pair of socks to sell to the hosiery shops in London.' She said the word 'London' as if it were some mysterious, magical place, and Non felt a flash of excitement.

'Is London a very big place?'

'*Duw*, it's so vast you could walk all day and never see the end of it. Course, we got to stop before we get there for the finishing of the animals.'

'Finishing?'

'Aye, cleaning the beasts and fattening them, so they look good to the dealers who are going to pay good money for them.'

Non sighed. She really was ignorant of the ways of the world. She had been cherished all her life, sheltered from the harsh reality of having to earn her own living. Now she was alone, and she realized with a sinking of her heart how much she had to learn about life as an independent woman. She glanced at Mary and smiled. 'Well, I think by the end of this drove I might be a little wiser than when I started it.'

'Good for you, girl. Now, less talking and more walking, or we'll never get to London.'

Non looked up at the sky, which was blue and beautiful. Suddenly, with the sun shining down on her, she felt happier than she'd done since the day she put her father into the ground.


## CHAPTER TEN

By the time they reached the Farmers' Arms, Non was so tired she could barely stand. She was shown to a tiny back room that contained only a pallet on the floor, a couple of none-too-clean blankets, and a rickety table. On the table stood a jug and basin, and the water in the jug, though cold, looked fresh.

By now the long days of walking were catching up with her. Non was young and strong, but even she was feeling the strain of constantly being on her feet. Still, she had more work to do. She'd promised Mary she would tend her feet before the women retired for the night. The men would be in the tap room, cheered by beer and singing in loud but harmonious voices.

Her supper was brought to her on a tray; it

consisted of a bowl of *cawl*, the tasty Welsh soup made of lamb and vegetables, freshly baked bread and a square of cheese. Non realized suddenly how hungry she was.

At last, she wiped the crumbs of bread from her lips and got to her feet. The accommodation might leave a lot to be desired but the food was good. She searched in her box for her remedies, but there was nothing she could use to soothe Mary's blistered feet. She would just have to go outside and hunt for what she needed.

It was almost dark in the fields outside the inn, but Non walked slowly, looking for a likely ditch where she might find some hay maids growing. It was an easy plant to spot by its round, hairy leaves and long flowers. Sometimes, in the dimness of evening, the petals appeared deep purple, but in the sunlight they were blue, with white spots on the tips.

Back in her small room, Non took out her mortar and pestle and began to grind the hay maids into a pulp. Then she mixed it with some fat left over from the lamb. It didn't smell very good, but the ointment should help heal Mary's feet. The leaves of the hay maids, chopped and infused in wine, would also help to ease the pain.

Non made her way down the rickety staircase to the tap room and peered in from the doorway. She could see the men of the drove standing round the bar, and behind them, close to the rear wall, was Caradoc. Non's heart quickened at the sight of his tall figure, his hair gleaming in the lamplight and his features thrown into sharp relief against the darkness of the wall behind him.

'Yes, Miss, can I do something for you?' The

landlord was looking at her closely, wondering what a decent young lady would want in the company of hard-working, hard-drinking men.

'I need a glass of wine,' Non said. 'It's not to drink, Landlord, it's to make up some medication for my friend. Her feet are so bad she can hardly walk.'

'You can make up a remedy for bad feet, then, can you?' The landlord came closer to where she was standing in the passageway. 'Do that mean you can make up medicines for all sorts of ills?'

'Well, some ills, certainly. Why, are you worried about anything?'

'It's my baby son, he's got the belly ache something awful. Sometimes he screams with the pain and the noise is enough to make a man deaf.'

'Give me the wine and I'll bring you something to soothe the colic in about half an hour.'

She returned to her room, feeling weariness wash over her. She looked longingly at the pallet, then shook her head. There was much to do before she could sleep.

Non used half the wine to infuse the hay maids, and then used the rest for the baby, mixing it with a potion which she'd found was a good remedy for windy colic. Armed with the medicine, she went back down the stairs and handed the bottle to the landlord.

'Just a few drops, mind, not too much. It should help relieve your baby's pains.'

'If it do work, you can come and eat by yer in the Farmers' Arms for free any time you like.'

It was warm out in the yard and, except for the low glint of light from the inn, the darkness was profound. Non eased her way across the ground, feeling her way carefully. After a few moments, she came to the door of a long low barn. She pushed the door open and it creaked on its hinges, the sound loud in the silence.

Mary was almost asleep, but she peeped over the edge of her rough blanket and after a moment sat up, putting her finger to her lips. 'Shush, they're all asleep 'cepts me.'

Non knelt down beside her. 'Look, I've made this for you.' She held out the pewter mug half full of the medicine. 'It will help make you sleepy.'

Mary took the drink without question and swallowed it down as obediently as a little child. She didn't protest when Non pushed back the blanket and began to smear her feet with ointment.

When Non had finished, Mary took her hand and smiled. 'You're a good girl, Non, just a bit simple in the ways of the world. But then, you're a vicar's daughter, after all, and can't be expected to know about life on the road. You stick to Mary, I'll put you right, you'll see.'

Mary settled herself down under the blanket and winked before closing her eyes. Non hid a smile; that was the nearest she was going to get to a 'thank you'. She patted Mary's shoulder and made her way silently out of the barn.

In her room, Non pulled off her boots and sank onto the pallet. Her own feet were sore from walking all day and her bones ached. It was a hot night and the air in the small room reeked of beer. Still, she was sheltered from the elements and she was free to undress and wash in private.

She slept almost as soon as her head touched the pillow, and through the thread of her dreams ran images of Caradoc, seated on a horse, galloping to her rescue and holding her close in his strong arms. She even felt the touch of his mouth on hers, and sat up abruptly to see the beginnings of daylight creeping into her room.

Downstairs, the drovers were eating a hearty breakfast of bacon, eggs and bread fried in fat. There was a long room beside the tap room where wooden tables were set up; this was where the women were seated.

Mary waved to her and, thankful to see she looked a great deal better, Non sat beside her on the rough wooden bench.

'*Duw fy merchi,* my feet are good as new!' Mary said.

Non hid a smile. Mary was referring to her as 'my girlie'—she acted like a maiden aunt although she was still only in her twenties.

'Well, I'm glad the medicine worked. Let's have a look.'

Mary lifted her sacking apron and her coarse skirt and showed her bare feet. 'See, the scabs are healing like magic and that ointment took the sting right out of them.' She let her skirt fall back into place. 'It's a pity they got into that state to start with, mind.' Mary looked at her levelly. 'If it wasn't for the stampede, I wouldn't have run over the rough stones. Mind you, it could be much worse— someone might have been killed. I'm just saying, so that you'll understand the importance of keeping the beasts calm.'

'I know, I've learned my lesson on that score,' Non said. She longed to repeat that the stampede was more Georgina's fault than hers, but then she should learn to keep her mouth shut: that was the message Mary was giving her.

'Get some food down you, Non,' Mary said. 'Sit by here with me and help yourself to some bacon and eggs. A bit of fried bread wouldn't do any harm, either.'

Non obeyed. She needed to keep up her strength, just as the other women did. The walk to Brecon was going to be a long one.

After breakfast, the women gathered at the front of the Farmers' Arms, waiting for the men to round up the cattle. Non watched in silence as Georgina Jones was helped into her seat in the carriage, her eyes barely glancing at the assembled women.

Non felt a pang of anger. Georgina was so smug, thinking herself superior when all she did was lounge around, waiting to get to London to buy herself fripperies to wear. As Miss Georgina Jones, she'd been given the best room the little inn could offer, and a proper bed, no doubt, with clean washed sheets. She had breakfasted in her room, and even now, with the openness of the hills and fields spread out before her, Georgina seemed sheltered and cosseted as she sat among her cushions.

'Take that look off your face, girl.' Mary's voice held a warning tone. 'If looks could kill, Miss Jones would be a goner.'

Non turned her back on Georgina, and stared at the inn as though it was her own dear home and she was sad to leave it. She would keep well clear of Miss High and Mighty Jones from now on.

Caradoc appeared suddenly in the doorway of the Farmers' Arms; behind him the landlord was smiling broadly.

'There's the clever girl!' The landlord pointed to Non. 'Your medicine did my baby the world of good, Miss. We 'ad a good night's sleep for the first time in months.'

'I'm glad about that.' Non felt absurdly proud, being praised for her skills with Caradoc looking intently into her eyes.

'She's a clever lady, in't she, Sir?' The landlord turned to Caradoc. 'I think you're lucky to have her along with the drove.'

Non waited breathlessly, wondering what Caradoc would say. His eyes held an amused look as he stared at her. 'It's only what we employed her for, Landlord,' he said at last. 'It certainly wasn't for her knitting or weeding, I can tell you.'

It was as if all the breath had left her. Non looked down at the ground, feeling her face glowing. How could he demean her in such a casual way? She suddenly felt worthless, as though she'd been employed as a gesture of charity, not as a working part of the drove.

'Come on, girl.' Mary took her arm. 'Look, the cattle are lined up on the road, the men are all mounted—it's time we got our legs moving, isn't it?'

Non fell into step with Mary, and then Flora came to join them.

'Lovely day,' Flora said. 'This beats working in a kitchen.' She glanced quickly at Non. 'No offence meant, mind.'

'None taken,' Non said, realizing that Flora had worked from morning till night in the vicarage. It was no wonder she was enjoying the freedom of the road, with the pale sun shining overhead.

\*     \*     \*

They had been walking for about two hours and the weather had turned chilly, the air heavy with the threat of thunder. Non knew enough now to be afraid of a thunderstorm. If lightning struck nearby or the thunder rolled too close, the herd would be spooked, and then what would happen? Probably another day's delay and time wasted while the animals were rounded up.

'Looks like we're taking a halt,' Mary said, pocketing her knitting. Non craned her neck to see over the heads of the other women. Mary was right, something was happening up at the front of the drove.

Non climbed up the grassy bank at the side of the road, from where she could see the cattle and the young ponies being driven into a field that was fenced and secure. Her heart sank. There would be a delay now; even if the storm passed them over, precious time would be lost.

But the storm did not pass them over. A mighty flash of lightning lit the glowering skies, and a few moments later thunder cracked overhead, rolling across the sky with frightening force. Suddenly the heavens opened and the rain came lashing down.

Non's skirt and shawl were soaked in a matter of seconds. She looked round to see the other women fleeing in the direction of a distant barn. Non followed them, but by the time she reached shelter she was wet through.

She stood in the doorway of the barn and shook the rain from her hair. Looking up, she saw Dennis driving towards her.

'Mr Jones says you're to come in by here with Miss Georgina,' he said, rising from his seat and extending his hand to her. Non was pulled up into the coach, and found herself sitting on the seat, looking into the hostile face of Caradoc's sister.

There was silence, except for the sound of the driving rain. Non lifted her skirts from her legs and shook them. 'It's a bit late to take cover now.' She glanced up. 'Though I am grateful to you for sharing your shelter with me, Miss Jones.'

'It's none of my doing,' Georgina said sulkily. 'Look at you, like a rat that's been dragged through a horse trough.'

Non bit back the angry words that sprang to her lips. She lifted her hand to her hair and found it had come loose from her ribbons; her bonnet was lost somewhere out on the road and she felt as bad as she obviously looked. She pulled her shawl, which clung wetly to her shoulders. She let it be; there was nowhere she could hang it without inconveniencing Miss Jones.

Georgina leaned as far away from Non as she could, and sighed heavily. 'My brother thinks you're too good to shelter in the barn with the other women. I say he's mad, all you are is a paid employee, the same as the rest of them. Lord, what a dreadful smell.'

'It's my shawl.' Non tried to be patient. 'Wool always smells bad when it gets wet.'

'Well, I don't see why I have to put up with it. I never liked you since the first time I set eyes on you. Flirting with my brother you were, then, and in my book that's why he brought you along on this trip.'

Non took a deep breath. 'The time might come when you'll need my help, and you just hope and pray I don't let my personal feelings cloud my judgement.'

Georgina stared at her coolly. 'I'm not gullible, like the rabble you normally deal with. I don't believe your potions and poisons do anything at all.'

Non pressed her lips together, determined not to get into an argument. She leaned forward to look through the window and saw to her relief that the rain was relenting and patches of blue sky were becoming visible through the cloud.

Dennis was still seated in the driving seat. He was soaked to the skin and his hat was dripping water onto his shoulders.

'All right, Dennis?' Non asked, angry at Georgina for not inviting Dennis to sit with them.

'I'm all right, Miss.' Dennis found it difficult to talk through his chattering teeth. 'It'll be all right when the sun breaks through—dry me off nicely, it will.'

'Shut up, boy,' Georgina said. 'Speak when I ask you to and not before.'

Non gave her a look that conveyed all the scorn and dislike she felt for Georgina. 'I'm getting out of here,' she said. 'I don't think I can stand the company any longer.'

She jumped to the ground and her boots sank into the mud. She looked up ahead, cheered to see the drovers were calling and herding the cattle towards the road. The women were coming out of the barn, shaking the rain from their shawls and taking out their knitting again.

The sun came out from behind the clouds and Non felt the warmth through her wet clothes. She took off her shawl and hung it over the side of the goods wagon. It would soon dry out in the sunshine.

At last, the cattle were on the move again, hooves sinking into the mud, but at least they had stopped bellowing in fear. Docile now, they joined the drovers' road and soon everything seemed normal. The sun shone, the women carried on with their knitting, and Non drifted away from the road, keeping a lookout for some more hay maids, or anything else that might come in useful.

'Nasty shower.' Caradoc rode up beside her, leaning over his saddle towards her, his eyes merry, his mouth curved into a smile. 'I see your clothes are steaming—you must have been soaked to the skin. Don't you think it would be a good idea to change into something dry?'

'I'll be all right,' Non said. 'It's Dennis I feel sorry for.'

'Dennis?'

'Your sister's driver,' Non said abruptly. 'He was the only one on the whole drove who didn't have cover.'

'Why on earth didn't the boy get in the coach with you and Georgina?'

'Because he wasn't allowed to.' She glanced up at him. 'You should know what a snob your sister is.'

'That's enough,' Caradoc said. 'You forget your manners, Miss Jenkins. It's my sister you're talking about.' He paused. 'Still, it was thoughtless of her to leave the boy outside in the rain.'

Non wanted to say that it wasn't thoughtlessness but sheer spitefulness on Georgina's part, but she'd already said enough.

'I don't understand why Dennis didn't climb down and shelter underneath the wheels,' Caradoc said thoughtfully. 'Perhaps the boy didn't have the

113

intelligence to think about it.'

'Oh, Dennis has the intelligence, don't you worry.' Non forgot her resolve not to say anything more about Georgina. 'Your sister is a stern and spiteful taskmaster, she wanted Dennis to make sure the horses didn't bolt in the storm.'

Caradoc slid down from the saddle. 'Again, you forget yourself.' His eyes flared as he looked down at her. All at once, Non saw him not as the carefree charmer she'd first thought him, but as a man with steel in his bones. The thought sent a thrill of desire through her body. 'Whatever your thoughts about my family, I would prefer you to keep them to yourself,' Caradoc said quietly. 'You've already caused trouble with your petty quarrelling, or have you forgotten that?'

'No, and I'm sorry, I let my tongue run away with me. But I'm very fond of Dennis,' she added lamely. 'He did work for my father once, and his behaviour was exemplary.' She shrugged. 'But there, you'll side with your sister, whoever else is insulted or hurt. It's in your nature.'

He came closer to her and his hands gripped her arms, bruising her flesh. 'And what do you presume to know about my nature?'

Non threw caution to the winds. 'I know you are proud, I know you are feckless, you flirt with every girl who catches your eye. I've seen you looking at young Flora, new on the drove as I am.'

'Not jealous are you, Miss Jenkins?' Non tried to pull away from him but he only gripped her harder. His face was close to hers, he smelt of sun and grass and the open air. Then he kissed her, and it was as though the sun was blotted out and the world ceased to exist.

She leaned against him, feeling his lips draw fire from her own. She stopped struggling and her arms crept around his broad shoulders. The kiss seemed to last an eternity. When at last he released her, he seemed as shaken as she was.

'That's enough from you.' He spoke roughly. 'I have more serious business than dallying with a vicar's daughter. I have a drove to run.'

She watched him walk away, her hands clenched into fists. 'I hate you!' she muttered, but she knew she lied. In truth, it was not hate but love she felt for Caradoc Jones: a love that could lead only to disaster.

## CHAPTER ELEVEN

At the next halt, the drove was met by a herd of fifty cattle, bringing the number of beasts to more than three hundred. The new stock comprised mostly of bulls, but there were about ten young heifers and a few milch cows. Non could see they were marked with the initials of their owner, cut into their hides just above the knee joint. Non could see Caradoc talking with two of the dealers. He had a notebook and pen in his hand, and his bearing was almost regal. He was so obviously in charge of the situation that she stood fixed to the spot, watching in admiration.

She put her hand to her lips, recalling the warmth of his mouth on hers, and she blushed, remembering how eagerly she'd responded to his touch. She'd never thought of herself as wanton, she'd never even considered the fact that she could

115

be so passionate, but Caradoc had aroused feelings in her that were new and a little frightening.

'Don't stare so, Non.' Mary appeared at her side. 'You shouldn't wear your heart on your sleeve, girl!'

Non looked at her quickly. 'I don't know what you mean.'

'I mean you're losing your head over Mr Jones, that's what I mean. The way you watch him all the time gives the show away.'

Non swallowed hard. She was aware of Mary's raised eyebrows, but ploughed on. 'He's a good drover, he takes care of his workers as well as his stock. I do admire him.'

'Oh aye, admiring is a new name for what you're feeling, my lovely. Now take my advice and turn your thoughts away from the likes of Mr Jones. He's not going to put a gold ring on the finger of a girl works for him, is he?'

Non sighed heavily. 'All right, Mary, you've made your point. Now please don't go on about it.' She hesitated. 'Do you think anyone else has noticed?'

'Noticed what?' There was a wicked gleam in Mary's eyes.

'You know exactly what I mean.'

'No, girl, I don't think anyone else has noticed; most of the women are out weeding and the rest they're knitting, but go on the way you are and the whole drove will know how you feel.' Mary put her knitting back in her pocket and settled herself down on a fallen tree trunk. '*Duw*, I'm that tired,' she said. 'I think I'm getting too old for all this traipsing around the countryside. I sometimes wish I 'ad a husband to keep me, then I wouldn't need to work.'

116

Non looked at Mary with new eyes. She was weathered by the sun, her skin brown, her dark hair tied up in a knot. She had fine bone structure and her eyes were heavy lidded, fringed with dark lashes. She was a lovely looking woman and must have had many suitors.

'Why haven't you married, Mary?' she said. 'I'm sure you must have been asked lots of times.'

'Aye, well maybe, but it was always by the wrong man.' She looked up at Non. 'If I was ten years younger I'd toss my cap at Morgan the smithy. He's a well-set-up man and comfortably off, what with all the work he gets shoeing the beasts . . . Just in case you're interested, he'll be joining us at Brecon. Some of the beasts have worn their *ciws* down too far.' She looked shrewdly at Non. 'You don't know what I'm talking about, do you? *Ciws* are the shoes fastened on to the cattle to save their feet from the hardness of the road.'

'And yet you women walk barefoot. Don't you think that's strange, Mary?'

'Beasts are worth money,' she shrugged, 'women workers are ten a penny. Do you know how clever Morgan is? It needs strength and skill to make the shoes. He's got to shape two separate pieces of metal for each hoof—you know why?'

Non shook her head. She'd talked to Morgan about his work and knew he was a skilled man, but she obviously didn't know as much as Mary.

'I'll tell you why, you ignorant girl. The cattle have cloven hooves, so they can't be shod like a horse. They have to be thrown to the ground first and that takes a man of great strength like our Morgan.' There was a hint of a smile in her voice. 'It's funny how some girls don't see a gift when it's

117

put under their noses. A handsome man is Morgan. We'll be seeing him soon and I expect you'll be all over him, won't you?'

Non was a little taken aback. Would she be pleased to see him or would Morgan's presence spoil the rapport she was building up with Caradoc? 'I didn't realize he'd be meeting us at Brecon,' she said.

'Well, if you wasn't interested enough to ask, then more fool you,' Mary said sharply.

Non was saved from replying by a shout from the head drover. He swivelled his horse around and called instructions to other men as they tried to merge the new herd with the old. Their task was difficult because both sets of animals were restless, turning in their tracks and stamping the dry earth into small puffs of dust. One of the bulls tried to mount a heifer and was beaten with a stick for his pains.

Mary got to her feet. 'Rest over, we'll be on the move again any time now.' She took out her knitting and held it up. 'See, Non, there'll be another nice pair of stockings made by nightfall. Why don't you take up knitting instead of looking for herbs and things all the time?'

'I don't *like* knitting and I *do* like herbs and things,' she smiled. 'Each to her own, eh, Mary?'

'Aye, fair play, you're right enough. I don't suppose you'd know how to turn the heel of a stocking, anyway.'

'And I don't suppose you'd know how to make a medicine out of herbs, either. Now come on, Mary, the cattle are beginning to move, we'd better get ready to follow.'

By the time the drove reached the next inn on

the route, Mary's blisters were playing up again. Non watched her limping as she reached the door. She would give Mary some freshly made ointment to cover her sores. Mary was not yet thirty, but she was coming to the end of her days walking the drovers' roads. And what would she do then, how would she earn her living?

That set Non to wondering about her own future. If she didn't marry, would she end up a lonely and embittered spinster? It was true that Morgan wanted her as his wife, but could she settle for second best now that she'd met Caradoc Jones?

Later, Non invited Mary to share her supper, and in the small attic room the two women sat side by side on the bed, eating game pie and fresh crusty bread.

'*Duw*, this is welcome, mind. By the time we got 'ere my stomach thought my throat was cut, I was so hungry.'

From her new perspective as a working girl, Non realized how privileged her upbringing had been. Even now, though she was part of the drove, she was still treated like a lady. Mary must think her fortunate to have her own room and her meals served to her, a benefit shared only by Caradoc's sister, Georgina. The rest of the women had to make do, like the men of the drove, either eating dried food or at best having bread and cheese from the taverns where they stopped for the night.

'You live well, mind,' Mary said, eyeing the clean linen on the bed and the small wash-stand holding a jug and basin. Her words seemed to echo Non's thoughts. 'You're treated well, by anyone's standards. Good food to put in your belly and a nice bed to sleep in.' She winked. 'Even if the man

119

you fancy isn't sharing it with you.'

'Mary!' Non shook her head. 'You forget I am a vicar's daughter. I wouldn't dream of sharing my bed with any man—not until I'm married.'

Mary sniffed. 'Good thing I don't think like that, else I'd die a virgin.'

'Mary!' Non said again, aware there was a half-admiring note in her voice. She glanced surreptitiously at Mary, wondering how she'd been brave enough to give herself to a man, with no wedding ring on her finger.

'No good looking at me like I got two heads, mind.' Mary popped a juicy bit of pie into her mouth, savouring the rich meat and gravy and the crusty pastry.

'Well then, tell me, were you in love with the man you took to your bed?' Non watched as Mary thoughtfully chewed her food, and when she swallowed, prompted her. 'Well?'

'I thought I was in love. I suppose I was in love, but then he wasn't, at least not with me. I found out he had a wife and five children living in Cardiganshire.' She shrugged. 'There, that's drovers for you. Never trust one of them is my advice.' She nodded. 'And that means the boss as well as the other men.'

'But the men seem so good to the girls. They're polite and decent and treat everyone the same.'

'You 'aven't got your eyes open, though. You're so taken up with the boss man that you don't see what's going on under your nose.'

Non frowned. 'I don't understand you.'

'Look, at least two of the girls are sleeping with drovers. I suppose they think the men will marry them, but most of 'em got wives at home.'

Non digested this information in silence as she tried to guess which of the girls would be daring enough to have an illicit affair. The eight women on the drove appeared to be respectable enough. One or two were a bit loud, but there had been no lewd talk from any of them. 'They seem like good girls to me,' she said.

'They're respectful enough in your company, but how often is that?' Mary said practically.

She was right. Non spent most of the day looking for fresh herbs, and at night she stayed in her room making potions, while the rest of the women slept in an outhouse or barn.

The men, there were ten of them, slept alongside the cattle, careful of the creatures that would eventually put money in their pockets. On reflection, it would be very easy for them to meet with the women during the night, especially after drinking in the tap room of whatever inn they were near.

'Come on, stop thinking about what I said and do my feet for me, there's a good girl,' Mary said. 'I'm sorry I spoke, now; you'll go watching all the girls and trying to make out who's up to what.'

Non shook her head and put the remains of her pie on the table. 'I'd better wash my hands first.' She went to the wash-stand and tipped some water from the jug into the basin.

'Duw, I never knew a girl for washing so much. I've seen you washing your plants in the streams we pass and dipping your hands in as well. Anyone can see you been brought up proper, like.'

'Stop talking for a minute and let's have a look at you.'

Fresh sores had broken out on Mary's feet and

Non clucked her tongue in dismay. Mary should be resting until her feet were healed.

'You're not really fit to carry on, Mary.' She rubbed an ointment made of bistort roots gently into Mary's wounds. 'Can't you do a bit of weeding at one of the farms, and meet us when we're on our way back?'

Mary winced with pain as the balm touched her sores. 'It's a thought, girl, but I'm all right to carry on for a few more days. I've had bad feet before; so have most of the other girls. We just have to put up with it. Part of the job, see?'

Non shook her head. Mary was stubborn, she would do what she wanted, there was no point in trying to change her mind.

'Look, why don't you stay up here with me for the night? The bed is big enough and you'll be more comfortable.'

Mary shook her head. 'Don't be daft, girl. I'd have them all talking about me getting soft. I'd be pensioned off at the next halt and then what would I do? No, you just leave Mary to make her own way, right?'

Mary picked up her boots from the uneven wooden floor and held them under the candlelight to re-do her laces. She swung the boots around her shoulders and smiled. 'Don't do to let your boots out of sight.' She went to the door. 'See you in the morning, and don't you go talking about Mary's bad feet to anyone, right?'

Non nodded. 'Goodnight, then, Mary. See you in the morning.' Non listened to Mary's soft footfall on the stairs and could tell that she was limping; she must be in great pain, with open sores that nothing but rest could really heal.

Non tidied up her food tray and put it outside the door. From downstairs in the smoky tap room she could hear the raised voices of the customers. The drovers would be joined in their drinking by local farm workers, all eager to listen to tales picked up on the roads. She wondered for a moment where Caradoc was. Would he be drinking with the men, or would he be with his sister? Georgina was like a spoilt child, she would demand attention, but would Caradoc humour her?

Suddenly Non was restless. It was lonely in the evenings, when she sat all alone in her room; a different room each time they stopped. She almost preferred it when the drove didn't reach a tavern and she, along with everyone else, was obliged to spend the night in the open.

It was at times like this, sitting alone in a strange room, that she missed her father most. His humour, his patience and his willingness to listen to her talk endlessly about her herbal remedies had been an essential part of their lives together. They had lived comfortably in the vicarage and eaten well, attended by loyal servants. She realized now that she'd taken it all for granted. Her father's death had changed her world; as well as losing her father, she had lost a way of life that was peaceful and safe. Would she have to marry to recapture all that?

A knock on the door startled her, and Non hesitated for a moment. The knocking became urgent, and she hurried to open the door.

'Help me! You've got to help me!' Flora pushed her way into the room, in tears.

'Please, Miss Non, you know these things— you've got to give me something to take, and quickly!'

'Try to calm yourself, Flora, and tell me what on earth's wrong.'

Flora's normally pretty face was blotched and reddened. It was clear she'd been crying for some time. She sniffed and tried to stop crying, but the tears continued to roll down her cheeks.

'I'm in trouble, Miss, real bad trouble. Say you'll help me, 'cos I daren't go home to my mam and dad in such a state.'

Non was puzzled. 'What is it? Have you hurt yourself in some way?'

'No, Miss. I'm with child, that's what I am, and the father a married man. You've got to help, you have, or I'm just going to die.'

Non took a deep breath. Her eyes ran over Flora's figure, but she was still as slim as ever. 'Whatever has happened to you, it didn't happen on the drove,' Non said quietly. 'We've only been on the road a matter of weeks.'

'I know that, Miss, but I never realized how I was until I came on the road, and when my curse didn't follow me I spoke to Mary and she told me I must be 'specting.'

'You didn't notice before that your courses weren't regular?' Non sat on the bed and gestured for Flora to take the chair.

'The curse haven't never been regular with me, Miss, and I haven't been sick in the morning, so it weren't until Mary spoke to me that I realized I was . . . you know.'

'And the father, is he with the drove?'

Flora nodded miserably. 'But he'll deny it, Miss. Men never do own up when they've got a girl ruined, do they?'

It was something Non had never needed to think about. Guarded as she had been by her father's position in the parish, she'd been ignorant of what happened in the outside world. Flora had been her maid and Non hadn't even known she was seeing a man.

'So, Miss, can you help me? Can you give me some medicine to take that will help me slip the baby?'

Non felt a rush of horror. 'I couldn't do any such thing!' she said quietly. 'You would be killing your child—you can't expect me to help do that.'

'But my dad will kill me if I go home with a baby on the way, and by the time we get back home I might be showing. I think I'm already three or four months gone. You do know what to give me, don't you, Miss? I can see by your face that you do.'

The root of the gladwin boiled and made into a pessary would cause a miscarriage, but Non had no intention of telling Flora that. She shook her head. 'Even if I did know of anything, I wouldn't risk it; your own life would be put in danger. I'm sorry, but I can't offer you any help.'

Flora sat doggedly where she was, her eyes fixed pleadingly on Non.

'Look, what I do suggest is that you go to the man and tell him he must look after you and the baby. It's his fault you're in this dreadful state now.'

Flora shook her head. 'You don't know the ways of men, mind. He'll say I'm a harlot, he'll say I threw myself into his arms.' She began to cry again. 'A man trapped is like a rat, see, he'll say and do anything to get himself out of a fix.'

'What if I talk to Mr Jones, then?' Non said. 'We could ask him for help.'

'No, Miss! No, he'll just send me home, that's all, and my Tom will have his marching orders as well.'

'Thomas is the man who took advantage of you, is he?'

'Yes, Miss.'

'Well, then he deserves to be dismissed,' Non said, frowning. 'I should think he deserves a good whipping too.'

'You don't understand, Miss. If Thomas loses his job, he won't be able to help anyone, will he?'

Non digested this in silence. Flora was right: without work, this man Thomas couldn't support his wife, let alone another woman and a child.

'So will you help me, Miss?'

'I'm sorry,' Non said firmly. 'I only try to ease folk's ills. My job isn't to endanger lives.'

'Then a pox on you!' Flora got to her feet and tugged her shawl around her. 'Then I'll kill myself, it's the only way out.'

'Wait,' Non said. 'Come and see me tomorrow night and I'll see what I can do to help you. But,' she added, 'I won't give you anything to take. I'll think of another way out of this trouble for you, but I won't be responsible for killing your child.'

'All right then, Miss, I'll see you tomorrow. You might have changed your mind by then, when you think of the trouble I'm in.'

Non sighed as she closed the door after Flora. What a silly girl, to let a man use her that way. She sank onto the bed. What on earth could she do to help? There was no way she'd supply the remedy Flora was asking for; it went against everything she believed in to take a life. And then her mood lightened. She'd speak to Caradoc in the morning. She wouldn't give him any names, just casually ask

126

what he would do in such a circumstance. He would surely have experienced such mishaps before. The thought cheered her, and she undressed, washed and climbed into bed, reassured that somehow Caradoc, in his wisdom, would know exactly how to deal with the situation.

## CHAPTER TWELVE

The next morning, Non had a taste of what it was like to get caught on the roads in the drenching rain with nowhere to run for shelter. The ground was turned into a muddy wasteland, so that the cattle lost all sense of direction and wandered into unfenced fields. The drovers were short tempered, shouting curses as they tried to guide the herd back onto the road.

Non could feel her skirt clinging uncomfortably to her legs, her shawl dripped water and rain slid from her bonnet onto her face.

Mary came up beside her. 'Now you know what a drove is really like.' She wiped her face with her sleeve. 'It isn't all hot nights and sunny days, is it? Life on the road can be hard.'

Non didn't reply. She knew she could climb into the goods wagon any time and shelter under the canvas, but she prided herself on being just like the other women who walked with the herds.

'So you didn't see fit to help Flora out then, *merchi*?'

Non spoke firmly. 'No, Mary, I did not. My medicines are to cure, not to kill.' She glanced at Mary. 'Do you blame me?'

127

Mary shook her head. 'No, I don't blame you at all. She's far too young to try any daft tricks, like swallowing something poisonous.'

Non didn't choose to tell Mary that the root of the gladwin, taken in the right way, would procure a miscarriage without poisoning the mother.

'I'm that sorry for the girl, though,' Mary said. 'She's walking the roads without a shawl to cover her. She's letting the rain soak her, hoping she'll catch a fever and lose the child that way.'

Non felt a pang of pity for Flora, but what she asked was impossible. 'She should have thought of that before she gave herself to a man, and her not wed.'

'Oh, mind now, Miss Hoity Toity!' Mary said sharply. 'Have you never felt the thrill of a man's lips on yours?'

Non bowed her head. She remembered Caradoc's kiss very well, remembered how she had trembled in his arms and how her nipples had tightened against the bodice of her gown. She thought of him now, his thighs strong against the flanks of the horse he rode, and there was a tingling inside her that frightened and appalled her.

'I'm human, like everyone else.' Non tried to catch her breath. 'But I hope I have the control to keep myself chaste until I marry.'

'I expect you have,' Mary said. 'But then you are an educated woman, you've had a good upbringing; not like poor Flora, born into poverty and likely to end up the same way.'

'She had a good life as maid in my father's house,' Non protested. 'We cared about our servants as though they were family.'

128

'Well then, you didn't watch Flora very well, did you? Otherwise she wouldn't have got in the state she is now.' Mary looked at her curiously. 'Have you never felt passion for a man, Non?'

'How are your feet?' Non changed the subject, hoping that the rain hid the hot colour in her cheeks. She had felt desire, knew how dangerous it could be, and she prayed to the Good Lord that she would never be so foolish as to let passion overrule her good sense.

'They're as bad as ever,' Mary said, 'but the drove will be stopping at the nearest shelter. It'll be a short trip today because of the weather, and tomorrow, if it's fine, we'll have to try to make up time by travelling a lot further.'

Non looked down at her boots; they were sinking deeper into the mud with every step she took. It was a wretched day, made more miserable by the fact that she'd had no opportunity to speak to Caradoc about Flora's predicament. She glanced over her shoulder and saw Flora walking, head bent against the rain, her dress clinging wetly to her small figure. Non sighed heavily. She must talk to Caradoc, but how was she going to manage it with the other drovers about?

At last, the animals were steered safely back onto the road; the fields they were passing now were closed in with dry-stone walls and the rain was easing a little.

Non made her way to the front of the drove, disobeying the rules laid down by Caradoc. He glanced at her from the saddle. 'Enjoying the weather?' he said. His hair, darkened by the rain, clung wetly to his forehead; droplets ran down his face and onto his mouth and Non had a sudden urge to kiss them away.

'I have to talk to you, it's important,' she said. 'When can I see you in private?'

'Tonight, with a bit of luck,' Caradoc said. 'Now fall back behind the animals, find out if my sister needs anything.' His tone was friendly but she could see his attention was focused on the animals.

'Right, tonight then.' She hardly noticed that Mary had fallen back to join Flora, who was plodding through the mud, head down as if she had all the cares of the world on her shoulders. And so she did; but it was her own fault.

By the afternoon, the rain had eased a little and Non saw Caradoc riding his horse towards her. 'Why are you walking in all this rain?' he said, looking down at her. 'Are you too proud to get up into the wagon and try to dry yourself?' He had touched a sensitive spot and she shook her head angrily.

'No, I'm not too proud. It's just that I don't want any of the other women to say I'm not fit enough to walk the drovers' roads.'

His eyes took in her breasts, revealed by the wetness of her bodice. 'You look pretty fit to me,' he said softly. Non pulled her shawl round her shoulders, feeling her cheeks turn scarlet. 'Go on,' Caradoc urged, 'get into the wagon, why don't you?'

'I'm wet enough now, so I might as well keep on the road. I like talking with the other women.' She looked up at him, wondering if this was the right time to tell him about Flora, but somehow she knew it would be a mistake, Caradoc wouldn't understand. Flora was right, he'd simply send her packing and her married lover with her.

130

'What are you thinking? Is there a problem?'

It was perceptive of him to see the question in her eyes, but she shook back her wet hair and kept her face turned away from him.

'No, there's not a problem, but it would be nice to know how long it will take us to reach shelter.'

'About another two hours,' Caradoc said. 'Look, I'm riding ahead to arrange accommodation at the Drovers' Inn. Why don't you come with me?'

'No, no really. I'm all right, I'll walk.'

'I thought you wanted to talk to me in private. Come on, hold on.' Caradoc held out his hand. 'You can get into some dry things at the tavern, you'll be much more comfortable then.'

Before she knew it, Non was lifted up and swung onto the saddle in front of Caradoc. She felt his breath against her hair, smelled the damp, clean scent of him and her heart began to beat faster. It was as if he was holding her in loving arms, and as he kicked the horse into a gallop, she relaxed against him.

She knew the women would be watching her and she flushed. They would be certain to talk about her now, especially Flora, who had taken to staring at her as though she hated the sight of her.

As Caradoc spurred his horse away from the herds, the wind and rain swept into Non's face, but she was happy to be close to him. She felt glowing, as if the sun was shining down on her. But her euphoria was short lived.

'Ah, there's Georgina catching up with us.' Caradoc spoke with his cheek close to Non's. 'She'll make sure she gets a hot bath as soon as possible.'

As the carriage drew level, Caradoc nodded at

131

Dennis. 'You know the way to the next tavern, do you?'

Dennis touched his cap and droplets of rain fell on his weather-reddened face. 'Yes, Sir, easy to follow was your directions, Mill Lane being the only way we could turn if we was not to be heading back home.'

'Good lad,' Caradoc said.

Georgina leaned forward and stared at Non through the carriage window. 'Looking after our vicar's daughter then, are we?' Her voice was heavy with sarcasm.

'Don't start,' Caradoc said easily.

'By the way, Miss Jenkins,' Georgina spoke in a friendlier tone, 'may I borrow your book for an hour or two?'

Non looked at her in surprise. 'Why do you want it?' She was reluctant to part with her herbal, if only for a short time, and yet it seemed churlish to refuse.

'I promise to take good care of it. There's just something I would like to look up for myself.'

'Yes, I suppose it will be all right,' Non said, still puzzled. 'But please don't keep it long—I use it every day for some cure or other.'

'I will return it to you tonight. Don't worry, I won't do your book any harm.'

Georgina held out her hand and Non fumbled in the bag hanging from her side and withdrew her herbal. Reluctantly, she handed it to Georgina. 'Please take care of it.'

'Not to worry.' Georgina disappeared into the gloom of the carriage and Caradoc, realizing that the conversation was over, urged his horse back into a gallop.

'We'll soon be there,' he said, his mouth dangerously close to her cheek again. 'I'll send a maidservant to your room with hot water for you to bathe. I can't have you catching a chill, can I?'

Non felt her heart beat faster. She was touched by Caradoc's thoughtfulness, but if she was honest it was not his concern for her health that moved her; it was the fact that she was falling in love with him.

She told herself she was a fool—Caradoc was not for her. The thought brought tears to her eyes; how could she bear to be so near him, to want him so much, knowing she could never have him as her own?

Sooner than she wished, the tavern came into view. It stood on a small rise of land, with the mountains towering behind.

'Welcome to the Brecon Beacons,' Caradoc said. 'Now they are shrouded in mist, but on a fine day these hills are magnificent.'

Caradoc reined in his horse and immediately a boy came to take the animal from him. 'Right, Sir,' he bowed almost double in front of Caradoc, 'I'll stable the animal, Sir.'

Caradoc swung himself to the ground and held up his hands to lift Non from the saddle. She felt his warm fingers tighten around her waist, and for a few seconds she stood almost thigh to thigh with him, her breasts pressed against him, his face close to hers. It was a moment of breathtaking silence, and then he released her.

'We'd better get in out of the rain.' He spoke easily, as though her touch had not moved him. Glancing at his face, though, gave her a different impression: his colour was high and his eyes avoided hers.

Within the hour, Non was luxuriating in a hot bath. The bath itself was old and rusting and had clearly seen better days, but the water was wonderfully soothing as it lapped her chilled flesh. On the floor beside her lay her bag, brought straight to her room by Dennis, and in it were fresh, dry clothes.

Suddenly she heard raised voices outside the room. The door sprung open and Georgina stood on the threshold, staring at her angrily. 'How dare you use the bath before me?' She moved further into the room, careless of the open door behind her. 'I'm of a delicate disposition and I need to get out of my mud-stained clothes at once.'

Angered and embarrassed by Georgina's abrupt entry into her room, Non stood up and wrapped a towel around her body. She stepped out of the bath onto the bare wooden floor, gesturing towards the cooling water. 'Help yourself,' she said. 'I've finished with it.'

Georgina backed towards the door. 'You think you're so clever and special because you mess around with herbs, but what you do anyone with the ability to read and a little common sense could do as well.'

'That's easy to say, but I've spent years studying the herbs. I know where they grow and when, I know how to dry them and save them for the winter months. You don't know the first thing about it.'

'I'll show you! You're not so clever as you think!' Georgina left the room, banging the door behind her.

Non shook her head. What on earth had she done to make Georgina dislike her so intensely?

She dressed quickly, anxious now that her precious herbal was in Georgina's hands. She might lose it, throw it on the fire or tear it to shreds, for all Non knew. She must get it back at once.

Non walked along the uneven wooden floor of the passage, wondering which room was Georgina's. It would be the best one, of course. She knocked on several doors, but with no response. At last, reluctantly, she returned to her own room and sat on the bed. She ran her fingers absently along the patchwork bedspread; it was freshly washed and smelled of the open air. The Drovers' Inn obviously cared about the comfort of its guests. She looked round the room: the wood of the old wash-stand was cracked in a few places, but it was polished and smelled of beeswax. The floor sloped towards the front of the building, but then the tavern was very old and had faced the ravages of many winters.

Non felt lost without her herbal, and wondered what on earth had made Georgina want to read it. Pique, most probably, because Non knew something that she, with all her education, did not.

When the maid came to her room with her evening meal on a tray, Non asked her which room was taken by Miss Georgina Jones. The maid, unsure of Non's position, gestured vaguely towards the landing.

'The one at the end of the corridor, Miss, the one with the big door.' She put the tray down and bobbed her way out, anxious not to offend and yet clearly wondering what Non's business was, riding with the drove.

Non hardly touched the soup or the cheese and crusty bread. She wanted her herbal back, and she

135

wanted it right away. She put down the tray and took a deep breath; if there was going to be a confrontation with Georgina, it might as well be now.

But Georgina's room was empty. Non stood in the open doorway, taking in the airiness of the room, the good drapes and the plumpness of the bed, before catching sight of the green cover of her herbal. With a quick look round, she slipped into the room and picked up her book. It was complete, no harm had come to it, and Non sighed in relief. It seemed she'd misjudged Georgina.

Back in her room, she put the book in her lap, and at once the pages flipped open to where the corner of one page was turned down. Clucking in annoyance, Non pressed out the crease, then read the words before her.

The root of the gladwin boiled in wine and drank, doth effectually procure women's courses; and used as a pessary worketh the same effect; but causeth abortion in women with child.

A terrible suspicion entered her mind. Georgina had boasted that she could use the herbal as well as Non could. Perhaps she'd heard the gossip that Flora was expecting and was planning to try to find the gladwin roots to give her?

Non carefully put her book into her bag, then hesitated for a moment before going downstairs. She would find Mary and tell her to watch that Flora didn't take any medicine, however desperate she felt. She slipped outside as quietly as she could; she didn't want to draw attention to herself. The

136

moon was sliding out from behind the trees, washing the ground in silver light. Across the yard, the old barn stood like a large shadow, the only illumination coming from the small windows lit by candles. Here, the women would be spending the night.

As soon as she entered the barn, Non heard the sounds of a woman groaning in pain, and with a stab of fear she realized she was too late. Flora was lying on a pallet, her face bathed in perspiration, her eyes wide with fright.

'Oh Gawd, Miss, help me!' She held up her hand when she saw Non. 'I'm dying with the pain, I am.'

'What have you taken, Flora?'

'Only the medicine you sent for me to take.'

'I never sent anything for you, Flora, it was too dangerous, I told you that.'

Mary moved quietly at her side. 'Dennis brought it, said it was from you.'

'Oh, no!' Non took a deep breath. It seemed Miss Jones had already done her worst. 'Mary, bring some candles so I can see what I'm doing.'

Flora was bleeding badly. 'Get blankets,' Non said to anyone who would listen. 'Mary, fetch my box of medicines from the store wagon.'

Non checked around the place where Flora was lying: there was no sign that the baby had been aborted, so it was essential now that the child be taken from the mother, otherwise they would both die.

When Mary brought her box, Non took out her essence of germander. Thankfully, the bottle was full. The medication, taken with honey, was commonly used for the easing of coughs and chills, but germander had other more powerful uses.

137

'Drink this, Flora. Come on now, lift up your head.' She held the bottle to Flora's pale lips. 'That's right, drink it all down.'

Flora gagged at the taste, but swallowed the medicine obediently. Almost at once, her belly began to convulse. 'Oh, dear God, help me!' Flora was pale and trembling with fear. 'What's happening to me?'

'The baby is coming, that's all,' Non said quietly. 'You must push with all your strength, Flora. The sooner the child comes from you the better.'

Flora began to wail. 'You're killing my baby!' She looked up at Non pleadingly. 'I know I've been bad, but I'm frightened to death now.'

'Stop whining!' Mary leaned over Non's shoulder and shook her finger at the girl on the ground. 'This is what you wanted, to slip the baby, that's what you've been telling us all for weeks. Now it's happening, and you just remember it's no one's fault but your own.'

Flora began to moan low in her throat; she was still convulsing, but she was growing weaker. Non kneaded her belly, pressing downwards, all the time willing the child to part from its mother.

Flora gave a huge gasp and then, at last, it was over: the tiny foetus and the afterbirth came slithering from Flora's trembling body.

'Now we need to lift her lower body high to stop the bleeding,' Non said. 'Someone fetch cold water and cloths, quickly!'

The hours dragged on as Non fought to save Flora's life. The candles burnt away and the thin fingers of a rosy dawn slid gently in through the windows. Non took a deep breath before examining Flora, then she sighed in relief.

138

'The bleeding's stopped, you're going to be all right. But you must have rest, you can't continue to walk the roads. Do you understand, Flora?'

'Aye, I do.' She looked sheepish. 'And thank you for helping me, Miss, there's grateful I am.'

Non straightened and rubbed the small of her back, realizing it was aching. This was a bad night's work and it was all Georgina's fault. She walked out into the fresh morning air and took a deep breath.

'You did well in there.' Mary had come to stand beside her. 'If it wasn't for you, Flora would have died.' She frowned. 'But you shouldn't have given her the medicine to slip a child in the first place. I thought you had more sense.'

Non looked at her in surprise. 'I didn't give her anything, Mary, though I know who did.'

'Who?'

'Miss Georgina borrowed my herbal. She told me whatever I could do she could do as well, if not better. She must have made up some sort of silly mixture, not really knowing what she was doing.'

'I believe you, *merchi*, but there's not a lot of folk round here as is trusting like me. You'll be the one to cop it for this night's work, you mark my words.'

Non sighed heavily. She had a sinking feeling that Mary would be proved right.


## CHAPTER THIRTEEN

It was early morning. The sun was barely showing over the horizon, the air was sweet, the grass

139

brushed with dew, but Non was unaware of her surroundings. She was standing in the doorway of the tavern, biting her lip in anticipation of her meeting with Caradoc. He had knocked on her door a few minutes ago and ordered rather than asked her to meet him outside. She didn't need two guesses to know why he wanted to see her. Flora was still weak and in pain, and Caradoc wanted to know exactly what had been going on.

The quiet of the morning was suddenly shattered by the whoops of the men as they guided the cattle onto the road. The animals milled around chaotically; it seemed a miracle to Non that the creatures were ever brought under control. One of the drovers shouted curses at a stubborn heifer and placed his huge boot against the cow's side, forcing the beast into line. Voices rang loudly on the morning air, making the strange sounds that the animals seemed to understand. At last the drove got underway. The noise of so many hooves pounding the earth gave Non a headache. The fact that she had not slept at all didn't help her feel any better.

She took a deep breath then as she saw Caradoc coming towards her. His head was bare and his features set in stern lines that boded ill. He stopped in front of her and his gaze met hers challengingly.

'Flora's been given a room in the Drovers' Inn. She's obviously not fit to travel, so I've decided that you will have to stay here with her. Georgina too.' He spoke in a hard voice. 'I'm delaying my own start until later. I intend to get this matter sorted out if it takes all day.'

Georgina came to the door of the tavern and stared up at her brother in surprise. 'I heard what

140

you said, Caradoc, and I refuse to stay behind! I haven't anything to do with the terrible business of Flora's illness.'

Non spun round to face Georgina. 'That's not true!' she said. 'Now I know why you borrowed my herbal book. You played with fire, meddling in things you know nothing about.'

'What on earth can she mean?' Georgina looked at her brother. 'I don't see how I can be blamed for anything.'

Non ignored her protests. 'Don't you realize the danger you put Flora in by your foolhardiness?'

Georgina glared at her. 'You're being silly,' she said. 'I haven't even read your precious herbal, you never let it out of your sight. I won't be blamed for your mistakes, Non Jenkins.'

'Georgina, shut up!' Caradoc said. 'I know you borrowed the herbal book, but I can't believe you'd use any recipes from it.'

'I didn't!' Georgina said angrily. 'I didn't give Flora anything. Who was with her when she lost the child? Her!' She pointed an accusing finger at Non. 'You are the one to blame for all this trouble.'

Caradoc sighed heavily. 'You're not getting out of this by telling lies. Admit it, Georgina, you did it because you wanted to prove you were as clever as Non. Well, you failed miserably.'

'That's just gossip!' Georgina said. 'I haven't even read this herbal book, so why is everyone blaming me?'

Caradoc gestured impatiently. 'Get inside, the both of you. Go on, let's see Flora and ask her what happened, shall we?'

'I don't think Flora should be troubled by any of this,' Non said quietly. 'She's still very weak and she's going to need a lot of care if she's to make a good recovery.'

'There, see?' Georgina said. 'I'm quite happy to talk to Flora, while *she* is trying to avoid a confrontation.'

'It wouldn't be a confrontation,' Caradoc said firmly. 'I just want to speak to Flora, hear her side of the story. Now come along, both of you, let's go upstairs and sort this mess out.'

Flora was sitting on the side of the bed, fully dressed, her boots hung around her neck. 'I'm all right,' she said. 'I'm fit to travel, really I am.'

Non shook her head. 'No, you're not, Flora.'

Flora's skin had taken on a greyish tinge and her hands were trembling. 'I got to work, mind.' She risked a glance up at Caradoc. 'If Mr Jones will let me.' She rubbed her hands together. 'Please don't send me home, Mr Jones. I'll be disgraced, no one will want to bother with me.'

'Well, you can't walk the roads in your state,' Caradoc said. 'You'll just have to stay here at the inn until we come back from London.'

'Oh no, Mr Jones, I want to come to London with you and . . .' she paused, 'and with the rest of the drove.' She looked down at her hands, beaten and ashamed. 'In any case, I haven't got any money.'

'There's no need to worry about any of that.' Caradoc shook his head. 'But you're certainly not well enough to travel. Anyone can see that.'

'I am—I can walk as good as the next girl.' She wiped her eyes, but the tears kept trickling down her face. 'I don't want to be separated from . . . well, the rest of the drove.'

'Now,' he ignored her protests, 'tell me exactly

what's been happening to you.'

She looked from Non to Georgina, and there was a fleeting expression of uncertainty before she spoke. 'I asked Non for something to take, some herbs to make me slip the baby.' The last words were spoken in a whisper.

'And what did I tell you, Flora?' Non said. 'I said that it was too risky. Tell Mr Jones what really happened.'

'I'm sorry, Miss, so very sorry.' She looked down at her hands again. 'Miss Jenkins gave me the drink, I took it and the baby went away, that's all.'

'Flora!' Non looked at the girl in disbelief. 'I only helped you when you were losing the baby, and I had to do that to save your life.'

Flora looked up at Georgina and shook her head. 'I can't say anything else, Miss. You gave me the stuff and I took it, that's all.'

Non bit her lip. She could see what had happened: Georgina had put pressure on Flora to lie and now the girl was too frightened to tell the truth.

'There, I told you!' Georgina said. 'You always want to think the worst of me, don't you, Caradoc?'

He shook his head. 'Hush Georgina, I'm not convinced that you are blameless, so just keep quiet. Now, I've made a decision. You women will stay here for a few weeks, and when the cattle have been delivered to London and I'm on the road with a new drove, I'll pick you up.' He smiled. 'So you'll still get to see London, Flora.'

'Well, I'm not staying behind like one of the common women,' Georgina said hotly. 'I'd be bored out of my mind.'

Flora seemed to gather her wits about her. She

looked directly at Georgina and spoke with more confidence than she'd shown before. 'If the truth be told, Miss . . .' Her voice trailed away as Georgina turned towards her.

'You're not too sick to travel, are you, girl?' Georgina spoke quickly. 'Surely you could ride one of the horses. That wouldn't do any harm, would it?'

'You go with the drove, Miss. Non will look after me—I trust her,' Flora said quietly.

Caradoc looked stern. 'You trust her when you've said with your own lips that she gave you bad medicine?'

Flora's colour rose. 'Well, it wasn't so bad. I mean she didn't . . .' Her words trailed into silence and Caradoc shook his head as he moved to the door. 'You women! Who am I to believe?' He put his hand on Flora's shoulder. 'You need a rest, Flora. I'm not even going to ask you who the father of your child was, but you'll have to rest here for a while, anyone can see you're not well enough to travel.'

He stepped out into the sloping passageway and paused. 'As for you, Georgina, you'll remain here too. Non is supposed to be your chaperone, so you'll stay together until I pick you up. In the meantime, I'll be leaving Dennis here with you—he'll look after you.'

'But what about Aunt Prudence?' Georgina said desperately. 'She'll be expecting me.'

'Well, Georgina, she'll just have to put up with it.'

He left the room and Non listened to the sound of his footsteps as he went down the rickety stairs. Then she turned to Flora. 'She made you say all

144

that,' she said, nodding at Georgina. 'She made you lie about who gave you the herbs, didn't she?'

'Look, Miss, I'm only a poor weeder, I can't afford to be sent home. I've got three brothers, all small, and Mam needs the wages I earn, see?'

'And Georgina threatened that you would be sent home if you told the truth—is that it?'

'Do you mind not talking about me as if I didn't exist?' Georgina said. No one took any notice of her.

'Well, Flora?'

The girl hung her head. It was obvious she had no intention of answering.

'I'm going outside to talk some sense into my brother,' Georgina said abruptly. 'I can't bear to be in the same room with you common women a moment longer.' She flounced out of the room and slammed the door behind her.

'I was scared to tell the truth, Miss,' Flora said quickly. 'And I'm that sorry I 'ad to let you down.'

Non sighed. 'Well, it's no matter now. We have to stay here for a while, so you and I might as well settle to it. You must rest as much as possible, do you hear me?'

Non went to the window and a half smile curved her lips as she saw Georgina Jones standing in the empty courtyard alone. Clearly she'd been too late to plead her case with Caradoc: he'd already left.

\*       \*       \*

As the days passed, Flora regained her health; her colour improved, the light came back into her eyes and soon she was her usual cheerful self. Georgina avoided Flora as much as she could, but took

145

pleasure in needling Non, making jokes about the herbal remedies, and when Non failed to rise to the bait, began to call her a witch. After that, Non avoided her whenever possible.

But early one morning, when Non had been out gathering herbs, she came upon Georgina, who was seated at the door of the Drovers' Inn with an expression of complete boredom on her face. Her eyes lit up when she saw Non.

'I see you've been rooting round in the ground for leaves and things again, it's really absurd.'

Non didn't answer. She lifted her basket higher on her arm and made to pass Georgina.

'I'm going to plant a rowan tree as soon as I get home; it's said they keep away witches, did you know?'

'Well then the tree will probably die through lack of love and care,' Non responded. 'Plants know good people from bad.'

'How foolish! And you an educated woman! Everyone knows plants don't have feelings.'

'Then why does the mandrake scream when it's pulled from the ground?'

'That's just rubbish.'

'Is it, then? You've never tried it, Miss Jones.'

Georgina got to her feet. 'You think you're so clever, don't you? You are just stupid, you think my brother cares anything for you? I've seen the way you look at him, but be warned—he'd have his way with you and then leave you flat. You don't know Caradoc as I do.'

Non suppressed the angry retort that rose to her lips. What was the use of arguing with Georgina when she was probably right?

It seemed the time would never pass. Even Non was weary of the same routine: eating breakfast at the large table in the tap room, then foraging for plants in the morning, and worst of all putting up with Georgina's sarcasm for the rest of the day.

But at last, the waiting was over. Non was on the grassy bank at the side of the inn one day when she saw Dennis hurrying towards her. 'Where's Miss Jones?' he panted, then crumpled his cap in his hand as Georgina appeared in the doorway.

'Miss Jones, one of the drovers has come from your brother. He's asking can we take to the road and meet up with the drove?'

'Thank heavens for that!' Georgina said. 'I'll get ready at once. You can pack my clothes for me, Non.'

'I'm your chaperone, not your servant, Miss Jones,' Non said. 'But if it will help us leave here I'll pack willingly.'

It took more than an hour to get ready, because Georgina kept changing her mind about which gown she was going to wear. But at last Non came out of the tavern carrying the bags. The carriage was ready and Dennis was waiting expectantly.

'Shall I help you, Non?'

'Thank you, Dennis, I'll come up into the driving seat with you. Flora had better go inside with Miss Georgina.'

He moved aside to accommodate her, the reins held loosely in his hands.

'I don't want Flora to come inside with me, thank you!' Georgina spoke sharply. 'She can sit up with you two.'

'But there's no room,' Non protested.

'Well, I won't move until you sort something out. I'm not riding with a smelly drover woman.'

Georgina turned away and disappeared into the gloom of the inn. Non shook her head and looked at Dennis. He shrugged his shoulders. 'I suppose we could squeeze Flora in by us.'

Non was about to reply when she heard the clip-clop of horse's hooves on the cobbled path outside the tavern. She looked up and her heart missed a beat as she saw Caradoc approaching the inn. He was staring down at her from the saddle, frowning in irritation. 'What on earth is the delay?' he asked. 'I expected you half an hour ago.'

She couldn't help noticing that his breeches were taut against his legs, outlining the muscles of his thighs. His hair fell across his brow and her heart lurched crazily.

'It's Georgina,' Non said flatly. 'She's not willing to share the coach with Flora, and there's no room for all of us in the driving seat.'

'For heaven's sake!' Caradoc said.

Georgina came out of the inn and pouted at her brother. 'Please, Caradoc, I can't bear to sit with Flora, surely she can walk?'

Caradoc sighed. 'I wish I'd never brought you on the roads, I knew it would give me problems. Look, Flora can sit with Dennis; you, Non, get up behind me, just until we catch up with the herd.' His voice was clipped and distant and he didn't meet her eyes.

She held onto his hand and he swung her into the saddle. Her heart was beating fast as she wrapped her arms around him. Carefully, she rested her cheek against his broad back, feeling his muscles move beneath her face as he shortened the reins of the horse. She closed her eyes, wishing that everything was different: that Caradoc had been born more humbly, as a man who would have found her suitable as a wife.

He rode swiftly, and before very long the dust from the herd showed they were drawing near the drove. Non closed her eyes, holding Caradoc tightly, savouring the moments when she could pretend he was hers.

When they reached the rear of the huge herd Non slipped down from the saddle, and realized how foolish her fancies about him had been because he simply left her standing on the roadway. She stood there, watching him, until she heard the rattle of wagon wheels behind her. She sighed heavily, the dream over, and turned to wait for Dennis to bring the carriage to a halt, then help Flora down from the driving seat.

Mary came towards the little group, smiling a welcome. 'How are you, Flora?' She hugged Flora and then held her at arm's length. 'She's looking ten times better, isn't she, Non?'

'She's recovered well, Mary,' Non said.

'Thanks to you, Non,' Flora chipped in quickly.

'She's done a good job of looking after you, but then you've had plenty of time to get better—we've been home to Carmarthen and halfway back to London while you been resting up.'

'Where are all the other women, Mary? Are they still gossiping about me?'

'All that's old news now. They've all got a job weeding on Dawson's Farm. Very proud of his gardens is Squire Dawson. We usually stop off there at least once every year. He pays well and gives the girls food.' She smiled. 'He's a randy old sod, mind, good thing he's getting too old to do any damage. Come on, we'd better get moving, or we'll be left behind.'

The women walked along in silence, the cattle moved slowly up ahead, the men called out to a recalcitrant bull from time to time, and Non realized that nothing had changed. Georgina still disliked her, and as for Caradoc, since the business with Flora he had had no time for her. Non fixed her eyes on the looming Welsh hills without really seeing them. Georgina was never going to be her friend, but now it was clear just how dangerous an enemy she really was.


## CHAPTER FOURTEEN

Morgan Lewis woke at first light and, immediately alert, got out of bed and poured water from the large china jug into a tin bowl. He had spent the night under the roof of the farmer Dai Morris. His room was comfortable; the bed was covered with a brightly worked quilt and on the deep window ledge stood a bowl of flowers. Morgan smiled. Dai Morris's wife made it plain she had a soft spot for him.

He went downstairs, drawn to the kitchen by the appetizing smell of frying bacon. He had breakfasted with the Morrises on many occasions and he knew that he would be well fed before he started his day's work.

'Come on in, Morgan, boy.' Sally Morris smoothed down her apron. 'I've got a lovely breakfast for you. There's a big job on for you today, isn't there?'

Morgan nodded. Today he had the task of shoeing some beasts that were to join Caradoc Jones's drove on its way to London. It was the second drove of the season, and this time Morgan hoped he would see Non Jenkins. On the first trip there had been delays and some kind of trouble. Flora, Non's former maid, had been sick, so it was natural that Non should stay behind to look after her. The thought of seeing Non warmed his heart. Surely by now she would be missing him too?

Morgan became aware that Sally was waiting for him to speak.

'Don't worry, I've been told about Big Awkward. I know the bull is a fiery creature and needs a firm hand if he's to be shod.'

'Aye, and the devil lives up to his name,' Sally grimaced, 'so you just go careful, mind, we don't want no accidents.'

'I'll be careful, don't you worry, Sally. I've been doing this job long enough to know how to handle any animal.'

'I hope you're right. That beast has been nothing but a right nuisance ever since it was born. I'll be glad to get rid of him. He gives me the evil eye every time I go near him. Anyway, don't let your breakfast go cold. A man is only as good as the food he puts in his belly, mind.'

A little while later, Morgan left the farmhouse and made his way to the top field. Dai Morris was already there, and with him was Caradoc Jones.

'Morning, Mr Jones, Dai.' Morgan nodded to both men. 'Better get right to it, then.'

As he approached the bull, Morgan took a deep

151

breath. Bringing a bull down was always a tricky procedure, and Big Awkward was notorious for resisting the strength of the fittest man.

He caught the bull's horns and twisted, but the beast was as stubborn as its name suggested. He twisted the horns again, and still the bull didn't move. Morgan brushed the hair back from his forehead. Felling the huge bull was proving even more difficult than he'd anticipated. Most bulls were hefty and put up a struggle, but this one, as Sally had told him, had a wicked look in its eye that boded ill for anyone who came within striking distance of those lethal horns.

'You got a job and a half there, Morgan.' Caradoc Jones leaned his elbows on the gatepost and watched Morgan from the safety of the other side of the fence.

'Aye, Mr Jones, this beast is a big 'un and needs careful handling, so be quiet now and let me get on with my work.' Morgan had respect for Caradoc, but this was a job that needed all his attention.

He seized the muzzle of the beast with his left hand and gripped the right horn with his other hand. With his heel firmly against the bull's right forefoot, he twisted the muzzle upwards. Taken off guard, the beast fell with a resounding thump to the ground, raising the dust.

Dai Morris ran into the field and bound the animal's hind feet together. 'Took you all your strength, did Big Awkward, but you bested him in the end. I never thought I'd see the day.' Dai attached the rope to an iron stake in the ground. The bull bellowed, its nose flapping like barn doors, but it was helpless.

Now that he had the creature trapped, Morgan

could put the *ciws*—the two pieces of metal that made up the shoes—on the cleft hooves of the bull. These would protect the animal's feet from the hardness of the road that led to Smithfield market in London. It was a job Morgan had done many times before, but today he was finding the task onerous. He was restless, and he knew full well why he felt that way: he was impatient to meet up with Non again.

He'd missed her badly. The days had seemed long without her, and if heaven was kind she would have felt the same. Morgan knew they were meant to be together, and he couldn't wait to ask her again to be his wife. He believed she liked him and trusted him; surely that was enough to make a good marriage?

Once the animal was shod, Morgan left the field and took a refreshing glass of lemon cordial from Sally Morris.

'You're one strong man, Morgan, boy,' she said admiringly, 'and handsome too, and you not yet married. Some girl is going to be very lucky to have you for a husband.'

'I'm not planning to get married just yet,' Morgan said evasively. 'I'm waiting for the right young lady to come along.'

'Then you'll wait for a very long time, boy. You have to go out looking and not expect a pretty young lady to be given to you as a gift.' She looked at him shrewdly. ' 'Tisn't true, then, what I've heard?'

'What have you heard?' Morgan said.

'Well, a little birdie told me that you have someone in mind.'

'Oh yes?' Morgan's tone was guarded. 'Well,

that's news to me.'

'Come on now, it's Sally Morris you're talking to, not some green girl with her hair in braids. You're after the hand of the vicar's daughter, aren't you? And I must say I approve. I've heard of Non Jenkins, she's a very clever girl and a good catch for anyone.'

Morgan smiled ruefully. 'Nothing is private in the world of the drover, is it?'

'You're right there. We've had some of the girls from the first drove weeding for us, and one of them told me you were after Non Jenkins long before you set out on the road.'

Morgan shook his head. 'Well, we'll have to see what happens, won't we? Even if I asked her to be my wife she might very well turn me down.'

Sally winked at him. 'She'd need her head read if she turned down a fine upstanding man like you. I saw you throwing that bull to the ground. Champion, it was. Big Awkward usually needs two strong men to fell him.'

Morgan rubbed his arms. Felling the bull hadn't been an easy task, and if he hadn't learned the trick of it from Taff Williams, a cattle man from North Wales, he couldn't have done it on his own. 'Right then, I'd better get on with it, pack up my belongings.'

'Going with Mr Jones, are you?'

'Aye, meeting up with the drove. They're resting in Vaughan's Tavern. I'll travel with them part of the way to London. When the cattle are delivered safely to the fattening fields I'll go back home to Wales.'

'And you might be taking a bride with you?'

'You never know,' Morgan said guardedly. 'You

'never know.'

*     *     *

Non sank down onto a grassy bank and rubbed her ankles. Her boots pinched and she loosened the laces, unhooking them from the eyelets.

'Feet killing you, are they?' Mary sat beside her and looked down at her own bare feet. 'God 'elp you if you went barefoot, then.'

'What's been happening on the drove, then?' Non asked. 'Any more excitement?'

'Not a lot, girl.' Mary bent her head. 'While you were stuck back at the inn with Miss Georgina, I took the chance to tell Mr Jones what I knew about what happened with Flora, and he just listened without saying a word.' She glanced towards Non. 'I think he knows it was all Miss Georgina's fault, but he's too loyal to his sister to admit it.' She brightened. 'Anyway, Flora is well on the mend now, isn't she, thanks to your good nursing.'

Non sighed. 'The worst part about staying behind was the way Georgina treated us. She's a very devious woman.'

'Too right! And she's got a tongue like a viper.' Mary looked at Non, her eyes shrewd. 'I know you wouldn't make mistakes with your medicines, that's what I feel in here.' She put her hand on her heart. 'As I said, I did speak up for you to Mr Jones, told him you weren't the one to blame.'

'That's good of you, Mary.' The women sat in silence for a time, watching the herd grazing in the field down below them. The cattle jostled each other, eager for the verdant grass.

Non suddenly felt she was in alien territory. The

stamp of hooves, the throwing up of dust from the road, the rigours of walking the Welsh hills—it all seemed unreal. What had happened to her comfortable lifestyle? At home in the vicarage, she'd been able to sit and read, to do a bit of sewing if the mood took her. She'd had hot water to bathe and clean pressed clothes to wear. Now all she had was the open fields and the rough terrain to contend with.

Mary pushed herself to her feet. 'Come on, then, let's start walking.' She took her knitting out of the large front pocket of her apron. 'I'll be glad when this drove is over, mind. I've had enough of the road, I'll not travel with the herd again.'

'What you need is a good husband, Mary,' Non said. 'You're a beautiful woman and so practical, you should find a man easily enough once you settle in one place.'

'I don' know. There's no one back in Carmarthen or Swansea that I'd want to marry. Perhaps I'm meant to be a spinster till the day I die.'

'Perhaps you'll meet some likely looking man in London, Mary.'

'Never did before! All the London men are snapped up as soon as they start shaving. At least, that's how it seems to me.' Mary held up the stocking she was knitting. 'Damn! I've dropped a stitch. That's gabbing too much, that is.' She glanced over her shoulder. 'Anyway, here comes Flora—better drop the subject of men, is it?'

Flora had a warm colour to her face. She looked well, but Non could see how deeply unhappy she was.

'What's the matter, Flora?' she asked quietly.

156

'You know you can talk to me in confidence.'

Flora looked uncertain for a moment, and then the words burst from her lips. 'It's Thomas. He's turned his back on me. He doesn't even look at me, let alone talk to me.'

'Why don't you try to put him out of your mind, Flora? He's married to a girl back in Five Saints, you're wasting your time on him.'

'Quite right,' Mary said. 'But you want to look at your own position, Non. Morgan's joining the drove today. He's a fine handsome man, he'd make a great husband for you.'

'Maybe.' Non spoke cagily; she knew how Mary would react if she told her the truth—that she had fallen hopelessly in love with Caradoc Jones.

'No "maybe" about it, that man is a good catch. He's well to do, an upstanding man with a good position in life. You'd not go short of anything if you married him.'

'For goodness' sake, Mary!' Non shook her head in exasperation. 'Stop talking about marriage! I don't think of Morgan in that way.'

Mary was silent for a moment, busy at her knitting, turning a heel in the stocking she was making. Non tried to read her expression and came to the conclusion that Mary was angry.

'Come on, out with it, tell me what's on your mind,' Non said.

'All right, I will. I know what keeps you from marrying Morgan—a foolish fancy for the boss, and let me tell you now, you've got no hope in that direction.'

'I don't know what you mean,' Non said slowly.

Mary's hands were suddenly still. 'You know exactly what I mean. You can't hide nothing from

157

Mary. I'm older and wiser than you, remember.'

'I'll remember, Mary. And don't worry about me, I'm a grown woman, I can make up my own mind who I'll marry and who I won't.'

The women fell silent. The atmosphere was strained, and Non was glad when a halt was called and the men began herding the cattle into a grassy field.

Mary sank onto the ground, sighing with relief. 'I don't know why I came on this blessed journey,' she grumbled. 'I should have stayed home when I had the chance. I should have had more sense at my age.' She shrugged her shoulders. 'But then, I got to have money to live. What I'm going to do when I give up travelling I just don't know.'

Non was glad Mary was speaking to her again. She sat down beside her and unlaced her boots. 'There's a stream over by the fence, see it, Mary? I think I'll go and wash my feet. What about you, Flora, are you coming?'

Flora shook her head. 'Me I'll just rest a bit, you go ahead.'

The stream was crystal clear, sending up a fine spray of water where it ran over the rocks just where Non settled herself on the bank. The water was icy cold and she gasped as it lapped over her feet.

'*Duw*, it's enough to freeze the skin off my bones.' Mary gingerly dipped her toes in the water. 'Oh, perhaps it's not so bad. I'm going to put my legs as far in the water as I can. There, that's lovely.' She hitched her skirt above her knees and leaned back, closing her eyes, her face turned up to the sun. 'It's lovely once you get used to it, isn't it, girl?'

Non followed Mary's example, hitching up her skirt and tipping her head back so that the sun shone on her face.

'Well now, two water nymphs. There's a fine sight to behold.'

Non hurriedly pulled down her skirt. Caradoc was standing behind her, a smile on his face. 'It looks so good I'm almost tempted to join you.'

She scrambled to her feet, her face scarlet with embarrassment as she saw Caradoc was not alone. Morgan was standing with him, a frown of disapproval on his face.

'I'm sorry, we didn't know anyone was there, did we, Mary?'

Mary shook her head and, unperturbed, continued to sit with her feet in the water. 'Don't fret yourself, Non,' she said. 'These two have seen more than one pair of legs, I'll warrant. S'cuse me, Sir,' she nodded to Caradoc, 'if I've offended anyone. I'm sorry, but you know me of old—I go my own way and do the work I'm expected to do, and after that I keep my own council.'

'Don't worry, ladies,' Caradoc said. 'I don't blame you for taking advantage of the lovely weather. In any case, we've done enough walking for today, the beasts must rest otherwise they won't be fit to walk again tomorrow.' He pointed to the hollow in the hills. 'You can't see it from here, but the tavern is just over the rise. There's a room booked for you as always, Non, and Mary, there's a fine dry barn where the rest of you can sleep.'

When Caradoc walked away, Morgan went with him. His shoulders were stiff and Non had the feeling he was angry with her.

Mary put her arm around Non and hugged her,

159

giggling like a girl. 'See Morgan's face, did you? You'd think he was married to you already, he had such a frown and all because another man saw your knees.' She paused. 'Mind, Mr Jones did have a good look while he was at it. Goodness knows how long the men had been standing there.' She aimed a mock punch at Non's arm. 'It doesn't do any harm to give the boys a treat now and again, let 'em see just what's on offer.'

'Nothing's on offer!' Non said. 'I'm just so embarrassed by the whole episode, I don't know how you can laugh it away like that.'

'Oh, dear, you are an old sober sides,' Mary sighed. 'But there, you're just a young thing with no knowledge of men. Once you're married, you'll see things differently.'

Non shook her head. 'Perhaps I'll never get married. If I can't have the one man I want then I won't have anyone.'

Mary looked at her sceptically. 'I believe you, many wouldn't. But come on now, let's get over to the tavern. I could murder a tankard of beer.'

Non walked barefoot beside Mary. She felt the soft grass cool against her feet, and suddenly she had tears in her eyes. Why was she such a hopeless fool, falling in love with the boss? Perhaps she should settle for a good man like Morgan, who loved her and would care for her always.

It was as if Mary had read her thoughts. 'You should grab Morgan by both hands while you have the chance. If you turn him down now there'll be plenty willing and happy to have him. Think, girl, you don't want to end up walking the roads till you're knocking thirty like me. Morgan might be your only chance of happiness, don't throw it away

160

because of a fancy that can never come true.'

Non walked on in silence. Her mind was in turmoil and her head had begun to ache. Well, she'd have to sort herself out, because if her instincts were right, Morgan meant to offer her marriage as soon as he had the opportunity.

## CHAPTER FIFTEEN

Non walked around the narrow streets of the small hillside town wondering what to do with her time. The other women, Mary included, had gone to do some weeding at one of the local farms; Caradoc and Georgina were having tea at one of the taverns and of Morgan there was no sign.

While Non realized she had no call on Morgan's time, she was piqued that he'd refused her invitation to accompany her around town. He'd been brusque to the point of rudeness, telling her he had something important to do. Somehow she felt he was punishing her for showing her legs to anyone who happened to pass by.

She paused to look into the window of a tiny shop that boasted a sign saying 'Milliner to the Gentry'. Non smiled, doubting if Georgina Jones would spend any time shopping here. She would pour scorn on the local fashions, preferring to wait until she reached the fine shops in London.

Walking aimlessly around the streets, Non suddenly felt lonely. She'd become used to having company for most of the day; the only time she spent alone was at night when she was in her bedroom, and then she was so tired she just wanted to sleep. At last, tired and bored, she returned to the tavern where she was to stay for the night. She might as well spend an hour or two browsing through her herbal, perhaps making up a few remedies to use on the next step of the cattle drove.

Vaughan's Tavern was furnished with solid but plain furniture. Simple tables and stools took up most of the bar room, the dark wooden floors were covered in sand for the sake of cleanliness, and in the huge hearth a good fire burned, the logs crackling mightily, shooting sparks into the room. It was chilly at this early hour and there were hardly any customers to be seen.

'Afternoon, Miss.' The landlord smiled, his plump face almost hidden by his tangled beard. 'Your room is ready, you're next to Miss Jones. I think you'll find it clean and tidy, this is a fine establishment, the best for miles around.'

Non smiled her thanks and paused at the foot of the stairs. The landlord saw her questioning look and waved his hand in the direction of the landing.

'You're on the right, just past the first door. Be careful, there's a board loose up by there, can't get a good carpenter in to fix it, see?'

Non smiled to herself. So much for the landlord's boasts about his 'fine establishment'. In her room, she sank onto the bed and fell back against the pillows. The flannel covers scraped against her skin and she winced; her cheeks were already burning with constant exposure to sun and wind. If she continued to walk the drovers' roads she would become weather-beaten and wrinkled and old before her time.

She didn't pick up her herbal straight away.

Instead she relaxed her tired legs, stretching out on her bed, and thought about London. She'd heard about the high life and rich pickings that, according to the other women, were to be had there. Perhaps she would stay behind in London, set up a business. It was a fine idea, but then she would have to say goodbye to Mary and Flora. Her heart skipped a beat. The one person in all the world she would hate to be parted from was Caradoc; she might as well admit it, if only to herself.

There was a sudden light rapping on her door and she sat up, her heart beating uncomfortably fast. Perhaps she'd drawn Caradoc to her with the force of her thoughts. But it was Morgan standing outside on the landing, giving her a smile that would charm women all the way from Llandovery to London.

Non tried to conceal her disappointment. 'Morgan, it's you.' She stepped back to allow him into her room.

'I've been given instructions to leave the door open,' he said. 'The landlord seems to think your reputation might be damaged if we are alone in a closed room together.'

'He's quite right.' Non sat in a small rickety chair that stood in the well of the window and indicated that Morgan take the seat opposite her.

'I want to apologize for the way I behaved earlier, but more importantly . . .' He came to her and knelt at her feet, pulling a soft calfskin pouch out of his waistcoat pocket. 'I think the time is right to ask for your hand in a proper manner. Non, will you agree to be my wife?'

She stiffened as he took a small gold ring out of the pouch and held it towards her. She noticed a pretty little ruby gleaming against the gold, and her heart softened towards him as she realized what his important task of the morning had been.

'I'm greatly honoured, Morgan,' she said gently. 'I think you are the most handsome of men and I know you to be honest and strong and willing to work hard to support a wife, but . . .'

'But,' he said, 'you do not want me for a husband?'

'I don't want anyone for a husband, not now— perhaps not for a very long time. I value your friendship greatly, but I can't pretend that I'll change my mind. I don't even know what I want to do with my life yet.'

The loose board outside her room creaked and Non looked up to see Caradoc and his sister looking into the room. Georgina was smiling in amusement at the scene before her, but Caradoc glowered darkly before walking on.

Non felt the rich colour flood into her face, but Morgan rose to his feet, completely at ease with the situation. 'I don't mind the whole world knowing about my feelings for you,' he said. 'I love you, Non, and I think I've always loved you, from when we were children together. I'll go now, if that's what you want, but I'll wait until you're ready, Non, because I know that one day you will marry me.'

He left her then, closing the door quietly behind him. Non put her hands to her hot cheeks, embarrassed that Caradoc had witnessed Morgan's proposal. She hardly gave a thought to Morgan's words; she was not ready to marry anyone.

Impatiently, she got to her feet. She would see if Mary was back from the weeding. The day had clouded over and the women wouldn't work in the

164

rain. Non hurried down the stairs and walked out into the soft drizzle that was falling. She sighed heavily; life was so strange. Morgan wanted her for his wife, and the only man she had room for in her heart was a man who would never marry her.

*    *    *

'Did you see that?' Georgina said. 'The blacksmith on his knees before that witch Manon Jenkins? I thought I'd die laughing. It was just like a scene from a play, and a bad play at that.'

'You're such a snob, Georgina.' Caradoc looked pointedly at his sister. 'And you are in my room. Why don't you go to your own room and give me a little peace?'

'You're such a grouch, Caradoc. I don't know why—after that pleasant walk this morning I thought you'd be in a better mood.'

'I'll be in a better mood when we arrive at Smithfield and I get paid for the cattle.' He looked at his sister sternly. 'And don't you ever ask to come on the drove with me again, because you've been nothing but trouble from the start.'

Georgina shook back her curls and removed her bonnet. 'I haven't been troublesome at all! I've put up with travelling in that awful makeshift carriage without a grumble, even you have to admit that. Remember, I'm not used to rough terrain and the constant stink of beasts. I think I've been very good in the circumstances.'

Caradoc took her arm and led her to the door. 'Out,' he said, 'I want to rest. Tomorrow we'll be travelling for a good many hours, we're behind schedule.'

'You can't be tired, Caradoc,' Georgina said. 'You're a young strong man, you should be enjoying life.'

'I've been to Carmarthen and back while you languished at the Drovers' Inn, remember?'

He pushed her gently from the room and shut the door, then stood at the window, staring out blindly at the grey landscape and the mist-clad mountains. In his mind's eye he could see Non with that fool Morgan Lewis kneeling at her feet, asking for her hand. The thought made him so angry that he felt like punching the blacksmith's handsome face. Morgan wasn't good enough to marry the likes of Manon Jenkins. She'd been gently raised and educated and she was an accomplished healer. Above all, she was a very beautiful woman.

He felt the fierce desire of a man wanting a woman. But Manon wasn't an ordinary woman. She was not to be dallied with. She was respectable, she needed a good husband, a man who could provide a decent home for her along with a comfortable standard of living. He could never have her, he realized that. She was so far below him in society, she would never be his equal, never be accepted into the rich drawing rooms of his father's friends. Did that matter? His common sense told him it did, but his heart told a different story.

He sat on the edge of the bed and stared out at the Black Mountains, misted now with a curtain of drizzle concealing the rugged peaks. Tomorrow he would be on the road again and he'd have other matters to concern himself with. But before that he would be spending the night alone, forced into celibacy, and that way of life did not suit him at all.

The next morning, the rain had ceased and a pale sun warmed the land. The drove got underway early, and for once the cattle were obedient and ambled along the roadway willingly.

It was a good day and yet Non's mind was full of chaotic thoughts. Why couldn't it have been Caradoc offering her a ring and not Morgan? She took a deep breath and looked up at the impressive peaks of the mountains, and realized how petty were her worries.

'We won't be long getting to Hereford at this rate.' Mary had come up behind Non, her bare feet making no sound in the soft grass.

'Goodness! You made me jump out of my skin,' Non said. 'How are you feeling today?'

'Very fine,' Mary said. 'But I've got some news for you.'

'What news?'

'Flora's decided to leave the drove. She and Thomas have made up their quarrel and are going back home to Five Saints together.'

Non looked at Mary in surprise. 'So Thomas is leaving his wife for Flora?'

'Aye, turn up for the book, isn't it? The man says he's in love with her, missed her when you stayed at the Drovers' Inn. He's talking about leaving his wife to set up home with Flora.'

Mary paused while she concentrated on a tricky piece of knitting. Non glanced at her, wondering what Mary really thought about Flora's affair. She was usually outspoken enough, but she'd said very little about Flora's troubles.

'Do you think he'll stay with Flora once they get back home?' She had to prompt Mary, who loved to impart a piece of gossip so long as it didn't concern herself.

'You never knows what folks will do. Take our lovely Morgan, now. He bought you a ring, did you the honour of wanting you for a wife, and you turned him down.' She shook her head. 'No accounting for folk's feelings, see?'

Non turned sharply. 'How do you know that Morgan offered me marriage?'

Mary winked. 'There's not much gets past Mary, mind. I've read the signs ever since you rejoined the drove. He worships the ground you walk on.'

Non shook her head. 'Well, Mary, just for you to know, I don't want to get married now, perhaps not ever.'

Mary frowned. 'Don't pin your hopes on Caradoc Jones, he's not going to buy you a gold ring.' She laughed when she saw Non's bewildered expression. 'It's all right, I'm not a witch, I'll leave all that to you. It was like this, see, I saw Morgan in town and he was going into a jewellery shop. I stood outside the window and watched him. I knew all along what he was up to.'

Non digested this bit of information and then began to laugh. 'Oh Mary, you're so funny!'

They walked along in silence for a moment and Non found herself thinking about Morgan on his knees before her and Caradoc witnessing the scene. He'd looked so angry, almost as though he was jealous. But that was silly. Caradoc probably disapproved of her having a man in her room, whatever the circumstances.

Later, when the men called a halt to the drove,

168

most of the women sat on the grassy verge, glad of the rest. Mary was rubbing the dirt from her feet.

'Not sore again, are they?' Non asked.

'I've been using that ointment you give me and my little feet are just fine. Come and sit by here, girl, and talk to me for a bit.'

Non shook her head. 'Sorry, Mary, I'm going to find some plants. I'm running out of supplies. I'll need to make up some more bottles of medicine when we stop for the night.'

'We won't get to the next inn until it's dark. Come on, Non, you need a break like the rest of us.'

Non gave in and sat down, pulling her skirts over her ankles. The weather was warm and she would have given anything for a cooling stream of water, but there weren't any streams, no sound of water over stones, only the folding hills and the high roads leading away from Brecon towards Hereford.

A shadow fell over her and she looked up quickly.

'I'd like a word, Miss Jenkins, if you please.' Caradoc's tone was formal.

'Is anything wrong, Mr Jones?' she asked as she scrambled to her feet.

He walked away from where the women were resting, and after a moment's hesitation, Non followed him. He walked into a canopy of trees and the greenness closed around them like encompassing arms.

'What is it?' she asked.

'I'm disappointed in your behaviour,' he said in a stern voice. 'I saw the blacksmith in your bedroom and it's just not proper. I didn't go to the expense of giving you shelter for the nights so that you could have trysts with a man.'

Non was taken aback by the tone of his voice and then, suddenly, she was angry. 'That's not fair!' she said, lifting her chin and straightening her shoulders. 'Nothing improper was taking place, as you could see when you stood in my doorway.'

'And what was the blacksmith proposing to you—an honourable marriage, or something more illicit as usually happens on the trail?'

Non's eyes were steely, and her voice was quiet. 'How dare you? How dare you say such things?'

'I just would like to know where I stand in this matter,' Caradoc said. 'I want to know if you'll be deserting the drove the way Flora and Thomas are doing and leaving my sister without a chaperone.'

'Your sister doesn't need a chaperone,' Non said. 'She needs a little slave who'll wait on her hand and foot.'

'Oh, we're getting personal now, are we?' Caradoc's face was white.

'Well, you were the one who got personal, Mr Jones, and please take note, I have no interest in leaving the drove, and I have no interest in marriage or a tryst, not that it's any of your business.'

She knew her face was red, but what she didn't know was that she looked very beautiful with her hair lifting in the breeze and her mouth trembling.

Slowly, Caradoc reached for her and took her in his arms. He looked down into her face for a long moment and she stood motionless, bewitched by him. Then his mouth came down on hers and she felt the whole world was exploding inside her head.

Her entire body tingled at his touch. Slowly, she put her arms around his neck and felt the crispness of his hair at the nape of his neck. She seemed to melt into him; her senses were reeling, she felt she no longer had any control as his hands slid down her back, softly, sensuously caressing her.

And then they were lying beneath the trees. He was kissing her eyelids, her throat and her breasts, his mouth warm, drinking her in to the spell of him. She wasn't aware of him rising above her but then he came towards her, closer and closer until he was within her.

She cried with pain as he entered her, but he was gentle, making soothing sounds as though she was some creature he was taming. And then the sensations began within her, like a conflagration rising to encompass her. Non clung to him, holding him close, kissing him with a passion she didn't know she possessed. She belonged to him, she was one with him and the very earth was witness to the glory of their love.

When it was over, Caradoc drew her bodice together and pulled her skirts down over her knees. 'My lovely, wonderful Non,' he said in a thick voice, 'you're so beautiful I can't take my eyes off you.'

She waited for him to say he loved her and that they would marry as soon as they reached a church, but he did no such thing. He tidied himself and then stood up, his hand outstretched to help her to her feet. It was then that the enormity of what she'd just done hit her. She'd given herself to a man without marriage vows being made. She was a disgraced woman, a fallen woman, just like Flora. And she was worse than Flora because she was educated, brought up to be ladylike, and now look at her. And look at Caradoc. The act over, he was in full possession of himself, looking through the

171

trees to where the rest of the drove was waiting.

'We'd better get back,' he said.

She waited for him to put his arms around her, tell her everything was going to be all right. But he didn't.

He said, 'I hope I was gentle enough with you. We can talk about it later. We'd better push on, get as far as we can before nightfall.'

As he took a step away from her, Non began to cry.

# CHAPTER SIXTEEN

It took five days for the drove to reach Hereford, when it should only have taken two and a half. As the cattle passed slowly through Eign Gate, rain and wind swept over the town, obscuring the way ahead. The animals became restless, pawing the ground, unwilling to move through the churned-up mud of the roads.

Non walked behind the drove, a little way back from the other women, feeling nothing but shame at the wanton way she'd behaved. She was grateful that no one wanted to talk because of the inclement weather. She still couldn't believe that she had given in to her passion. Her father would have been shocked to his very soul if he was alive to see she'd become a fallen woman.

Mary had guessed from the start: she'd given Non a long look and shaken her head. Morgan had been too busy to pay her much attention, for which Non was grateful. As for Caradoc, he behaved as though nothing had happened at all. She was so

172

hurt by his attitude, so humiliated, that she hardly looked him in the eye.

Perhaps now that they were inside the walls of Hereford, Caradoc would make an opportunity to talk to her about what had happened. She hoped so, but her heart was heavy.

'See that church spire there.' Mary had stopped to wait for Non, her hair bedraggled under her hat and her cheeks red from the wind. She pointed towards the tall spire of a church. 'See that's near the Lamb and Flag tavern, where you'll be sleeping in comfort tonight.'

'What about you and the other women?' Non avoided meeting Mary's eyes.

'We'll be all right there. The barn is well built, the roof don't leak and the place is halfway tidy by any standards. We'll all be provided with a hot meal, a nice dish of *cawl*, most likely. Lovely soup the landlady makes, mind, real lamb and good fresh vegetables and not the leftovers from yesterday's meal, like we get in some places.' She put her hand on Non's shoulder. 'You going to talk about it?'

'What?' Non asked, startled.

'About what happened between you and the boss, girl, what else?'

'You are too knowing for your own good, Mary, but now you've asked me outright, I'll tell you. I'm so ashamed of myself I could die!'

'*Duw, duw*, girl, you don't die of shame over a thing like that. I know you was brought up to be respectable like, but you can't punish yourself forever for giving in to your feelings. It was a mistake, and one best forgotten.'

Non looked at Mary and felt such misery well up

173

inside her that it was hardly bearable. Even Mary, wordly wise as she was, believed she had made a mistake. 'How could I allow it, Mary?' she said softly. 'I feel so . . . so . . . *sullied*.' She swallowed hard. 'And what makes it worse, he hasn't paid me any attention at all for days.'

'You can't expect too much of the man. The drove has been hell this last few days and he's needed all his strength to keep us on course.'

They walked in silence for a while. The little town of Hereford was a pretty place, or it would be when the sun was shining. She would look around later, but the first thing Non wanted was a hot bath. Her clothes were soaked by the rain and clung uncomfortably to her body.

Mary sighed heavily. 'I should mind my own business, Non, but I feel I must warn you again about Caradoc Jones. I've been on many droves with him over the years and you must not expect a ring on your finger. But I suppose you know that without me telling you.'

Non hung her head. She *had* expected marriage, she couldn't deny it; once Caradoc had taken her virginity she had thought he would make an honest woman of her.

'Oh, you silly little girl!' Mary's voice was so full of compassion that Non felt tears spring to her eyes. 'You thought it was special, that Mr Jones would marry you. Now that was the biggest mistake you could ever make.'

Non didn't reply. She still had a tiny flame of hope in her heart that once they were settled in Hereford for the night, Caradoc would come to her and tell her he loved her and would marry her as soon as it could be arranged.

'Hey, you there!' Georgina's carriage drew up alongside Non. 'I've got a chill coming on with all this dratted rain. I wish I'd never set out with the drove at all. A fine sight I'm going to look in London, with my nose all red and my eyes streaming.'

Non looked at Georgina and saw that her normally pale skin was flushed, sweat beaded her forehead and her eyes were almost closed. 'I can find you a good syrup to take,' Non said. 'Do you want to wait until we get to the tavern?'

'Can't you give me something now?'

'I've got some tincture of sage in my box. I'll go and get it if you like.'

'Well, hurry up then.' Georgina began to cough and Non took a deep breath, trying not to get angry. Even now, when she was asking for help, Georgina was hostile and demanding.

'I'll be as quick as I can.'

The supply wagon was a little way back behind the drove, and as she approached it, Non could see that one wheel had sunk into the mud at the side of the road. Her heart began to pound as she caught sight of Caradoc overseeing the efforts to free the wagon. Non stared at his broad back and longed to wind her arms around him and hold him close.

Morgan was there too and he was being practical, forcing a sack beneath the wheel and getting the men to push it free of the mud. Caradoc glanced at her and nodded distantly, like a boss to a worker. Non averted her eyes and made her way round the back of the wagon, her face flushed. She was so hurt by his casual attitude towards her that hot bitter tears welled in her eyes.

The wagon was pulled free and Non was able to

175

retrieve her box and select the bottle she needed. Caradoc was chastising the driver, telling him to keep to the middle of the roadway, and he still didn't look her way.

'I haven't seen much of you these past days.' Morgan's voice sounded in her ear and Non jumped. 'Is everything all right?' He looked down at her, a puzzled frown on his face. 'I hope you've not taken offence, Non. An offer of marriage is a compliment, not an insult, mind.'

'It's this awful weather.' Non felt awkward, knowing that Caradoc was still standing alongside the wagon. 'I've hardly been able to pick any plants, let alone talk.' She gestured helplessly, not knowing what else to say in the face of Morgan's honest concern. How would he feel if he knew the truth about her?

'I hope you'll think it over, Non. You could do a lot worse than marry me, even though I am just a blacksmith.'

'It's nothing to do with that,' Non said quickly. 'I just don't feel ready for marriage right now. Perhaps when the drove is over I can think about my future.'

'So you've not ruled it out altogether?' The entreaty in Morgan's eyes touched her heart.

'No, I haven't ruled anything out, Morgan.'

Now why had she said that? She was only giving him false hope. She looked away quickly as Caradoc strode towards her.

'Non, I want to talk to you,' he said, gesturing for her to follow him. Her heart began to beat so loudly she thought everyone would hear it as she followed him a little way along the road.

She could feel Morgan's eyes boring into her

back. She knew she'd left him standing there without excusing herself, but she was trembling so much she could hardly think straight.

'It's about Georgie. Is she fit to travel?'

Non's heart dipped; she'd been sure he was going to talk about their relationship. She took a deep breath and held out the bottle in her hand. 'I'm just going to give her some tincture. I'll see how she feels then, but I fear she might be coming down with a fever.'

'In that case I'd better rest the drove here, where we can at least enjoy good food and shelter.' He shook his head. 'I didn't really want to stop more than a night, we're way behind our schedule already. Will this fever break by morning?'

'It might. I'm sure that once Miss Jones has rested for the night she'll feel much better.' She looked up at him, willing him to say something more, to tell her he loved her and that she was special to him.

He stared down into her eyes and then, for a brief moment, his fingers grazed her cheek. 'I'd better get on with my work. I'll speak to you tonight—I'll come to your room.'

Non heaved a sigh of relief. He was going to make things right between them, after all. She watched as he walked away and her heart was so full of gratitude that she could have cried.

She became aware that Morgan was still staring at her and his face was dark with disapproval. She attempted to smile at him, but he looked away and suddenly she felt as though she'd cheapened herself. If Morgan felt angry about one small touch, how horrified he'd be if he knew the whole story.

Once again, shame swept over her. How could she be so wanton? She had allowed Caradoc liberties that no woman should allow outside the marriage bed. She'd known it was wrong, she realized how foolish she'd been, she wished she could go back in time and change everything, and yet she still was shaken by a glancing touch from Caradoc's fingers.

She was no better than poor Flora, who had nearly lost her life because she'd trusted a man from the drove, a man who already had a wife and family. No good could come of that situation, and by the same token no good could come of her alliance with Caradoc. Impatient with her own thoughts, she hurried to catch up with Georgina's wagon. When Dennis saw her, he drew the horses to a stop so that Non could climb up on the wheel and into the carriage.

'About time!' Georgina was lying now amongst the cushions. 'I could die while I waited for you to attend me.' Her voice was thick and slow and Non knew the girl must be suffering the soreness that chills and fevers bring to the throat. So long as it didn't spread to her lungs, Georgina would soon recover.

Non offered the bottle to Georgina. 'Take a sip of this tincture,' she said, 'and then take more in about an hour's time. Once we stop, I'll come to see you in your room and bring you more medicine.'

Georgina looked at the bottle as though she could barely see it, and after a moment Non drew out the cork and held the bottle to Georgina's mouth.

Non was relieved when the drove reached the

Lamb and Flag. She climbed the stairs to her room, thankful to be indoors. She took off her wet clothes and put on her nightgown, before putting her petticoats near the fire to dry. She would rest for a while, she was tired and her legs ached. She leaned back against the pillows, smelling the clean scent of lavender and linen. She closed her eyes, and before she knew it she was asleep.

Non woke to the sound of rapping on the door. She scrambled off the bed and opened the door to find Caradoc standing there. The hot colour rose to her cheeks as she let him into her room.

She looked at his tall lean figure, longing to be in his arms, wanting to hear his words of reassurance that she was more to him than a passing fancy.

'I hope this won't take long,' she said quickly. 'I've promised to see your sister to give her more medication.'

'Never mind Georgina.' He closed the door carefully behind him. 'I want to see you—be with you—there's been no opportunity until now.'

Her heart lifted. He was going to tell her he loved her, that everything was going to be all right.

He took her in his arms and she lay her head against his chest, feeling the beating of his heart against her face.

'My little Non, how I've waited to be close to you again.' He swept her up and carried her to the bed.

Startled, Non struggled out of his arms. 'Have you just come here to lay with me, or have you anything to say to me?'

He looked at her, a puzzled frown on his face. 'What's wrong, what do you want me to say to you?'

'I want you to tell me you love me.' The words

came out boldly and Caradoc moved slightly away from her. Then his face softened.

'Of course I love you. Look, Non, there are women in plenty I could enjoy for a night of lust, but you are special to me. Our lovemaking was magical, I can hardly wait to have you in my arms again, to touch your lips with mine and to know you belong to me.'

Relief swept through her at his words. He did love her, he wanted her not just for a night but for ever. He took her in his arms again and she clung to him, clasping her hands behind his neck, feeling the softness of his hair against her fingers. Love flowed like a hot fire in her veins, and then Caradoc was above her, pushing up her nightgown, kissing her pale thighs. She sighed, she knew she should stop him, but then she couldn't stop herself.

She felt a sensation of exquisite passion as he took her; she heard her own voice moaning low in her throat with pleasure. The joy seemed endless, until at last a starburst of sensation began at her thighs and flushed her whole body, making her shudder with pleasure.

When it was over, he held her and kissed her mouth gently. 'I must go,' he said softly. 'I've got so much to do, but don't worry about a thing, little Non, I meant it when I said I loved you.'

He was gone before she could think of anything to say that would stop him. Alone, she felt as if she'd fallen from a great height. Her stomach lurched as she thought over every moment they'd spent together. He'd said he loved her, but Caradoc had said nothing at all about marriage.

Non wondered what he was thinking. Did he want to make her his mistress? Her heart almost stopped beating at the prospect. Her father had wanted her to make a respectable marriage; he'd even named Morgan as a prospective husband. He would turn over in his grave if he knew how she was behaving now.

Non stripped off her nightgown and poured water from the jug into a huge flower-painted basin. She needed to bathe, but tonight she was not offered the luxury of a bath. She needed to wash her hair, but she would wait until the drove passed a suitable pool or river, somewhere private, secluded, away from prying eyes.

She washed carefully, as if she was washing Caradoc out of her system. But it was no use. She loved him and wanted him with a passion that was frightening.

When she'd dressed, she rummaged in her box of medicines looking for the right bottle. It was fortunate that she had more of her tincture of sage; the remedy was excellent for soothing sore throats and combating chills.

Non went next door to Georgina's room, where she found her in bed. The girl's eyes were clearer and some of the heat had left her skin.

'You should be all right to travel by morning,' Non said, handing her the bottle. 'The sage seems to be doing you good.'

'Well, put it in a cup for me,' Georgina said sulkily. 'It's the least you can do.' She appeared to be watching Non's every movement. 'I can see you're falling in love with my brother.' Her words fell like stones into the quietness of the room. 'It won't do you any good, you know. I've seen his women come and go, he even fathered a child by one of his paramours—be careful that doesn't

181

happen to you.'

'I don't know what you mean.' Non spoke quickly, too quickly.

'I think you know exactly what I mean.' Georgina stared at her with hostile eyes. 'You're a fool to trust him. He uses his charm to get everything he wants, so don't say you weren't warned.'

'I still don't know what you're talking about.' Non slipped the bottle of tincture back into her box. 'In any case, you're not my chaperone, I'm yours, or have you forgotten?'

'Oh, such insolence! Well you'll be laughing on the other side of your face once we reach London, because then Caradoc will act as though he never knew you.' She smiled. 'I think you know what I mean by the term "knew", or are you completely stupid?'

Non left without answering, and when she reached the privacy of her own room, she closed the door and leaned against it, her eyes filling with tears.

Then there was a gentle knocking on the door; Non rubbed her eyes fiercely, then opened the door to a young girl of about fifteen, with food on a tray. She was drably dressed in a dark-brown gown covered by an apron made of sacking.

'Here, Miss, there's some good boiled lamb and a nice chunk of freshly baked bread. You need filling up after a day on the trail in this weather.'

'Thank you, just put the tray on the table there.'

'You look awful pale, Miss. Shall I bring you a nice hot toddy? Keep the cold out, it will, mind.'

'No, thank you very much but I'm quite all right.' Non forced a smile as she closed the door behind the girl, and looked at the food knowing she couldn't eat one morsel of it.

She was almost asleep when she was roused by the sound of knocking again on her door. She sighed, expecting a summons from Georgina, but when she opened the door it was Morgan standing there on the landing, his eyes searching her face. 'Can I come in?'

She stepped back. 'Of course you can, Morgan. Please, sit down there near the fire. Your clothes are still soaking from the rain, why haven't you changed into something dry?'

'I'm all right,' Morgan said. He didn't sit, but paced back and forth across the small space before the fire. 'It's you I'm worried about.'

'Why are you worried about me? I'm well enough, as you can see.'

'It's not your health, it's your state of mind,' Morgan said. 'What is going on between you and Mr Jones?'

Non felt the colour flood into her face. 'There's nothing going on.' Even as she spoke she knew her voice carried no conviction.

'Don't lie to me, Non, I know you too well and in any case I saw the way Caradoc Jones looked at you and touched you. I hope you're not hoping for an offer of marriage from that quarter.'

Suddenly Non was angry. Everyone seemed to be minding her business. 'Look, I've had a tiring day, and if you've only come here to accuse me of goodness knows what, you can leave right away.' She walked to the door. 'Please, Morgan, I want to rest for a while now. Will you please go?'

He sighed heavily and walked to the door. 'Non, don't let your feelings run away with you. Life on

183

the road can seem romantic, with the bright moon above and the soft grass under your feet, but there's a real life to be faced once the drove ends.'

'I know that!' Non said. 'I do know that, Morgan, I'm not a half-wit. Now please go away and leave me in peace.'

She closed the door behind him, almost kicking it in her fury. She stared at the closed door, seeing only Morgan's troubled expression. Suddenly her anger was gone; she went to the bed and curled up on it, putting her hands over her eyes, as if by that gesture she could blot out her shame. But it was there, inside her, making her heart race and her pulses leap. She was a wanton fool and nothing except marriage to Caradoc would make her an honest woman.

## CHAPTER SEVENTEEN

The morning dawned with the skies a clear untroubled blue. Non slipped out of bed and stepped over to the window to open it wide. The fragrant air drifted into the bedroom; once the drove began, the smell of the beasts would be all-pervading; the noise of hooves and the mournful bellow of the animals would accompany the drove all the way to the next halt.

Looking down into the forecourt of the inn, Non caught a glimpse of Caradoc striding towards the stables. He looked so handsome, so strong, and her heart ached with love for him. As if sensing her presence, he looked up and caught her eye, and lifted his hand in a small gesture of recognition.

She drew back quickly, embarrassed to be seen watching him.

When she was dressed, Non went into Georgina's room; the walls attested to the age of the building, the heavy stonework whitewashed and peeling. Even the floor seemed to slope, as though the building was leaning to one side, driven like the trees by the easterly wind.

Georgina was sitting up in bed, enjoying a breakfast of toasted bread and strawberry jam. She was looking much better; the hot redness of fever had vanished in the night.

'Excuse me, Miss Jones,' Non said. 'Do you think you're up to travelling this morning?'

Georgina sucked the jam from her fingers. 'I saw my brother earlier and he says we're to wait behind if that's what I want.'

Non took a sharp breath. 'But you're looking so much better, I think your fever has broken.'

'Oh that,' Georgina said dismissively. 'Well, whether I'm well enough to travel is beside the point. I'd do anything rather than stay behind in this old inn with you as my only companion. We wouldn't even have Flora with us, now that she's run off with her lover.' She smiled spitefully. 'My dear brother is not very keen to have you along on the drove, do you see?'

'I don't believe that,' Non said quickly. 'Caradoc has said nothing to me about staying behind.' She paused; she must be careful not to reveal too much of her feelings to Georgina.

'My brother is Mr Jones, to you. Do you understand? And what he does and what I do, come to that, has nothing to do with you. Now get out of my room and leave me in peace.'

As Non closed the door, her hands were clenched and her emotions torn between anger and pain. Would Caradoc have liked to leave her behind? Was he sorry he'd made love to her again? The thought made her feel ill. But then she was a fool, putting her trust in a man she hardly knew. She'd acted like a child grasping at an impossible dream. Georgina was right, Caradoc would never marry her. To him she was just a diversion from the boredom of the road.

Her mood changed from despair to anger. She folded her nightgown and packed her bag in a mood of determination. She would leave the drove, forget about Caradoc and his odious sister. She would put her mistakes behind her and start again.

\*     \*     \*

'What is going on between you and that girl?' Georgina stared at her brother, seeing how the sun lifted his bright hair and realizing what a handsome man he was. 'She's all of a shake at the mere mention of your name.'

'I don't know what you're talking about.' Caradoc sounded bored. 'I've got work to do, Georgina, so if you've nothing sensible to say to me I'd be obliged if you'd get ready to leave.'

'I am ready,' Georgina said, 'but there's no sign of your little harlot, is there?'

'You are talking foolish nonsense,' Caradoc said. 'And you should be grateful to Non, she's cured you of the fever, hasn't she?'

'There we are! You know exactly who I'm talking about, and let me tell you, you're playing with fire there. She's not an ignorant peasant girl,

186

remember. Non Jenkins wouldn't be paid off with a little bit of money, oh no, she'd want a ring on her finger, that one. Just be careful you're not caught out by her cleverness and trickery.'

'How could I be "caught out", as you put it? What could Non possibly do to hurt me?'

'She could tell you the oldest lie in the book.'

'And what's that?'

'That she's expecting your child. That's what women usually say in order to trap a man.'

'That won't happen,' Caradoc said, frowning at her angrily, 'because nothing is going on between us. It's all in your fertile imagination.'

'You don't fool me, brother, I know you too well. You think you're falling in love, but you know what life is like on the trail. How many liaisons have been formed between the men and the girls who walk the drovers' roads? I've seen them come back to Swansea, lives ruined by a silly affair. Take Flora and Thomas, they think life is going to be wonderful, but wait until they get back home and have to face reality.'

'All that has nothing to do with me.' Caradoc spoke brusquely. 'I hire people to work for me, I'm not a keeper of other folk's morals.'

'But you are the keeper of your own,' Georgina said triumphantly. 'You're an educated man, you should know better than to trifle with the feelings of someone so far beneath you.'

'I've told you before, Georgina, mind your own business. Now are you ready to go on or do you want me to leave you behind?'

Georgina sensed that her brother would like very much for her to stay behind. 'And what about our little herbalist, would she have to stay behind

187

too?'

'No, she would not! I told you earlier this morning that I'd need her on the drove. She's proved how useful she can be.'

'I expect she has.' Georgina's tone was laced with sarcasm. 'But no, I shan't stay here in this awful place, I'm coming to London with you, so don't try to get rid of me.'

'We leave in an hour.' Caradoc walked away, striding out angrily.

Georgina smiled. It was so easy to rile him, Caradoc always rose to the bait whenever she chose to dangle it before him. This time, it was perfect. He was carrying on with the vicar's daughter and he was a fool if he thought no one would notice.

Later, as she rode in her carriage well to the rear of the herd of cattle, Georgina sighed with boredom. Then she caught sight of Non talking to one of the other women and she smiled.

'You there, Non, come over here, I need some medication.' She lay back against the cushions, feeling like an empress from ancient Egypt. Dennis glanced back at her. 'Want me to stop the horses, Miss Jones?'

'Of course, you idiot. I can't reach over the side of the carriage while it's moving, it would be far too dangerous.'

Dennis began to dismount and Georgina stopped him. 'Where do you think you're going?'

'Just to put down the steps for Miss Non.'

'Nonsense! She can climb up on the wheel. She's not to be spoiled, do you hear me?'

She watched as Non drew nearer, and then she stared down at her, noticing how pale the girl was and how troubled her expression. Still, she felt no pity. The girl was acting the harlot, she was just as much of a strumpet as that fool Flora, and there was no excuse for her behaviour. She was poor but educated, and should have made a suitable marriage by now. It would pass the time nicely if she could tease Non a little.

'What can I get you, Miss Jones?' Non asked quietly, standing with her head bowed and her eyes averted.

'Climb up into the coach,' Georgina spoke pleasantly, 'I think you have walked far enough.'

She caught Non's upward glance of surprise and smiled inwardly. 'Come along, I won't bite, for heaven's sake!'

Non lifted her skirts and put her foot on the wheel, swinging herself into the coach with ease.

Georgina smiled. 'You peasant people are not at all delicate, are you? Why, I saw not only your calf but your entire knee as you climbed aboard.'

Non ignored the insult. 'What's wrong, do you feel feverish again?' She put the back of her hand against Georgina's face. 'You're quite cool, so what *is* wrong with you?'

'Just sit down, that's right, over the other side of the coach—you smell of cattle.'

Non sat down and looked warily at her.

Georgina's smile was spiteful. 'Are you going to marry him?' She saw Non start and a frown of displeasure crossed her face.

It was a long time before Non answered. 'Who do you mean?'

'Why, the blacksmith Morgan, of course. Who else could possibly wish to marry you?'

'It really is none of your business who I marry, if I ever do.' Non's voice was calm and level, but

189

Georgina could tell she was angry. The thought pleased her.

'Oh, you'll marry,' she said with confidence. 'Women like you always do.'

'Women like me?'

'Yes,' Georgina paused, choosing her words well. 'The sort of woman who lies with one man and when she is discarded finds some dullard who'll make an honest woman of her.'

Non jumped from the carriage, landing lightly on the ground. 'If you've anything serious to say to me, call me. Until then, please leave me strictly alone.'

'Why should I?' Georgina challenged. 'You're a servant, here for my benefit. Who else would put up with your foolish ideas of medicine?'

'You'd better not mock,' Non said. 'I can make bad medicine as well as good, mind.'

Georgina leaned back. 'Are you threatening me?' She was annoyed to hear a quiver of fear in her voice.

'Of course not,' Non was looking up at her with a strange expression on her face, 'but don't keep trying to goad me, you never know where it might lead.'

Georgina watched as Non walked away, then she glanced at Dennis and leaned forward to prod him in the back. 'Did you hear that?' she said, her voice high with indignation. 'Did you hear that girl threaten me?'

'Sorry, Miss,' Dennis said. 'I didn't hear anything except the drumming of the herd.'

Georgina bit her lip. Non was clever, but she was a woman in the thrall of a man, and a man as fickle as Caradoc. Well, Non would soon learn that

Caradoc was only trifling with her, and serve her right.

* * *

'You look as though you lost a shilling and found a ha'penny.' Mary glanced at Non. 'Don't let that bitch of a woman get you down.'

Non sighed. 'She's insufferable, she tries to goad me whenever she can.'

'And you are letting her,' Mary said. 'You'll have to grow a shell, my girl. You been spoilt by your father, he's brought you up so well, coddled you like a baby and now you're let loose into a world that's full of bad people as well as good. Get used to it, Non, or you'll sink under it all.'

'I don't know why Georgina hates me so much.' Non shook her head. 'I've never done her any harm, I've only tried to help her when she's been sick.'

'Well, don't expect thanks from the likes of her,' Mary said. 'She's a spoiled rich girl. She can't wait to get to the bright lights of London. She's likely hoping for marriage to a rich young man and a fine town house to live in.'

Non forced a smile. It was foolish to let Georgina goad her into saying things she didn't mean. 'You're right, Mary, as always.'

'No, love, not always. But I'm right in this: give up any grand ideas you may have and marry Morgan while you still can. No man is going to wait for ever, mind.'

Non didn't reply. She knew that Morgan had guessed her feelings; he could see she didn't love him and never would. No, Morgan wouldn't want to marry her now, even if she said yes.

'I won't ever get married,' she said. 'I'll earn my own living and make something of my life. I don't need a man to keep me, thank you.'

Mary looked at her shrewdly. 'Fine words, but I don't believe any of them. You'll want children, a good man to care for you, you'll not be content with the life of a spinster.'

'You seem content enough.'

'Ah well, I'm regretting it all now.' She shrugged. 'What will I do when the droving is over? I can hardly live the rest of my life on the money I'll get this season.' She smiled. 'Maybe I'll find a rich widower in London, a man who'll treat me like a princess, but I doubt it.'

'Oh, Mary! You talk as if you're ancient! You'll have plenty more offers of marriage, you'll see.'

Mary's look spoke volumes. 'And pigs might fly.'

They walked a few miles in silence, and Non's thoughts turned to her own future. She wondered what she was going to do when she reached London. Perhaps she should forget Caradoc, and Morgan too, be what she wanted to be, an independent woman. She wondered what London would be like: a huge, sprawling place, according to Mary, the greatest cattle market in the country. Non had a vision of a big green field with cows and bullocks grazing peacefully together, waiting patiently to be bought by some rich landowner.

'So, Smithfield, is it a lovely place?' Non asked.

Mary shook her head and a stray curl flew loose from under her bonnet.

'Wait and see, my lovely, you just wait and see. You won't be able to believe your eyes, I can tell you that.'

Non felt stirred with excitement, feelings that had nothing to do with Caradoc Jones.

'But first, before we gets to London, the animals got to be finished.'

'Finished?'

'Aye, haven't you noticed how scrawny the beasts are? The long walk takes all the meat off their bones and the animals have to be fattened before the buyers will pay good money out. That's what we call "finishing".'

Non realized there was a great deal more to cattle droving than she'd dreamed of. She was so ignorant of so many things, the ways of beasts, but more importantly the ways of men.

'Aye, girl, you've a lot to learn.' Mary spoke as though she'd read Non's thoughts. 'Now listen to me, good girl, leave that Caradoc Jones alone while you're still safe.'

Non blinked. 'Safe?'

'Aye, safe. Right now you're a free woman, you've got your whole life in front of you. Don't mess it all up because of a bit of passion.'

Non wanted to tell Mary that what she felt for Caradoc was much more than passion. She loved him, loved his smile, his touch, the very essence of him. And if Mary was right and Caradoc had no intention of marrying her, then she was content to be alone.

The drove was called to a halt. The men and the animals needed a rest. The day was hot, the sun burning mercilessly down and the ground was baked hard and dry.

'Look,' Mary said, 'they've stopped us by a good wide river. What do you say about us taking a bathe here, my girl?'

193

Non looked down at her dusty boots and the dirt that clung to the edge of her skirts. 'I'd love to have a good wash, but what if we're seen?'

'We'll walk down the bank a way, find some place that's sheltered by the trees. We'll be all right, the men are used to us women taking a bathe wherever we find some good clean water.'

It seemed that the other women on the drove had the same idea. Like children, they discarded their dusty clothes and slipped into the crystal river. Non hesitated; she was able to wash almost every night, secluded in a room of her own with a girl to bring her water—her need to bathe was not so pressing. And yet it looked so much fun.

'Oh come on, forget you're a vicar's daughter for a while and get your clothes off.'

Non glanced behind her. The men seemed a fair distance away, and anyway, why worry about modesty when there was clean cool water to be enjoyed?

As she slipped into the river, she gasped as the water closed over her thighs, her breasts and then her shoulders. She loosened her ribbons and lay back so that her hair waved like fronds of rushes in the water. It was so beautiful, the sun hot above her and the water cool against her naked limbs.

'That's the spirit!' Mary waved her arms and drifted towards her, her dark eyes alight with merriment. 'You'll be one of us before this trip finishes, you'll see.'

Non relaxed and let the orange particles of light dazzle through her closed eyelids. This was heaven. Her spirits lifted. She was young, she was in love and she was on her way to the magical streets of London.

# CHAPTER EIGHTEEN

Caradoc sat in the sunshine flipping the pages of his notebook, adding up the cost of the drove so far. Beside him Georgina, a happy smile on her face for once, sat leaning against the bole of an oak tree.

'You know those coarse women are bathing naked, don't you?' she said. 'I do wish I could go in the river with them.'

He didn't reply. It was best to say nothing to some of Georgina's remarks.

She tried again. 'So how's the cost of the drove working out, brother?'

He decided to humour her, and put his book down with a sigh. 'Well, you know I pay the men one shilling a day, except for the head drover who gets two shillings, and what with the price of grass for the beasts and accommodation for us, it adds up over the season to a fair bit of money.'

Georgina sniffed. 'Thomas was your head drover. Now he's chosen to go home with his trollop, why should you pay anyone else two whole shillings? You do most of the work yourself.'

Caradoc shook his head. 'I need to employ a new head drover—I can't do everything myself. Now if you want me to go on talking about the price of droving, why don't you keep your remarks to yourself?'

'Well, I'm just trying to help, that's all. I think you're far too generous.'

'Not at all. I pay the going rate, and if the men have worked exceptionally hard they receive a bonus of six shillings when we reach London.'

Georgina tutted her disapproval. 'Far too generous,' she repeated. 'I don't know how you manage to make a profit.'

'I manage very well, thank you.' He expected the cattle to bring in five pounds ten shillings per head, and a large bullock like Big Awkward might even fetch seven pounds, but that was something his sister didn't need to know.

'Listen to those women, will you?' Georgina's smile vanished. 'They sound like a lot of hooligans, calling and shrieking like that.'

Caradoc lifted his head, registering the happy cries of the women as they bathed in the river hidden by a deep copse of trees. 'They deserve some fun; the long walk from Wales to London is tough on everyone.' He calculated in his head the price of the grazing at Hereford, trying to keep his mind free from thoughts of Non. 'I think I'll just take a walk. I've been riding hard and need to stretch my legs.' The stop was an enforced one. A couple of the beasts had lost shoes and the stony ground beyond Hereford had made the animals' hooves tender. 'Good thing Morgan is riding with us. He'll have the cattle back on the road in no time. Anyway, I'm off, I'll talk with you later.'

He left his sister pouting at his departure and strolled beneath the trees, avoiding the heat of the sun. Georgina had been as much of a nuisance as he'd expected; she'd meddled in the business of Flora and Thomas, with disastrous results, and for some reason best known to herself she'd taken a dislike to Non. Even when Non cured her of the fever, Georgina still complained about her to anyone who would listen.

The swift rush of the river leaping over stones drew him towards the riverbank, the sound of running water giving the day an element of calm. Caradoc stepped through the trees and stopped abruptly as he caught sight of Non coming out of the river.

Her curves were outlined against the green of the foliage. She was like a water sprite, her dripping hair hanging down her shapely back, her breasts small and pert, the nipples proud where the coldness of the river had touched them. He felt a surge of something strange—not merely lust, but surely not love?

He turned away and walked back the way he'd come. The women were dressing now, they would only be a few minutes and then the drove could continue on the last few miles to the inn where he would bed down for the night. Alone, he told himself firmly.

He was becoming far too interested in Non Jenkins. He felt her draw him as if she'd cast a spell on him. He held no truck with foolishness of that sort, but in some way she had bemused him, made him care about her. Perhaps there was no great harm done. If he stopped the affair right now she would soon forget him. After all, Morgan the blacksmith wanted her for a wife. Strangely, the thought made him angry.

He tried to shake off the image of Non coming out of the water, her cool breasts, her shapely hips and her slender thighs gleaming in the sunlight, but the picture of her remained firmly fixed in his mind. He had been a fool to become involved with her. He knew she was not like the other women; she was a lady, brought up to be respectable, and she'd sacrificed a great deal when she'd let him make love to her.

He had a choice—he could make an honest woman of her. He knew his family wouldn't approve, but then he never did crave the approval of others. He tried to imagine Non as mistress of a big house, wondering how she would adapt to the ways of the gentry, how comfortable she would be with all the tinkering and fussing involved in entertaining guests, and he knew she would be out of her depth.

'Fool!' he said out loud. 'You damn fool!'

He smelt the cattle before he came upon them, most of them sitting now, in the smooth grass of the English countryside. He could see Morgan, his strong back bent as he worked on a beast that had thrown a shoe. He would make Non a fine husband, he was young and strong and handsome, and though he was only a blacksmith he was intelligent and hard working.

'Morning, Morgan.' Caradoc stopped and thrust his hands in his pockets. 'Nearly finished with the beasts?'

'Aye, shouldn't be long now, there's one more to *ciw* and then we can be on our way.' He straightened and Caradoc noticed that Morgan was taller than him by several inches. The thought did not please him.

'The women seem to be having a good time.' Morgan rubbed his hands against his canvas apron. 'I only wish I could join them. A dip in the river is what we all need in this hot weather.'

Caradoc ignored the remark. Deep in thought, he could see the image of Non, naked and lovely, standing like a goddess, her skin wet and gleaming.

'Give me another half-hour,' Morgan was saying. 'We'll be ready to move by then.'

Caradoc nodded and walked away. He could hear the voices of the women as they drew nearer, and somehow he didn't feel ready to see Non face to face.

'Caradoc!' The high-pitched voice of his sister stopped him in his tracks. 'Caradoc, how long are we to stay in this awful place?'

'Good old Georgina, moaning as usual.' He forced a smile. 'Morgan reckons we can be on our way in about half an hour. In any case, what's the hurry?'

'I just want to get to some sort of civilization,' she said. 'I'm so tired of riding the roads, seeing only the backsides of the animals as I get bumped about in that awful wagon. I'm sure Dennis looks for every hole in the road.'

'And why would he do that?'

'He doesn't like me, that's why!' Georgina sounded pettish. 'I have no friends on this drove, not one.'

'Well, you could try talking to some of the women.' Caradoc knew the suggestion would infuriate his sister.

'Them!' Her tone spoke volumes. 'I'm sure they can't even read and write, so what would I talk to them about?'

'Why don't you try to make friends with Non Jenkins? She's an educated lady—more learned than you, I dare say.'

Georgina shook her head. 'You know very well I don't even like her! I wish I'd never come with you. I should have taken the mail and arrived in London smelling sweet, instead of stinking of cattle.'

'I couldn't agree more.' Caradoc smiled as he walked away, ignoring the angry voice of his sister. It served her right. She'd insisted on coming with him, and now she knew exactly how hard life on the road could be.

* * *

Non felt clean and fresh. Her skin tingled and her hair, twisted now into a knot, was curling in tendrils round her face.

'*Duw*, that swim was lovely, wasn't it?' Mary said. 'It's good to wash away the dust and dirt of the road. It makes a girl feel more 'uman.' She paused, rubbing at her hair with her apron. 'Mind, I swear we was being watched.'

Non looked at her in amazement. 'What makes you say that?'

'I saw something—a man—just like a shadow, really.'

'I'm sure none of the men would be allowed to spy on us, Mary.'

'Maybe, maybe not, but whoever it was, they 'ad a good eyeful.'

The thought made Non feel uncomfortable; she didn't want anyone to see her naked. She thought of Caradoc, then—he'd seen her naked. He'd been intimate with her and she could see his eyes, dark with passion, as his hands traced the outline of her body.

'You're gone all red. Thinking of your lover, are you?' Mary's shrewd eyes were upon her and Non turned away without answering. She knew it was wrong to give her virginity to a man who had no intention of marrying her, and yet if he came to her

200

room tonight, she would lie with him again; she wouldn't be able to stop herself.

'There we are, then, back with the blessed smelly cattle.' Mary stood with her arms folded. 'It looks like we're on our way again. The men are rounding the beasts up, see?'

Non did see. She saw Caradoc astride his horse, looking like a knight of old with his hair gleaming in the sunlight. She felt a jolt in her heart. She knew why she couldn't resist him, it was because she was hopelessly in love with him.

'I've told you before, don't wear your heart on your sleeve, girl.' Mary spoke in a scolding voice. 'From the way you look at Mr Jones, even a child would know you're mad about him. Look, there's Morgan coming to talk to you. Concentrate on him, my lovely.'

'I'm not wearing my heart on my sleeve, Mary, so don't keep on about it.'

'Look, *merchi*, you should think carefully about what you're doing. Don't ruin your life for a man who only wants a roll in the hay.'

Her words were like a knife in Non's heart, and she felt the colour rush to her face. She wanted to scream at Mary that they were in love, it was not a sordid affair but a true meeting of souls. She saw Morgan drawing closer and kept silent.

'Enjoy your splash in the stream, did you?' He was speaking to both women, but his eyes were on Non.

She took a deep breath. 'It was lovely, the water was so clean and fresh.' She glanced up at Morgan and met his eyes. 'Finished the shoeing, have you?'

'Aye, not much to do, really. Some of the young heifers were a bit skittish, but I made good time.'

201

She stood before him, not knowing how to talk to him. It was as though he could read her thoughts, knew her weaknesses.

'What's wrong, Non?' Morgan put his hands on her shoulders. 'I can see you're troubled, can't you talk to me about it?'

'There's nothing wrong with me,' she said, feeling the heat of his hands through her gown. She knew he wanted her, wanted her for a wife. He was honest and good, and it was her own fault that she didn't love him.

'You can talk to me about anything,' Morgan said softly. 'I care about you, Non, and I can see you're not happy. Do you want to go back home? If you do, just say the word and I'll take you.' He paused, trying to look into her eyes. 'I'm not a wealthy man, Non, but I do make a fair living. I could look after you, give you a home of your own. We've known each other a long time, so you know you can trust me.'

When she didn't answer, he spoke again. 'If you want to go back to Swansea, just say the word and we'll set off first thing in the morning.'

'No!' Non spoke quickly. 'I don't want to go home, I want to stay with the drove, and see London for myself. I want some excitement in my life, Morgan, before I'm too old to enjoy it.'

His hands dropped to his sides. 'Well, when you're ready, when you've had enough of the road and enough of London, remember I'll always be waiting for you.'

He left her, then, and as she watched him walk away she wished she could love him. Life would be so easy then, uncomplicated by emotions she couldn't control.

202

By the time the drove reached the inn, Non was exhausted. For the first time she felt weary of the road. The endless days when all she seemed to do was walk were only lightened by the thought that Caradoc would come to her in the night, hold her in his arms and make her feel like a real woman.

In her room, Non sank onto the bed and fell back against the pillows. The room was a good one, sweet smelling, with clean curtains at the window and fresh bed linen to lie on. Caradoc must care about her, if only a little, because he made sure she was comfortable each night they found shelter.

But later, when Non had eaten her supper of bread and cheese and a bowl of thick rich broth, and she'd read her herbal until her eyes ached, she felt lonely. She wasn't sleepy; her mind was full of chaotic thoughts, her heart full of hope and love. And yet she knew her love for Caradoc was pointless, their liaison doomed to failure.

She slipped from the bed, went to the door and looked along the corridor. She could hear the voices of the men in the room downstairs and occasional bursts of laughter. There, with all those other men, was the only man she would ever want. She doused her candle and sat near the door, with it open just a crack, waiting for Caradoc to come upstairs. She knew she was weak, she was a fool to herself, but she wanted the warmth of his arms around her. She needed him to tell her he loved her and would take care of her always.

She was almost asleep when she heard the creak of footsteps on the stairs. She waited and watched until she was sure it was Caradoc making his way into one of the bedrooms. She crouched near the door a little while longer until everything was quiet, and then she crept along the passageway, holding her breath, fearful that her breathing would give her away.

He looked up in surprise when he saw her, his eyes bright in the candlelight as he stood there looking at her. He was unashamed of his nakedness. He was so handsome and strong that Non felt tears of love brim in her eyes. She closed the door behind her and slipped the bolt home. Tonight there would be no hasty departure from his room, tonight she would sleep with him until morning poked her prying fingers through the window panes.

## CHAPTER NINETEEN

Non opened her eyes as the morning light filtered into the room. She turned to look at Caradoc. He was still asleep, his hair tousled over his brow, his lashes long against his cheeks. She felt weak with love for him and, leaning over him, she lightly touched his lips with her own. He woke up then and reached for her, holding her close to him as though he would never let her go.

He made love to her with such tenderness that Non knew in her heart that he loved her. Whatever difficulties they encountered, he would always love her. She clung to him, feeling his hardness within her; she kissed his shoulder and moaned as he caressed her. Her heart was singing. She was in love, and the most wonderful thing in the world had happened—she was loved in return.

When it was over, they lay sated side by side and

it was then that Caradoc said the words she longed to hear.

'I've fallen in love with you, Manon Jenkins.' His voice was tender. 'I can't imagine my life without you.' He kissed her brow. 'You've cast a spell on me, tangled me in your lovely hair, bewitched me with your kisses.'

She lay in the hollow of his shoulder, tears springing to her eyes. Her heart was full of love and thankfulness. Now everything would be all right, Caradoc would marry her when they reached London.

There was a loud knocking on the door and Caradoc sat up. 'It's probably the landlord. I asked him to bring me an early breakfast.'

He slid out of bed and drew on his trews, and from where she lay, Non looked lovingly at the breadth of his shoulders and the firmness of his body.

'Let me in, Caradoc!' Georgina burst into the room, her eyes glowing with malice. 'I knew I'd catch you out if I was patient.'

Caradoc caught her shoulders. 'How dare you spy on me? Get out of my room before I throw you out.'

'You're a fool! Why can't you behave like a man, instead of a greedy boy? Do you have to have a woman wherever you go?'

She looked at Non, and there was scorn in her voice when she spoke. 'You're an even greater fool to trust him.' She pointed to her brother. 'He takes a woman as casually as he takes a sip of wine. If you think you'll get your claws into our family by demeaning yourself, you're very much mistaken.'

Non sat up in bed, hugging the blankets to her

breasts. 'Caradoc loves me. We'll be married once we get to London.'

Caradoc spun round to look at her. 'Hold on there, Non, you're moving too fast. I didn't say anything about marriage.'

She swallowed hard. 'I thought that's what you meant when you told me you loved me.'

'I do love you, but marriage is a different proposition. Just wait a minute. Georgina, you're leaving.' He pushed Georgina from the room, closed the door and stood looking at her, running his hand through his hair. 'I'm so sorry.' He sat on the bed beside her. 'I do love you, Non,' he took her hand. 'I want to set you up in a nice house where we can be together like man and wife.'

Non didn't cry. Her heart was breaking but she held her head high. 'If you're not offering me marriage, then you're not offering me anything.'

Caradoc sighed heavily. 'I don't know what you mean.'

'You want to "set me up" like some common whore. How could you, Caradoc? How could you do that to me?'

She slipped from the bed, aware of him watching as she pulled on her clothes. Her lip was trembling and she fought for control as she went to the door. 'I woke up thinking this was the happiest day of my life, and it's turned out to be the worst.'

She closed the door quietly behind her and hurried back to her room. She fell onto the bed and let the tears flow. 'Oh, Caradoc, how could you treat me like this?' The sobs were hard and painful and she tried to stifle the violence of them against her pillow. She had believed him when he said he loved her; it was as if her wildest dreams had come

206

true, only to find that his promises were like dust.

After a time, she sat up and dried her tears. Now she'd seen Caradoc in his true colours, she'd keep as far away from him as she could. If only he hadn't said he loved her she might have been content to lie in his arms with the promise of nothing more than a moment of warmth and passion. Then he'd raised her expectations. She'd believed he would make an honest woman of her—what a fool she'd been.

She lay wide-eyed, staring into the brightness of the morning but not seeing anything of the lovely day. The sounds of the men preparing for the drove scarcely penetrated her feeling of doom. What was going to become of her now? Perhaps she should take Morgan at his word and let him take her home.

But then she'd be giving in. She would never see London, never find out what sort of life she could make for herself. If she went with Morgan, he would expect her to marry him. He was an honest, upright man; he didn't deserve spoiled goods, another man's leavings. She was crying bitter tears again as she slid from the bed and began to wash, dress and make herself ready for whatever the day ahead held.

\*　　　\*　　　\*

Non walked along the drovers' road with her head down, avoiding the eyes of the women, who clearly knew what had taken place the night before. Georgina had wasted no time in spreading gossip. It was only Mary who looked at her with compassion; everyone else clearly thought her a whore, a woman of easy virtue.

Mary touched her arm. 'Look, *merchi*, you're not the first nor the last to have a little adventure. Most of these other girls would jump into bed with the boss man if it was offered to them, so lift up your head and be proud.'

Non squeezed Mary's hand. 'Thank you, Mary, but I've been a fool, and you tried to tell me that more than once. I'm going to take your advice and forget Caradoc Jones. I'll concentrate on my career—I'll make myself the best-known herbalist in the whole of London.'

Mary beamed. 'That's the spirit!'

Non heard the noise of wheels against the rough ground and knew, with a sinking of her heart, that Georgina's carriage was about to pull up beside her. She stared straight ahead, but Georgina would not be ignored.

'Well then, what a pale face we have this morning. Has too much rolling round in the hay taken it out of you?'

There was a murmur of laughter from some of the women, and Non felt the colour flood into her face. She glanced at Dennis, whose embarrassment was obvious by the way his eyes slid away from hers.

'Like being the boss man's strumpet, do you?' Georgina leaned over and prodded Non with her whip. 'Well, don't get too used to it. My brother isn't known for his discretion in this sort of affair. No doubt he'll meet some other fancy piece when we get to London.'

Non stopped walking and looked up at Georgina. 'I've made a mistake, I'll grant you that,' she said clearly. 'I trusted that at least one member of the Jones family was able to keep his word.'

Georgina laughed, her head thrown back, her bonnet slipping from her head. 'Then you're a bigger fool than I took you for.'

'Look,' Mary shook her arm. 'Look, Non, the boss is coming. Prepare yourself now, have some dignity, right?'

Caradoc rode closer to the carriage and waved for Dennis to go on. 'We're hoping to be halfway to Aylesbury by tonight,' he said, 'so we don't want any delays, all right?' He looked hard at his sister, and she made a face at him before leaning back against her cushions. 'You women all right? How are your feet, Mary? Holding up fine this trip, are they?' Mary nodded, but Caradoc hardly noticed. 'And Non, I'd like to speak with you.'

Non kept her eyes fixed firmly in front of her. 'I'm busy, Sir,' she said.

'Well, there's a small matter I have to discuss with you. Can you stop walking for a moment and just listen to me?'

'Very well, Sir.' She waited until the women were in front of her, then turned to Caradoc. 'What can you say now to make everything all right again? There's nothing you can do except offer me marriage, and we both know you're not going to do that.'

'I'm sorry for what happened this morning,' he said quickly. 'You didn't give me time to think. I've a great deal hanging in the balance right now, not the least being my need to see this drove safely to London. I didn't mean what I said, you must realize that.'

She looked up at him. 'You'll marry me, then?'

He looked away from her, his mouth set in a

209

grim line. She could see his jaw twitching and knew he was angry with her, but now she'd begun to talk to him she couldn't stop.

'I thought when you said you loved me you meant it.' The words came out hard, like stones hitting the ground. 'Now I realize I'm only a temporary diversion, someone to sleep with to pass away the long hours on the road.'

'No!' He pushed his hand through his hair. 'Look, I do love you, Non, but I'm not ready for marriage, not yet.'

Non was shaken by his words. They were the same ones she'd said to Morgan. Did that mean Caradoc didn't love her? The thought was a bitter one.

'Of course, you'll marry one day. You need heirs, fine sons to take over the business, as you've taken over from your father.' She felt a lump in her throat. 'I would have been honoured to bear you sons, Caradoc.'

'Non, just let me get this drove over and done with, and then I'll be able to give my attention to other matters.'

Non drew a deep breath. 'You do what you must, I won't be bothering you again. Now if you'll excuse me, Sir, I've work to do, too, and I've wasted enough time already.'

She watched him ride away and suddenly she was alone. The sun was overhead, the green fields were all around her, the waving branches of the trees cast patterns on the roadway. It was a lovely day, and Non had never felt so miserable in all her life.

Non spent the afternoon gathering herbs, then caught up with the drove at the next halt. Some of the women had gone to work for the local landowners, and the cattle had been driven into the fields to graze and rest. The men were doubtless enjoying themselves in the bar; Non was glad—she didn't think she could face anyone right now.

She'd collected some leaves and roots of St John's wort, as well as a special kind of ivy; both were recommended to calm the nerves. A quick look at her herbal told her that the mixture was beneficial taken inwardly as well as applied outwardly. Non went round the back of the inn and peered into the kitchen. A large woman wrapped in an apron was kneading dough on the wooden table.

'Excuse me,' Non stood in the doorway, 'I'm with the cattle drove. Can I come in and use your kitchen for a few moments?'

The woman didn't stop kneading the dough, but threw Non a quick look. 'I don't know about that. What do you want in my kitchen, anyway?'

'I'm a herbalist. I'd like to make up some tinctures here, if you'll kindly allow it.'

'Oh,' the woman's eyes brightened, 'come on in, then, and welcome.'

Non found a corner of the table that was clear of flour and began to tear the plants into small pieces.

The woman glanced at her. 'What you making?'

'An infusion of these herbs,' Non said. 'That's my job while I'm on the drove, looking after folk who fall sick. Well, that's the easy part of it.'

'I'm Mrs Deacon, owner of this establishment.' The woman stopped kneading and put a clean cloth over the dough. She placed it on the hearth near the fire, and then sank into a chair, her floury hands held out before her. 'And you're Manon Jenkins. I've heard a lot about you.'

211

Non looked at her in surprise. 'Have you?'

'I have indeed. You're supposed to be looking after Miss Georgina Jones, but I hear you've been a bad girl.'

Non's fingers were still. The greenness of the herbs was staining her skin and she stared at her hands in silence for a moment. Would everyone know of her sins? 'Well, you've probably heard the gossip from Miss Georgina's own lips, then.' Her voice was tinged with bitterness.

Mrs Deacon didn't reply directly. 'News we're short of round here, we rely on the drovers to tell us what's going on in the big world outside.'

Non continued shredding the leaves and roots. She couldn't think of anything to say in her own defence. She'd slept with the boss man, and in the eyes of everyone she was a fallen woman. It was strange how something as wonderful as the love she'd shared with Caradoc could make her feel so cheap.

'It's none of my business and I'm not one to pass judgement, but you're the daughter of a parson, by all accounts, and you should know better, if you don't mind me saying.' She paused. 'Now how about a nice drink of cool apple water?'

Non suddenly felt like crying. 'Please,' she nodded her head. 'I'll soak my herbs in the apple water and try them out, they're supposed to lighten the spirits.'

Mrs Deacon poured the drink into pewter mugs and handed one to Non. 'They must be good,' she nodded in the direction of the herbs, 'if you take them yourself.'

'Herbs are powerful medicine,' Non said. 'They can cure most ills.'

Mrs Deacon sat down. 'Can they cure my bad veins, then, Miss?'

'I can recommend bistort, or snakeweed. Taken in a little wine, it has proved good for disorders of the blood.'

Mrs Deacon nodded. 'You got some of that, then?'

'I've got some in my box. I'll go out and get a bottle for you, if you like.'

'That's very good of you. I'll get some wine by the time you come back.'

Non's box was in the supply wagon, which was hitched up outside the inn. She climbed into the well of the cart and rummaged in her box. Above her the sky was darkening, and the clouds were beginning to race. Non hoped it wouldn't rain. She didn't want the weather holding up the drove tomorrow; all she wanted now was to get to London, to try to make her living there far away from any contact with Caradoc Jones.

Mrs Deacon was waiting for her when she returned to the cheerful warmth of the kitchen. 'Have you got the medicine for me?'

Non held up the bottle. 'Pour some of it into the wine to sweeten it, the herbs can be somewhat bitter.'

The two women sat in silence for a moment, and as Mrs Deacon drank the medicine, she made a wry face. 'Well, this stuff tastes so bad it should cure the veins of a dray horse!' She grimaced as she put down her mug. 'Now, Miss, it's none of my business, but I'm an outsider and I might be able to see things more clearly than you.' She hesitated. 'What makes a fine young woman like you fall in love with a man who takes liberties?'

Non sighed deeply. 'I've been very foolish,' she said. 'I thought he meant to marry me.'

'Ah, well, that's one of the oldest tricks known to mankind.' Mrs Deacon shook her head. 'Why do women believe men when they're lying through their naughty little teeth? Don't you know that a man will say anything if it lets him get his hand on your chastity?'

Non nodded. 'I know that now. Pity I didn't realize before I let him . . .' She shrugged. 'Well, you know.'

'Aye, I know.' Mrs Deacon sniffed. 'Never did it myself, mind. Never trusted any man long enough to let him under my petticoats.'

'So you're not Mrs Deacon, then?'

'I'm not, but don't you go telling anybody that, do you hear? They all thinks I'm a widow woman, respectable an' all that. It don't do to let the men get too free in the bar. I won't even have spittin' and bad language, that's my rules, and any man who don't obey them get's chucked out.'

Non didn't need to ask who did the chucking. She could see by the strength of Mrs Deacon's arms that she'd have no problems dealing with awkward customers.

'Right,' Non said softly, 'I'd better go and see to my things now. What room am I to have, Mrs Deacon?'

Mrs Deacon smiled slyly. 'I was giving you the small back room, but when you was out there I switched you round with the hoity toity Miss Georgina, who's done nothing but complain since she arrived. I could wring her neck.' She made a twisting movement with her big hands, and Non smiled wryly.

'I don't think you're on your own there, Mrs Deacon.'

'Well, anyway, you got the big front bedroom, looks out over the hills and fields, and the bed is fit for a king. Come on, I'll show you myself. The girls who help me out here are all busy in the bar serving my good beer to the drovers.'

Her heavy feet plodded up the stairs and each board creaked as she trod on it with her considerable weight. 'Hey, I think that medicine is working—my veins feel better already.'

The room was comfortable, the big front window framing the view of the green and yellow patchwork of fields. The skies seemed clearer too, so with any luck, first thing in the morning, the drove could make straight for Aylesbury.

'This is lovely,' Non said. 'Thank you, Mrs Deacon, I'll be very comfortable here.'

'I should think so.' She turned back towards the landing. 'Now, you shall have a bit of supper when it's ready and don't forget my advice. You just leave those sinful lusts to the gentry, they got the money to pay for their mistakes.'

As she spoke, Morgan was standing in the narrow passage waiting to pass. He looked inside the room, saw Non and held her gaze. He didn't speak, he didn't need to: the pain in his eyes told her he knew all the sordid details of her liaison with Caradoc. Non hung her head. She was an outcast, a loose woman, and now everyone on the drove knew the truth she would never live it down. With her reputation in shreds, she would never be able to return to Swansea. She would have to make her home in London, whether she liked it or not.

# CHAPTER TWENTY

The rest of the trip through Aylesbury and onward to Tring seemed to pass in a haze, and Non felt so much of an outcast that she scarcely lifted her head to look up at the clear skies and the soft green fields of England. She sometimes heard the women giggling behind her back as they walked and a feeling of deep shame would fill her. She had been foolish and sinful, lying with a man who wasn't her husband, and now she was reaping her just rewards.

Caradoc seemed set on avoiding her. He'd scarcely spoken a word to her lately, and for her part, she had nothing to say to him. The thought made Non thoroughly miserable. Even Morgan turned away whenever he saw her, and Non prayed the drove would reach London quickly, for there she could make a new start for herself. Alone.

Mary, loyal, faithful Mary, was staying behind for a day or two at Tring, and Non missed her loyal cheerfulness. Mary and the rest of the women were employed weeding a big patch of land for one of the local farmers and would not catch up with the drove until they reached Barnet fair.

'Why don't you take some of your precious herbs?' Georgina's voice startled her out of her reverie and Non looked up.

'What?'

Georgina was for once walking instead of riding in her carriage like a princess. She was swinging her bonnet in her hand, and her hair was lifting in the breeze. She could be a pretty girl if it wasn't for the mocking twist of her lips.

'Surely your herbal remedies will cure anything, even the shame of being labelled a sinful woman?'

'Please,' Non didn't feel like a row with Georgina, 'I don't really want to talk about any of it.'

'Ah, well, you're the only one, then. The rest of the camp are enjoying your fall from grace and talking about it all the time. Fancy, a vicar's daughter becoming a plaything for a rich man, who'd have thought it?'

Non looked down at the muddy, well-trampled road beneath her feet. The sun was high and the smell of the animals was overpowering. Non wished herself anywhere other than walking the drovers' road to London.

'Cat got your tongue?' Georgina's spiteful voice was like a barb. 'Well, I did try to warn you about my dear brother, but being headstrong and silly, you chose not to listen to me, more fool you!'

'Just leave me alone, will you?' Non's voice was low. 'I know how silly I've been, I don't need you to rub it in.'

Georgina caught her arm and drew her to a halt. 'Did you really think my brother would marry you? Not even you could be that stupid.' She laughed, a light tinkling laugh. 'He's got his sights set on Elizabeth Pugh, a rich lady from Swansea, and I mean a *lady*, not some trollop of a girl like you.'

Non jerked her arm away. 'Will you stop taunting me?' she said, her voice rising. 'I know I was a fool to trust your brother, he's proved that to me without any help from you.'

'Oh, the little trollop is getting angry, is she?' Georgina made a wry face. 'Have I at last

217

convinced you how stupid you are?'

Non shook her head. 'Just leave me alone, is that too much to ask?'

'But I can't leave you alone. You are my chaperone, or have you forgotten?'

'You are a vixen, you don't need a chaperone, any man would run a mile away from your spiteful tongue. You may look sweet and pretty from the outside, but you're bitter and twisted and you're incapable of being nice to anyone.'

'How dare you speak to me like that?'

'You don't like the truth?' Non stared angrily at Georgina. 'Well, you're quick enough to hand out advice, so let me give you some. Try a little kindness to people once in a while: it may surprise you how easy it is to praise rather than criticize all the time. Then some man might even fall in love with you.'

Georgina lifted her hand, and it came down hard across Non's face. Non reacted quickly, pushing Georgina away with all her strength. Georgina, taken by surprise, staggered and fell to her knees in the mud and muck of the road. She looked down in horror at her ruined skirts, then lifted them up with her fingertips, an expression of distaste on her face. Slowly, she got to her feet and glared at Non. 'You won't get away with this, you stupid whore!' She walked away, climbing the grassy bank at the side of the road, skirting the slowly moving herd of cattle. No doubt she was anxious to find her brother and tell him what Non had done to her.

Non's shoulders drooped. It seemed she could do nothing right. The trip she had embarked on with such high hopes had turned into a disaster. She tried to remember how it had felt to be in

Caradoc's arms, to be sure of his love, but all she could hear was his denial of her, destroying her dreams in one moment of truthfulness, making it plain he'd never intended to marry her.

She didn't look up when she heard the sound of horse's hooves thudding along the verge of the roadway. She knew with a sinking of her heart that Caradoc had come to remonstrate with her.

He reined in his animal and slid from the saddle. 'Non,' he said, his voice hard, 'why do you have to cause trouble?'

She lifted her head and stared at him, trying to be angry, but all she could see was the sweetness of his mouth, the clearness of his blue eyes and the noble way he carried himself.

'I didn't want to quarrel with your sister,' she said quietly. 'But she goaded me, telling me how stupid I was to believe you would ever want to marry me.'

'Look, Non,' he put his hand on her arm, but she pulled away from him. 'I'm sorry, I wasn't thinking straight, I should never have allowed things to go so far.'

'And I should have known better than to believe you loved me,' Non said softly. She held back her tears, not wanting him to see how much she cared. 'I've learned a valuable lesson: never believe any man when he says he loves you, when all he means to do is get into your bed.'

Caradoc frowned. 'I do love you, Non. But I have obligations. I'm not free to make such choices. All I can say is I'm sorry if I hurt you.'

Non turned away from him, unable to bear the pleading look in his eyes. If she softened now, he would lie her down in the grass and make love to

219

her as if nothing mattered but possessing her.

'Well, once we get to London I'll be out of your way,' she said. 'I intend to make a good life there as a herbalist, so you needn't worry your head about me.'

'Non . . .' He tried to touch her cheek, but she moved away from him.

'No!' she said. 'You've made it clear where we both stand. You don't want marriage and I do. We both made a mistake, let's leave it at that. Now I've got work to do, I need to replenish my stock of herbs.' She glanced up at him. 'That's if I still have a job with the Jones's cattle drove.'

'Of course you have a job. I wouldn't leave you in the middle of nowhere alone. But one word of advice—just keep out of Georgina's way. She told me how you attacked her, and all of this has nothing to do with her, it's between you and me.'

Non shook her head, not bothering to explain to him what had really happened. The Joneses would stick together, come hell or high water.

She watched him ride away, so straight, so tall and so unobtainable, and tears came tumbling down her cheeks. 'Oh, Caradoc,' she murmured, 'how could you treat me like this?'

By the time she'd cried herself out, the herd had moved out of sight round a bend in the road. She began to walk; she was tired and heavy hearted, but somehow she must summon enough strength to follow the drove until they reached London.

\*　　\*　　\*

Caradoc was tempted to glance back, but he knew Non would be crying and how could he resist her

220

then? He loved her, he admitted that much to himself. But as his sister pointed out, Non did not have the makings of a mistress of a big establishment.

He hated facing her, hated himself for playing her false. He should never have given in to the temptation of sleeping with her. She was not a sophisticated society widow, like the mistresses he'd had back home. She was a green, innocent girl and he'd taken her chastity away from her.

He rode to the head of the herd and spoke briefly to one of the men. 'Bevan, prepare me a fresh horse, and one for my sister. I'll ride to the next inn and book us accommodation for the night. When I'm gone I want you to keep your eye on Manon Jenkins for me. She's the only woman on the drove right now, and I don't want any harm coming to her, do you understand?'

The man nodded and, satisfied, Caradoc fell back, waiting for his sister to catch him up. As soon as she set eyes on him, Georgina began to cry.

'I hope you've sent that hussy packing!' she said. 'I don't know why we had to bring the dreadful creature with us in the first place.'

Caradoc didn't reply. He took the reins of the fresh horses from Bevan and indicated that the man help Georgina into the saddle. She grumbled constantly about her ruined skirts, and at last Caradoc turned to look at her.

'Will you just be quiet?' He spoke sharply. 'I've had enough of your carping on about how bad things are on the road. You're thoroughly spoilt. You should know a bit of cattle manure is unavoidable on a trip like this.'

'I didn't expect to be pushed into the mire,

221

though, did I?' Georgina sounded pettish. 'And you haven't answered my question. Did you send the girl home or not?'

'How could I send her home?' Caradoc was exasperated by his sister's endless whining. 'I couldn't spare a man to go with her. I've already allowed Thomas to go back to Five Saints with Flora, all because of your interference in affairs that don't concern you. I can't afford to be another man short, and I certainly couldn't leave the girl alone in the middle of nowhere, could I?'

Georgina sighed heavily. 'You're so blind, Caradoc. Can't you see that Manon Jenkins set her cap at you long before we came on the drove. She's a wicked scheming hussy.' She lifted her stained skirts and grimaced. 'See this gown? It's ruined! All because of that witch's spitefulness.'

Caradoc shook his head. 'It's not like Non to use violence.'

'You don't see her the way I do,' Georgina said. 'You only see a pretty face and a willing bedfellow. She's spiteful and evil, and for all we know she's in league with the devil.'

'Now you're being silly.'

'Am I, Caradoc? Well how does she cure folk of their sickness? She grinds roots and things in that special bowl of hers and all the time she's doing it she's murmuring to herself. I don't trust her, Caradoc. I think you should leave her behind at this next halt.'

'Just be quiet, Georgina.' His voice held a warning that even Georgina could not ignore. 'I've been a master drover for a few years now, and I don't need any help from anyone, certainly you.'

Caradoc was relieved when he saw the chimneys

of the Welsh Road Inn come into view. Smoke rose like fingers of grey mist against the blue sky, and as he drew nearer he saw the door standing open, and the welcoming smell of roast beef carried towards him on the fine air.

'Well, this place looks halfway decent,' Georgina said. 'At least the windows are cleaned and the step's been scrubbed. Perhaps I can look forward to a comfortable bed tonight, for a change.'

Caradoc didn't reply. He drew the horses to a halt and a boy came running out to take the reins.

'Give the animals a good rub down and there'll be sixpence in it for you,' he said as he slid from the saddle. He turned to Georgina and lifted her down onto the forecourt of the inn.

The landlord's plump wife came to greet them, exclaiming as she saw Georgina's mire-stained gown. 'Oh, you've had a fall, poor dear! Let me take you to your room. I'll get the maid to bring some hot water to you straight away.'

Georgina stood looking at the woman for a moment. 'It wasn't a fall,' she said. 'A wicked evil woman deliberately pushed me into a cowpat.'

Carodoc couldn't conceal his amusement. 'Don't listen to her, Mrs Moon,' he said. 'My dear sister didn't fall into a cowpat, as she so quaintly put it, she fell into a whole heap of cow dung.'

He left Georgina fuming and strode into the tap room. The first thing he wanted was a good drink of beer, and then he would be free of women and glad of the company of some of the local men.

\*       \*       \*

Non felt ill at ease as she walked alone along the

road. She had fallen behind the herd as she stopped to pick some gilliflowers for making into a cordial. Far in front of her, she could see the dust from the hooves of the animals as they picked up pace, sensing that soon they would be allowed to graze and rest.

She paused as she saw a figure riding towards her, and as he drew nearer, she breathed a sigh of relief as she recognized the strong features and broad shoulders.

'Morgan, it's good to see you.'

'I've come back for you,' he said. 'I don't like the idea of you walking alone, especially as it's getting dark.'

He slipped from the horse and stood beside her, hardly able to meet her eyes. She could see by his expression that her fall from grace had hurt him very badly.

'Morgan, try not to judge me too harshly.' She put her hand on his arm. 'We've always been good friends, surely that hasn't changed?'

'I saw you more as a wife than a friend,' Morgan said. 'I wanted to marry you, make an honest woman of you.' His tone grew sharper. 'How could you do it, Non? How could you give away your chastity so lightly, and to a man who takes women as easily as you pick these?' He gestured towards the gilliflowers. 'I cared so deeply about you, Non, so very deeply.'

'I know.' Non was close to tears. 'And I'm sorry I've hurt you, but I fell in love with him, that's the way it is.'

'And does he love you?'

'I think he does.'

'But will he marry you, make an honest woman

of you?'

She looked down at the ground, knowing that Caradoc had no intention of marrying her. 'No, he won't marry me, he's told me that in no uncertain terms.' She felt tears burn her eyes. 'I didn't know that, not at first, and since I found out the truth, I've not lain with him.'

Morgan was quiet, and the air was so still that the only sound was the clip-clop of the horse's hooves against the road. Morgan looked straight ahead, his face grim, and Non touched his arm.

'Please, Morgan, speak to me. We can still be friends, can't we?'

He took a long time to answer. 'I can try to think of you as a friend, but it will be difficult, Non, very difficult.'

Non suddenly felt weary. 'I've made some stupid mistakes in my life and I know I'm guilty of a great many things, but I can't regret loving Caradoc.' She spoke in a low voice. She saw Morgan wince, and she felt like throwing her arms around him and holding him to her breast as though he was a child, not a grown man. 'I'm sorry about one thing, though. Very sorry,' she said. 'I'll always regret hurting you. I never meant to, please believe me.'

Morgan didn't reply, and Non was glad when she saw the sprawling grey walls and the smoking chimneys of the Welsh Road Inn in the distance.

By the time Non and Morgan reached the door of the inn, the animals had been put into the fields to graze. Caradoc would pay the farmer for the grass the beasts ate, and the accommodation for himself and his sister as well as for Non. It would cost extra for the men to stay in nearby outhouses, but Caradoc Jones was known for the care he took

225

of his drovers.

At the door of the inn, Morgan paused. 'I'll say goodnight to you, Non.' He didn't look at her. 'And I'll try, I'll really try to be a friend to you.'

She watched as he walked his horse around to the stables, and then, when she was alone in the gathering dark, she let her tears fall. What a mess she'd made of her life. She squared her shoulders. Well, she would learn from her mistakes, she would be a success and prove to the world that Manon Jenkins was a woman to be reckoned with.

## CHAPTER TWENTY-ONE

It was a fine sunny day; the sky was cloudless, with little wind, and Non took off her bonnet, lifting her hair between her fingers and wishing she was anywhere but at Barnet fair. She felt like an outcast now that hardly anyone was speaking to her.

'Why don't you smile now and then? I'm getting tired of that long face.' Mary rubbed her hands, which were stained green from all the weeding she'd done over the past days. 'Cheer up, I'll see you enjoy the fair. You'll be able to buy some new ribbons for your hair, or even have your fortune told.'

Non glanced at her. She was glad Mary was back from the weeding, but her heart was still heavy when she thought of the way Caradoc had treated her. 'What fortune?' she said dryly.

'I'd never have thought it of you.' Mary's voice was stern.

'Never thought what of me?'

'Never thought you was one for self-pity.'

'Well, I've got nothing to be cheerful about, have I?' Non said flatly. 'No one is speaking to me, except you. All the other girls talk about my foolishness in falling in love with the boss.'

'And don't you think they might just be right? Any of us could have told you about Caradoc Jones; he's a good boss, but a bad man when it comes to the women. If you hadn't been so innocent, brought up nicely like you was, you'd have seen through his charm right away.'

Non digested this in silence. Mary was right, but that didn't make things any easier. Since their affair had been discovered, he'd been distant, and in spite of that she still wanted him. Wanted his arms around her, his hot passionate mouth on hers. She shivered.

'Walked over someone's grave, have you?' Mary asked. 'You're shivering like it's cold winter, not beautiful summer.'

Non didn't reply. There was nothing to say that she hadn't said a million times before.

'All right,' Mary said, 'I won't keep harping on about the mistakes you've made, but I would like to know what you're going to do when we reach London. It's only a few miles away now, mind.'

Non lifted her head. 'I'll stay there, find work. I'll have my own shop before too long, you'll see.'

'Fine words don't make for a fine dinner,' Mary said. 'London is a tough place. You haven't been there before, and I have.'

Non turned to look at her. 'What's it really like, Mary?'

'It's big and noisy and there's more people than you've seen in your whole life.' She paused. 'But then, a good little herbalist like you shouldn't do too badly, providing you get a lucky start.'

Non made a wry face. She wouldn't need luck, she'd need to work hard. She'd have her pay from Caradoc, and perhaps it would be enough to rent a room with a nice big front window.

'Anyway, let's get a move on,' Mary said. 'I can hear someone playing a fiddle, it makes your feet want to tap. Look, there's a cart with pots and pans hanging on it, and a ribbon stand. See there, a fortune-teller! I told you, didn't I?'

The noise of the crowd was deafening. Mary spoke again, but Non could only see her lips move, she couldn't hear any of the words. The cattle installed in the nearby fields eating the verdant grass added an occasional angry bellow to the cacophony of sound. Non put her hands over her ears. 'I've never heard anything like it!' she shouted.

Mary pulled her arm and spoke into her ear. 'I'm going to have my fortune told, are you coming?' She winked. 'You never know, there might be a young man in the offing for me.'

Non smiled. 'I thought you didn't need a man to make you happy.'

'Well, a girl can change her mind, can't she?'

A woman with long hair tied in ribbons came to the flap of the tent and beckoned to Mary.

Mary's eyes gleamed. 'Are you Madam Zeta?'

The woman nodded and Mary followed her inside the tent, stopping only to wink saucily at Non.

Non moved away. She didn't want anyone meddling in her fortune. Father had said often enough that such people were wicked, that it was sinful to probe into the unknown. She threaded her way through the throng, conscious of the smell of toffee apples, and her spirits lightened. It was time to forget her problems and enjoy herself, if only for a short time.

She stopped at a tent with a small stage set up in front of it. A very tall man in a bright coat was talking to the crowd, but Non had difficulty understanding him. With a sweep of his arm he stood to one side, and then the smallest woman Non had ever seen stepped onto the stage.

She was no more than two feet high and yet she was perfectly formed, with swelling breasts and a tiny waist. She had pink rouge on her cheeks and mouth and her hair was light silver, as if it had been bathed in moonlight.

Non paused, enchanted as the woman began to sing. Her voice was thin, like a child's, but sweet and high. When her song was finished, people clapped and some threw money, and Non was suddenly aware that she had no money to throw. Surely Caradoc would have given the women some of their wages to spend at the fair? If so, he'd left her out deliberately. Was he purposely trying to humiliate her?

She felt her arm jogged and she turned to see a small boy with a scarf tied around his head standing close to her. He swore and frowned at her.

'There's nothing in your pockets but bleedin' fresh air,' he said in disgust.

Non surprised herself by laughing. 'You've probably got more money than I have. I can't even buy myself a pretty ribbon.'

He looked surprised; he stood back from her and eyed her from head to toe. She knew her clothes were dusty and her bonnet faded by the sun, and smiled. 'You see? I'm no richer than you.' She held out her hand. 'I'm Non Jenkins, who are you?'

He grimaced. 'I'm just Albie. What's your favourite colour, Miss?'

'Well, Albie, let me see. Blue, I think.'

'Right you are.' He disappeared into the crowd and Non shook her head, not knowing what to make of the strange people who populated Barnet fair. She was just about to move away from the stage when she felt a tug on her arm. 'Here, Miss, something for you.' Albie was looking up at her, his dirty face alight with pleasure. He pushed a shining blue ribbon into her hand and grinned, revealing surprisingly white teeth.

'You haven't stolen it, have you, Albie?'

'No, Miss!' He looked indignant. 'I paid for it with money I got from some rich gent this morning.'

'Well, thank you kindly, Albie.' Non pushed her bonnet back onto her shoulders and tied the blue ribbon in her hair. 'There, Albie, do I look pretty now?'

He rubbed his naked feet in the dust. 'You are pretty as the sunshine, Miss.'

'And you're a poet, Albie. Do you live here, in Barnet?'

He spat on the ground. 'Not me, I live in the best place on earth.'

'And where's that?'

'London town, Miss.'

'I'm impressed,' Non smiled. 'I'm making for London myself, I might even see you there.'

'You might, Miss, but London's a big place. Still,

I'll look out for you.'

Non held her hand out to him. 'Thank you for the ribbon, Albie. I hope I'll see you again one day.'

He looked at her hand and then, slowly, he curled his grubby fingers in hers. 'You're a real lady, Miss, even if you do talk funny.'

Non laughed. '*I* talk funny? You should listen to yourself!'

She was still laughing when Albie let her hand go and touched his cap, before disappearing into the crowd.

Non looked round for Mary, but there was no sign of her. It was getting hot and she needed a drink. She stood on tiptoe, trying to see over the heads of the crowd, looking for a stall where she might buy some cordial. Then she remembered she had no money.

On the edge of the fair, she stopped and sank onto the grassy bank. Her boots were covered in dust and so was the hem of her skirt. She wondered if she smelt of cattle; she'd got so used to being around the beasts that she no longer noticed the smell herself.

'What's a pretty girl like you doing sitting here alone?' The voice was deep and the accent strange. Non scrambled to her feet to face a young man who was doffing his hat to her.

She brushed down her skirts self-consciously. 'I'm not alone,' she said defensively. 'I'm with friends, but we seem to have missed each other in the crowd.'

'Oh, you're a girl from the country, aren't you?' he said. 'Never seen anything like Barnet fair, I'll wager.'

Non looked round, hoping to catch sight of someone from the drove. 'No, it's very impressive,' she said. 'But if you'll excuse me, I'll go and look for my friends.'

He put out his arm so that she couldn't pass. 'Don't run away, it's a shame to see a little lady like you on your own. I'll look after you.'

'No, really,' Non said firmly, 'I've got to go.' She caught sight of Morgan and waved to him. 'Look, there's my friend now. Morgan!' She waved again and this time he saw her. He pushed his way through the crowd, his eyes hostile as they rested on the young man.

'Are you bothering my young lady?' His shoulders were hunched and his fists clenched, and the young man hurriedly backed away.

'I was just offering my help, that's all. Sorry if I've given offence.'

Morgan caught Non's arm. 'Haven't you the good sense to stay with the womenfolk?' He sounded angry. 'This place can be dangerous, there are cut-throats and pickpockets everywhere.'

'I came with Mary,' Non said. 'None of the other women are talking to me. Come to think of it, this is the first time *you've* spoken to me in ages.' She smiled up at him. 'But now we seem to be friends again, could you do me a favour and buy me a cold drink?'

He took her arm and guided her through the press of people, leading her expertly towards a small public house on the perimeter of the fairground.

'I expect you'll find the other women in here. They usually go into the small back room reserved for the ladies when they've had enough of the fair.'

He was right; the first person Non saw was Mary. 'Go talk to her while I get us something to drink,' Morgan said.

'*Duw*, where have you been, girl?' Mary said. 'I've been searching for you all over.'

'I can see that.' Non spoke dryly: Mary had a full tankard of beer clutched in her hand. 'Did Madam Zeta give you any good news?'

Mary shook her head. '*I* could tell fortunes better than that woman!' she said scathingly. 'Told me I had four children and another on the way. *I* told *her* that would be a miracle, since I had no man. You should have seen her face! And then she had the cheek to tell me that a woman my age should be married with a clutch of children! A woman "my age", and her older than me by at least ten years.'

'Never mind,' Non said. 'I suppose you refused to pay her, did you?'

'Oh, no!' Mary was shocked. 'I couldn't do that, she might put a spell on me or something.'

Non hid a smile. 'I expect you're right, it doesn't do to owe anyone anything.'

Just then Morgan came back, holding a cup of strawberry cordial for her, and Non drank thirstily.

'I'll go into the bar with the men,' he said. 'I can't sit with a clutch of women.'

'All right, see you later—and thank you, Morgan.' She watched his broad frame as he walked away, and wished again that she could fall in love with him. He was such a good, fine man.

'Don't know when you're well off, you don't,' Mary said. 'As I've told you many times, you should jump at the chance of a man like that.'

Non pretended she hadn't heard, and looked

round curiously. The public house was small and cramped, and looked as if at one time it had been an ordinary dwelling house. The room she was in had dark beams across the smoke-blackened ceiling, and sand grated underneath her boots.

'Nice in here, isn't it?' Mary changed tactics. 'Just the place to rest, out of the sun and the noise and the stink of the fair. Good of Morgan to bring you here, wasn't it?'

'Aye, it was.' Non was determined not to be drawn into a discussion about Morgan's virtues. 'Did you know Mr Jones hasn't given me any money?'

'Well, that's not unusual, we don't get paid properly until we deliver the cattle to Smithfield. Still, when we get as far as Barnet the boss gives us a little in hand to be going on with.' She paused and looked warily at Non. 'I 'spect he was too shamed to give you any money. Might look funny, as if he was paying you for . . . well, you know.'

Non felt the heat rise in her face. 'Are you saying he thinks I'm a whore, then?'

'No, no, course not!' Mary was flustered. 'But it was awkward for him, can't you see that?'

'No, I can't!' Non put down her cup and squared her shoulders. 'Where is Mr Jones now?'

'Why, he's back at the fair seeing to the sale of the ponies, I think. Why?'

Non shook her head. 'I'm going to see him. He should have paid me as well as the rest of you. How did he expect me to manage without money?'

'I wouldn't go over the fair now, it's man's work selling animals and Mr Jones won't like being disturbed.'

'That's just too bad, then, isn't it?'

Non left the public house and made her way back to the fairground, her heart thumping, her mind seething with angry questions. If Caradoc meant to hurt and embarrass her, he'd succeeded. She fought back the tears; she wouldn't give him the satisfaction of seeing her crying.

By the time Non found the field where the ponies were kept, the sale was over. Caradoc came towards her, head down, shoulders hunched, his hands thrust into his pockets.

'Good afternoon, Mr Jones.' There was more than a hint of sarcasm in Non's voice.

Caradoc looked up, surprised to see her, and half smiled. 'Non, what are you doing here? Why aren't you in the inn with the rest of the girls?'

Non stared at him. His eyes avoided hers; he was glancing around as though afraid she would cause a scene when there were so many people around.

'One simple reason.' Non felt as though she was going to burst into tears. Here he was, the man who'd told her he loved her, treating her like a common street girl. 'I didn't have any money.'

He put his hand on her shoulder and then removed it quickly, as though the heat of her skin burnt him. 'I'm sorry about that, I didn't think.'

'No, you were too busy avoiding me.' Non spoke bitterly. 'You've had your bit of fun with a foolish virgin girl and now you don't want to even know me. Well, don't worry, I'll be off your hands once we get to London.'

'Non!' He looked down at her, meeting her eye for the first time. 'It's impossible for us to be together, can't you see that?'

'What a pity you didn't think of that before crawling into my bed!'

235

She turned away from him and started to run. Where she was going she didn't know or care, she just wanted to put as much distance between them as possible. He didn't come after her as she'd half hoped he would. At last, when she stopped running, she leaned against the cool bole of a tree and, closing her eyes, tried to picture his face as he'd made love to her. It was a memory she would cling on to, for he would never be allowed to touch her ever again.

## CHAPTER TWENTY-TWO

The night sky was full of stars, and Non stood in the window of the small back bedroom in the Barnet Inn, holding the curtains aside. From downstairs came the sound of men talking loudly, laughing, having a good time. Caradoc was there among them. He would have forgotten all about her, why should he remember? She was only another foolish woman who'd given in to his charms.

The cattle had rested and had eaten the rich grass, for which Caradoc would pay before they left the finishing fields. And when they got to London, she would never see Caradoc Jones again.

At last, she climbed into bed and pulled the blankets up under her chin. She felt utterly alone, as if the whole world had turned against her. She needed love and reassurance, but there was no one she could turn to for comfort.

And then she thought of Morgan. He still cared about her, but she couldn't go to him, he was too kind and good and she would only be using him. She tried to snuggle down and get some sleep. Tomorrow was the final leg of their journey; then she would see London in all its glory. But every time she closed her eyes, she pictured Caradoc, his smile as he took her in his arms, the tenderness with which he held her and made love to her.

How could he put all that aside for the sake of what he called 'a good marriage': marriage to some woman who was wealthy and respectable, who wouldn't lie with him without the security of a gold ring on her finger?

It was almost morning before she fell into a restless sleep, and when she woke she felt tired and downhearted. Not even the prospect of arriving at her destination could lift her spirits. Instead she was frightened when she thought of living in London alone.

Caradoc would find a place for them to stay for a few days. But then, when his business was concluded, he and the rest of the drovers would be making their way home.

Non ate only a little breakfast. Her stomach was churning as she imagined Caradoc casually leaving her behind and going home to Five Saints. A small flame of hope flickered in her heart: perhaps he'd try to persuade her to go with him. But as soon as the thought was born, it died. Caradoc had his own life, a life with no place in it for her. He'd made that clear.

It was a sunny day, but with a sharp wind that caught Non unawares as she stepped outside into the courtyard of the inn. The first person she saw was Georgina. For once she was smiling, and Non watched as Caradoc came into view and bent to kiss his sister's cheek.

'Well, Georgie, you'll soon be off my hands. Good old Aunt Prudence is welcome to you!' Although Non couldn't see his face, she knew Caradoc was smiling. However cross he was at times with his sister, his love for her was evident. The thought was like a barb in her heart. If only he loved *her* half as much, he would marry her whatever her station.

Georgina's lips stiffened in disapproval as she caught sight of Non. She turned and walked away swiftly, but not before Caradoc had seen the look on her face. He spun round.

'Morning, Non. We'll be on our way soon. Are you all ready to face the might of London town, then?' His expression was guarded, and his voice was falsely hearty. 'You'll see great sights in London, and you'll have a few days there before we return home. I'll make sure you have a comfortable room before I take Georgina off to my Aunt Prudence's house.'

'Thank you, Mr Jones.' Non didn't look at him.

'Non, look, I'm sorry—call it summer madness. I should have exercised more control, I don't know what to say to you.'

'You knew what to say when you wanted to possess me. You told me you loved me. Was that "summer madness" too, Caradoc, or was it downright lies?'

He sighed heavily and then shrugged. 'Dennis will be bringing the horses any minute now. I hope you're ready to go.'

'I'm ready.' Non spoke unsteadily, but if he noticed the quiver in her voice, Caradoc didn't say anything.

'It'll be an easier journey going home,' he said. 'Georgina won't be with us, so we'll have a chance to talk properly then.'

'I won't be going back home,' Non said quietly. 'I've decided to stay in London, find work as a herbalist.'

Caradoc shook his head. 'That's madness!'

'Why is it madness?' Non asked. 'I have to earn my living somewhere. It might as well be London.'

'But you won't know anyone there, you'll be alone. Why don't you come home with me and settle down in Swansea? There you might find yourself . . .' He stopped speaking abruptly.

'Find myself a husband?' Non shook her head. 'Who would want me now? I'm damaged goods, remember?'

'Oh, Non!' he said remorsefully. 'I'm sorry, so sorry.'

'It's a bit late to be sorry.' She turned away from him. 'Go on, the hands are waiting, the cattle has been rounded up, you're needed elsewhere.'

'We'll talk later, when we reach London,' he said.

'Perhaps. I'd better go and get my bag from my room. Goodbye, Caradoc.'

She fought back tears as she climbed up the rickety staircase to her bedroom. Inside, everything was tidy, the bed was remade and there was fresh water in the jug on the side table. The room was impersonal, as if no one had ever been there, breathed, slept, made love. It was just another room in another inn.

She took up her bag and made her way downstairs. Soon she would be starting a new life, and she must try to look to the future now and not the past.

*     *     *

'You're very quiet, Non.' Mary's knitting needles were clicking away and the stocking she was knitting was almost finished.

Non glanced at her and forced a smile. 'Well, our journey's almost over. Soon it'll be time for you to go back home, Mary.'

'I think you should come as well,' Mary said, without pausing a moment from her knitting. 'You don' want to be by yourself in London, believe me.'

Non didn't reply. She'd already had this conversation with Caradoc and she was tired of arguing. She pulled her shawl closer round her shoulders; the wind had a chill in it today, as if it heralded a bleak time ahead.

'Cold?' Mary asked. 'Never mind, it'll be warmer in London. The streets are so crowded, see?'

Non tried to imagine the scene. Would the streets of London be like Swansea on market day? She'd struggled through the traffic of milk carts and wagons pulled by huge dray horses every time she went to sell her remedies in the busy Swansea market.

'Morgan's gone back home, then,' Mary said quietly.

Non looked at her in surprise. 'Has he? I didn't know. He never said a word to me.'

'Can you blame the man, when all you've done is give him black looks and long silences?'

Non felt as though she'd been punched in the stomach. 'I wish he'd told me he was leaving. I'd have liked to have said my goodbyes to him.'

240

'Look, why don't you come back to Swansea with us? The journey home is always lovely—no stinking cows to think about, just soft nights under the stars and plenty of money in your pocket.'

'I've made up my mind,' Non said. 'I'm staying in London.'

'You might change your mind once you see the place,' Mary said.

Non shook her head. She couldn't go home where everyone would be talking about her.

It was as though Mary read her mind. 'Look, *merchi*, folk soon forget gossip. Even if it did get round that you and Mr Jones—well, you know— it'll soon be stale news.'

'It'll get round all right, the other women will see to that.'

'Maybe. But you're not like the other women he's had, you're special to him. I'm sure Mr Jones cares about you.'

'As much as he cares for the cattle he sells.' Non heard the bitterness in her voice and swallowed hard. 'How could he do it to me, Mary? He took my innocence and then made it plain he didn't want to marry me.'

Mary sighed. 'Who knows how the minds of the gentry work? They're different to you and me, they think they're a law unto themselves.'

Non rubbed her eyes with her fingers, and Mary, observant as ever, was watching her. She didn't say anything, but she put her knitting carefully in the pocket of her apron and linked arms with Non.

'Never mind men. We can do without them, can't we?'

'Looks as if we'll have to,' Non said dryly. She squeezed Mary's arm, grateful for her loyalty.

241

'You wait till we see London. We'll have a high old time there before we go home.'

'I'm not going home,' Non said. 'I mean it.'

'Well, we'll see what you make of the place first, is it? You might not like London, not to live in, mind.'

'I'll like it, Mary,' Non said. 'I'll make myself like it, because I'm not going back to Swansea ever again.'

Mary turned to look at her. 'Never is a long time, Non. Better say you don't know what you'll do in the future. In any case, haven't you got folks in Five Saints village? You could always go there.'

Non shook her head. Mary didn't know what village life was like. People lived so close to each other that even the slightest hint of scandal was carried from house to house in no time. But Mary was right about one thing: Non couldn't foresee what the future would hold. Perhaps she would make her fortune in London, and then she could return home a rich woman. On the other hand, perhaps that was a dream that would never come to fruition.

\*          \*          \*

Morgan loaded his tools into his leather bag and left the room in the inn without looking back. He was leaving more than the drove; he was leaving his dreams behind, his dreams of taking Non home as his bride.

Anger bit deep into his soul. How could she give herself to Caradoc Jones, a man who had no intention of making an honest woman of her? It had been torture to ride as far as Barnet with

Caradoc, when all he wanted to do was put his fist in the man's face.

Soon the cattle would be sold. Caradoc Jones would take a rich purse with him when he returned to Wales. And no doubt there he'd make a fine marriage and enhance his fortune even more. The man had the luck of the very devil.

Morgan thought achingly of Non; with her face pale, her eyes shadowed by dark circles, her suffering was apparent to anyone who cared to look. Even now, he would take her for his wife if she would have him. But she would never know that, he'd never tell her. Still, she would return home to Swansea some time; perhaps when she'd had her fill of London, realized that the streets there were as dirty as any other streets and that not one of them was paved with gold, the way the storytellers had it.

Morgan collected his horse from the stables behind the Barnet Inn and, slipping his foot into the stirrup, he swung himself into the saddle, and set off at a steady pace back along the trail towards home.

\*　　　\*　　　\*

Non felt weary. Her eyes ached, her back ached, and all she wanted to do was to fall down in the soft grass and fall asleep.

'How far is London now, Mary?' she asked.

'*Duw, merchi*, we've only walked about two miles, there's another ten to go yet.'

Non looked ahead of her at the fields of rich grass and the road running between them like a ribbon. The cattle were far ahead; all she could see

243

of the drove was the small patch of dust thrown up by many hooves. Occasionally, she would hear the distant sound of a drover's call, carried to her on the breeze.

'I'm going to miss you, Non,' Mary said, 'and I'll be worried about you.' She laughed. 'Oh dear, hark at me—I'm getting to sound as posh as you.'

'You speak very nicely, Mary,' Non said. 'You have a lovely soft voice.'

'Now you're teasing me!' Mary replied. 'But I don't mind. It's been a real treat being your friend, Non. Are you sure you won't come home to Swansea with me? We could set up in business together—I could sell my knitted wares and you your remedies. How about it?'

'I'm staying in London,' Non said. 'You are welcome to stay with me, Mary. We could find lodgings together.'

'No fear! I wouldn't stay in London for all the tea in China. It's a place you got to be born to. A rich place, mind, and the people are friendly enough, but . . . no, I couldn't live there.'

'Why? What's wrong with it?'

'Nothing wrong, but like I said, you have to be born to it. Now no more questions, you just wait and see for yourself.'

Non shrugged. 'All right, I will, but I don't know why you're being so mysterious.'

'Not mysterious, just cautious. I'm not going to be the one who puts you off a life in London, you must decide that for yourself when you gets there.'

'Get there,' Non said.

'What?'

'You said "gets there" and you should be saying "get there"—that's if you want to speak correctly.'

'Didn't say I wanted to speak correctly.' Mary's face was suddenly wreathed in smiles as she copied Non's accent. 'But you know what, Non? You could always find a place as a governess, you're so good at all that teaching sort of thing.'

'Well thank you, Mary, but my heart's set on being a herbalist.'

'Well, you're good at that too,' Mary conceded. 'You cured my foot ache good and proper. But come on now, we're falling too far behind the herd. We don't want to be attacked by footpads, do we?'

Non forced herself to walk a little faster. Somehow she was reluctant, after all, to reach London. There she would be saying goodbye to all she knew, and starting life afresh without Mary's friendship. And, she thought dismally, without seeing Caradoc ever again.

It seemed a long time until they caught up with the herd. The constant bellowing of the animals and the calls of the men as they kept the drove in order were so familiar to her now. Suddenly, Non was on the point of tears. She was afraid of what lay ahead, a life alone in a strange town.

'Only about five miles to go now,' Mary said. 'Up ahead there's the carriage with Miss Georgina in. She'll have an easy life in London, I'll bet a penny.'

Non could see Caradoc talking to his sister. They were rich and cultured and one as selfish as the other. She would be better off without them, she told herself. But somehow, she didn't quite believe it.

# CHAPTER TWENTY-THREE

London was a place of noise and movement, where the crowds seemed to be like a restless sea, constantly changing. As Non walked down St John Street and into the huge area that was Smithfield market, she heard strange-sounding voices calling out the price of beef on the hoof. Groups of men haggled over the prices of the beasts; the merits of the black runt from Wales against the larger-built stock from the fields of England caused heated debates. It was a chaotic, exciting place, and Non's spirits rose.

Non had spent the night in a clean, rather splendid room in a house in Bartholomew Close, and even there, the rattle of the carriage wheels, the calls of the lamplighters and the evil smell of the city had overwhelmed her. But Caradoc was taking care of her; he'd made sure she was safe and comfortable.

She stood on tiptoe and searched the crowd for a sight of him. He'd told her in no uncertain terms to stay in her lodgings, but she was too restless to sit idly by while the whole panoply of London was just outside her window. She looked round at the huge crowds and sighed in despair. It would be almost impossible to find anyone in this melee. She saw a drover prod a beast into a pen that was already overcrowded with animals. The animal bellowed and was beaten for its pains.

Averting her eyes, Non skirted the pens and began to search in earnest for Caradoc; what he'd still failed to do was give her the wages she was due. He didn't seem to realize that she was penniless. Once she'd received her money, she would start to make a new life for herself, find a reasonably priced building to rent, begin her career as a herbalist. And forget Caradoc Jones ever existed.

As she walked, her boots sank ankle deep in the mire dropped by the animals; she held her shawl over her mouth and tasted the damp misty air that hung like a pall over the place. Would she ever come to love London? Would she be able to make a living here? These were questions to which she had no answer.

'Hey there, Non, I've been looking for you everywhere. But I must say, this is the last place I expected to find you. Didn't Mr Jones tell you that women seldom come here when it's market day.'

'Mary, thank goodness!' Non clutched her friend's arm. 'And yes, Caradoc told me to stay indoors, but he's not my keeper, he can't boss me around, not now the drove is over.'

She pointed to a pen where sheep were herded so close together the creatures must have found it difficult to breathe. 'Is it always like this at Smithfield, so noisy and dark? Surely the sun shines some of the time.'

'Well, of course it does. Today there's a "London Particular" come down, but don't worry, the fog will soon lift. This is only one part of London, remember. There's a lot to see of the town, it's pretty marvellous, but I think you'll find that out for yourself.'

'But it's dirty and smelly and there are so many people!'

Mary shook her head. 'You must be patient.

247

Given time, you'll find it's really a magical place, a place where you see things never seen before. You wait until St Bartholomew's fair, that'll open your eyes—it's even better than the fair at Barnet.' She took a deep breath and rushed on. 'And then, when you go to Covent Garden you'll think you're in heaven; the flowers, the herbs, the beauty of the place just gets into your heart.'

'Why don't you want to live here then, Mary, since you think so much of it?'

Mary shook her head. 'It's the young who make a success of business here, and if I'm to find a husband, it won't be here.'

'But I thought you didn't want a husband, Mary.' Non lifted her foot from a deep pile of manure and clucked her tongue in disgust. Mary was walking with ease, as though she were stepping on streets of gold. She had become so used to the sights and sounds of London that she took the dirt and stink for granted.

'I suppose I'll have to give in, find a good kind man and settle down,' Mary said. 'Now I'm getting too old for the road I'll have to find a smithy, or perhaps a farmer, they're always on the lookout for wives. I don't mind if he's rich or poor so long as he'll look after me.'

She looked sideways at Non and smiled. 'It's a shock at first, I'll grant you. But somehow London gets into your blood, you don't even notice the smell after a while.'

'So it's only here in the cattle market that it smells like this, is it?'

'You'll have to find out for yourself. London is a lucky place for folk who really try their best. Some of the little hosiery and drapers' shops even in posh parts of the town are run by Welshmen who've made good here.'

'Well then, if others can do it, so can I.' Non looked around. She was becoming accustomed to the constant shouting of the dealers and the bellowing and complaining of the animals. Even the smell of the huge area of Smithfield didn't seem so bad. She felt it in her bones: here, she could make a success of her life.

A sudden scream rent the air. Non spun round, her heart thumping. There were figures flying in all directions, men were scattering like leaves in autumn and a child fell into the mire beside them, howling in misery.

Non picked the girl up and held her close, frightened and confused. Then there was a sound of thunder and out of the cloud of dust and filth, Non saw Big Awkward, the prize bull, head down, eyes rolling, charging towards them.

'Oh God, Mary! The bull's broken free and he's heading straight for us!'

The animal's horns pointed towards them like spears. The beast was so angry that saliva spilled from its jaws and its hooves stamped in the mud, sending up sprays of filth.

Non froze as the bull headed straight for her and the child she was holding. She saw its huge eyes roll, red and evil, and tried to move, but her feet seemed fastened in the mire.

At the last minute, with the animal bearing down on her, Non felt a fierce push from behind. Still holding the child, she staggered and fell, and then she was on her hands and knees in the mud with the little girl clinging tightly round her neck.

And then it seemed as if she was living in a

nightmare. Big Awkward had slewed to a halt, foam running down the sides of his jaw. The beast bent its great neck, looked around as though choosing a target, and for a moment was still. Suddenly a bellow rent the air, then the bull raised its head and charged.

'Mary!' Non screamed, but she was too late—the bull caught Mary with a jabbing thrust of its horns and tossed her high into the air. After what seemed an eternity, Mary fell to the ground as if she was no more than a rag doll.

Non tried to get to her feet, but everything seemed to be happening in a haze of slowness. She watched as Big Awkward stood over Mary, letting out a terrible bellow of anger. And then the beast's horns were lowered threateningly, pausing for a moment before knifing into Mary as she writhed on the ground.

Non struggled to her feet and tried to move towards the animal, but strong hands held her back. 'Leave it, I'll deal with it.'

'Caradoc, thank God!' She watched as he advanced on Big Awkward, with only a stick and a rope to restrain the beast. Non's heart beat so hard she thought it would stop from sheer fright. Feeling the whip of the stick, the bull turned evil eyes on Caradoc before returning to his prey on the ground. Caradoc stung the beast across its malevolent eyes with the stick, and while the bull turned its great neck, moved in to loop the rope over the blood-stained horns.

For a moment it seemed that Caradoc too would be thrown to the ground, and then the London drovers moved in, eager to help. Rope was tied around the bull's hooves, bringing the great animal crashing into the mire. There it lay, twisting and bellowing, struggling against its bonds.

Fearfully, Non looked to where Mary lay on the ground. She was very pale and still, blood was soaking her skirts and her hands were clasped over her stomach as though to stop the flow.

Non knelt beside her. 'Mary, my lovely, can you speak to me?'

Mary's eyes flickered open. 'I don't suppose I'll be needing that 'usband, after all.' Her voice was little more than a whisper. 'But you'll make your fortune by here in London, so don't go letting me down now.'

'Mary, you'll be all right, someone is fetching a doctor. Just lie still and quiet and you'll soon be in safe hands, don't worry.'

'No need of no doctor, I'm slipping away, I can feel my sight fading. Do you think there's a heaven, Non? If there is, I'll wait there for you.'

'Don't die, Mary,' Non said in a choked voice. 'Please don't die.'

'Tell me there's a heaven, Non. Your father was a holy man, just tell me I'm going to a better place.'

Non touched Mary's cold cheek. 'Of course there's a heaven. But you're not going to die, Mary, you're not!'

A smile touched Mary's blue lips. 'You never was any good at lying, *merchi*.' Her eyelids fluttered for a moment, and then, with eyes wide, she looked up at Non as if she was going to speak again. But as Non watched, the light faded from Mary's eyes and her head rolled to one side.

Strong hands were lifting Non to her feet. A mother came and took the little girl by the hand, thanking Non profusely for saving her child. Non looked up into Caradoc's white face and stared at him as though she didn't recognize him.

'Come away,' he said softly. 'There's nothing you can do for Mary now.' He put his arms around her and she leaned against him, feeling tired and beaten. The pain was so deep that even her bitter tears didn't give her ease.

'Mary!' she said softly. 'My poor, dear Mary, I'm going to miss you so much.'

\*       \*       \*

Later, sitting in her room in the tall house in Bartholomew Close, Non was still in shock. She remembered Caradoc bringing her home, and remembered he'd sat holding her hand for what seemed hours. She still couldn't believe that Mary was gone out of her life for ever; Mary, who had been so full of life, so full of wisdom.

Strangely, she couldn't cry any more. Her eyes were hot and dry and she wanted the relief of tears, but they wouldn't come. She remembered her father's death months before and the bitter tears that had rolled down her cheeks. But for Mary, there were no tears; just emptiness, and a feeling of a life wasted.

There was a gentle knocking on the door and Caradoc came into the room. He was carrying a tray, which he set down on the table beside her.

'It's just a little broth,' he said. 'Please try to eat something.' He sat on the edge of the bed and Non quickly averted her eyes from the bruises on his face. 'She'll have a proper Christian burial,' he said. 'I've seen to it all, so there's no need for you to worry.'

·252

She covered her face with her hands and Caradoc knelt down beside her, drawing her hands into his. 'I'm so sorry, Non. I know you've lost a good friend, and so have I.'

'She only came to the market to find me,' Non said dully. 'I'm to blame and I feel so guilty.'

'Non, let me hold you, just for a minute.' He put his arms around her, and she rested her head wearily against his shoulder. It was then the tears came. Great, gulping sobs shook her, and Caradoc held her tightly, patting her back as if she was a child.

'There, it's good to cry it out,' he said softly. 'It's all been a terrible shock for you. But soon you'll be home. I'll take you myself and the journey will be much quicker than you think.'

She sat up away from him and rubbed her eyes with her fingers. 'I'm not going back,' she said in a low voice. 'I'm going to stay and work hard to establish myself as a good herbalist. I owe it to Mary to make a success of my life here.'

'But you can't stay in London alone.' Caradoc was outraged. 'You're a single woman.'

'And what do you think my life was like before I joined the drove?' Non pushed him away. 'When my father died, I was turned out of my home. I was a woman alone then, but I didn't sit around bemoaning my fate.'

'But I'll be paying you good wages, and you can set up in a fine little place in Swansea. Money doesn't go very far in London.'

'It's not your concern,' she said. 'You've made it plain that I'm to expect nothing from you.'

'Non,' he took her hands, 'if I could marry you, I would. I love you, but it's out of the question.'

'No need to tell me why.' Non's voice was bitter. 'I'm not good enough for you.'

Caradoc got to his feet, running his hands through his hair. 'Of course you're good enough for me! Oh Non, don't make this more difficult than it already is.' He looked at the clock on the wall. 'I have to go, Aunt Prudence will be waiting for me.'

Non looked up at him. 'No doubt she'll be introducing you to ladies of a suitable station in life, girls with rich fathers willing to be generous to a suitor who is rich already.'

'Try to understand, Non. If I was a free agent I'd marry you tomorrow, but my father expects me to make a good marriage.'

'We've had this discussion so many times already,' Non said, 'and it all seems so trivial with Mary gone.' She rubbed away a tear. 'And if you're not man enough to make your own decisions, then you're not good enough for me.' She stood up and faced him, her hands clenched into fists. 'Go then, meet your rich heiresses. And whatever you do, don't keep your Aunt Prudence waiting. To be late for dinner would be unforgivable.'

He left her then, closing the door quietly behind him. Trembling, Non sank back into her chair and pushed the bowl of soup away. She put her hands over her face and let the tears flow. They were tears for Mary, but also for herself.

*     *     *

Georgina sat beside her aunt at the long dining table, trying to hide her disappointment at the lack of guests. She'd hoped for some handsome gentlemen visitors; even the company of young

254

women would have been preferable to dining alone with Aunt Prudence.

The door opened, and Georgina smiled as her brother walked into the room. 'Caradoc, so you're here at last!' She allowed him to kiss her cheek. 'I suppose you've been tied up with some boring business deal.'

Caradoc kissed his aunt and sat down beside her. 'Sorry to keep you waiting, Aunt Prudence, but there was a nasty accident at the market and I had arrangements to make.'

Georgina leaned forward. 'I heard there was quite a scene there, with Big Awkward running wild. Tell us all about it, Caradoc.'

'Not much to tell,' Caradoc said.

'Oh, come on,' Georgina prompted eagerly. 'We're just ready for a bit of gossip, aren't we, Aunt Prudence?'

Caradoc frowned and shook his head, but Georgina wasn't going to be put off. 'What happened, was anyone hurt?'

'As it happens, a woman was killed.' He spoke abruptly, and Georgina sat back in her chair with her hands to her mouth. 'It was one of our women,' Caradoc said. 'A good woman.'

'Who? Don't keep us hanging on, for goodness' sake!'

'It was Mary. Now are you going to shut up about it? I'd like to eat dinner in peace, if you don't mind.'

'Oh, all right.' Georgina lost interest at once. Mary was no great loss: she was just one of the women walking the drovers' roads.

Georgina watched as her aunt gestured to the servants to bring in the dinner. She admired Aunt

255

Prudence, who was a lady to the tips of her fingers and handled her staff with just the right amount of imperiousness to command respect.

'Good food,' Georgina said as a platter of steaming beef was placed on the table. 'I've almost forgotten what a proper meal tastes like.'

'Well, you would ride with the cattle,' Aunt Prudence said sharply. 'A most undignified mode of travel for any young lady.'

'But Aunt Prudence, Father was going to marry me off to some old man. I had to get out of Swansea quickly, surely you can see that.'

'Well, maybe so, but you were always wayward, even as a child. Now Georgina, don't talk in front of the servants. You never know what tales get carried.'

Georgina nodded. She couldn't agree more; servants were a breed apart and they thrived on gossip.

The meal progressed slowly and with little conversation. Caradoc was morose, eating his food as though lost in thought. Georgina felt a little prickle of alarm. Surely he hadn't been associating with that awful witch Manon Jenkins again?

She waited until the servants had left the room and then tapped her aunt on the wrist. 'I suppose I needn't tell you that Caradoc got mixed up with a woman from the lower orders, need I?'

Aunt Prudence looked at her nephew, her eyes glinting with laughter. 'It's only what young men do, Georgina, and you must remember, women from the lower orders are not like us.'

'What do you mean?' Georgina asked, hoping her aunt would make some derogatory remark about the women, because that would include

256

Manon Jenkins and perhaps then Caradoc would realize how foolish he'd been to encourage the girl.

'They have no inhibitions.' Aunt Prudence dabbed her lips with her napkin. 'Just remember, Georgina, that once a man tastes the fruit he no longer wants the tree. I'll be introducing you to eligible young gentlemen, but I'm warning you, don't allow any man to take liberties with you, that's all I'm saying. Now be quiet and eat your dinner, it's an early night for you after travelling all this way.'

Georgina sat back in her chair and took up her knife and fork with a feeling of wellbeing. She was here in London, living in a huge house much grander than anything back home, and soon, very soon, she would meet a dashing young man with plenty of money which he would be happy to spend on her. And as for Manon Jenkins—without her friend Mary to show her the ropes she would be lost, and she would soon crawl back to her humble roots where she belonged. If Georgina's smile was a little smug, there was no one but her aunt and her brother to see it.

# CHAPTER TWENTY-FOUR

Non sat near the window of her room in Bartholomew Close and stared out at the buildings greyed by the pall of rain and fog. London seemed a forbidding place, a place where the sun never shone. She turned back into the room, trying to gain comfort from the glow of coals in the fire. But never had she felt so alone.

Her mind constantly turned to Mary and her tragic death. True to his word, Caradoc had arranged the funeral and attended to the burial of Mary's body. He'd comforted Non, holding her in his strong arms when she cried. But where was he now? Probably enjoying a happy evening with his aunt and her guests in a better part of London.

Non sighed in exasperation. Here she was, worrying about a worthless man like Caradoc, while her best friend was lying dead. How could she be so heartless?

Tears threatened to spill over as Non remembered Mary and the way she had clasped her hand as she lay in the mire, blood all over her clothes. With her last breath she'd urged Non to make a success of her life. Poor Mary, she would never more see the sun, never enjoy a breath of air or hear the birds sing in the spring. She'd not asked much from life: a few weeks in London and then a comfortable trip home to Swansea to find herself a kind man to marry.

Non rose to her feet. She felt restless, trapped in the room that was becoming stuffy. She was tired of looking into the fire, trying to make sense of all that had happened over the past days. She dabbed at her tears; they were useless and didn't bring relief. The pain was still there, and it seemed too much for one person to bear.

From downstairs she heard the muffled sound of the bell that heralded supper. She had no appetite, and yet anything was better than sitting alone in her room, quietly going mad.

When she entered the cosy dining room, the other guests—all women—nodded and smiled in recognition. Mrs Summers, who owned the house, sat at the head of the table and bowed her capped head in a regal manner as each person took their seat.

'Good evening, ladies.' She spoke softly, but with an accent that had a faintly foreign sound. 'I trust you are settling in, Miss Jenkins.' She spoke the name awkwardly and Non smiled.

'Please just call me Non—it's short and easy to manage.'

Mrs Summers bowed her head again. 'Very well, Non. I trust you are comfortable in my house.'

'I'm very comfortable, thank you.' And she was, she felt safe and secure in the elegant close. She wasn't quite sure how long she would be staying; it was really up to Caradoc.

As if reading her thoughts, Mrs Summers spoke again. 'Your gentleman friend, Mr Jones, will be calling here later this evening to see you.' Her shrewd eyes rested on Non's face, trying to read any tell-tale signs of embarrassment.

'Mr Jones is very kind,' Non said quickly. 'He employed me to travel to London as a chaperone to his sister.' She returned Mrs Summers' look. 'He will be returning to Swansea in a few days' time, and I shall be staying here in London.'

Mrs Summers made no comment, but began to ladle soup into bowls and pass it round the table. The soup, followed by a large slice of beef with boiled potatoes, was adequate but not very appetizing. The food provided by the small taverns where Non had stayed on the way to London had been of a better quality.

For the first time, Non studied the three other women seated at the table. One wore the dark clothes of a widow and the other two were so alike that they must be sisters.

'I'm Mrs Richards,' the older woman caught her eye and smiled, 'and these are my daughters, Florence and Lottie. We haven't liked to speak to you before, especially as you've taken your meals in your room, but you have all our sympathy on the loss of your friend, I assure you.'

Non felt she should attempt to make conversation. 'Are you staying long in London, Mrs Richards?'

'Bless you!' Mrs Summers spoke up before anyone else could reply. 'These ladies are my regulars, they stay with me all the year round.'

'Well, that just goes to show what good lodgings they have here,' Non said politely.

The tea when it was served was strong and sweet, and Non savoured the taste. 'This is the best cup of tea I've had since I left home,' she said, and Mrs Summers looked pleased.

'I like my tea to be refreshing, not like that watery stuff served up by some of the cheaper lodging houses.' Mrs Summers leaned forward and touched Non's hand. 'I'm not prying, you understand, but I hear you lost your friend in a fatal accident at the Smithfield market.'

Non took a quick breath. 'Yes, that's right, but if you don't mind I'd rather not talk about it.'

'Of course, of course,' Mrs Summers said. 'But what a terrible fate, to be gored to death by an angry bull.'

'It really is too sad,' Mrs Richards said, her eyes full of curiosity. 'My Florence was out shopping and heard the terrible news from one of the street traders. Poor girl, and very young too, I understand?'

'Yes,' Non kept her head bowed, 'quite young.' She pushed away her cup. 'If you will excuse me, Mrs Summers, ladies, I think I'll retire to my room.'

'Yes, go on my dear, I can see you're upset,' Mrs Richards said sympathetically. 'What a dreadful scene to have witnessed. I hear you held your friend's hand until she passed from this life to the next.'

'Excuse me.' Non swallowed hard, trying to suppress the tears that brimmed in her eyes. 'I'll say goodnight then. Forgive me, I'm a little distressed.'

'Don't forget that Mr Jones is calling to see you,' Mrs Summers said quickly. 'You can talk with him in the best room. There's no fire lit in there, but then that would be wasteful for a room hardly used. However, I trust you will be comfortable enough for what I suspect is a small matter of business.'

'Thank you, Mrs Summers. Perhaps you'll be good enough to call me when Mr Jones arrives?'

Mrs Summers bowed her head in acquiescence and Non left the small dining room with a sigh of relief.

She sat in her room, where the fire was gradually dying away, and somehow she knew that it wouldn't be replenished with coal, not tonight. Mrs Summers would no doubt consider it a waste.

It was about an hour later, the longest hour Non had ever spent, when Mrs Summers called up the stairs to tell her Caradoc had arrived.

He was standing near the fireplace in what Mrs Summers called 'the best room', where the coals lay grey and dead. He looked tired, and Non gestured for him to sit down.

'What did you want to see me about?' she asked. 'It's rather late to come calling. Haven't you got a gaggle of eligible young women waiting to dance attendance on you?'

He remained on his feet and looked at her long and hard. 'You must think me very shallow.'

'Well, what else am I to think about a man who declares his love one minute and with the next breath says marriage is out of the question?'

He took a bag of coins out of his pocket. 'Here, you'll be needing this.' He handed it to her and for a brief moment their hands touched. 'You'll need all the help you can get if you're to stay in London.' He hesitated. 'I will be up with the next drove in a few weeks, and by then you might well have changed your mind.'

When Non didn't reply, his voice softened. 'Non, I would rather you came back home with me. But as you're determined to make a life for yourself here, there's not a great deal I can say.'

'No, there's nothing you can say,' Non agreed, her voice tinged with sarcasm. She saw Caradoc turn his head away from her, as though he couldn't meet her eyes.

'What I did was wrong.' His voice was low. 'I shouldn't have lain with you, I know that, but believe me when I say I love you.'

'And a fat lot of good that's going to do me, isn't it?' Non was angry. 'You treated me as if I was the most precious thing in your life, and then once you'd had your way with me you cast me aside with excuses.'

'I haven't cast you aside, Non. I've told you I'd keep you in luxury if you came home to Swansea.'

'As a mistress!' Non shook her head. 'I'm too

262

good for that, Caradoc. I'll be no man's kept woman.'

'I can only repeat that I'm sorry,' Caradoc said.

'Sorry!' Non's voice rose and she took a deep breath in an attempt to steady herself. 'I'm a ruined woman. No man will want me now—don't you understand what you have done?'

'I would offer you marriage if only . . .' His voice trailed away.

'If only I had money and position, that's what you mean, isn't it?'

'I'd better go.'

'Yes, I think that's best.' Non felt a constriction in her throat. 'I hope you have a safe journey back home.'

At the door he paused and gestured to the money bag Non had dropped on the table. 'There's quite a bit of money there. Enough, I should think, to keep you here for a few months. At least you'll have a chance to get on your feet.'

'Please don't offer me charity. I only want what I've earned.' Non spoke quietly, but her heart was fluttering like a butterfly inside her.

Caradoc smiled ruefully. 'After putting up with my sister, I think you've earned every penny you've got.'

He took a deep breath as if he was about to say something more, but Non forestalled him. 'Well, thank you, Mr Jones, and I'll bid you goodnight.'

Caradoc straightened his shoulders. 'Well, goodnight, Non, and may I wish you good luck in your enterprise.'

He left the room and Non rubbed her hands together: they were cold and she felt that the chill of the room had seeped through to her bones. She heard the murmur of voices in the hall and the sound of the heavy front door being closed and locked. She waited a few more minutes, not wanting to see anyone, and then made her way quietly up the stairs to her room.

She dropped the bag of coins onto the small bedside table and sat on the bed, feeling too weary and miserable even to cry. She had lost her best friend in the most terrible accident, and if that wasn't enough to bear, Caradoc had casually paid her off as though she was a common whore; it was not a very promising start to her new life in London.

Her night-time ablutions were hasty; the room was too cold to linger around in her underwear. She crawled beneath the heavy blankets and the patchwork quilt and rubbed her limbs, trying to get some warmth into them. It was a long time before she slept. She kept seeing Mary, tossed like a rag doll and flung to the ground, and the light going from her friend's eyes. When she did sleep, it was to dream that Mary was alive and well again.

When she woke the next morning, it was to the realization that she would never see Mary again. She sat up with a heavy heart, blinking as the sun pointed fingers of light into her room.

The young maid was on her knees setting the fire, and she glanced over her shoulder and smiled when she saw that Non was awake.

'Morning, Miss, I'm Bella. I'm just lighting your fire, for the room to be warm when you get up.' She sat back on her heels. 'Tell you the truth, Miss, not everyone in the house gets such treatment.'

'What do you mean?' Non hugged the bedclothes around her shoulders. In spite of the sun shining in through the window, the room was cold.

'Well, the gent who called last night, he gave Mrs Summers the money to look after you.'

Non sighed. Caradoc thought money could solve everything. Still, her heart was warmed a little; Caradoc had thought about taking care of her before he went off to his rich life in his aunt's house in a fashionable part of London. It was a small comfort, but right now it was all she had to hold on to.

\*　　　\*　　　\*

Caradoc held the newspaper in front of him, hoping to deter his sister from making conversation. All through breakfast she had talked incessantly about clothes and bonnets and shoes, and he'd had enough of all that. Aunt Prudence had the good sense to take her breakfast in her room.

'Caradoc!' Georgina pulled the paper away from him. 'Why aren't you listening to me?'

'I have been listening to you,' he said wryly, 'ever since I sat down at the table. All I've heard is your voice chanting a litany of the new wardrobe you're going to buy.'

'Well, would you rather I talk about your latest paramour?' There was a spiteful edge to Georgina's voice. 'I'm so glad she's staying in London; she'll soon learn what life is all about when she has to earn her own living.'

'And you'd know all about that, wouldn't you?' Caradoc folded the newspaper carefully and put it down on the table. 'Look, Georgie, I don't want to quarrel.'

She touched his hand. 'Neither do I, darling, but you seem so miserable, so wrapped up in yourself. You should enjoy London while you're here.' She paused. 'And for goodness' sake, stop thinking about Manon Jenkins.'

'Actually, I was reading another article about the accident at Smithfield.' Caradoc was losing patience. 'Have you forgotten that a woman was killed, and by one of my own bulls? Don't you realize what a tragedy that is? Mary was a good and loyal worker.'

'Well, I'm sorry about that, of course!' Georgina said hesitantly. 'But no one is going to blame you for it, are they?'

'No, it was an accident. Such things happen when a large herd of animals become so crowded together they can scarcely breathe.'

For once Georgina was silent. She drank her tea and looked thoughtfully down at her hands. Perhaps she was grieved about Mary; after all, she was not entirely heartless.

Aunt Prudence came into the room, her skirts swishing around her ankles. 'Good morning, my two beautiful darlings.' She kissed Caradoc, and then with less enthusiasm bent her head towards Georgina. 'It looks as if it's going to be a beautiful day for shopping. What are you going to buy, Georgina? New gloves, a few bonnets?'

Georgina perked up at once. 'Oh, Aunt Prudence, thank goodness you're here, because all my brother does is go on about matters that depress me.'

Caradoc rose from the table and took his aunt's hand. 'I'll leave you two ladies to talk. I've got business in town, I might be out all day.'

'Don't worry, dear boy, we shall be out all day, too!' Aunt Prudence raised her eyebrows at him. 'I've got a feeling Georgina will want to visit every shop in town before we're done.'

'See you this evening, then.' Caradoc bowed to the two women and with a sigh of relief stepped into the hall. He took his hat and coat from a tiny girl who seemed too young for service, but then she was probably privileged to work in such a fine household. It was strange, he'd never thought much about the plight of the lower orders before. Not until Non came into his life.

He waited patiently while the groom brought the carriage round to the front of the house; it was a fine sunny day, in contrast to the day he'd arrived in London, when it had been grey and dull. What a pity Non's first sight of London had had to be so painful. He wondered for a moment if he'd go and see her; he could picture her face, her clear eyes, the tilt of her head. Even now he could feel the softness of her body as she'd yielded to him. He brushed the thoughts aside. He had business to see to, and it was no use hankering after something he could never have.

*     *     *

A few days later, Mrs Summers came up to Non's room to see her. 'I have to ask you for your rent, dear,' she said. 'I seem to have gone through most of what Mr Jones left here. I don't know where the money goes these days—I thought I'd have enough to keep you for at least a month.' She shrugged. 'But then, the servants need paying, there's

267

supplies to be bought, I suppose it all costs money.'

'Come in, Mrs Summers.' Non held the door wide. 'I'll pay you a month in advance, how will that be?' She went to the drawer where she'd put her wages, and stared in dismay when she saw that the bag of money wasn't there. 'I'm sure I put it in this drawer,' she said, frowning. Non opened the rest of the drawers one by one, but they contained only the clothing she'd brought with her. 'It's gone!' Fear was like an icicle sliding down her spine. 'My money, it's gone!'

Mrs Summers crossed the room to look into the drawer. 'Are you sure you put it here, dear?'

'Yes, I'm sure, but I'll look around just in case I've made a mistake.' Non opened the cupboard and pulled out her bag of medicines. It was just possible she'd put the money in there for safekeeping. She carried the bag to the bed and rummaged through it, becoming more frightened as she realized the money was not there. She shook her head. 'It's gone, Mrs Summers, it's gone.'

Mrs Summers sank into a chair and fanned herself with her hand. 'I think I know the answer, my dear.' She took a deep breath. 'Bella has quitted my service. We had a small, very small falling-out and she stormed out in a fury. I have the strangest feeling that both your money and mine have gone with her.'

'Is there anything we can do to get it back?' Non clenched her hands together in fear; she'd been depending on her wages to get started. She'd intended to rent small premises from where she could sell her medicines.

Mrs Summers shook her head. 'Nothing, dear. Folk can disappear in London without trace.' She got to her feet. 'Anyway, I have to get on.' At the door she stopped and looked back at Non. 'I can keep you here for another week, but without money I can't run a business. You do understand, don't you, dear?'

When Mrs Summers had gone, Non sank onto the bed and stared down at the carpet without seeing the pattern dulled by age. What would she do now? She had no money, and soon, very soon, she wouldn't even have a roof over her head. Fear curled like a snake inside her, but she wouldn't give way to it. She raised her chin and straightened her shoulders. She mustn't fail at the first hurdle. 'Don't worry, Mary,' she whispered. 'If I'm to go down, I'll go down fighting.'

# CHAPTER TWENTY-FIVE

As Non stood at the window looking over the sun-dappled street, she felt an ache in her heart, knowing that soon she would have to leave the security of the house in Bartholomew Close and look for work. She hoped she could find a position that offered her free lodgings, because she had no money to pay for rent.

There was a knock on the door and Mrs Summers looked into the room. 'My dear,' she said, 'there's a gentleman to see you.'

Non's heart lifted. 'Is it Mr Jones?'

Mrs Summers shook her head. 'It's a Mr Morgan Lewis, I believe. Perhaps you would like to come downstairs and talk to the gentleman?'

Downstairs in the best room the air was chill;

although the afternoon sun shone outside, the windows were heavily curtained to prevent people from looking in. Morgan was standing uneasily near the door, his hat in his hand.

'Non,' he smiled warmly at her and took her hands. 'I'm sorry I haven't been to see you before this. I've been in London these last few days and I'll be leaving for home tomorrow, but I felt I must come to talk to you before I go back to Swansea. Are you keeping well?'

His words were stilted and he spoke formally, as though they were strangers rather than old friends.

'That's very thoughtful of you, Morgan. It's lovely to see you.' Non smiled warmly at him, realizing she was glad to see him. She drew her hands away and sat on the uncomfortable sofa. 'Sit down, Morgan. You'll be staying a little while, won't you?'

'Well, I'd like you to come out to tea with me. Will you come, Non?'

Mrs Summers appeared in the doorway. 'Go on, Miss Jenkins, you might as well have a good talk to the young man, it's good to mull over your troubles with an old friend.' She looked meaningfully at Non, nodding rather pointedly towards Morgan's pockets.

'I'd love to come out with you,' Non said. 'Don't keep supper for me, Mrs Summers. I'll have something while I'm out.'

'Very good,' Mrs Summers said. 'The other ladies are going to be out this evening too, visiting relatives, I believe.' She smiled, no doubt relieved to be spared the expense of at least one meal.

Outside it was warmer than in the cloistered best room of the house. Morgan held his arm towards

Non and she took it, smiling up at him, glad of his company.

'How did you know where I was staying?' she asked.

'I asked Caradoc Jones. He didn't seem too keen to give me the address, mind. Quite posh, Bartholomew Close, isn't it?'

'I suppose so, but I won't be staying there for much longer. I need to find premises where I can work.'

Morgan frowned down at her. 'You're looking a bit peaky, is anything wrong?' He was genuinely concerned, and if she told him that she'd been robbed he'd have given her his last penny. But somehow she couldn't bring herself to speak about it. Needy though she was, she could hardly put her burdens on Morgan.

'I'm all right. I'm missing Mary, of course. I still feel desolate at the loss of her.'

Morgan squeezed her hand. 'I know, it was a terrible sight for you to witness. Some stupid drover prodded Big Awkward with a stick. The beast is bad tempered enough to be a nuisance, but I've never known him attack anyone before.'

They walked in silence for a time, and Non struggled to keep the tears at bay. She had been so fond of Mary; so happy to think she'd have her company in a world that was so different from the one she was used to.

'There's a little place where we can drink some tea.' Morgan pointed to a shop with a tiny doorway. It looked very small for a tea-house, but when Non was guided through the passageway she saw the room beyond was a fair size, with a large mullioned window looking out onto a narrow court.

The court was crowded with people: a knife-grinder was at his wheel, and beside him a thin woman with a baby in her arms leaned against the wall. A lone pig rutted around for food and was kicked aside by a drunken man, who hurled abuse at no one in particular.

All at once, Non felt ashamed. She thought she was ill used because she had been robbed, but these people were ragged, hungry-looking and without hope. She had her herbal knowledge, and thanks to her father she was able to read and write. She might be penniless right now, but as soon as she found work she would be all right.

'Sit here, Non,' Morgan spoke her name softly. 'We'll order tea and then we can talk.'

He waited until the china pot was put on the table, watched as Non poured the tea, then leaned forward. 'I know you're not happy here. Why don't you come home with me?'

She shook her head. 'Thank you, Morgan, but I've come to London to carve out a living for myself. I don't want to give up and go home without at least trying to make a success of things.'

'You don't need to make a living for yourself. Come home and marry me, let me take care of you. I'm fearful for your safety here in London, all alone.'

Non put her hand on his arm. 'Let me be, Morgan. Enough about talk of going home.'

Morgan looked at her doubtfully. 'All right, I suppose you must have your own way. But I'll be travelling up to London again in a few weeks' time with another cattle drove. Leave an address with Mrs Summers, will you?'

'We'll see.' Non was afraid to tell him that she

wouldn't have an address unless she began to earn good money in the next few days. Suddenly fear clawed at her. She glanced out of the window into the dimness of the court outside, half afraid to look at the ragged people who stood there. How would she live? She couldn't sleep on the streets like a beggar.

Morgan put his hand over hers and she was comforted by his big presence. 'Why so thoughtful? Not changing your mind about coming home, are you?' His voice held a hopeful note.

'I have to give it a try here in London,' she said. 'You'll see, I'll make my fortune and when I come home it will be as a rich lady.' She sounded sure, confident, but as she hid her trembling hands under the table she knew she wasn't sure or confident at all.

*       *       *

'I don't know why the smithy wanted Non's address.' Caradoc looked sternly at his sister. 'Seeing as he didn't ride with our family's drove this trip, I wasn't obliged to tell him anything.'

Georgina gazed up slyly from under half-closed lids. 'Then why did you? And what does it matter?' She paused. 'I think you're jealous because the smithy's looking for that little whore.'

'Don't be so stupid, Georgina.' Caradoc turned away from his sister's penetrating gaze. 'I hope she had company when he called on her, I wouldn't like her to receive him on her own.'

'The handsome smithy is from the lower orders and you can't expect him to live by the same rules we do. The same goes for Manon Jenkins; she's not

273

a lady, is she?' She arched her eyebrows meaningfully, but Caradoc pretended not to notice. Georgina wouldn't let the matter rest. 'I mean to say, no lady would part with her chastity out in the open fields like a common harlot. What's to say she didn't welcome Morgan into her bed like the whore she is?'

'Keep your nose out of matters that don't concern you, Georgina.' Caradoc was angry and made no attempt to hide it. 'I'm sick and tired of your sharp tongue. I pity any man who has the misfortune to marry a shrew like you.'

'Touched a raw spot, have I? Well, I expect your precious Non will be lying in the arms of the smithy right now. He's probably promising her a wedding ring, which is more than you did.'

If ever Caradoc had felt like striking a woman, it was now. 'Shut up! Just shut up!'

Georgina drew back, frightened by the intensity of his anger, and Caradoc pointed towards the door. 'Just go to your room and leave me alone.'

'Why should I go to my room?' The words were brave, but Georgina was already moving towards the door.

'You'll go if you know what's good for you.'

Georgina, characteristically, slammed the door behind her. Caradoc sank into a chair and stared into the huge grate, watching sparks shoot from the crackling logs. He tried not to think of Non and the smithy together. Surely she wouldn't allow Morgan to take liberties? But then she'd come into his arms eagerly enough, surrendering herself to him so willingly. He swallowed hard. The memory was so bittersweet it almost hurt. He ran his fingers through his hair, wishing he could stop thinking

274

about Non. She wasn't the bride for him, and he knew that better than anyone. He would be returning home to Five Saints soon, and then he might never see her again. The thought was alarming rather than comforting.

He took a deep breath. He would be running another drove to Smithfield in a few weeks' time, and if he still felt the same way about her he could talk to her then. The money he'd given Mrs Summers would be enough to take care of Non's needs for a few months; she would be safe in Bartholomew Close, she could try out her herbal remedies to her heart's content, and by the time he returned she might view life differently. She might come to realize that life as his mistress would not be such a bad one after all.

*       *       *

Non was filled with apprehension as she took a seat in the big drawing room. Mrs Summers had requested her presence for what she termed a 'private talk'.

'I'm sorry to say this, my dear, and I do worry about you, but I will have to ask you to vacate your room as soon as possible. The only income I have since my dear husband passed away is from the rooms I rent. You do see my problem, don't you?'

Non nodded. 'I know, but please give me a little time, a day or two, and I'll find somewhere cheaper to live. I'll be all right, don't worry about me.'

'Why didn't you ask your young man for money while you had the chance? It was rather foolish of you.'

'I couldn't do that. Morgan isn't my "young

275

man", and I can't be beholden to him.'

'Then how are you going to live, my dear? Where are you going to get money from to buy you a rented room, however cheap it might be?'

'Just give me a few days,' Non said. 'I won't be a burden on you, I promise. I'll sell some of my remedies, and then I'll be able to afford another room somewhere.'

'Well, good luck to you, dear, but I still think you should have taken that handsome young man into your confidence.'

Mrs Summers rose to her feet, her beads rattling on her plump bosom. She took a dainty handkerchief out of her sleeve and dabbed her eyes with it. 'I'm so sorry to have this conversation with you, my dear, but now I've made myself clear I'll need you to move out of here by the end of the week.'

Non saw that the interview was at an end. She got up from her chair. 'Thank you for your patience, Mrs Summers, I'm very grateful to you.'

Back in her room, she stood looking round her, wondering how she was going to survive. She felt tears burn her eyes and wished for a brief moment that she had confided in Morgan. But then he would have insisted that she go home with him. Non took her box out of the cupboard and picked out some of the bottles and a few packets of dried herbs. She must try to sell them at once, it was the only way to make the money she'd need for halfway decent lodgings.

She put on her jacket and braced herself to go out onto the street. She hung the strap of her bag over her shoulder and placed the remedies inside, and then she stood at the door of her room, trying to pluck up enough courage to venture forth into the crowded noisy streets of London.

## CHAPTER TWENTY-SIX

As Non walked along Giltspur Street, she heard the few shillings she'd earned rattling in her pocket. Her eyes were misted with tears and the road seemed to be a ribbon of light wavering before her eyes. Leaving the house in Bartholomew Close had seemed to be the hardest thing she'd ever done.

Mrs Summers had been reluctant to let her go, but she'd had no other choice; the new guest had arrived early that morning and had required the privacy of her room right away.

Non skirted the periphery of Smithfield market and stood for a long time, looking at the busy scene before her. The animals were enclosed in small pens, as they'd been on the day she'd first arrived in London. Standing looking into the melee, she remembered the awful day when Mary had been killed by the maddened bull; the sights and the smells brought everything back into focus. She bit her lip, suddenly feeling that she couldn't face life in London alone.

She caught sight of a tall man with bright hair, leaning over one of the pens examining the beasts. Her heart began to beat swiftly. Caradoc was here—he hadn't left London without her. And then he turned, and she saw that it was not Caradoc, but a stranger who stared right through her.

'Wot you selling, Missus?'

Non looked up, startled to see an elderly man in a big overcoat standing beside her. 'I'm selling herbal remedies,' she said. 'Do you need anything?'

'I don't, but cover your head or folk will take you for a dollymop.'

Quickly, Non tied the ribbons of her bonnet tightly under her chin. She didn't know what a dollymop was, but she could hazard a guess that it was a woman of poor character.

'Now, Miss, what you doing here? The market is for men and boys, not for women. Another thing, this is my spot. I sell my Lucifer matches here, always have done.' He held out a tray filled with small boxes. 'Hold this for me and I'll show you how the matches work.'

Non put down her bag and held the tray. She tried not to show her impatience, but she wished the man would just go away and leave her alone. Still, he was clean and neat and he only meant to be friendly.

'See, you dip the match in the tin and pick up some phosphorous.' He demonstrated, and then ran the match along the rough edge of the wall, where it exploded into light.

Non was suitably impressed. 'I'm sure you do a good trade in matches, and I'm not here to sell my herbs.' She returned his tray. 'I'm looking for lodgings. I only stopped for a moment to look at the market.'

'Lodgings, is it? Well, you don't want to go into a pack,' he said. 'Those places are for the scavengers and gonophs. You watch yourself, little lady.'

He might have been talking another language. 'I don't know what you mean,' she said. 'What's a pack?'

'Are you soft in the head, girl? A pack is one of them low lodging houses, and before you asks, a gonoph is a pickpocket. I can see you're not from these parts, so look out for yourself and guard your box of tricks, whatever you do.' He smiled and tipped his hat to her before melting into the crowd.

Non's hand brushed her skirt: there was no chinking of money. She quickly slipped her hand into her pocket and her worst fears were confirmed—her few shillings had gone. She'd learned the hard way that London gonophs were smooth plausible thieves.

She looked once more around the market, but there were no familiar faces. She began to walk away, feeling she was turning her back on everything she knew. She suddenly felt very small, lost in the rabbit warren of streets she was passing through. Around her, ragged children held out grimy hands for money, a look of hopelessness etched on small faces.

She seemed to walk for most of the day. Mrs Summers' new maid had given her the address of a lodging house. She'd spoken apologetically, telling Non it was a far cry from Bartholomew Close, but it was clean and the charge was about two shillings for the week. It had seemed just what Non was looking for, but now she wasn't so sure. The broad elegant streets were lost behind her. Now she was walking through grimy courts enclosed by the high walls of adjacent buildings. No sunlight penetrated the gloom, and the few windows she saw were covered in grime and filth.

She was used to walking—she'd walked all the way from Swansea to Smithfield—but the hard cobbles seemed to bruise her feet. She would need to use some of her own balm to cure the blisters before she could sleep that night.

Non stopped at the end of a narrow turning and saw that she'd reached her destination. The house was in a small square; outside was an upturned cart, the shafts pointing to the skies, and crouched under the cart was a ragged boy, his eyes large in his thin face. Non wished she had a few pence to give him, but she had none for herself.

As she drew nearer to the door of the lodging house, Non saw that the building was crumbling. It looked as though it would fall down at any minute. It was a tall house, narrow and mean, and the windows were hung with grimy curtains, the colours dulled with dust from the street.

A young woman answered the door and looked at Non without interest. 'Wot you want?'

'A room, please. This lodging house was recommended to me by Mrs Summers' maid.'

The woman shrugged. 'I've never 'eard of her. Still, come in, there's one room going spare, you might as well have it as anyone else.' Her eyes narrowed. 'You got money to pay, have you?'

Non shook her head. 'I was robbed. I stopped at the market for a few minutes and an old man stole my money.'

'Aye, there's plenty of thieves around Smithfield, all right. Good place for rich pickings. Still, if you ain't got money I can't let you have the room.'

Non noticed the woman was rubbing her hands; they were swollen and red, with the nails split on the edges. 'I could give you some good medicine to take the pain away from your hands,' she said quickly. 'That's what I do to make a living, sell my medicines.' She took out a small jar of cream. 'This ointment is made from leaves of the beech tree. Just try a little.'

The woman looked at her doubtfully.

'Go on, it won't harm you,' Non urged.

The woman opened the pot and cautiously rubbed a little of the ointment into her fingers. 'Well, it's lovely and soft, I grant you that.' She held her hands before her. 'That feels better already.' The young woman looked at her in awe. 'All right then, come in, I'll trust you till you sell some more of them things. I'm Ruby, you can call me that if you like.'

'I'm Non Jenkins, and you won't regret trusting me, I promise you.'

'We'll see. The room is back here, the only one I got spare. You can like it or lump it. I can see you talk nice an' all, so I suppose I can trust you. But there's to be no sub-letting, you got that?'

She showed Non into a room at the back of the house. It was bare except for a bed, a chair and a rickety table.

Non put her bag on the floor and looked round, her heart sinking. The place stunk to high heaven and the small window was hung with a grimy cloth. 'What's that smell?' Non blurted out the words before she had time to stop and think.

'Oh that, it's the Thames, you dull or wot?'

The smell was overpowering, and Non realized the house must be very close to the river. She put her hand to draw back the cloth, but Ruby stopped her.

'Leave it, it's soaked in ammonia to kill the smell of the water. If you takes it down the pong will be much the worse.'

Non stood as if dazed, her senses reeling. How

281

could she live in such a place? She would be better off going home to Swansea. 'I'll take it,' she said. She had no choice. Where else would she get a room with no money to put down for rent?

'I'll need rent before the week's out.' Ruby went to the door. 'I'll have a bit more of that ointment before I go to bed, too.'

'Here, take it, I can always make up some more.' Non gave Ruby the round tin. 'I'll be out at first light looking for more herbs,' she said. 'Should I have a key?'

Ruby put her hands on her hips and laughed so hard that tears came to her eyes. 'Keys round here? You must be soft in the head. There's nothing to steal, who'd want a rickety table and an old bed?'

She left Non alone then as, still laughing, she made her way along the passage, her boots creaking as she walked. She'd been impressed with the ointment, but even offering her more wouldn't change her mind about having the rent by the weekend.

Non sat down on the plain wooden-backed chair and put her bag on the bare boards beside her. She wanted to cry as she felt the chill of dampness creeping through the wall. She wished with all her heart she was back in the comfort of Mrs Summers' house in Bartholomew Close. She put her head in her hands and pressed back the tears. Crying would solve nothing at all.

\*       \*       \*

Georgina was bored. Aunt Prudence had turned out to be a stringent keeper of the purse strings, and allowed her only just enough money to buy the required garments to take home with her.

At first Georgina had planned to stay in London until next spring, but a few weeks in the dreariness of the tall house closeted with her aunt had made her change her mind. Georgina had not met any charming young men: it was only dried-up old crones just like Aunt Prudence who visited the house. Still, Caradoc would be here again before too long, bringing the next drove from Five Saints. Then she would have to make up her mind if she would go home with him or not.

The door opened and Georgina heard the swish of her aunt's expensive gown sweeping the carpets. She braced herself for the lecture that was sure to come. But she was to be pleasantly surprised.

'Look, Georgie, I've brought a fine young man to see you.' Aunt Prudence spoke coquettishly, like a young, flirtatious girl.

Georgina rose at once and turned to greet the man, and then she recognized him. 'We've met before!' she said. 'Back home in Swansea.'

Aunt Prudence swept forward with the young man in tow. 'Clive is the cousin of my great friend Lady Langland. I thought he would be good company for you. As it's such a lovely day, why don't we take a turn around the park? Will that cheer you up, Georgina?'

Georgina forced herself to smile coolly, even though her heart was racing. Clive Langland was an answer to her prayers. Why had Aunt Prudence taken so long to introduce him?

He bowed over her hand and she had the urge to run her fingers through his thick dark hair. He looked up and met her eyes, and his were sparkling with amusement; in spite of her assumed coolness,

283

he seemed to know exactly how she was feeling.

'Do say you'll honour me with your company, Miss Georgina,' he said smoothly. 'It would be a great pleasure to walk in the park with such a beautiful young lady.' He turned, and his look included Aunt Prudence. 'Pardon me, *two* beautiful young ladies.'

'I would like that very much.' Georgina hoped she sounded suitably unimpressed by his flattery.

'Go and take your coat from the maid, then,' her aunt pushed her towards the door impatiently. 'If you dither about too long, the sun will have gone behind the clouds and we won't be walking anywhere.'

When Georgina stepped outside the pillared door of the house, she felt the sun hot against her face. It was a lovely day, made even better by the young man at her side.

'How long are you staying in London?' Clive Langland asked. His voice was deep and very masculine, and though he might be a touch shorter in stature than she could have wished, his chiselled features made up for any shortcoming of height.

'Oh, she can stay as long as she likes,' Aunt Prudence interjected. 'The dear girl is tired of the country; even though her father's estate is enormous and she had every luxury at home, Georgina needs more sophisticated company these days.'

Georgina wished her aunt would fall into a hole. 'What line of work are you in, Mr Langland?' Georgina hoped her question sounded polite rather than plain nosy.

'Don't be silly, my dear!' Aunt Prudence tapped her arm. 'Mr Langland is from an excellent family and has private means. He doesn't need to work. What a suggestion!'

Georgina felt her colour rising. Trust Aunt Prudence to make her sound like an ignorant country bumpkin.

'I dabble a little at writing poetry,' Clive Langland said easily. 'I would like to see myself as a great writer, but alas, my work is very modest.'

'I'm sure your work is very fine.' Georgina was impressed. A poet, and a rich one at that: Clive Langland was quite a catch.

The park was unusually quiet. The birds were singing and the pathways were dappled with sunlight streaming through the trees. Georgina felt inspired, renewed; perhaps staying in London wasn't such a bad idea, after all. She smiled at Mr Langland, uncomfortably aware that she was approximately the same height as him. Still, that aside, he had a great deal to recommend him.

The walk was over all too soon; a brief shower drove Aunt Prudence towards home. At the door, she looked at Mr Langland and smiled brightly. 'Perhaps you would like to come in and take some refreshment?'

Clive Langland bowed slightly, and Georgina found herself looking at his fine luxurious hair with a feeling of longing.

'Alas, dear ladies, I have to be somewhere else very shortly, though I do hope I might call again?'

Aunt Prudence tapped his shoulder playfully. 'We shall expect you tomorrow, at the same time, if you please.'

'I do please.' He took Aunt Prudence's gloved hand and kissed it. Hastily, Georgina drew off her glove, and felt the thrill of his lips pressing against her bare hand. And then he lifted his hat and began to walk quickly along the street without looking back.

'Tut tut, come along inside, Georgina. Don't stand there gawping after Mr Langland like a foolish child.'

'He's very nice to look at,' Georgina said shamelessly. 'He's a very handsome man, I can't imagine why you didn't introduce him to me sooner.'

Aunt Prudence gave her hat and coat to the hovering maid. 'I didn't introduce you to him because he's been out of the country.' She swept into the drawing room and Georgina followed her.

'Oh? Where has he been?'

'I believe he's travelled the world, though what bit of it this time I'm not certain.' She sat down and stared shrewdly at Georgina. 'A potential husband, I think.'

Georgina took a seat. 'He's well worth considering, and he's a sight better than the old man Father wanted to land me with.'

'Well then, this has been a good day's work. Shall we have some tea?'

Georgina nodded. Her thoughts were already on tomorrow, when Mr Clive Langland would be calling on her. If she had her way, today's little outing would be the first of many, and hopefully might lead to wedding bells. The thought made her shiver with delight. 'You're not such a bad old stick, are you, Auntie?'

'Really! The expressions you young people use today are so disrespectful.' Her tone was severe, but Aunt Prudence's eyes were twinkling. 'Let's have that tea, shall we?'

Georgina would have agreed to anything at that moment, she was so grateful to Aunt Prudence for thinking about her future. Clive Langland was handsome and charming, and as a husband he would suit her very well.

## CHAPTER TWENTY-SEVEN

It was early, the sun barely showing over the horizon, but Non had been outdoors for hours searching for clove gilliflowers to make a syrup for the ease of heart pains. She'd also managed to find some deep purple germander for healing chesty coughs; these remedies she would sell without any trouble. Folk in London seemed to cough a great deal, due perhaps to the fog that frequently clung like a garment to the chimneytops of the buildings.

Non was in good spirits. In the last few days she'd been successful in peddling her remedies around the local lodging houses as well as at the Welcome Inn, an old barn of a building that stood on the corner of Westbury Court. She had earned herself enough money to pay her rent and have a little over to buy food.

Thinking of food reminded her that she needed bread and cheese for her breakfast. As she was feeling rich, she stopped the pie man and bought two pies for supper, one for herself and one for Ruby. She and Ruby had become friends; though blunt to the point of rudeness, Ruby had a generous heart and a great respect for Non's knowledge of healing remedies. And Non would always be grateful to Ruby for giving her the benefit of the doubt when she had no money to pay the rent.

On the way back to Westbury Court, Non passed the meat market, and as she always did, she looked around hoping to catch sight of someone from home. If she was honest, the one person she wanted to see was Caradoc. At the thought of him, her heart beat faster and she felt tears spring to her eyes. She was so much in love with him, and she couldn't believe he didn't love her too. She remembered the hot nights lying with him on the drove, his tenderness as he made love to her, the way his mouth had tasted against hers. Surely it meant something more than a passing fancy to him?

When she returned to the lodging house, Ruby was there to meet her. She was greatly excited and her dark eyes gleamed merrily as she took Non's arm.

'A handsome gent's been here looking for you,' she said. 'A very fine gent, good clothes from the best tailors in London, I'd say. He gave me a whole tevess just for telling him you lodged here. Did you hear me, he gave me a *shilling*, and he said there was more where that came from.'

'Caradoc!' Non said. 'Was his name Caradoc Jones?'

'I don' know, do I? He talked fancy, like a real gentleman. I didn't catch his name, though. Why? What's this man to you?'

'Oh Ruby, if only you knew!'

'Well, I'll know if you tell me, so come into my nice warm kitchen and I'll make us a brew.'

Non followed Ruby to the back of the house and sat in the oak rocking chair, her hands pressed against her breast. 'Tell me what he looked like, Ruby.'

'Well, he looked rich, a man with plenty of money and plenty of sense to go with it.'

'But his hair, was it dark or light? And what colour eyes did he have?'

'Well, he had a hat on, but I think his hair was light coloured. And he was tall, I remember that. As for the rest, I don't go gazing into the eyes of any strange man who comes my way, do I?'

Non took the mug of tea and held it with both hands. She was trembling so much she could hardly speak.

'He's keen on seeing you, I do know that much.' Ruby sat down close to the table. 'And if I had a good-looker like that one after me, I wouldn't be sitting in a kitchen drinking tea, I'd be leading him up the aisle, or at least up to bed!'

Ruby's laughter was infectious and Non relaxed a little. 'Perhaps it was just someone calling for one of my remedies. The word is getting around now, you know that as well as I do.'

'No, he wasn't a customer. This gentleman wanted you, he called you by name. "Is Miss Manon Jenkins in?" he said. Now do strange men calling for medicine ask for you by name?'

Non took a deep breath. She hardly dared believe that Caradoc had come here looking for her. 'How did he know where to find me?' she asked, looking at Ruby with anxious eyes.

'The maid from Bartholomew Close gave you my address, so she probably passed it on to the gent as well.'

Non nodded. 'Yes, that's right. Caradoc was paying for the rooms I had there, so he would find

289

out easily enough where I'd gone to.'

'Now you're thinking with your head and not with your heart.' Ruby crossed her arms. 'I tell you something, now. If this man wants you for a wife you'll be drowned in riches. Mind you, he did look a bit on the old side for a girl like you.'

Non shook her head, her heart sinking. 'Caradoc is a young man,' she said, 'barely older than me. It couldn't be him.'

Ruby flapped her hands in a dismissive gesture. 'Never mind, it isn't every day a rich gent comes calling at my house. You *will* see him when he comes back, won't you?'

'Of course I will. But it's as I thought, he's a customer, that's all.'

'Well, you ain't going to look a gift horse in the mouth, my girl! Customer or no customer, this man has money and you can help him spend it.'

Non sighed and put down her empty mug. 'I'd better start making some syrup.' She got up from the chair and it swung to and fro, the rockers creaking as though a ghost was sitting in it.

'Well, do it in my kitchen,' Ruby said. 'I won't watch you and steal your precious remedies, don't you worry about that.'

'Can I?' Non smiled. 'That's good of you, Ruby. It will be easier if I can work on a corner of your kitchen table. I won't be any trouble.'

Non rolled up her sleeves and fetched a bowl of water to wash the earth from the herbs. Ruby was making bread on the other side of the table, kneading the dough with her fingers. 'This dough gasps like a landed fish when I push the air out of it,' she said, 'but at least it tastes nice when it's baked.'

Non took a knife from the drawer and began to chop the leaves and flowers of the germander plant. There was a companionable silence in the kitchen that made Non feel at home for the first time since she had come to London. She shredded the herbs and began to pulp them, and looked up as Ruby put the dough in the fireplace with a spotless cloth over it. She came and stood beside Non, watching as she worked with her pestle and mortar.

'Them are pretty flowers, such a deep purple. What are they?'

'They're called germander flowers. I'm going to mix some water and sugar with them and make a syrup. Very good for coughs.'

Ruby made a wry face. 'I gets enough of coughs myself, perhaps you'll give some to me when it's done.'

Non nodded and continued to work, cutting and mixing the herbs until it was time to stand them on the window-sill.

'Smells lovely,' Ruby said. 'What do you do with it now?'

'I let the mixture stand and then I put it into little bottles. You've seen the bottles in my box, Ruby.'

'Aye, I have that, but mind you I wouldn't know what bottle was for what medicine. You're lucky you can read and write. I've seen you sticking little labels on the stuff, but it's all a foreign language to me.' Ruby laughed. 'I can't even *speak* proper, me.'

'And I can't cook a loaf of bread like you. We've all got our talents, Ruby.'

'I suppose you're right. There's the door, must be the rich gent back again. Want me to show him to your room, Non?'

Non shook her head. 'I don't want to leave my work just now. Bring him in here, Ruby. If he doesn't like it, that's too bad.'

In spite of her brave words, Non waited with a feeling of apprehension as Ruby answered the door. She heard footsteps coming towards the kitchen, and braced herself as her heartbeat quickened.

The man who came through the door was, as Ruby said, an older man. His hair was turning grey, but he was upright in posture and his eyes were a steely blue as they looked into hers.

'Mr Jones!' Non said. 'What are you doing here?'

'Could we talk in private, Miss Jenkins?' He spoke imperiously and Non felt a flash of resentment.

'I'd prefer it if you say what you've come for right here in the kitchen,' she said coldly. She saw him glance at Ruby. 'It's all right,' she said. 'Ruby is a friend, you can speak in front of her.'

'Very well. May I sit down?' He took the rocking chair and stretched his long legs out before him. He looked so much like Caradoc that Non felt her hands begin to tremble. 'It is about my son. He believes himself to be in love with you, but that's just the foolish nonsense of a young man. He'll be heading a new drove into London soon, and I want you to tell him in no uncertain terms that you will not marry him.'

Non put her hand on her breast as though she could steady the fast beating of her heart. 'And why should I do that?' She leaned forward. 'If what you say is true, and Caradoc does love me, what would he think of you meddling in our affairs?'

Mr Jones looked down at his boots for a long moment, and then his clear blue eyes met hers again. 'He doesn't know I'm here. But I'll tell you this, I don't want you ruining his life. If you love him you'll send him away.'

Non breathed deeply and steadied herself against the table. 'How would I ruin his life? If he loves me, surely that's all that matters?'

'Caradoc is to marry a lady back home, a fine lady with a good background. The mingling of the wealth of both families will make our droving industry the strongest in the country.'

'And I'm nothing but the daughter of a poor cleric. I'm not fit to be his wife, is that what you're trying to say, Mr Jones? Tell me, what's more important to you—money or your son's happiness?'

His eyes deepened until the colour seemed almost as dark as the crushed germander flowers. 'You allowed my son to bed you, young lady. Who is to say you haven't slept with other men since you came to London?'

'How dare you!' Non's hands clenched into fists. She was angry, she was no longer in awe of Caradoc's father. 'You have insulted me in the worst way possible. I am no whore! I love your son and I will always love him. There will be no other man for me.'

Mr Jones stood up and looked down at her. 'Perhaps the offer of a hundred pounds will tempt you?' he said brusquely. 'You could set yourself up in a fine business, make a new start, marry well. Come along, my dear, you must be tempted by my offer. A hundred pounds is a great deal of money.'

Non moved to the door of the kitchen, her

senses suddenly sharp: she was aware of the aroma of the crushed flowers, the smell of the dough proving in the grate. She saw the sunlight shine unexpectedly through the window and it was as if the world had stopped spinning.

'I think it's time you left, Mr Jones.' She was surprised at the calmness of her voice. 'I will not be bribed, not even if you offered me a thousand pounds. Hear this and hear it well, Mr Jones, I am not to be bought.'

'We will speak again.' He was undeterred by her anger. 'I shall be staying with my sister. Here is the address, should you change your mind.'

Non turned her head away as he held a slip of paper towards her. He placed it on the table, and for a moment rested his hand on hers. 'I can see you are a fine woman, Miss Jenkins, but you are not the one for my son, believe me.'

She heard his footsteps die away as he left the house, and then Non sank into a chair and put her hands over her eyes. Hot tears gushed through her fingers and spilled down her cheeks. She had never felt so besmirched in all her life.

'Blimey, Non, why didn't you take the money?' Ruby put her arms around her shoulders. 'There's nothing sure in this life, but an 'undred pounds would sure make things a lot easier for you.'

Non was too upset to speak. She shook her head and the room seemed to spin around her.

Ruby rubbed her shoulders with gentle hands. 'Look, luvvie, don't let an old bloater like him upset you, he's just an old man with more money than sense. Now you hold on, I'll brew us another pot of tea and I'll soon have you feeling better.'

Ruby busied herself round the kitchen, looking

anxiously at Non from time to time, until at last she put a mug of tea on the table and sat down with a determined look on her face. 'It's not all bad. Blimey, if some rich old geezer said his son was in love with me, I'd be over the moon and back to earth before you could say bread.'

Non looked up at her. 'Thanks for the tea, Ruby. You're a good pal, but why didn't Caradoc come to see me himself? Why send his father?'

Ruby spooned sugar into her cup and made a wry face. 'Aye, you're right. This Caradoc Jones is a grown man, he should know his own mind, and if *he* says he loves you, that's good enough, ain't it?'

Non felt a warmth run through her. What if it was true? What if Caradoc stood up to his father and said he wanted her for his wife?

'He might come knocking on the door for you any day now. The cattle are on sale in Smithfield on Friday, so he can't be far away,' Ruby said excitedly. 'That would be something, wouldn't it? A bit of romance on me own doorstep.'

'Don't get carried away, now,' Non said cautiously. 'We don't know if Caradoc has left Five Saints yet.' It was true, and yet hope burned brightly inside her. She would be counting the days, wondering when Caradoc would come for her.

'The market is only two days away, it's a fair guess he's going to be there,' Ruby said. 'You must get yourself a pretty gown—something with sprigs of flowers—and a new bonnet, just in case he comes calling.'

Non smiled ruefully. 'And where do you think the money's coming from?'

'You've made some good sales. Get out there and make more. And Non, for this month you needn't pay me any rent.'

Non looked at her. She saw the kindness in Ruby's face and wanted to cry. 'Why would you do that for me? You hardly know me.'

Ruby sniffed and rubbed her eyes. 'Well, you've brought me luck. People have 'eard of your remedies and they come here to buy them. You've made my little place famous, Non. I've had no rooms empty since you came, haven't you noticed?'

Non hugged her. 'Thank you, Ruby, but Caradoc has seen me at my worst, blown about by the wind and rain and covered in mud. He'll have to take me as he finds me.'

'Then he'll find a girl with a good heart and a pretty face, and no man's got the right to expect anything more.'

Later, as Non lay in her bed, she looked through the window at the star-studded night. The sky was clear; there had been no haze of fog for days. The sun had been shining late into the evening and summer was at its highest point. Non covered her face with the sheet; the hot weather had made the smell of the river much worse, but she was becoming accustomed to it. Only now, when the night was hot and still, was she aware of it.

It was a long time before she slept, and when she did, she dreamed of Caradoc taking her hand and slipping a plain gold band on her finger. And when she woke there was a smile of anticipation on her lips.

# CHAPTER TWENTY-EIGHT

Caradoc looked up at the sky: the clouds were gathering above him, fearsome and dark, threatening wind and rain. The cattle were already restless as the drove passed through the town of Hereford.

The last drove had yielded a good profit, but Caradoc couldn't concentrate his mind on business. He had thought of nothing but Manon Jenkins since he'd left her behind in London. There was no getting away from it: he was in love with her.

''Scuse me, Mr Jones.' The voice startled him out of his reverie and he looked down from his horse to see Flora hurrying to keep up with him. She was thinner now; she was no longer the young girl she'd been. The loss of her baby and her betrayal by Thomas, who had gone back to his wife, had taken the bloom of youth from her. ''Scuse me, but the women want to take shelter. See, there's a barn over by that hill there.'

'But you're all used to a bit of rain. Not turning into a bunch of softies, are you?'

'No, Sir, but if it rains the wool gets wet and it stinks to high heaven, and what's more we can't get any knitting done in the rain, anyway.'

Caradoc smiled. Flora, it seemed, had taken over the position Mary used to hold: she was now the woman in charge, the one who made the decisions. The happy-go-lucky girl had gone, leaving a strong, decisive woman.

'It's up to you, Flora, I trust you to know what you're doing.'

Flora nodded. 'That's what we'll do then, Sir. We'll catch up with you when the weather clears or when you stop for the night.'

He nodded. 'Right then. I'd better head the cattle towards Tewkesbury. We'll have to pay a toll but it will cut the journey by a good few hours.' He took his watch from his pocket. 'If I don't see you before, I'll meet you at the Black Bull in a few hours.'

In spite of his doubts about the weather, the day improved; the clouds shifted across the heavens and the sun shone. Caradoc turned in the saddle to look behind him, and saw with satisfaction that the animals were more docile now that the threat of a storm had passed. In the distance, he could see the women trailing way behind the animals, hurrying to catch up, and smiled. Flora was doing her work well, she had noted the change in the weather and had the women moving again. He settled back into the saddle and concentrated on the direction he was taking; he didn't often take the Tewkesbury route, but sometimes a diversion was necessary.

As he rode on, Caradoc's thoughts turned once again to Non. He remembered teasing her at the market; he remembered her father, the vicar of the parish, a good and upright man, and he felt guilty. He had taken Non's innocent sweetness and made her a woman, a passionate woman, and the thought that she might give that passion to another man nearly killed him. Once he arrived in London he'd find her and ask her to be his wife.

A smile curved his lips. The effect such a marriage would have on his family would be interesting to see. His father would be outraged, but he no longer cared. He wanted Non and by

298

heaven he would have her.

\*　　　\*　　　\*

Flora put her knitting in her pocket and held up her hand for the other women to stop walking. 'It's time to rest,' she said. 'Once we're in Tewkesbury it will be all go until the cattle are safely through the town. Come on, Jessie, I know you're only sixteen but you need to pace yourself, mind. Don't forget, this is your first time with the drove and you got a lot to learn.'

Flora settled herself on a grassy bank and, lifting her skirts, rubbed her ankles. She was used to walking now and she had grown up a great deal. She felt there was a new life waiting for her in London. There, she might find fresh opportunities. Perhaps she could meet up with Non Jenkins. One thing was sure, she would never trust a man again.

Thomas had let her down in the worst possible way. As soon as they'd returned home, he'd gone moody and taken to drink. In a way she was relieved when he went back to his wife to beg her forgiveness. He didn't give a thought to Flora and how she would manage.

Flora looked at the rest of the women: young, unmarried girls, innocent, laughing together as though they didn't have a care in the world. How lucky they were, and how she wished she could warn them not to let any man touch them without being churched first. She lay back on the bank and closed her eyes, and the sun dazzled through her eyelids. The world seemed bright and wonderful, and yet she knew it to be cruel and hard. When she'd lost the baby, she'd thought everything would

299

return to normal. Now she knew different. She could hear the other women talking quietly to each other, and sighed. It was time to be on the move again. 'No rest for the wicked,' she said, and Jessie looked at her through slanted eyes.

'You're not wicked, Flora. You was jest let down by a bad man, that's all.'

'Thank you, Jessie, and you mind the same thing don't happen to you. A couple of nights in a man's arms and what you got to show for it? An empty pocket and a full belly.'

\*　　　\*　　　\*

Caradoc paid the toll with little grace; the price for movement of cattle through the towns was increasing by the day. Soon it would be better to take the hill roads and bypass the towns altogether.

The skies had darkened again and thunder began to roll overhead, and as the drove approached the crossroads on the outskirts of the town, the beasts became restless, jostling and stomping on each other, bellowing in panic. The sooner the drove was outside the boundaries of Tewkesbury the better he'd be pleased. On the open land the cattle were easier to control, and there was no fear of innocent bystanders getting hurt.

A fork of lightning lit the sky and one of the young heifers began to run straight at the crossroads. Caradoc could see a farm cart coming down the hill, unaware of the herd of cattle moving towards it like a restless sea. He called a warning, and too late the farmhand looked up. He pulled hard on the reins and his horse reared, whinnying in fright. The cart began to tip, spilling a load of hay onto the road, and the driver jumped clear.

Caradoc pressed his way towards the head of the stampeding cattle, using his whip to move the animals towards the open hillside that led out of town. The hill was steep, and soon the animals grew tired; the pounding of many feet against the wet ground subsided as the cattle slowed their pace. Caradoc handed his whip to one of his men.

'Here, Jack, I'll go back and settle with the farmer for the loss of his load. We're lucky that's all I have to settle. This damn weather frightens the cattle out of the few wits they have.'

As he returned down the hill, Caradoc saw the farmhand sitting on the roadside, his hands covering his face. Caradoc dismounted from his horse and put a hand on the young boy's shoulders. 'Come on, you're not hurt.'

'No thanks to you . . . Sir,' he added as an afterthought.

'No thanks to you, either,' Caradoc said easily. 'You should look where you're going.'

'Well, my load is ruined,' the boy said ruefully. 'I'll have a right tongue-lashing when I get back to the farm.'

Caradoc dipped into his pocket and took out some coins. 'Here, this should settle matters. It's enough to pay the farmer for the load and for you to buy a drink of beer to calm your nerves. A word of warning, though—in future be aware there are others on the road beside you.'

'Thank you, Sir.' The boy's face brightened. 'There's more than enough here to buy me a drink or two.'

'Well, be sure to give most of the money to your

employer, or you might just find yourself out of a job.'

'Right, Sir, I'll do that, Sir.'

Caradoc turned his animal, pulling gently on the reins, and the horse responded, setting off at a trot back up the hill. The sky was darkening again, but soon the drove would reach the Black Bull, where they would spend the night. A smile curved his lips. It was at night he could dream of Non, feel the softness of her skin against his and taste the sweetness of her lips. Impatiently, he urged his animal into a gallop; the journey could not go quick enough for him.

*       *       *

Flora lay in the warmth of the barn and stretched her legs under her blanket. She was tired; they had been on the road for days now, days spent walking on the soft grassy banks at the side of the drovers' roads. Days that should have been easy; but she had never quite regained her strength after losing the baby.

'You sleeping, Flora?' Jessie's hoarse whisper seemed to penetrate the darkness.

'No I'm not, but if I was you would have woken me up anyway, wouldn't you? What's wrong?'

'I'm scared of the dark. I don't like the owls swooping around us when we settle down for the night.'

'They might not be owls, they might be bats.' Flora smothered a laugh.

'That's even worse! Creepy crawly bats are just like mice with wings.' There was a pause. 'Can I bring my bed alongside yours?'

302

'All right, anything to shut you up. But be quiet about it, you don't want to wake the rest of the women, do you?'

Flora heard a rustling in the darkness and then Jessie settled down beside her. Slowly, she put out her hand and touched Flora's arm. 'Will you hug me like my mam used to do?'

Flora put her arms around Jessie's slim body, realizing that she wasn't the only one on the drove to feel miserable.

'Your mam dead, then?' Flora whispered, and she felt Jessie nod.

'Aye, this past six months, and I got no father either. That's why I joined the drove, but I don't like sleeping in barns in the dark, it frightens me to death.'

'You'll be all right. Just think of us women as family, soon you'll know everyone. There's little enough privacy for washing and such, so you gets used to each other.'

'Tell me about Manon Jenkins,' Jessie said. 'I've heard she's a witch, but she can cure folk of their sicknesses.'

'Oh, Manan, is it? If you ask me, you want to talk about anything so that you don't have to go to sleep.'

'Aw, go on, just tell me a bit about Manon and I'll shut up. Is it true she picks flowers and such and makes them into a syrup?'

'Non is a very clever woman, well clever about herbs and things. But, like me, she's not so smart about the men she fancies.'

Flora made a wry face in the darkness. Now was as good a time as any to warn Jessie about the dangers of getting involved with any of the men on the drove. Not that she'd listen, she would go her own way like most women, but at least she couldn't say she hadn't been warned.

'It's funny how it affects you. Lying in the heat of the summer nights surrounded by stars somehow makes a girl lose her senses. You know about me, I was fool enough to let a man take liberties with me and I ended up with a full belly.'

'Did that happen to Manon Jenkins, then?'

'Well, she didn't get with child, as far as I know, but she did fall in love with a man and did the same as me, slept with him. We're fools, all of us. Men just want to have their way with us and then walk away free as a bird.'

Jessie sighed. 'I want a man of my own, Flora, someone to love just me, to care about the little everyday things like me having a bad back or sore feet. Are there any men out there like that?'

'If there are you won't find them on the road.' Flora shifted her arm from round Jessie's shoulder. 'Now, listen, why don't you find a nice job in service, ask Mr Jones to find a good position for you. You're too delicate to walk all the way to London a couple of times a year.'

'Do you think he'd give me a place?' Jessie asked eagerly.

'Well, you can only ask. Now go to sleep, there's a good girl, or we'll both be fit for nothing in the morning.'

Flora turned away from Jessie and put her hand to her mouth as she felt the tears form a lump in her throat. Jessie's words had touched a chord in her. She too wanted a man who would care about her, what woman didn't? But who would take her now? She was soiled goods. Flora turned her face into her blanket and let the hot tears roll unchecked down her face.

# CHAPTER TWENTY-NINE

Non put away her book and rubbed her eyes. The light had faded and the candles were almost burnt out. She put her hand to her brow; her head was beginning to ache, the result of straining her eyes in the dim light.

There was a gentle knocking on the door and Ruby appeared, carrying a tray. 'Some hot milk to help you sleep. Mind if I sit with you a while?' She seemed a bit edgy.

'Of course I don't mind, it's nice to have company.' Non put more coal on the fire and the two women sat in silence for a time. There was no sound except for the shifting of coals in the hearth and the ticking of the clock. Then Non heard Ruby sigh.

'I've heard there's animals sick of some mysterious disease been brought into Barnet—it could be the drovers from your part of the world.'

'It can't be the Jones's cattle drove,' Non said, with more certainty than she felt. Surely Caradoc would be more careful than to bring sickly animals so near to London.

She hoped his herds were still in the finishing fields, well and strong, putting on fat from the good grass they were eating. But the image persisted of animals falling sick of the cattle plague. Caradoc would lose thousands of pounds of other people's money.

'All the meat will be scarce, and folk are saying the sickness can affect humans as well as animals.'

'Don't worry, Ruby,' Non said. 'It could all be idle gossip. We aren't likely to catch anything from the animals.'

'Thank Gawd for that.' Ruby finished her milk and put the mug back on the tray. 'I'd better go to my bed.' She stood up and stretched her arms above her head. She looked a bit more cheerful. 'You're right, we can't worry about something that might never 'appen. We could get run down by a horse and cart tomorrow, eh?'

'Nothing's going to happen to us. Goodnight, Ruby.'

When Ruby had gone, Non took up her herbal and lit a fresh candle. She wanted to find herbs to treat animal sickness, just in case some disease had been brought into London. If the animals were isolated and left alone, the sickness would probably run its course. But if she had some herbs that would help them recover, so much the better.

She rubbed her eyes. Her headache had grown worse, and reluctantly Non put aside her book. She washed and climbed into her bed, but she lay there a long time, wakeful and worried. She longed to see Caradoc, to be in his arms, to know he was safe and well, but she'd heard no word from him. He'd no doubt forgotten her. His father was worrying himself about nothing, Caradoc would never marry her.

At last she fell asleep, only to dream of Caradoc. With him was Morgan. Both men lay drowning in a river and she was torn between them, not knowing which one to care for. She woke early to the sound of the rain beating against the window and thin

306

light creeping into her room.

She sat up, wrinkling her nose in disgust. The smell from the Thames was overpowering—the rain must have swollen the river, bringing the water nearer the houses. She heard the wind howl down the chimney and knew there would be no chance of picking herbs today. She pushed aside the bedclothes and stood looking in horror at the uncarpeted floor, where effluent was seeping between the floorboards. She dressed quickly and pulled on her boots, trying not to look at the mire beneath her feet.

Ruby was already in the kitchen, where the smell was a little better, helped no doubt by the pan of bacon sizzling on the hob.

'You'd think it was autumn; the weather's turned spiteful on us,' she said, 'and the rain's brought the stink in from the river.' She shifted the bacon with her fork, turning it to brown the other side. 'You gets used to it, love, and once the rain stops it won't be so bad. Want some breakfast?'

'I'll just make a piece of toast for myself.' Non pushed back her hair. 'What about your guests, have they complained about the awful smell?'

Ruby shook her head. 'No, they have lived in London long enough to put up with the smell. In any case, they're all on the upper floor. They won't see the muck that seeps into the house.'

'Lucky people!' Non waited until Ruby had served the breakfasts, and then she cut a thick slice of bread and held it before the fire. The coals were hot, but the warmth was pleasant and the cosy room seemed to make the weather outside more bearable.

Ruby returned to the kitchen. 'Make me some

toast, Non, I'm starving hungry.' She looked at Non. 'Do you think this animal sickness will come into London?'

Non handed the toasted bread to Ruby. 'There's very little we can do about it, so try and put it out of your mind.'

'But you'll look after us if the sickness comes our way, won't you? I trust you and your remedies, Non. I know how good a medicine woman you are.'

'Ruby, you must keep a sense of proportion. All you've heard is that a few animals have fallen sick in Barnet—that's about twelve or more miles away.'

'Aye, you're right. Want some more tea?' Without waiting for a reply, she poured the golden liquid into Non's mug.

'The rain's stopped,' Non lifted her head to listen, 'and I do believe the wind is dropping. I might be able to collect some herbs, after all.'

Ruby made a wry face. 'I wish you could stay indoors today. I don't want you catching anything and bringing it home to me.' She popped the last piece of her toast into her mouth and licked her fingers.

'I've told you not to worry,' Non said. 'And I promise I won't be out too long.'

Ruby's expression was hard to read. 'I've come to depend on you, Non,' she said. 'You're not a boarder any more, you're my best friend.'

Non hugged her. 'And you're my best friend, too, but you're getting upset for nothing.'

'Well, see what gossip you hear when you're out,' Ruby said, 'and I promise I'll try not to go on about it.'

Later, as Non left the house, a pale sun was

beginning to shine through the clouds. The air was foul and she wrinkled her nose in disgust. The water of the Thames was turgid and she hurried away from the stink as quickly as she could. She had a great deal to do today, herbs to be picked and medicines to be made. Her reputation was growing, and she felt she was on the first step of the ladder towards the successful career she'd planned. She would even have been happy if it weren't for thoughts of Caradoc and the way he'd held her and kissed her and told her he loved her. Suddenly, without warning, she was weeping hot, bitter tears.

*     *     *

'We've lost above two thousand pounds, Father.' Caradoc was standing near the fireplace in Aunt Prudence's elegant drawing room. 'The animals infected with rinderpest have been slaughtered and there's nothing to do but cut our losses. I'll have to go back home and put a new herd together, but there's something I must do first.'

'I'll be staying in London for a while.' His father looked at him shrewdly. 'But I really want you to get another herd up here without delay, so we can make good our losses. Think about it, Caradoc; it will take you a few days to get home and then say sixteen days to bring a new herd to London. Can't any other business wait a little?'

'No, it can't,' Caradoc said sternly. It was time his father realized he was no longer a child.

'It's that girl, isn't it? You mean to see her.'

'Father, I don't ask about your private life, so I'd appreciate it if you wouldn't ask after mine.'

'She's a pretty little thing, but she's the sort who

309

wants a wedding ring on her finger. I gave her some money to keep away and she soon changed her mind about trapping you into marriage. In any case, Georgina told me the girl is betrothed to Morgan the smithy, so let well alone, Caradoc.'

Caradoc felt anger build up within him. 'You went to see her? How dare you interfere in my private affairs?'

'I'm sorry, but it's best to get these things out in the open. Morgan has probably tasted the sins of the flesh with the girl, her sort don't have the moral values that we hold so dear.'

'Well, you had no right.' Caradoc went closer to his father and met him eye to eye. 'Keep out of my affairs, Father. I'm warning you, I won't put up with any more interference, is that clear?'

'Don't talk to me in that tone of voice. Are you forgetting you're my son, my only son and heir to all I possess?'

'And are you forgetting I'm a grown man? Another thing, much of the money salted away in the Bank of the Black Ox has been accrued by me. I've worked hard to keep our business flourishing. Are you trying to tell me that if I see Manon Jenkins, you'll cut me out of your will?'

'No, son.' His father stepped away from him. 'Of course I'm not saying that. You're right, you've earned a lot of that money by the sweat of your brow, and I wouldn't try to deprive you of it, whatever you do.'

'Good, then we understand each other. Father, I must shape my own future, just as you shaped yours.'

The door opened abruptly and Georgina came into the room, a look of concern on her face. 'Why

310

are you two quarrelling? I can hear you from the other side of the house. Have you forgotten we have a guest?'

Caradoc frowned at her. 'Don't be alarmed, Georgie. We're just discussing business. Nothing for you to worry about. And as for our guest, I don't think Clive Langland has come to see Father or me, it's you he's sweet on.'

'What's that?' George Jones looked at his daughter, his expression stern. 'Not entertaining a young man, are you, Georgina?'

She looked uncomfortable for a brief moment and then she smiled. 'No, Father, Auntie is doing the entertaining. But I do find Mr Langland good company, I must say.'

'Are you forgetting you're promised to a fine man back in Swansea, where we'll be returning very shortly?' her father said.

Caradoc caught his sister's beseeching look. 'Surely, Father, Georgie has the right to meet men her own age?' He put his arm around his sister's shoulders. 'Aunt Prudence wouldn't have brought this Langland fellow into her house if he wasn't respectable.' He smiled. 'And rich.'

George Jones shook his head. 'I don't understand you youngsters of today. I had to obey my father in everything—who I worked with, who I walked out with, everything.'

'And yet you married my mother against Grandpapa's wishes,' Georgina said quickly. 'And you know how devoted you were to Mother.'

'Oh, well, I give up trying to guide you. These days children are headstrong and unmanageable, and I just wash my hands of both of you.'

Caradoc watched his sister hug her father's arm.

311

'Come and meet Mr Langland, Papa, please do, and then you'll see what a fine young man he really is.'

'Go on, Father, I'll be with you in a minute,' Caradoc said. He stood for a long time staring out at the grand square beyond the window. A milkmaid carrying a yoke was making her way along the street, and on the other side of the road a cow-keeper was urging his animals to hurry with the aid of a stick.

Caradoc regretted the loss of his own animals very deeply. It was not only the lost money that worried him, but the fact that he'd failed to bring the herds to London in good shape. Perhaps he should go straight home, bring back a healthy herd of beasts. Then Father would have nothing to complain of.

The Bank of the Black Ox was strong enough to bear a few losses, but Caradoc pitied the farmers back home, who relied on the money in order to secure next year's stock of animals and grain. His father was right in one thing: another herd had to be put together quickly. He would go back to Five Saints, do his duty by the farmers who trusted him, and then he could settle his own affairs.

He turned from the window and directed his thoughts to more enjoyable memories. He felt again Non's soft lips part under his own. He had tasted her sweetness and knew that she would be the only woman for him. He would go home first, he decided, then he and Non could have a quiet wedding in London on his return. A cloud seemed to pass over the sun of his thoughts. The problem was, after the way he had treated her, would Manon Jenkins still want him?

# CHAPTER THIRTY

Non lifted her head and rubbed her back. She seemed to have been hours gathering angelica and bluebottle leaves, to make a potion that might be as effective on animals as it was on human illnesses. The autumn sun had vanished behind grey clouds and the chill wind seemed to seep into her very bones. Non shivered. It was high time she made her way back home.

Briefly, she thought of her real home, the home she had shared with her father. There had been love and kindness as well as godliness, and the house had always been a place of welcome and warmth. Now, lodging with Ruby, she had no real home. Perhaps it was about time she took stock of her life and made plans for the future.

Non had seen a few vacant properties on her travels, but none of them had seemed suitable. Now, with her options running out, she might have to lower her sights and choose something cheaper: a few rooms on the riverside, perhaps—although blighted by the smell of the Thames, they would be cheap and convenient. Once she was earning a good living, she could move somewhere more select.

She had done well with her herbal remedies over the past few months. She'd gathered a faithful following among the Londoners, some who could pay only a few pence, but others, from the richer parts of town, who were willing to pay generously to relieve the pain of gout or the heat of a fever.

She deliberately walked along the streets near

the river, where she had spotted a house a few days ago, its blank windows testifying to its vacancy. It was conveniently placed in Orange Street, not far from Ruby's guest-house. It would provide a place to work, and at night she could lock up and return to Ruby's house for her meals.

She located the house and knocked loudly on the door, hoping the landlord might be there. After a few moments the door opened, and a young boy stood looking at her with open curiosity. He seemed familiar, and then she remembered him from the fair at Barnet.

'Albie!' she said. 'What are you doing here?'

He stared at her strangely for a moment, and then his thin face brightened. 'I remember you, Miss. You're the lady with the ribbons, you was kind to me.'

'And you were kind to me.'

'Wot can I do for you, Miss?' Albie seemed very grown up. He was taller than she remembered, but still as thin as a stick.

'I'm looking for a room where I can set up shop.' She lifted her basket higher on her arm. 'I saw the front room of the house was empty and wondered if I could rent it.'

'Well, Miss, I don't rightly know. Me and Grandpa we only rent the rooms at the back, but I can take you to the landlord if you like.'

'I would like that very much. Can we go now?'

'Aye, I'll fetch me cap and we'll be off. It's quite a ways to walk, mind.'

Non smiled. 'That's all right, I'm used to walking. I've walked all the way from Swansea to London with the cattle drove.'

He grinned and she saw that one tooth was

missing. 'Come in, Miss, look about and see what you think of the bleedin' place before you speak to the landlord.'

Non walked into the gloom of the narrow passage and waited as Albie flung open the door to the front room. She stepped inside and was pleasantly surprised by its size. The room was square and the window facing the street was large, with a deep window-sill where she could display her bottles of potions quite neatly.

'What sort of money does the landlord charge you, Albie?'

'My grandpa knows, but he ain't here now.' He chewed his fingernail. 'I think it's about a shilling a week, but then we got the kitchen and the two bedrooms for that.'

Non bit her lip. A shilling was a great deal of money, but then she'd been earning three times that since her reputation as a healer had grown. It was well worth a visit to the landlord, just to see what terms he would offer.

Soon she was walking away with Albie at her side. He was taller than her now, his thin legs protruding from too-short trousers. But his grin was cheerful as he led her away from the mean streets towards the more opulent houses in the richer parts of town.

Albie pointed to a tall house, with a wide door flanked by pillars. 'This is it, Miss. It's called Bloomsbury and it's where the toffs live.'

'What's the landlord's name, Albie?'

'Mr Langland. He's all right so long as we don't fall behind with the rent. Not that he comes collecting the rent 'imself. Oh no, one of his men does that—a bloke called Billy, a real big bully of a man.'

'All right then, let's ring the bell and see what happens, shall we?' Non pulled on the bell, and after a long time the door was opened by a heavily built young man.

'Mr Billy,' Albie said, 'this lady's come to ask about renting some rooms in our place.'

Non stared at the man anxiously. She was tempted to walk away and forget the whole thing. Come to think of it, could she take the risk of opening a shop? What if no one came to buy her products? She would have Billy to deal with, and she had the feeling that that might not be pleasant.

The more she studied Billy, the more worried she became. He looked down at her through half-closed eyes. He had large ears, bruises on his knuckles, and as he moved forward Non instinctively stepped back apace. He didn't speak and he looked every inch the bully Albie claimed him to be. He towered over her, his huge arms crossed over his chest, his jaw jutting towards her as if he expected a fight.

'I just would like to know if it is possible for me to rent a room in Mr Langland's house in Orange Street.' Non raised her chin and held the man's gaze. 'It's just the front room, you understand?'

He seemed taken aback by her well-modulated voice, and the pugnacious jaw was lowered a bit. 'I don't rightly know,' he said. 'I'd have to speak with my master about that.'

'Well, is he at home?' Non spoke imperiously, aware that the man had no idea of her place in society. She was well dressed in comparison to most of the women who rented properties in that area, and he was uncertain how he should deal with her.

'I'll speak to the master. Wait here—Miss,' he added as an afterthought.

Within a few minutes, a well-dressed man entered the hallway and peered out at her. Reassured by her dress and manner, he gestured for her to enter the house.

'I'm Clive Langland. I understand you wish to rent a property?'

'Well, it's a room, really,' Non said, 'at the front of the house in Orange Street. I want to set up as a herbalist there. I'm already well-known in the area, I can give you testimonials if they are required.'

'That won't be necessary,' Mr Langland said, and Non was uncomfortably aware of his scrutiny. His eyes seemed to look through her gown to the flesh beneath. She moved slightly and he looked away. 'It's a shilling a week,' he said. 'Billy, take the rent in advance from Miss . . . ?' he looked back at Non enquiringly.

'Miss Jenkins,' she said and dipped her hand into her bag to count out one shilling. Mr Langland was taking no chances.

A key was brought for her and then Non found herself dismissed, the door closed in her face. She looked at Albie and smiled. 'Right then, Albie, you and I are neighbours. What do you think of that?'

He smiled and hugged her arm, then backed away shyly. 'It's bleedin' lovely!' he said, a flush spreading across his thin face. 'You'll like me old grandpa, he's a right yarner.'

Non looked at Albie questioningly. 'What's a yarner?'

'You know, Miss, he spins a good yarn, that's what a yarner is. You'll hear enough of his stories

317

once you're settled in with us.'

'That's something I can look forward to, then.' Non rubbed her fingers over the surface of the key, and a warm feeling of achievement settled over her. She'd made the first step towards owning her own shop. 'Come on, Albie, we're on our way.'

\*      \*      \*

Morgan leaned on the fence in Smithfield market and ran an approving eye over the cattle standing patiently in their pens. These were beasts from England, not as fine as the Welsh Blacks, but they were healthy, free from disease and, above all, about half of them needed to have new shoes tapped onto their cloven hooves. Once shod, they would be taken to new owners, some as milch cows. The rest of the beasts would provide meat for the whole of London.

Hearing his name called, he stood up and touched his cap. 'Mr Jones, Sir, it's a pleasure to see you. Sorry about your animals, must have been a great loss to you.'

'Aye, bad enough, but we'll survive.' Caradoc looked at the fresh stock of animals in the pens. 'Good-looking lot—someone is going to make a lot of money out of these beasts. As for me, I'm going home to get a new herd, try to make good the losses.'

'If Non had been with the drove she'd have spotted the rinderpest straight away,' Morgan said easily.

'I've no doubt she would.' He looked at Morgan questioningly. 'Haven't seen anything of her, have you?'

318

Morgan felt a tension creep into his muscles. His jaw was set and he had to force the words from his mouth. 'I haven't seen hide nor hair of her.'

'Just as well, because when I come back to London I'm going to see her, talk to her seriously about marriage.'

Morgan looked levelly at Caradoc. The man was rich, handsome, and had a great deal of power, but none of that would sway Non if her mind was set against him.

'I mean to marry her myself.' Morgan spoke bluntly. 'I've always been fond of Non, and I think she'd be better off with a man like me.'

Caradoc laughed. 'You? You're not worthy of her, she needs someone who will treat her like a princess, shower her with luxuries. What have you to offer her?'

'A real and sincere love.' Morgan had difficulty restraining himself, he longed to punch Caradoc Jones squarely in the face. 'You treated Non like a whore, and she won't forget or forgive you easily, if I know her.'

'What's wrong with you, man? You know full well she's lain with me. Are you willing then to take secondhand goods?'

Morgan grasped Caradoc's jacket and thrust his fist against the other man's jaw. 'Don't talk about her like that. Manon is more of a lady than any woman I know.'

Caradoc loosened Morgan's hold; he shook him away and straightened his collar. 'I respect you, Morgan, and I apologize for the words I used in regard to Manon. She is every inch a lady, as you say, and I wouldn't disrespect her for the world. Surely the fact that I intend to make her my wife tells you that.'

Morgan stepped back from him. 'And *I* intend to make Manon *my* wife.' He strode away, anger still burning inside him. He had been a fool. He should have played a cunning game, found out if Caradoc knew where Non was living, rather than let his temper get the better of him. He took a deep breath. He had work to do: if he intended to ask Non again to be his wife, he would need all the money he could earn.

Morgan caught sight of the head drover, who was waving impatiently at him, obviously wanting some work done on his beasts. Morgan pushed his cap back on his head and rolled up his sleeves. He would work hard until the sun set, and then he would try to find where Manon Jenkins was living. It shouldn't be too difficult, her fame as a healer was spreading round the town. But first he had to earn enough money to offer her the best life he could.

\*　　\*　　\*

'You've done wot?' Ruby was looking at Non with large eyes. 'Rented a *shop*?' She sank into a chair in the small kitchen and waved her hands in front of her face. 'Oh my Gawd, that don't mean you're leaving my place, does it? I'd miss you like hell if you went away.'

Non put her basket on the shelf and took off her coat. 'I'm staying here for as long as you'll have me,' she said. 'I've only rented one room, so I'll need a place to eat and sleep, and you, my dear friend, are the best cook for miles around.'

She sat down abruptly. Suddenly the room

320

seemed to darken, everything was receding from her vision and she realized she was about to faint. Next thing she knew, she was on the cold stone floor and Ruby was bending over her, holding a burnt feather under her nose.

'Wot's up with you, Non?' There was a fearful note in her voice. 'You ain't been near the market and caught the animal plague, have you?'

Non struggled to sit up. She shook her head. 'No, it's all right, I'm quite well, I've just walked a long way today.'

Ruby seemed to accept her excuse. She nodded her head and helped Non to her feet. 'Come on, sit down, have a nice cuppa tea and rest a bit, then you'll feel better.'

Non watched as Ruby made the tea, and clasped her hands together to stop them trembling. What she'd suspected for some weeks was now almost a certainty. She'd thickened in the middle, she'd missed her monthly courses and now she couldn't walk a few miles without fainting.

'Ruby,' she said quietly, 'I think I'm with child.'

## CHAPTER THIRTY-ONE

It was a bright sunny day; the rain clouds of the past week had gone and the air outside was clear and sparkling. Georgina was walking with her father in the park behind Aunt Prudence's house. The thought of going home with Papa and meeting up with the odious Mr Mapleton again filled her with dread.

'What did you think of Mr Langland, Papa?' she

asked in a small voice.

Her father looked down at her with a twinkle in his eye. 'He's very handsome, and from what I've heard he has an eye for the ladies. Not that there's anything wrong with that, of course,' he added hastily, and Georgina hid a smile. Her father was well known for his fondness of the fairer sex; everyone knew he'd had several mistresses.

'Well, Papa, Mr Langland is very rich and very attentive, and I think he would make me a better husband than Mr Mapleton, who is, after all, stuck in the backwaters of Swansea. And,' she added slyly, 'he's very old and perhaps wouldn't give me a good healthy brood of children.'

'All right, Georgina, no need to labour the point. I can see you're very much taken with Clive Langland.'

'So I have your permission for him to call on me, do I?'

'I suppose so. You always get your way in the end, don't you?' He put his arm around her shoulders. 'But a word of warning: take things slowly. After all, none of us knows very much about our Mr Langland except what your Aunt Prudence tells us.'

Georgina hugged herself. She had what she wanted and now there was a chance to supply her father with a little titbit of gossip. 'You went to see that trollop Manon Jenkins, didn't you, Papa?' She spoke innocently, her eyes wide as they looked up at her father.

'Now, Georgina, do keep your own council about things you don't understand.' George Jones spoke coldly. Even though she was his beloved daughter, Georgina sometimes had to tread warily

322

where he was concerned.

'It's just that one of Auntie's maids was shopping for me in Covent Garden, and she met up with a friend of hers.'

George yawned, demonstrating that chatter about servants bored him. But Georgina congratulated herself that he wouldn't be bored once he heard her news. 'Well, Beryl was talking to a woman who rents a room to Manon Jenkins.'

Her father looked down at her and shook his head. 'So what's your point, Georgina? You're clearly set on telling me some bit of juicy gossip.'

'It's not just gossip, Papa. It seems that Manon is with child. She has all the symptoms.'

'And what would you know about such things?'

'Only what I was told, but the hussy must have been playing fast and loose since she came to London.'

'If this is true, the child must be Caradoc's,' her father said slowly. 'I've had the girl watched and she's kept very much to herself.' He stopped walking and took his daughter by the shoulders. 'She must be well gone by now, but say nothing of this to anyone. If that girl is having my grandson then she must give him up to me the minute he's born.'

Georgina couldn't believe what she was hearing. She'd expected her father to condemn Manon, to be contemptuous of a woman who would put herself in such a position, but all he was concerned about was the unborn brat.

'Well, I know Manon was very friendly with Morgan the smithy on the way up from home. Perhaps the child is his?'

Her father shook his head. 'You forget,

Georgina, I keep myself well informed about the drove and anything to do with it. I might not have been with you personally, but I had eyes and ears there, watching and listening to everything that was going on.'

Georgina didn't doubt it. Her father was formidable when he chose to be. He was head of the Bank of the Black Ox, he was very rich and influential, he was a man to be reckoned with and she had sadly misjudged his reaction to her news.

'Come along, our walk is over. You must stay indoors today, I won't have you repeating idle gossip to anyone you come across. Come on, hurry, I have things to do.'

Georgina looked up at him with a feeling of exasperation. He had forgotten all about her problems. All he cared about was Caradoc and the possibility of that witch Manon Jenkins providing him with an heir. Well, one day Manon Jenkins would get her just desserts, and Georgina hoped she would be there to see it.

\*    \*    \*

The little shop in Orange Street was doing well. Trade was brisk and Non was kept busy mixing potions and grinding roots with her pestle and mortar. So busy that sometimes Albie was drawn in to work in the shop.

Now Non wore an apron to conceal her burgeoning waistline. She had no idea what she was going to do when the baby was born, but for the time being, the best thing seemed to be to make a good living. She had stocked up on herbs by drying them over the big mantelshelf, ready for use in the

324

winter months.

She would need help from Ruby when the baby was born, and Ruby was very willing, a good friend; in a way she'd taken Mary's place since Non had come to live in London. And she needed friends now as she'd never needed them before.

The small bell she'd had placed on the door tinkled as a big man entered the shop. Non looked up, and felt a shock as she saw Mr George Jones standing behind her table looking down at her, his eyes on her apron.

He knew! Somehow George Jones had learned she was with child. She lifted her chin and took a deep breath. 'Yes, Sir, what can I do for you this morning?'

'You can talk,' he said bluntly. 'You can tell me how far gone you are with my son's child.'

'How dare you?' Non's voice was hard. 'My private life has nothing to do with you. I thought I'd made that clear when we last met.'

'You don't understand, I want to help,' he said. 'I'll willingly take responsibility for my son's actions. I'll bring the child up as one of the family.'

Non looked at him in disbelief. Did he really think he could take her child away from her so easily? 'There's no need for you to take any responsibility for anything to do with me,' she said. 'I am making a good living here and I can provide for myself and my baby without your help.'

'Don't be foolish, girl,' he said. 'Don't you realize what sort of privileged life I could give the child? He would have the best of everything—a good education and a thriving business to inherit when the time was right.'

'He would have everything except a mother,'

Non said. 'Well, forget it, Mr Jones. I am keeping my child, and I don't want or need any favours from you.' She walked to the door and opened it. 'Good day to you, Mr Jones.'

He stood beside her for a moment, looking down at her, and Non felt a rush of anger. 'If your family is so concerned, why isn't Caradoc here himself? Is it that he can't face the consequences of his actions?'

'My son has other things on his mind,' George Jones said. 'I persuaded him to leave at once for home. I don't want him delayed by the news that you are carrying his child.'

'When is he coming back?'

'That's nothing to do with you.' George Jones looked down at her with a scowl on his face. 'And I'm telling you now, I'll get that child away from you, whatever it takes.'

Non went to the shelf where she kept her bottles of medicines. 'Take this mixture of briony and wild vine,' she said cuttingly, 'it might help calm you down.'

He backed away from her. Non followed him and closed the door behind him with a resounding bang.

By the time she reached home that evening, Non was worn out. She felt a chill every time she thought of Mr Jones's visit. The determined way he'd spoken to her about her baby frightened her.

Ruby knew at once that something was wrong. 'You're very pale, Non. Should you be working so hard in your condition? Sit down and I'll make you a nice cup of tea. Put your feet up, girl, you're looking washed out.'

Ruby made the tea and brought it to Non, who

was sitting in the rocking chair. 'Now what's upset you? Because something 'as.'

'It's nothing. Just an awkward customer, that's all.'

'Don't tell me lies, Non. I know you too well for that. Come on, who has upset you?'

'Caradoc Jones, leader of the drove, is the father of my child.' Non looked for any sign of disapproval from Ruby, but she just shrugged.

'So? He's not rushing round here to help exactly, is he? Forget him. Just you look after yourself.'

'I don't think Caradoc even knows about my condition, but his father found out about the baby somehow and he wants to take it away from me.'

Ruby looked shame-faced. 'Then it's all my fault,' she said, shaking her head. 'I gossiped to a friend in the market, she's a maid in one of the big houses. I told her about you, that I was worried an' all, and she must have carried the tale.'

Non sighed. It wasn't important how Mr Jones knew, but if he thought he could interfere in her life, well, he would have to think again.

\*     \*     \*

Georgina stood near the fireplace in Aunt Prudence's drawing room, looking over at Mr Langland with a feeling of pride; he was holding court in a roomful of young ladies and yet his eyes were constantly on her. Georgina felt the colour come into her face as he caught her eye and winked saucily at her. How she wished she could be alone with him. She wanted to feel his mouth on hers, to have his strong arms hold her close.

Her colour deepened as Aunt Prudence came

327

into the room and bustled towards her, ploughing through the assorted company as though she was a battleship at sea.

'What's this, Georgina? Standing in a corner dreaming will get you nowhere. For heaven's sake, go and talk to Mr Langland. You'll not make your dreams come true by being too coy.'

Aunt Prudence would be scandalized if she knew just how intimate she and Clive had become; they had shared stolen kisses on more than one occasion.

'I can't just walk boldly up to Mr Langland as though I was eager for his attention,' she said with a shyness she didn't feel.

'Well then, I'll take you myself. Listen, there's the music starting up; he'll want to dance with you, I'm sure.'

Georgina allowed her aunt to draw her across the room, and watched as she caught Mr Langland's arm. 'My dear boy, do dance with my niece. She's such a shy little thing, and not at all used to the smart society one finds in London. You must enlighten her to our ways, Mr Langland, show her around our fair city and such.'

'I would do that gladly.' He smiled at Georgina and her heart began to pound. He held out his arms and she went into them eagerly. He laughed, and she noticed the dimples that appeared in his cheeks with a feeling of tenderness.

'Come along and relax, Miss Jones,' he said. 'You are a timid little thing, aren't you?' He bent close and whispered in her ear. 'I am always happy to "enlighten you to our ways", Georgina.'

She smiled up at him. 'If you can spare the time from your other admirers,' Georgina said teasingly.

'I have all the time in the world, and I will gladly spend it with you.' He took her hand and kissed it, and looking up into his sparkling eyes, Georgina realized with a rush like the tide sweeping the shore that not only did she desire Clive Langland, but she had fallen in love with him.


# CHAPTER THIRTY-TWO

Non stood at the table, sleeves rolled up above her elbows as she ground angelica into a paste. She looked up as Albie appeared in the doorway. He was sniffling miserably.

'We've got to get out of our house, Miss.'

'What do you mean, get out of the house? Who's been telling you that?'

'My grandpa got a letter. Here, you read it, Miss. Perhaps there's bin a mistake, Grandpa isn't very good at reading.'

Non took the folded letter and opened it. The writing was bold, the tone clipped. Albie was right: it was a notice terminating the tenancy. She looked at the foot of the document and saw that the signature was that of a solicitor. It was a name she didn't recognize, but she knew at once who was behind this sudden decision to throw them out of the house.

She folded the letter carefully and handed it back to Albie. 'Don't worry, I'll see what I can do.' She took her shawl from behind the door. 'Try not to be upset. I'm sure this is all just a silly mistake.'

She took a cab across London, and though she was reluctant to spend good money on the fare, she felt the expense was justified. She stared out of the window at the long, wide roads, lined by fine buildings, that were opening up into large, stately squares. Looking round her at the houses, all the same, all elegant, large and imposing, she felt suddenly afraid. What if Caradoc was there, what would her reception be? He must know by now that she was going to have his child—how would he react?

When she alighted from the cab, she looked around, trying to get her bearings. And then she saw it: number 83, a house like all the others. And yet she could not stop the fast beating of her heart as she thought that Caradoc might be inside.

The butler who opened the door stared down at her coldly, and when she asked to speak to Mr George Jones, he frowned. 'Have you an appointment, Miss?' he asked haughtily.

'No,' Non said. 'But if you give Mr Jones my name, I'm sure he'll want to see me.'

'I'm sorry, Miss, we are not accustomed to strange women arriving on the doorstep wanting to see the Master without an appointment.'

'Well,' Non stepped into the hallway, 'I shan't move until you tell him I'm here.' She stood firmly inside the door. 'I was chaperone to Miss Georgina when we travelled up from Wales, and Mr Jones will be happy to see me, I assure you.'

'Wait here, I'll see if Mr Jones is at home.' The man walked away, the stiffness of his shoulders attesting to his indignation. Non could almost hear him grumbling about 'strange women', but she didn't care. She had to see Mr Jones and try to withdraw the notice terminating Albie's grandfather's tenancy.

After what seemed an eternity, the butler reappeared and gestured for Non to follow him. His expression was a mask of disapproval and Non resisted the temptation to make a face behind his back.

George Jones was seated at his desk in the big room at the front of the house. He must have seen her arrive at the door, but he'd played a cat and mouse game, keeping her waiting until he was ready to see her. Standing beside him was a man who was strangely familiar to Non. He was well dressed, almost foppish, and his eyes narrowed as they took in her appearance.

'I know why you've come,' George Jones said. 'Please, Miss Jenkins, take a seat, and might I add that you shouldn't be gadding about London in your condition.'

'Never mind about me.' Non remained standing. 'I'm here to ask why you want to turn Albie and his grandfather out of the house they rent. It's a poor enough premises and you get your rent regularly.'

'That's where you are wrong.' Mr Jones waved his hand towards the other man. 'Mr Langland here owns the premises you mention, it's nothing to do with me.'

'You might not own the house, but you are behind this.' She waved the letter at him.

Mr Langland smiled thinly. 'We meet again, Miss Jenkins. It was my decision to terminate the tenancy. There have been complaints from some of the neighbours about the unsuitability of a pregnant woman and two men inhabiting the same house. There are many tenants out there just waiting for an opportunity to take over the building. I agree. In any case, I can charge a new

331

tenant a higher rent. This is business, it's nothing personal.'

'Don't insult my intelligence, Mr Langland!' Non took a deep breath; she would get nowhere by being angry. 'Look, I'll move my things out at once, will that suit you?'

George Jones held up his hand. 'Perhaps I can help,' he said. He picked up a pen and tapped his teeth with it. 'I'm sure Mr Langland will agree with me that the boy and the old man can stay where they are on one condition.'

'And that is?'

'Simply that you move to a place of my choosing, a comfortable house with your own servants. You will not have to lift a finger, you will be taken care of, and then, when my grandson is born, you must hand him over to me.'

Non sighed in despair. 'Look, Mr Jones, please don't take out your anger on innocent people. I'll move my shop out of there right away, but I can't and won't give up my child.' She moved closer to the desk. 'What does Caradoc have to say about all this? If you are so concerned about your grandson, why don't you send Caradoc to see me, and then we could talk things over like civilized people.'

'My son is busy at the moment. In any case, I don't think he wishes to discuss the matter with you.' He got to his feet and stared at her coldly. 'Now, if you won't agree to my terms, you, the boy and the old man have until the end of the week to vacate the premises. Is that clear?'

'But that's so unfair!' Non took a deep breath. 'I thought you were a man of the people yourself, so why punish an innocent boy and an old man when the only one you are angry at is me?'

He walked round the desk and stood close to her. 'I'm not angry with you, I don't care enough about you to feel angry. All I want is for you to hand over my son's child. Once you've done that you can go your own way to hell.'

Non walked to the door and stood for a moment looking back at George Jones. He had already turned his back to her and was settling in his seat. She could see where Georgina got her spiteful nature; she'd inherited it from her father.

'Thank you for your time, Mr Jones,' her voice was edged with sarcasm, 'and you, Mr Langland, good day to you.'

When she returned to the narrow house on Orange Street, Albie was there to greet her. 'Is everything all right? Have you sorted it out, Miss?'

She shook her head. 'No, Albie, but don't be upset, I'll think of something.'

'But what, Miss?'

'Look, first thing in the morning I'll find us other lodgings. It will be a bit of an upheaval, but it'll work out all right, you'll see.'

Albie bit his lip. It was clear he didn't want to leave the home he shared with his grandpa, but he met her eye bravely. She rested her hand on his shoulder for a moment. 'We'll be all right, I promise you.'

'But Miss, people know where to find you now. How will your customers find you when we move?'

'When I've got us a place, I'll tell everyone who comes into the shop where to find me. It will work out just fine, you'll see.'

Her words were brave, but Non felt sick when she thought of leaving the house where she'd made such a success of her business, and where Albie and his grandfather had lived so comfortably.

The next morning, she spoke to Ruby. 'I have to ask you a favour.' She sat at the kitchen table and looked up at her friend anxiously. 'Because of me, Albie and his grandfather are to be evicted from their home. Could you possibly put them up here for a few days until I find somewhere else?'

Ruby sat opposite her and looked down at her hands. 'Well, there aren't any rooms free, but they could stay in the kitchen for a few nights, I suppose.'

'What if they have my room? I can sleep on the sofa in the sitting room.'

'Well, that would be all right,' Ruby said reluctantly, 'but only for a night or two.' She looked into the fire, avoiding Non's eyes. 'I don't suppose I dare ask how they makes their living.'

'No,' Non half smiled, 'they were getting by on the little Albie and the old man could earn.'

'Bleedin' steal, you means, girl.'

'Aye, I suppose that's what I mean. Well, is it all right then, Ruby? I promise I'll start looking for rooms right away.'

Ruby nodded reluctantly. 'All right, bring them over and we'll see what's what. Now, I don't know about you, but I got work to do.'

On an impulse, Non hugged Ruby. 'You're the kindest person I know,' she said softly, 'and I won't let you down. I'll go out right away and find somewhere to rent. I've got a little money saved, so it shouldn't be too hard.' She paused in the doorway. 'Thank you, Ruby, from the bottom of my heart.'

\* \* \*

334

Caradoc looked out into the gloomy rain-filled sky, wishing now that he'd not sent the drove to London ahead of him. Still, he had to meet with the farmers on the trail: every one of them was feeling the pinch after the last disastrous trip. He was staying at one of the better inns at Tring, at a loose end waiting for the mail coach to arrive the next morning. He couldn't wait to get to London and speak to Non. The last time he'd made love to her had left an indelible image of her on his mind. She was so perfect in every way; how could he have waited so long to see it?

He looked up as the landlord brought a letter to him. 'This is for you, Sir.'

Caradoc knew by the writing that his sister had taken a few minutes of her precious time to contact him. Whatever she had to say, it must be important. 'Thank you, landlord.'

He had some important news too, about her precious Clive Langland. The man was all but bankrupt. Caradoc's solicitor had contacts in London, and it had needed only the exchange of a few letters to find out that the man was a fool and a liar.

Georgina's letter began plainly enough, asking when could she expect to see him in London, as she was going to be married very soon.

'Not if I can help it.' Caradoc said the words aloud and strode to the window, holding the letter tightly between his fingers as though he was holding the man by the throat. He returned to the letter, and the last few lines drove all other thoughts from his mind. He looked carefully at the words again.

Your floosy Manon Jenkins is with child and Father, poor fool, believes that you are responsible. He intends to get the infant from her as soon as it is born.

> Love,
> From your sister Georgina.

Caradoc crumpled the letter in his hand. Non expecting a child—could it be true? The sooner he reached London and found out for himself what was really going on, the better.


## CHAPTER THIRTY-THREE

Georgina stood in the hallway, staring at the closed door of the drawing room. Clive was inside with Papa, asking for her hand in marriage. The two of them had been closeted there for almost an hour and Georgina feared her father was making difficulties.

Several minutes later, the door opened and Clive emerged, smiling. Georgina ran into his arms. He kissed her chastely on the cheek. 'Your father has consented to our marriage,' he said, holding her away from him. 'I rather think your Aunt Prudence convinced him I was a man to be trusted.'

'Good old Auntie!'

George Jones came into the hall and took his daughter's hand. 'To tell you the truth, my dear,' he said with a twinkle in his eye, 'I'll be happy to see you safely married.'

'Oh, Papa, don't be silly!' Georgina kissed him.

'I'm so happy!' She turned to look at Clive. 'Can the wedding be soon?' She felt she couldn't wait to be Clive's wife, to be in charge of his large house, with servants to wait on her hand and foot. Clive was not only handsome but he was a good catch. Georgina mentally hugged herself in delight.

'As soon as it can be arranged, my darling.' Clive gazed at her, and she blushed with pleasure, wondering how she would feel when she was truly a married lady.

She watched as her father shook Clive's hand. 'I suppose an early marriage is all right with you, young Langland?'

'Perfectly, Sir. I couldn't ask for a more beautiful or accomplished lady to be my wife.'

Later, when Clive had gone home, Georgina sought out her father. 'I'm so pleased you like him,' she said, putting her hand through his arm. 'And you needn't worry about grandsons, I should think Clive and I will provide you with as many as you can handle.'

He kissed her cheek fondly. 'And I will love them all. But you must remember that if Caradoc fathers a son, the boy will be my heir.'

Georgina felt her spirits drop. Her marriage would be a momentous occasion, but all Papa could think of was Caradoc and the bastard child he was bringing into the world. She wanted to stamp her feet and scream for attention, but for a well-born lady that was out of the question. Instead, she promised herself that once she was married, no one would ever dictate to her again.

\*　　　\*　　　\*

Non felt a sense of homecoming as she let herself into Ruby's house. It was familiar and inviting, and the stench from the river was overridden by the smell of freshly baked bread.

Ruby was sitting in a chair near the fire. She looked up when she saw Non, and dabbed her face with her apron. 'There's a letter come.' She handed Non a sheet of paper. 'I can't read it, but I have a feeling it's going to be bad news. I never had a letter before.'

Non took it and quickly read the curt sentences; after a moment she sat down opposite Ruby. 'As you thought, it's bad news.'

'Tell me then,' Ruby said, ' 'as somebody died?'

'No, it's nothing like that. It's about the house— it's been sold.' She reached out and touched Ruby's hand. 'I thought you owned it, Ruby.'

'I do. Well, put it like this, me and my brother Bernie own it between us.' She shook her head. 'It can't be sold, I haven't signed any papers or anything like that.'

'It seems your brother's done it for you. It says here you're to have half of the proceeds.'

'But this is my 'ome!' Ruby fanned her face with her hand. 'I can't be chucked out of my own place, can I?'

Non knew who was behind the plan to buy the house. It looked as if George Jones would go to any lengths to get his own way.

'We've got till the end of the week, that's all,' she said quietly. 'But don't worry, Ruby, I'll find us somewhere to live.'

Ruby began to cry. 'But I don't want to leave here! I don't want to be chucked out of the only home I've ever known.'

Non rubbed her head; she felt a pain across her brow. 'I'm sorry, Ruby, I really am sorry.'

'Well, it's not your fault,' Ruby said. 'It's that brother of mine, he's daft as a brush and I don't suppose he got a fair price for the place, either.'

In that, Ruby was wrong. Her brother arrived later that night, looking jubilant. He bustled into the kitchen and kissed his sister on the cheek.

Ruby pushed him away. 'What the 'ell do you think you were doing, selling me 'ouse over me 'ead?'

'I made a good deal, Ruby,' Bernie spoke eagerly. 'The bloke who bought the old place from me paid me twice what it's worth.'

'Have you got the money, then?'

'Well, no,' he said. 'But it'll be in the bank first thing in the morning.'

'You fool, Bernie!' Ruby was flushed with anger. 'You should have got the money straight away. I don't trust banks. Another thing—I never wanted to sell the house. I was born here and I thought I'd bleedin' die here.'

'But we can buy a house each out of the money we made,' Bernie said. 'I thought I was doing the right thing.'

'Well, you should have talked to me,' Ruby said. 'I haven't signed anything. I'll see one of them solicitors, get the sale cancelled.'

'You can't do that,' Bernie said. 'I wrote your mark for you, it's all legal, like.'

Ruby looked at Non. 'Is he right, do you think?'

'I'm afraid so.' Non took Ruby's hand. 'Mr Jones would have made sure of that.'

'Mr Jones—the toff who came here looking for you? And to think I made him welcome in my

339

house. If I'd known what he was after, I'd have poured the cabbage water all over him.'

She began to cry in earnest. 'I'm frightened of living anywhere else. And if we don't find a nice place, what'll I do?'

Non put her arms around Ruby's shoulders. 'Don't worry, I'll see us all right, I promise you.'

'I hope you're right, otherwise we'll all be sleeping rough in the streets.' Ruby glared at her brother. 'And it will be all your fault, Bernard Simkins!'

*       *       *

'I don't see what the big rush is.' George Jones eased himself back in the chair and frowned at his daughter. 'I knew you wanted to be married soon, but next week is out of the question. There is a great deal to be arranged. I want your wedding to be a fine affair.' He looked at her closely, his eyes pausing at her waistline. 'There isn't something you're not telling me, is there, Georgie?'

'Of course not, Papa. It's just that I love Clive so much and he'd like the wedding to be soon and so would I. So why wait?'

George Jones sighed, and ruffled his daughter's hair. 'I suppose you'll be happy living here in town. At least you'll be near Aunt Prudence.'

Georgina looked startled. 'I suppose you're right, I'd never thought about that. Of course, Clive will want to live in London, he has a fine house in Bloomsbury.'

'You don't sound too sure of yourself, girl.' George looked at her sternly. 'Now is this wedding what you really want?'

340

She rushed into his arms and buried her face against his neck. 'I'm sure, Papa. I love Clive so much it hurts.'

'Well then, you just remember to be obedient to your husband in all things. I can't talk women's talk, but anything you don't know about the duties of a wife you can ask your Aunt Prudence.' He held her away from him. 'Now, let's settle down and talk about the practicalities.'

He took his daughter's hand and kissed it. He wasn't often given to shows of affection, but he would miss Georgie; she was such a sweet, loving girl. Still, she had chosen well. There hadn't been time yet to check her prospective husband out, but if he owned a prime piece of property in Bloomsbury he must be a rich man. Clive Langland seemed to be a good catch for his daughter, and if Prudence recommended him then he must be all right. Still, it wouldn't do any harm to look more closely into the man's prospects; it was a father's duty and George Jones was never a man to shirk his duty.

\*       \*       \*

'I've found us a house!' Non burst into the kitchen, anxious to tell everyone her good news. 'I've put a deposit on it. It's not very big, but it's cheap and there's a front room I can turn into a shop.'

'Stop rushing about like that, Non. You're in a delicate state and you shouldn't be taking any risks. And what did you say? A house you're renting—a whole house? How are you going to pay for it?' Ruby rubbed her hands in her apron, her forehead creased into lines of worry.

341

'I'm going to let out rooms, of course. There's young Albie and his grandpa, they are happy to lodge with us, and there'll be you and me, all of us contributing to the rent. I've cleared it with the landlord. It will be all right, don't you worry.'

'I got a right to worry. I won't have any money until my brother tells me the bank has paid up. Bleedin' banks, never did understand them.'

Non hugged her. 'You took me in when I couldn't pay you rent, remember? Well, now I'm going to do the same for you. Once the bank pays you we can square the rent. Later on, when I'm earning a regular living, we might even be able to buy a house between us.'

Ruby sank into her chair. She put her head in her hands and large tears rolled down her cheeks. 'You're a real diamond, Non Jenkins, a real diamond. I should have known I could count on you.' After a moment she brushed away her tears. 'I can't sit here crying like a baby, there's packing to be done and all sorts of things to sort out. I don't know if I'm coming or going.'

Non took her arm and guided her to the door. 'First thing you're going to do is look at our new home. I want to know what you think of it.'

Ruby pulled away. 'Your word is good enough for me. If you says it's fit to live in then it must be. Is the house near the river?'

'I'm afraid so,' Non said, 'but we can put cloths soaked in ammonia over the windows, just as you've done here. In any case, I think I've become quite used to the smell now.' She hugged Ruby's arm. 'First thing in the morning we'll go over there. It will be light then and you can choose which room is to be yours.'

'And can I work in the kitchen, like always?'

Non smiled. 'I promise you, the kitchen is all yours. How else am I going to feed the lodgers?'

'Let's have a mug of my gooseberry wine to celebrate, shall we?' Ruby's face brightened. 'I think we deserve a little pick-me-up.' She went across the kitchen into the larder, where the wine stood in thick bottles on the cold slab.

'This will soon make everything seem rosy and good. We'll be singing, mind, if we drink too much of it. Strong stuff, is my gooseberry wine.'

They sat talking and drinking and making plans, and at last Ruby yawned widely. 'I better get off to my bed,' she said. 'I think the drink is gone to me 'ead.' She touched Non on the shoulder. 'And you need your rest too, wot with a little one growing in your belly. Sleep tight, Non, tomorrow is another day.'

*       *       *

The house was tall and narrow, with small steps leading up to the door. The address was grand, but the building showed signs of neglect. Non stood with Ruby on the pavement, looking up at the begrimed windows. Then she led the way to the door and unlocked it.

'Our new home, Ruby.' She led the way down the dimness of the passage and into the kitchen.

'Gawd, wot a size on a kitchen! And look at that table—big enough to roll out pastry for at least two dozen lodgers.' She beamed at Non. 'We're going to do well here, I can feel it in my water.'

Ruby was right. Within a week, most of the rooms were occupied: Albie and his grandfather

343

took the ones on the first floor, and the floor above was soon let to an elderly shoemaker and his wife. It was only the two attic rooms that stood empty.

Meanwhile, Non was making good use of the front room. It had a big mullioned window facing the narrow street outside, and served as a fine shop. Most of her old customers had followed her from Orange Street and placed regular orders for her herbal syrups and infusions.

She was in her back room mixing some ginger root when the doorbell rang, echoing through the house. It was a Friday morning and the cattle market would be in full swing, so Non expected to be busy; she'd prepared some ready-bottled remedies for everything from a chesty cough to bunions on the foot. She bustled into the shop, wiping her hands on her apron, a polite smile on her face as she greeted the two women. 'What can I do for you, ladies?'

'*Duw*, Non, it's me, Flora, and this is Jessie. You haven't forgotten me already, have you?'

'Of course not!' Non went to the other side of her counter and hugged Flora. 'What are you doing here in London?'

'What do you think?' Flora said. 'We've come up with another drove. We didn't expect a job so quick, but the Joneses had bad luck with the last herd. They had to be slaughtered, it was the rinderpest, didn't you know?'

'I had heard something,' Non said, reluctant to talk about Caradoc and his troubles.

'Well, of course there was no money in it for Mr Caradoc Jones, he had to come back to Five Saints and build up another herd to make a fresh start, didn't he?' Flora fanned her hand across her nose.

'*Duw*, it stinks round here. It's the river, I 'spects. The Tawe back home is just as bad, something should be done about it.'

Jessie nudged Flora. 'Go on, ask her.'

Flora nodded. 'All right, give me time. Look, Non, we haven't come here to chatter about home or to buy any medicine. We've heard you got rooms going empty, and as we want to stay in London for a bit we thought we'd take them, if you'll have us, mind.'

'Of course I'll have you!' Non said. 'I'll be delighted to have you living here, but you have to pay your rent like everyone else, mind.'

'That's all right, Mr Jones has paid us our money. It'll tide us over until we find work in London, won't it, Flora?' said Jessie.

'Well, Non,' Flora said, her sharp eyes missing nothing. 'What's been happening to you, girl? You're a might different from the girl who joined the drove all those months ago.' She looked meaningfully at Non's stomach.

'It's a long story and a common one, I'm afraid.' Non held out her hand and showed the brass ring on her third finger. 'I'm called Mrs Jenkins by folk around here.'

'I think I know who planted that seed,' Flora said. 'Anyone could see you were head over heels about Mr Jones, so it don't take much working out. Does he know?'

'Well, I'm not sure. His father knows and so does Miss Georgina. I expect Caradoc will know everything by now.'

'Well, he's a decent boss,' Jessie said. 'I think he'll do right by you and give you money to keep the child.'

345

Non shook her head. 'I don't want the Jones family coming anywhere near me or my baby. I'll take care of things myself. Now, do you want to see these attic rooms before I get busy in the shop?'

As she led the way up the uncarpeted stairs, Non's spirits were low. In spite of her efforts to make a success of her life, the shadow of Mr Jones and his threats to take the child away from her were making her miserable. But the Joneses had no rights over her or her baby; she would see them all in hell before she would let them take what was rightfully hers.

She forced a smile. 'It will be like old times, all of us together. I'm glad of my friends now, Flora.' She spoke the truth, for she knew that she was going to need friends when her child was born as she'd never needed them before.

# CHAPTER THIRTY-FOUR

Georgina was standing in the sunny drawing room, staring out into the garden. Aunt Prudence's house had a fine garden at the back of the building, which sported trees, mature shrubs and a large area of green lawn.

The doorbell rang, echoing through the hall. She heard the maid answer it, and then, with her heart beating fast, she heard Clive's voice. He'd come for her.

'My dear Georgina.' He bowed over her hand and kissed her fingers, and Georgina resisted the urge to fall into his arms and hold him close. 'Are you ready, my darling?'

She was—her bag was packed, hidden behind the curtains. No one had noticed that some of her clothes were no longer in the wardrobe in her bedroom.

'Oh Clive, we are doing the right thing, aren't we?'

'Of course we are, darling. If we wait for all the pomp and ceremony of a big wedding it won't happen for months.' He leaned closer. 'And I can't wait any longer to call you my wife and take care of you the way a husband should.'

Georgina leaned against him. She was impatient too, but part of her wanted the big wedding, the elegant coaches, the church full of people. But there was a snag: Papa had decided that he wanted her married in the big church in Swansea, and that would take ages to arrange. Clive was right, an elopement was the quickest solution. It was also very romantic, she told herself.

'The coach is waiting outside,' Clive said persuasively, 'and I have everything arranged for our wedding this afternoon.' He smiled his charming smile. 'I have a gift for you.' He took a pouch out of his pocket and shook a ring onto the palm of his hand. It was a small ring, but set with fine diamonds and rubies that sparkled in the sunlight. 'This was my mother's,' he said. 'She would be so pleased for you to have it, God rest her soul.'

'It's beautiful.' Georgina was suddenly filled with the excitement of the occasion: tonight she would be Mrs Clive Langland and mistress of a large establishment. And if her papa had any qualms about such a hasty marriage, it would be too late for him to do anything about it. Not that he was all that interested in her marriage, he was more concerned with taking the bastard child from Manon Jenkins.

'We'd better leave right away,' she said, 'while Aunt Prudence is out. Otherwise she'll insist we take a chaperone.' She thought suddenly about Manon Jenkins, who had chaperoned her all the way from Swansea and all that was familiar. For a moment she wavered. Was she doing the right thing? Would she regret leaving Five Saints for good?

Clive touched her cheek. 'Are you all right, Georgina?'

'Of course I am,' she said stoutly. 'I want to spend the rest of my life with you, Clive, wherever that might be.'

She left the house with her head bowed. The maid who opened the door for her was frowning, but she was too timid to ask any questions. As Georgina took her place in the carriage, she glanced up at the elegant square and reassured herself that she would be coming back as Clive's bride. Once her papa and her dear Aunt Prue got over the shock, all would be well.

Clive took her hand. 'Well, my dear, we're on our way to good fortune.' He smiled and kissed her.

She glanced up at him. 'Good fortune, what a funny thing to say!'

'Well, it's my good fortune to have met and fallen in love with such a wonderful lady, that's all I meant, my dearest darling.'

He shouted an order to the driver and the coach jogged into motion. Georgina felt as though a thousand butterflies were fluttering within her, but the touch of Clive's hand on hers gave her courage.

'Clive,' she looked up at him, admiring his dark good looks, 'you do love me, don't you?'

He leaned forward and his lips touched hers, and all doubts vanished from her head.

\*     \*     \*

Non leaned against the table, pausing in her work of grinding gladwin roots into pulp to make yet another syrup. This time the medication was for her own use; it helped ease the stomach cramps she sometimes experienced at the end of the day, when she'd been on her feet too much.

The doorbell chimed and a flurry of customers entered together, a group of well-dressed servants. They made regular visits, buying syrups and elixirs for their mistresses who lived in the big houses in the richer parts of London.

Non took her time serving. It was imperative that she make the correct selection of medication for the variety of complaints she was presented with. It was by this means that she was building her reputation as a reliable herbalist.

When her customers had departed, Non sank into the chair she kept near the counter. Her belly was larger now, and she was feeling more tired as each day passed. She closed her eyes and rested for a moment, but the bell rang sharply again and the door opened to admit a tall, familiar figure.

'Caradoc!' The child within her kicked, as though in response to her feelings of shock and pleasure.

He stood looking down. 'My dear, dear Non.' He came around the counter and took her hands in his.

'I love you, Non. I came as soon as I heard about the baby.'

'You've told me you loved me before, but it didn't really mean anything, did it? Did you know that your father has threatened to take the child from me? I expect you know exactly what's been going on and you're hoping to dupe me into believing you love me, so that you can claim your son.'

He smiled. 'You're convinced it's going to be a boy, then?'

Non shook her head. 'No, but your father is, he is a strong man. Tell me the truth, Caradoc, has your father sent you round here to talk me into parting with the baby?'

'Of course not!' Caradoc said. He lifted her fingers to his lips and kissed them. 'I've come here to see you because I wanted to make sure you were all right. I meant it when I said I love you. I can't get you out of my head, Non, I want to—'

Not waiting for him to continue, she pulled her hands away. He had said nothing about marriage, not even now. All he wanted, like his father, was to take the baby from her and bring it up as part of the Jones family. Well, she wouldn't fall for his charms this time.

'You're wasting your breath,' she said firmly. 'The child isn't yours.'

He stepped back from her. 'But he must be mine. I'm the only man you've lain with.'

'You're wrong, you are forgetting about Morgan the smithy. He's what you call a real man, his intention always was to make an honest woman of me, which is more than you can say.'

'But I do want to marry you, Non. I love you, I

want to make you my wife.'

'I don't believe you. In any case, it's too late for that.' Non held out her hand. 'I'm already married.'

Caradoc's face shadowed. 'And the child is definitely not mine?'

'The child is not yours,' she said slowly and clearly. 'I don't want anything more to do with you or your father. Please tell him that for me, will you?'

Slowly, the light of happiness dying from his eyes, Caradoc left the shop. When he'd gone, Non sank into her chair and closed her eyes against the feelings of grief and pain. How could he have been so cruel, pretending he loved her, telling her he wanted to marry her? His family had made it plain to her that he had a fiancée waiting at home for him. A woman with money, position, someone who would grace his fine house and give him all the children he desired. Why then was Caradoc so eager to take her child from her?

'Is everything all right?' Ruby had come into the little shop. 'You look bleedin' worn out. Come on, shut up shop now, I'll make us a nice cup of tea.'

Non nodded. 'I'll lock up now and then I'll come through into the kitchen.' She opened the door for a moment, looking out into the twilight of the evening. The smell from the river was bad tonight; all day the sun had shone on the thick water, drawing from it the stench of the effluent that constantly flowed into it. But yet she had a feeling for London; now it had caught her it might never let her go.

She closed the door and walked slowly through the passage towards the light of the candles flickering in the large kitchen. The glow from the

351

fire reflected on the walls, and at that moment Non felt she was truly at home.

*     *     *

'And you believed her?' George Jones rose from his chair and confronted his son. 'You are a fool, Caradoc, more of a fool than I thought.'

His son frowned. 'Father, I talked to Non. She is married to Morgan Lewis, she tells me the child is his. There's nothing I can do about it.'

George shook his head. 'The girl was feeding you lies, Caradoc. She hasn't seen a great deal of Morgan, has she? He's been with the droves back and forth to Swansea, when would he have had time to get married?'

Caradoc shook his head. 'Non wouldn't lie to me.'

'And you have never lied to her? Come on, Caradoc, you must have sweet-talked her to get her into bed. Of course she's not married. The child she is carrying is yours, I have no doubts about it at all.' He could see by the fleeting expression crossing his son's face that his words had touched a raw spot. 'Talk to Morgan, ask him about this so-called marriage. I think you'll find I'm right.'

Caradoc looked at his father. 'I suppose you'll know where to find him?'

'You'll find him where the drovers always stay when they are in London. Use your brains, boy. Think with your head for once and not with what's in your trews.'

He watched his son leave, then took out his pocket-watch and frowned. Where in heaven's name was Georgina? It was almost time for supper;

she should be downstairs, not preening herself in her bedroom.

The door opened and Prudence came into the room, wringing her hands together. 'George, I don't know how to tell you this.' Tears welled in her eyes and she brushed them away.

'Tell me what, woman? Stop blubbering and speak sense, will you?'

'It's Georgie—she's gone!'

'What do you mean, gone? Is she out visiting? Is she at some ball or other with Clive Langland? Speak plainly, Prudence, for heaven's sake.'

Prudence took a crumpled note from her pocket and handed it to him. She was trembling from head to foot. 'The shame of it. Oh, George, what have I done to deserve this?'

George took the note and read it, and the paper fluttered from his hands onto the floor. He stared down at it as though mesmerized.

'Say something, George. Your daughter's eloped with Clive Langland. What are you going to do about it?'

'Do? I'm not going to do anything. The girl's made her bed, now just let her lie on it.'

## CHAPTER THIRTY-FIVE

Georgina stood close to the window, staring out at the hotel grounds outside Bath. She glanced down at her hand and saw the wedding band glint in the lamplight, and waited excitedly for Clive to join her. At the moment, he was fortifying himself with a stiff whisky. Georgina smiled, the consummating of a marriage was as new to him as it was to her. He'd held her, kissed and even caressed her when they'd managed to sneak a few minutes alone. She'd behaved in a way some would think immodest, but now they were man and wife she didn't know what to expect.

She heard his step and sat abruptly down on the bed. She'd undressed herself from sheer necessity—there had been no time to arrange for a maid to accompany her. She looked down at her nightgown: it was made of fine linen, with an edging of handmade lace. She loosened her hair so that it hung over her shoulders, covering the swell of her breasts beneath her gown.

There was a brief knock on the door and then Clive came into the bedroom. He looked down at her with a glint in his eyes that she found a little disconcerting.

'Are you ready for me, my love?' He stood before her and rested his hands on her shoulders. 'I hope so, because you are looking very beautiful, my sweet.'

He went into the dressing room and she heard him taking off his clothes. She was anxious, wondering if she would be the sort of wife he wanted. She twisted her wedding band, praying he would not be disappointed. When he came back into the room, he was naked. Georgina averted her eyes; she felt absurdly shy as her husband, his arousal obvious, came towards the bed.

He flung back the sheets and slid into the bed beside her. She lay there, not knowing what to expect. She knew what happened in the marriage bed, of course, but she really didn't know how to conduct herself.

'Clive,' she said in a small voice, 'tell me what I must do.'

'No need, my sweet, leave it all to me.' He rolled on top of her, pushing up her nightgown, and then his mouth was hot against her throat. Georgina liked his kisses, she wanted him to kiss her mouth, but he was too intent on other things. Before she knew it, he was pushing into her and she cried out in pain.

'There, there,' he said. 'It always hurts first time, so I'm told.' He leaned on his elbow and looked into her face. 'But I've never had a virgin before, so we'll just have to see how it goes. Be quiet now and let me get on with it.'

It seemed to last for hours. The pain, the blood that stained the bed, none of it stopped Clive from taking his pleasure again and again, until at last, exhausted, he rolled away from her.

Georgina stifled the tears that threatened to overflow.

'Was that good enough for you, eh?' Clive said, stretching his arms above his head as though he'd won some sort of victory. 'I must say I was on form tonight. Count yourself lucky, not every bride has a husband with such staying power.'

She wanted to tell him that love should be tender, that she would have liked a little more consideration of her feelings, but by the time she had composed the words in her mind, Clive had turned away from her and begun to snore. She would have ample time to talk to him, to ask him to teach her the duties of a wife but also give her pleasure in what should be a meeting of souls. At last, Georgina fell asleep with the tears still glistening on her lashes.

*     *     *

He'd gone out first thing in the morning, and now, with the sun casting a mellow evening glow over the fields, Clive had still not come home. Georgina sighed and moved away from the window. She stood for a moment staring into the mirror over the mantelshelf. There was nothing different about her appearance—she was the same Georgina who had stood before the priest to confirm the hastily arranged marriage only yesterday—and yet there was a difference. The eager, happy glow had left her eyes. Was her disappointment evident to Clive? If so, it didn't bother him. A tiny worry niggled at her. Had she made a mistake in marrying so hastily? She pushed the thought out of her mind, telling herself she was a very lucky girl to have such a fine handsome husband.

At last, when he did come home to her, Clive was clearly the worse for drink. He fell asleep at once and Georgina felt nothing but a sense of relief.

The next day, Clive took her home to his elegant house in Bloomsbury. All the staff were lined up in the hall, waiting to welcome their new mistress. At last, Georgina felt that her dreams were coming true. She had married well, to a man who was handsome and witty when in company. If, as yet, she'd received little warmth from him, surely that would grow in time?

Once she was settled in her new home, Georgina sent a message to her father and Aunt Prudence, assuring them that she was well and happy. But she received no response, and although she waited several days there was no communication from her family.

When, after a week, there was still no news from him, Georgina decided she would visit her father and ask him to give his blessing to her marriage. She found Clive in his study and rested her hands on his fine broad shoulders, and a feeling of pride rose within her. 'Will you come with me to see my family, Clive?'

Her husband was studying some papers, household accounts and other bills, but he looked up at her with a half smile on his lips. 'Do you really think that's wise, my dear? Shouldn't we give your father a little time to calm down?'

'Well, we have to face him some time. I'm sure he'll forgive us the minute he sees us.'

Clive rose from his chair and pushed the bills aside impatiently. 'I think you'd better go on your own, just to test the water. Once your father is used to the idea of our marriage, I'll come with you to see him, I promise.'

Georgina hid her disappointment. 'Very well, I'll go alone. Will you at least have the carriage brought round for me?'

He rang the bell and stared at his wife. 'You look very comely today, Georgina.' He took her in his arms and pulled her close. 'Your breasts are very lovely, have I ever told you that?'

'Clive!' Georgina pulled away from him. 'Such talk should be kept for the bedroom.'

He pushed her away abruptly. 'You can be such a prude! Well, go on, run back to your father. Stay with him if you like, I won't miss you.'

His petulance came as a surprise, and Georgina frowned at him. 'Clive, I really don't think you

357

mean that.'

He turned away without answering.

'Well, if you do, I might just take you at your word and stay with Papa and never come back. Think of the scandal that would cause.'

He smiled at her then. 'Of course I didn't mean it, my dear. You are my wife and I love you very much. Indeed, I'll swear on oath I couldn't go on without you.' He held her gently and kissed her mouth, and she forgave him his harsh words. 'Now go and see your father. Prepare the way, tell him I'll come to see him soon.'

As she left, Georgina was smiling. Clive was just like a little boy: threaten to take his toys away from him and he capitulated at once. Well, she was beginning to learn what it was to be a wife, and if Clive was lacking in finesse in the bedroom then that was something she must put up with. All in all, life was good, and once she'd spoken to Papa, everything in her garden would be lovely again.

\*       \*       \*

Non restocked her shelves and stood back to admire the tall, elegantly labelled bottles that contained her supply of common herbal medicines. Her little shop had blossomed; now she had a fine new table and some solid chairs where her customers could sit and talk at their leisure. Business was good, very good, and with Ruby's help she was making a fair living.

The door opened and Jessie came into the shop, her bonnet flying, her hair dishevelled. She fell against the table and tried to catch her breath, one hand to her breasts and the other supporting her small frame.

'What on earth is wrong?' Non hurried towards her. 'What's got you into this state? For heaven's sake, sit down and rest a minute.'

Jessie sank gratefully into a chair. 'It's terrible news, Non! All over the streets around Smithfield folk are falling sick, they're saying it's the cholera.'

Non felt a chill pass over her. 'I doubt that. Perhaps some more ordinary pestilence is about, some fever or the lung congestion.'

Jessie shook her head, her eyes were wide. '*Duw*, I wish it was, but one woman at the Smithfield market saw a man die of it. Blue he was, with terrible convulsions of his body. I'm frightened, Non.'

Non felt the baby leap in her womb as if mirroring her own fear. She swallowed hard, not sure what to say. The symptoms Jessie described matched what Non had read about the cholera, which was a dreadful disease and almost impossible to cure.

'Non! Non, where are you?' Flora came running down the stairs. 'What's all this crying about? What terrible thing has happened?'

Jessie turned to her. 'It's the cholera, here in London! What are we to do, Flora? I don't want to die so far away from home.'

Non took charge. 'Right, have any of you been near Smithfield in the last few days?'

'Well I haven't,' Jessie said quickly.

'Nor have I.' Flora bit her lip and put her hand on Jessie's shoulder. 'We've been too busy taking your medicines around these parts to wander far.'

'Then you must both go home to Five Saints,' Non said. 'Go and pack your belongings at once and I'll give you the fare for the mail back to Swansea.'

'You must come with us,' Jessie said, clutching Non's arm. 'Think of your baby, you can't bring him into the world where there's an awful sickness.'

'I will be needed here,' Non said firmly.

Ruby came into the room and looked around at the worried faces. 'What's wrong?'

'It's the cholera,' Jessie said. 'People are turning blue and dying within hours. It's a plague like what happened to Mr Jones's cattle, that's what it is.'

Ruby sat down abruptly on one of the chairs. 'Oh my Gawd!' She looked up at Non with frightened eyes. 'Will we get it, Non?'

Non tried to smile. 'I doubt it. We're far enough away from Smithfield, we should be all right.' But she wasn't at all sure of that. Cholera was practically unknown to her; she knew the symptoms and knew what possibly could cure them, but she had no direct experience of it herself. 'Ruby,' she said, 'I'm sending Jessie and Flora home on the next mail. You can go with them if you like.'

'No, I'll have none of that.' Ruby regained her composure and stood up, her hands planted firmly on her hips. 'London is where I was born and it will be where I die. You go, Non, go with your friends. There's no need for you to stop here.'

'I'm staying,' Non said. 'Now Jessie, Flora, get ready to leave. At once.'

In the flurry of activity that followed, Non had little time to think about the danger to herself and her child. In any case, she knew that Caradoc was in London, and what if he fell sick? To go home would be like leaving him to his fate.

It was only an hour later that Non and Ruby

360

stood waving goodbye to the girls as the mail coach left the Blackwoods Inn. Non waved until it was out of sight, wondering if she should have gone with them. But no, she was needed here in London. She had the gift of healing and she would do her level best to use it wisely.

*     *     *

Georgina walked into the hall of Aunt Prudence's house and immediately compared it to where she now lived with Clive. Clive's beautiful home was full of rich paintings and heavy furniture, and she realized how well off she was to have married him.

The maid took her coat, and then she was shown into the room where her father sat alone. He gestured for her to be seated opposite him. His face was grim and it was clear he was not in a forgiving mood.

'Well, what have you done, Georgina?' He studied her face. 'What foolish thing have you done this time?'

'I've married Clive,' Georgina said in surprise. 'It's a good marriage, Papa. I love Clive and he has a beautiful home where there are staff enough to supply all my needs.' She looked at her father imploringly. 'I know I should have waited for the big wedding, Papa, but it was so romantic to elope.'

'You are quite right, you should have waited. Then you would have known that your precious husband is a pauper.'

'What do you mean, Papa? He has beautiful things in his house and the building itself must be worth a fortune.'

'I've had him checked out, Georgina. He's in

361

debt up to his neck, the bailiffs are going to move in any day. He no doubt hoped that marriage to you would save him, but he's wrong, Georgina, I won't give the man one single penny.'

Georgina felt the blood drain from her face. 'Do you mean that I'm going to be poor?' Her voice was little more than a whisper.

'That's exactly what I mean, Georgina. Now return to your husband, there's no place here for you.'

'Papa, you can't mean it!' Tears formed in Georgina's eyes and trembled on her lashes.

But her father would not be moved. He held the door open for her and gestured for the maid to bring her outdoor clothes. 'Goodbye, Georgina,' he said, and with that he turned away and closed the door on her.

She stood there forlornly, her hopes and dreams smashed into tiny pieces. Then, with halting steps, she made her way back to the carriage that was emblazoned with Clive's monogram. Everything he'd told her was a lie: he had no fortune, would soon have no home, and with tears blurring her eyes, she realized that even his protestations of love had been nothing but a sham.

## CHAPTER THIRTY-SIX

Non stood in the hallway of the annex of St Bartholomew's hospital, her heart pounding as she tied the belt of the stiff white apron around her waist and looked at the nurse in charge. 'What is the man's name, Nurse, and why is he here instead of being taken to the main hospital where he could get proper treatment?'

'It's a gentleman, a cattle drover I believe, and he's here because it's expedient. We don't want to infect people with the scourge of cholera whilst they are already sick, now do we? This building is to be demolished once the epidemic is over, and all traces of cholera with it.'

Sister Messenger looked at Non with a practised eye. 'I'm aware that this patient is asking for you and we do need all the help we can get, but are you sure you're fit to be here, Mrs Jenkins?'

'I'm well and strong,' Non said. 'The baby isn't due for a while yet.'

'That's all well and good, but babies don't come to order, that's my experience.'

'I'll be all right. I won't be any bother to you, I promise.'

'Well then, dear, you'd better see this man at once. I'm sorry to say his condition has worsened over the last hour.'

Sister Messenger was once more the professional nurse in charge. 'He was clear headed when he was brought in and asked for you, even told us your address, but now the fever's taken hold no one can understand a word he says.'

A cold hand seemed to touch Non's heart. All Albie could say when he came running to the house was he'd heard talk that a Welshman from the drove had been taken into the fever hospital. 'What's the patient's name, Sister?'

'I don't know. As I said, no one can understand him. Run along and see him, he's in the room just along the corridor, first on the right. There are other patients too—if you can give them anything you think might help, then do so.' She sniffed. 'Not that I believe in this herbal medication myself, but as I said, we're desperate for help here.'

Non picked up her bag of medicines as though she was completely in charge of the situation, but inside she was trembling. Even though she told herself that any one of the drovers might have fallen prey to the sickness, she couldn't swallow her fear that Caradoc might be the one struck down.

The doors of the room were wide open and as she entered it was strangely quiet. Some patients were already past help: one old man lay inert, his face pinched, his skin a dusky blue. As Non walked along the row of beds, her heart was in her mouth. And then she saw him. His hair clung wetly to his brow and his eyes seemed sunken into his head.

'Morgan!' She sat beside him and took his hand. He opened his eyes for a brief moment, but then he drifted away again into unconsciousness. She was ashamed of her sudden feeling of relief that it was Morgan, not Caradoc, who was sick.

Non dipped into her bag and took out a syrup she'd made of angelica roots. Gently, she fed the liquid into Morgan's mouth, then smoothed his throat with a delicate touch, encouraging him to swallow.

He was burning up, his lips tinged with blue. Non found the large unused kitchen and brought a bowl of water from the stand outside. Carefully, she bathed the dry skin of Morgan's face, holding him close when his body contorted with sudden cramps.

'Non,' he opened his eyes, '*cariad*, go home. You can't do anything to help me now.' Non felt tears spring to her eyes. He was calling her his love, his sweetheart, and even now, sick as he was, he was thinking of her safety.

A young girl came into the room, wrapped in a large white apron that rustled with starch as she walked around the beds. She bent over a patient to whisper words of comfort and then glanced at Non, watching as she administered more medication to Morgan. After a moment the girl came over to her.

'What are you giving our patient?' she asked in a subdued voice. 'I thought there was nothing that could help cure the cholera but bed rest and God's good will.'

'I'm a herbalist,' Non said. 'I make up medicines from herbs following Mr Culpeper's recipes.'

'Will you be able to save him?' She nodded to where Morgan was lying. 'I thought all the men in here were not long for this world.'

'I don't know if I can help at all,' Non said. 'I've never treated anyone with cholera before. I've never even seen a case, but Mr Culpeper recommends certain roots and flowers, and all I can do is try them.'

The nurse held out her hand. 'I'm Sarah. I commend you for being so brave and so determined to help, especially in your condition. Tell me what to do and I'll administer the medication to the rest of the men.'

Non smiled for the first time since she'd entered the 'house of death', as the townsfolk now called it. She took a large bottle from her bag. 'Look, there's quite a lot of infused angelica leaves and flowers here. Use it at your discretion. Apart from that, just do your best to keep the men cool. Oh, and Sarah,' she indicated that the nurse lean closer, 'only help those who are not too far gone, understand?'

The next hour passed with dreadful slowness and Morgan's condition did not seem to improve. Non stretched her aching back. It was hot in the annex and the smell of sickness dominated the room. She felt Morgan's forehead: he was still consumed with fever.

She stepped outside, desperate for a breath of air. A small group of people were standing round the doorway; Non guessed they were the families of the patients inside.

'Are you a nurse? Can you tell us what's happening in there?' A woman touched her arm. 'It's my son, he's sick, with terrible cramps in his belly. Nothing I could do to ease it.'

'Where do you live?' Non asked. 'I'm wondering if the sickness is confined to one area.'

'No, I don't think so. There's a father over there brought his daughter in this morning, he lives about two miles away from me. What good will it do you to know where we live?'

Non sighed. 'I thought the sickness might be contagious, but in light of what you say, I don't think that's the case.' She talked with the father of the sick girl and then with a few of the other relatives, and at last she found what linked them: they had all used the same source of drinking water.

She excused herself and hurried back indoors. Sister Messenger was crossing the hall and Non stopped her. 'I think the water supply is the source of contamination,' she said. 'All the people outside have used the same standpipe.'

'Don't talk nonsense, girl!' Sister Messenger said crossly. 'Everyone knows the sickness is airborne.

It's carried by rotting vegetables and other unmentionable effluents. Now, if you'll excuse me, I've patients to see.'

Non returned to Morgan's bedside. He was still feverish, and Non kept herself busy bathing his face and body, and administering the medication to him whenever she could force a drop through his parched lips.

She closed her eyes for a moment, feeling unutterably weary. She felt she could sleep for a week. Then she heard footsteps approaching, and was alert at once. Sister Messenger was standing before her, a stern expression on her face.

'This is most irregular,' she said, waving what looked like a letter. 'A woman named Ruby Simkins is outside, asking for you. She handed me this letter and it seems you've been summoned, yes *summoned* to care for a rich gentleman, who at least had the good sense to fall sick in his own well-equipped home.'

'But I can't leave Morgan,' Non said quickly. 'I think we're getting the better of the fever, his colour has improved a little.'

Sister Messenger stepped towards the bed and put the back of her hand against Morgan's brow. 'Yes,' she said almost reluctantly, 'he does seem a mite cooler.' She straightened up, folding her hands across her starched apron. 'Nevertheless you should go to . . .' she consulted the letter, 'here's the address. The patient has a very strange name—Caradoc Jones—does that ring a bell with you?'

Non took a deep breath. She looked from Morgan to the Sister and nodded her head. Tears rolled down her cheeks, and Sister Messenger backed away as though horrified at such a show of

367

emotion.

The young nurse came to her side and put an arm around Non's shoulders. 'There, there,' Sarah said. 'Don't fret now. If you have to go, I'll look after your friend for you.'

'Oh, Sarah, what am I to do?' She put her hands over her eyes, knowing she was faced with an impossible task. How could she choose between her dear old friend Morgan and Caradoc, the man she loved?

\*　　　\*　　　\*

Georgina stood in the elegant drawing room, looking up at her husband with a feeling of sheer panic. 'The cholera is here in London?' She could hardly speak the words. 'Are we all going to die?'

'Not me,' Clive said, 'I'm getting out of here. I'll stay somewhere in the country, anywhere away from here.'

'And what about me?'

'Well, do what you like. Go home to your little village, you'll be safe there.'

'But you—our marriage—I thought you loved me.'

He came to her and put his hands on her shoulders. 'I am fond of you in my way, but you have no money. You see, I need a woman with money if I'm to keep up this lifestyle.' He waved his hand in a gesture that encompassed all the luxuries of his elegant home, and Georgina felt as though a giant hand was squeezing her heart.

'You're just *fond* of me? Oh, Clive, how cruel you are! I thought you were the husband I've always wanted, and yet you would desert me like

368

this. How could you?'

'Now don't turn on the waterworks. I can't stand it when a woman cries, such shows of emotion are not at all endearing.'

Georgina followed him as he ordered his man to pack his boxes; she still couldn't believe he meant to leave her behind. 'Shall I get one of the maids to pack some clothes for me, Clive?'

He sighed. 'Do as you please, go home or go back to your father's house, go anywhere, but just leave me alone.' He turned to stare at her, and for the first time she noticed the cruel twist to his lips. 'Just stop bothering me, Georgina.'

'But Clive . . .'

'But nothing! How on earth did I believe, even for a moment, that I could live with you? All you've done is nag and criticize.'

Georgina put her hand to her lips. 'When have I ever nagged or criticized you, Clive?' Her voice was small, pleading, and she hated the weakness that made her want to beg him to take her away with him.

'If you want particulars, think of our wedding night, when you lay still like a lifeless doll,' he shrugged, 'when all I did was try to please you.'

'But you were rough with me, Clive. I wasn't used to the ways a wife should behave, but I'll do better in the future, you'll see.'

Clive took no notice of her. He ordered his man to carry the boxes downstairs and then he left the house. He turned once before climbing into the coach. 'Forget what I said about going back to your father's house.'

'Why?' Georgina asked, hopeful even now that he would take her with him.

'I've heard that cholera has struck in that area, so if I were you I'd get the mail back to Swansea as soon as you can.'

He closed the door of the coach and leaned back in his seat so that Georgina could no longer see his face. And then the horses were whipped into motion and the carriage rolled away, taking all Georgina's hopes and dreams with it.

\*     \*     \*

Non sat beside Morgan, willing him to recover from the sickness that was tearing him apart. Although he'd rallied for a short while, his condition had suddenly taken a turn for the worse and he lay against his pillows so quietly that Non could scarcely hear him breathing.

'Aren't you going along to see to this Mr Jones?' Sister Messenger appeared beside her and looked at Non with a stern face. 'You can leave the care of this young man to me and my staff. We are used to looking after the sick, after all.'

'How can I leave him?' Non's voice was little more than a whisper. 'He's my dear friend.'

'Well, he's not your husband, is he? No one asked you to come here, and what's more, I don't believe you're even married. Perhaps in the circumstances you would be better off working in a private residence, out of sight.' She stalked away, her chin high.

Non looked round at the walls, windows and doors, anywhere but at Morgan's tortured face. She longed with all her heart to go to Caradoc, but how could she leave Morgan?

Sarah came to the bedside. 'I can see you want

370

to go. Look, I'll take special care of your friend, don't worry about him. I'll keep treating him the way you have, I promise.'

Non gathered up her belongings. 'Thank you, Sarah, you don't know what this means to me.'

She looked back at Morgan and he opened his eyes. 'I'm going to be all right,' he said in a hoarse whisper. 'The worst is over now, thanks to you.'

Non hoped he was right, but as she left she couldn't help feeling that she'd betrayed her best friend.

## CHAPTER THIRTY-SEVEN

The hallway was elegant, the rich carpet glowing in the light from many lamps. Non stood near the front door, waiting nervously for George Jones to appear. He had practically demanded that she come to the house, and yet now he was leaving her standing around like a beggar.

At last, George Jones came down the stairs towards her. He looked pale, his strong features lined with worry. His eyes met hers, and then he had the grace to look away.

'My son, you must save him—he's caught the cholera from somewhere. I warned him not to go visiting the poorer quarters of the town, where you live.'

Non ignored the barbed words. 'I'll go to him at once. Which room is he in?' It was pointless trying to explain to George Jones that cholera was not contagious but was the result of drinking bad water. He, along with the rest of the world, would

371

not trust the beliefs of a mere herbalist, and a woman to boot.

'At the top of the stairs, the bedroom to the right of the landing.' He stood aside and watched her as she climbed the stairs. She felt antagonism emanating from him and knew she was only here as a last resort.

Caradoc was quiet, his skin pale but dry, and with no tinge of dusky blue. Non opened the window to let in fresh air: the room was too hot for a man with a fever. She sat beside the bed to open her bag and selected a full bottle of angelica. She saw a bell pull and rang the bell for the maid.

'Bring me a spoon,' she said. 'And tell me, where do you draw your water?'

'We have a pump at the back, Miss,' the maid said, her eyebrows lifting in surprise.

'Good. Fill up the china bowl with water, cold water. Quickly!' she added, as the maid hesitated.

'Do I understand you're giving my servants orders, Miss?' An elegant woman stood just outside the door, hovering as if afraid to come inside. 'Who are you and what are you doing here?'

Non guessed at once that this formidable-looking woman was Caradoc's Aunt Prudence. She was frowning heavily, and yet her pale eyes were anxious as they rested on her nephew.

'Mr George Jones sent for me,' Non said quietly. 'I'm trying to help Caradoc. I have some herbal medication here, I'm hoping it will cure him. Didn't you know I was coming?'

'No, I did not! And in future I should like to be consulted on these matters.'

'Well, you'll have to talk to Mr Jones about that. Now if you'll excuse me, I have work to do.'

The maid came back to the room and, with a worried glance at Aunt Prudence, placed the bowl of water beside the bed. 'Here's the spoon, Miss,' she whispered. 'I didn't know what size you wanted, so I brought a teaspoon.'

'That will do nicely.' Non carefully measured out the syrup and held the spoon to Caradoc's mouth. She fed him the medication a little at a time and saw, with a sense of relief, that he swallowed it easily, which she took as an encouraging sign. She bathed his face and neck and the hot skin of his arms, and he seemed to stir a little.

'Is he going to be all right?' Prudence asked from the doorway.

Non had forgotten the woman was there; she glanced over her shoulder. 'It's safe to come in,' she said. 'I don't believe the cholera is a contagious disease, but carried through bad water.' She shook her head. 'Unfortunately, no one else appears to think the same.'

'But you, have you been in contact with the cholera yourself?'

Non fought against the constriction that tightened her throat. 'I have just spent several hours at the annex to St Bartholomew's hospital, nursing a dear friend of mine. I've left him to come here.' She eased her cramped position, rubbing at the small of her back as she became aware that she was aching.

Prudence stepped back into the shadows of the corridor. 'I don't know what George is thinking, bringing you here like this. You could be carrying the disease with you.'

Non sighed; it was impossible to get through to people that the disease was not carried from one

373

person to another. If it were, all the nurses at St Bartholomew's annex would be sick themselves, as well as the relatives she'd seen waiting outside for news of their loved ones.

Prudence disappeared along the corridor, leaving Non free to give all her attention to Caradoc. He was so handsome even now that her heart ached for him. She sent up a prayer for the return of his good health. Then she held his hand, talking to him softly. 'You must get well,' she whispered. 'Our baby needs you, I need you.' He didn't stir, and after a while she gave him more of the angelica syrup. She really didn't know if it would do any good; all she could do was try her best to cure him.

At last, he seemed to relax and the lines of pain that had etched his mouth faded, leaving his lips a healthy colour: lips that had kissed hers with achingly sweet passion.

At last, exhausted, Non sat back in her chair. She must have dozed for a moment, because she was suddenly aware of fingers curling round hers. She opened her eyes and saw that Caradoc was awake. He looked up at her and then raised her hand to his lips. He was much cooler now, and Non bent to kiss his forehead. 'Are you better, my darling?' she asked in a low voice. His eyelids fluttered for a moment, his mouth twitched into a smile, and then he was asleep again.

Non sat with him until dawn spread a rosy light across the room, snatching moments of sleep, although she woke to every movement Caradoc made. Feeling the pale morning sun on her face, she bent forward and placed her hand against his cheek. Her heart leapt with joy; his skin was cool—

the fever had gone.

He opened his eyes and his mouth curled into a smile. 'My little guardian angel,' he said softly. 'Don't leave me, Non. Promise you won't leave me.'

'I promise I won't leave you.' Her heart was filled with gladness. He was alive, and, though weak, he would recover his strength, given a few days' bed rest. She smiled down at him, but already he was asleep again: not a fever-induced sleep but sound, healing rest.

She got up quietly and went to the door. She must tell George Jones that his son was going to recover.

He was standing in the spacious hallway, and looked up when he saw her. She softened towards him as she saw the tension in his face.

'He's all right,' she said quickly. 'Caradoc is going to live.'

'Thank God!' George Jones said, watching her as she came towards him.

As she reached the bottom step, Non felt a searing pain across her back. She cried out and held out her hand.

'What is it?' he asked abruptly. 'What's wrong with you?'

'The baby!' she gasped. 'The baby is coming—it's too early.'

George Jones took charge at once. He ordered two of the servants to take Non upstairs to one of the guest bedrooms, and sent a footman for a doctor. 'Hurry!' he commanded. 'And don't come back without him. Tell him I'll pay double the fee.'

Everything was happening in a haze of pain. Non had known that childbirth was going to be difficult, but she could never have imagined the harshness of the contractions as her child battled to come into the world.

As Non drew breath between the pains, she heard Prudence Jones talking outside the room.

'You mean to allow a bastard child to be born in my house? How dare you take such liberties, George?'

He answered in a low voice, and Non, engulfed by another contraction, didn't hear his reply. She had a preparation of columbine seeds in her bag, but she didn't know where her things had been taken. She tried to raise herself up in the bed, but the pain was swamping her, sapping her will.

Some time later, she felt hands touching her swollen stomach. She forced her eyes open and saw an elderly man with grey hair sprouting from his ears bending over her. 'Not long now, my girl,' he said. 'I've examined you and you are almost fully dilated.' He smiled. 'Now don't frown at me. I'm old enough to be your grandfather, but I'm used to childbirth, unlike these modern young doctors who leave it all to the midwives.'

Non felt reassured. The doctor was thorough but gentle, he had a kindly smile and his hands were sure as he felt her belly. 'Head's well down, that's a good sign, me dear. Won't be long now, the pain will soon be over and you'll give birth to the most handsome child in the world.' He smiled. 'But then every child that's born is handsome to its mother.'

Non felt a contraction begin at her back and travel round to her stomach. She bit her lip, trying not to scream.

'Bear down, child, bear down,' the doctor encouraged. 'Come along, the head is almost here, just push a little bit harder—there, that's it!'

The baby was born, and Non fell back against the pillows, exhausted. She turned her head with an effort and looked at the baby cradled in the doctor's arms.

'It's a boy. He's small, but he's a healthy little boy. Here, hold him.'

'Let the nurse see to the boy.' George Jones came into the room and Non looked at him in terror.

'Don't take my baby from me! Please don't take my baby!' She began to cry weak tears, that ran unchecked down her cheeks. A nurse in crisp white uniform took the baby and Non could hear the sound of water and the angry cries of her child.

'Doctor, what's happening to my son?' Non lifted her head from the pillow. 'Is he all right?'

'He's fine and dandy, me dear, he's having his first wash, that's all. Now you just rest and recover your strength, that's my advice.' He turned to George Jones. 'Have someone bring her a dish of beef broth later on; that will help her feel stronger.'

The doctor was ushered from the room and Non closed her eyes, too weary to work out what she was going to do next.

The nurse came to the bedside and smiled down at her. 'The first one is always the hardest,' she said. 'Let me just clean you up and then you can sleep all you want. I'll take good care of your son, I promise you.'

Non knew she should thank George Jones for all he'd done, bringing in a doctor and a nurse to care for her. She would thank him later, but for now she was too tired to do anything but sleep.

# CHAPTER THIRTY-EIGHT

Ruby stood back and admired her handywork. She'd made one of the rooms into a nursery, with pretty print curtains at the windows and the same design for the bedcovers. Albie and his grandpa had worked on the furniture, scrubbing and painting until the place shone. The room was at the far end of the house, away from the smell of the river, and looked pleasant now with the morning sun creeping through the blinds. Ruby was determined that Non Jenkins and the baby when he was born would have every comfort. She'd managed to borrow a crib from one of the neighbours, and had made a little quilt and a pillowcase. Sewing, she found, helped to pass the long hours of waiting. She was surprised how much she missed Non's company, and though she wasn't the maternal type, she'd welcome the child for his mother's sake.

She went downstairs to the kitchen and sat in her favourite chair. The room smelled of stew, good lamb stew that would build up Non's strength. She would need it if she was going to work at her herbs and be a mother.

Non had been hailed as a heroine. The news had quickly spread among her customers that she'd saved the life of Caradoc Jones, son of the rich cattle drover from Wales. People were praising her to the skies, saying she knew better than the doctors.

Ruby took the stew off the fire and put it on the hob to keep warm. She was smiling with happiness because she was hoping to bring Non home today. The gossips said that Caradoc Jones was well on the mend, but Ruby had heard nothing from the Jones family direct. But she was going to look after Non herself, whatever plans the Joneses might have.

When all her preparations were made, she borrowed a horse and trap from John Freeman, who owned the stables at the end of the road, and set off towards Bloomsbury. The roads were quiet in the light of early morning; a lone milk cart rumbled past her but none of the street traders were about, so Ruby crossed London at a fair pace. Slowing the horse, she stopped outside a grand-looking house with stone pillars outside the door.

'Whoa, boy.' She dismounted, tying the reins of the horse to a post. With her heart in her mouth, she went round the back of the house and knocked on the door.

At first, the kitchen maid tried to turn her away. 'We don't want itinerants around here. You run along now or you'll have Mrs Finsbury after you.'

'I've come to see Non Jenkins,' Ruby insisted. 'If I don't see her I'll make such a row that your neighbours will all complain. I'm not going and that's that.'

The maid hesitated, and seizing her chance Ruby pushed past her and found her way into the large warm kitchen. 'All I wants is to find out if Non Jenkins is all right. I'm not out to cause a fuss, but I will if no one talks to me.' She sat on a chair and planted her feet firmly on the flags. 'No one will bleeding shift me, so there!'

Cook tried to coax her to leave, the footman suggested she'd be best off sending a letter, and still Ruby was unmoved by their efforts. At last, a sniff-nosed housekeeper beckoned her out into the corridor.

'I don't know who you are or what you want, but if you're asking after Mr Caradoc Jones he is almost well again, so do not concern yourself on that score.'

'I'm not,' Ruby said bluntly. 'I'm "concerned" for Non Jenkins. I know she's due to have her baby and I won't leave until I've seen her for myself.'

The woman glanced uneasily over her shoulder. Quite clearly she had no intention of letting the other servants know what was going on. 'She's had the baby. It's a boy, and mother and child are doing well. Now go away at once or I'll set the dogs on you.'

'Well that settles it. If she's had the baby I'm not shiftin', not until I've seen her for myself.' Ruby folded her arms and out-stared Mrs Finsbury, who backed away from her.

'I'll see what I can do,' she said, and Ruby was content. She was going to see for herself if Non was ready to come home with her or not.

\*       \*       \*

Non was sitting in the coolness of the drawing room, suckling her son. With the morning light shining on his hair, he looked achingly like his father. There had been some sort of commotion below stairs, and the nurse who was always in attendance had gone away for a moment. Non was glad of the peace; she was rarely alone with her son.

She looked up, startled, as the front doorbell

rang, breaking the stillness of the day. Then there were voices and a woman dressed in a smart coat and a feathered hat came into the room. Non recognized her at once, even though she was not in uniform.

'Sister Messenger! What are you doing here?'

'Well, first I think I should congratulate you on the birth of your son. I told you babies arrive whenever they've a mind to, didn't I?' She didn't wait for a reply. 'I've come to ask you for your notes on the medication you used, if you can spare them. It worked on your friend Morgan—he's well on the road to recovery now.' She paused for breath. 'Fortunately, I had kept the note Mr Jones sent summoning you to care for his son, so I knew exactly where to find you.'

'I'm so glad about Morgan,' Non said softly. 'I felt so guilty leaving him like that.'

'You did your best for him before you left, so don't feel guilty, my dear.' Sister Messenger clasped her gloved hands together. 'Everyone is talking about your cures, you know. You won't be able to handle all the business that will come your way after this.' She smiled a frosty smile, but nevertheless her eyes were sparkling. 'I think you were right all along about the cholera being spread by bad water. I've observed that the victims were indeed drinking from the same source.' She rested her hand on Non's shoulder. 'If only the doctors would listen to me, we could all work for proper sanitation. Cholera and many other sicknesses would be a thing of the past.'

George Jones came into the room and nodded to the Sister. 'Has your business been concluded?' he asked bluntly.

'Ah, yes, business.' She looked down at Non. 'I can see you have your hands full, but if you could give me your recipes I can have them made up at the hospital.'

'They are upstairs with my things,' Non said.

George stepped forward at once. 'Give the child to me.'

'But I'm still feeding him,' Non protested.

'I've employed a wet nurse for him,' George Jones said easily, 'so that you can get your strength back all the sooner.'

Non was outraged at his high-handedness, but she had no intention of arguing with him in front of Sister Messenger. She hurried upstairs, and on her way across the landing glanced at the closed door of Caradoc's room. Since he'd recovered, she'd not been allowed to see him. Perhaps, she thought gloomily, he did not want to see her. She fetched the papers from her bag: she'd passed the time while she sat with Morgan carefully copying out the remedies. Sarah had requested them, and Non couldn't part with her Culpeper's herbal, even to help Sarah.

Sister Messenger was delighted when Non handed her the sheaf of papers. 'Thank you so much, Mrs Jenkins. I know we can't save all the sufferers, but with a little help from you some might overcome this dreadful sickness.'

George Jones hovered, looking pointedly at her, and at last she took a deep breath and held out her hand. 'I'd better be off, then. Thank you for all you've done. I'm so proud that your gift for healing is being recognized, at least by the patients, if not the doctors.'

When she had gone, George Jones moved closer

382

to Non and stared down at her as though she was a stranger, not the mother of his grandson. 'You are keeping my staff busy this morning,' he said, and there was an iciness in his tone that set Non's teeth on edge. 'A friend has come for you, a Mrs Ruby something or other.'

Non felt her heart lift with pleasure. Ruby was here—she would have come in a horse and trap—she must have known Non wanted to go home. She thought briefly of the closed door of Caradoc's room. Well, if he didn't want to see her or his child, then the sooner she left the better.

'Your few belongings have been packed in readiness,' George said. 'Your presence has been a trial to my sister Prudence, she keeps a respectable house.' He half smiled. 'And as you've no doubt observed, Caradoc wants nothing to do with you.'

'I'm ready to leave at once, Mr Jones,' Non said stiffly. 'I suppose I should thank you for taking care of me and my son up until now, but I'm quite capable of looking after him.'

'You are not taking the boy.'

The words hit her in the face like hard stones. 'What do you mean? Of course I'm taking my son!' She stood and faced George Jones, but he waved his hand as though dismissing her.

'What can you offer him?' he asked. 'You scratch a living at the side of a stinking river, selling your herbal rubbish to the gullible public. That's no way for the boy to be brought up.'

'I help a great many people, Mr Jones,' Non replied defensively. 'And in any case, it's nothing to do with you how I make a living.'

'Not even the doctors recognize your so-called medicines, Miss Jenkins. Look,' he said more quietly, 'don't be so selfish. You can give the boy nothing. I, on the other hand, can give him all his heart desires, excellent schooling, good clothes to wear and the heartiest food to put in his belly. He'll have the best of everything. Once Caradoc is fully recovered, he'll tell you that himself.'

'But he's my son,' Non said. 'I won't give him up.'

'Here, let me help you with your coat.' George Jones guided her firmly into the hallway and the maid held her coat for her.

'I've told you,' Non said weakly, 'I won't go without my son.'

He ignored her and pushed her through the open front door. 'Your friend is outside with a pony and trap. You just go with her and think about what I said. The boy can have a life of luxury with me or a life of poverty with you.'

The door was slammed behind her and Non stood on the step, not knowing what to do.

'Non!' Ruby climbed down from the cart. 'What is it, my chick? Why, you're as white as a ghost! One of the servants said you'd had your baby. Where is he?'

Non felt tears tremble on her lashes. 'They've taken him from me,' she said. 'I don't know what to do, Ruby. Perhaps he is better off with the Joneses. I know he'll never go short of anything while he's with them.'

'Come on,' Ruby took her arm. 'Let's get back home and have a cup of tea, and then you can think this thing through properly.'

Listlessly, Non climbed into the trap and sat looking at the house where her son had been born. It was an elegant building, warmed by the sun into a mellow brightness. Perhaps she was selfish to want to keep her son, when she could give him nothing but hardship. And yet even as she thought about leaving him behind, the milk flowed into her breasts and her body ached for him.

*     *     *

Caradoc sat up in bed, blinking against the light flooding in through the window. There had been a great deal of activity downstairs, a lot of banging of doors and loud voices. Once Caradoc thought he'd heard Non's voice, and he longed for her to come to see him.

She'd nursed him back to health. According to Father, she'd left Morgan's side to be with him, and yet now that he was getting stronger she seemed to be avoiding him. He looked towards the door as his father came into the room.

'How are you feeling, Caradoc? By the look of it you'll be fit enough to get up for a while today.'

'That will be pleasant.' Caradoc almost laughed at his own understatement. Once he was out of bed he could talk to Non, see for himself if she was well. He had not seen his son yet: Father had thought it best to wait until they were sure there was no sign of the cholera returning, and Caradoc had agreed with him. Still, now he was recovered he'd be able to hold his son in his arms and see for himself the likeness everyone said there was between them.

'Will you send Non to me, Father?' Caradoc asked. 'I haven't seen her for several days.'

His father walked over to the window. 'She's gone,' he said flatly.

385

'What do you mean, "gone"? Where has she gone? I need to see her to speak to her about . . . well, about a lot of things.'

'She left quite happily this morning with her friend Ruby.' George spun round. 'But don't worry, the boy is still here with us. We'll take care of him from now on.'

Caradoc pushed aside the bedclothes and rang for his man to attend him.

His father frowned and shook his head in disapproval. 'What are you doing, Caradoc? There's no need for you to get dressed, no need at all.'

Caradoc faced his father, trying to control his anger. 'You seem to forget that we owe Non everything. I wouldn't be alive if she hadn't nursed me. There is no way Non would willingly leave her child behind. You've forced her to leave, Father. You never would accept that I cared about her.' He paused, but his father seemed to have nothing to say. 'Have you sunk so low, Father? What's become of our family? You've cast Georgina aside, left her to face ruin alone, and now you're trying to run my life. I don't know how you can live with yourself.'

'The girl has no money,' George Jones protested. 'What could she give the boy?'

'It's a strange little thing called love, Father, but you wouldn't know anything about that, would you?'

'The girl left quietly, she must have thought I'd made the right decision.'

'Well, I'm going to find her,' Caradoc said in a hard voice, 'and there's nothing you can do to stop me.'

Non had spent a sleepless night. Her arms were empty and her heart seemed empty too. She rose early and sat in Ruby's kitchen, staring into the fire. Her arms seemed to ache with emptiness, her heart was breaking and yet the tears would not fall. She could still see George Jones's face as he told her she was no good for her son, she could hear the sharpness in his voice and feel his hands pushing her away. And Caradoc had never even seen his son: that just showed how little he cared.

There was a tap on the door and Ruby looked at Non. 'If it's a customer, I'll tell them to come back tomorrow, shall I?'

Non felt so tired, so very tired. 'Non!' Ruby called. 'It's not a customer, it's your friend Morgan.'

Non was on her feet at once as Morgan came into the room. He looked thinner and his face was pale, but he was smiling.

'Non! I've come to thank you for caring for me while I was ill.' He took her hands in his and kissed them. 'Without you I wouldn't be alive, I'm sure of that.'

'I only did my best for you, Morgan, but I'm so glad to see you.' She sat down abruptly in her chair.

Morgan looked down at her in concern. 'But you're not well yourself, tell me what's been happening.'

'I've given birth to a beautiful son,' her voice broke, 'the Joneses have taken him from me.' She swallowed her tears. 'Perhaps he will be better off with them but I ache for him, Morgan.'

'He should be with his mother,' Morgan said.

'Caradoc has no right to keep your son from you. Where's your fighting spirit gone? Come on, get your coat, I'll come with you to fetch the boy home.'

Suddenly Non's heart was filled with hope. 'Thank you, Morgan.' She looked up as Ruby came into the kitchen. 'Do you think you can borrow a horse and cart again?'

Ruby nodded. 'I dare say I could.'

'Well, as Morgan's pointed out, I've been weak. How could I leave my son to grow up with such a selfish family? I'm going to get him back, Ruby. I've got a clear head now and I know my son should be with me.'

'Good for you, girl!' Ruby said. 'I thought you'd get your dander up once you felt better. I'll run down the street right away.'

Non took Morgan's hand. 'You've always been a good friend and I can never repay you for standing by me now.'

'I'm the one who owes a debt of gratitude. I wouldn't be here today if it wasn't for you and your cures.'

A few minutes later, Albie came into the room. 'Ruby's outside with the horse and cart,' he said. 'Are you going to be all right, Non?'

'I'm going to be just fine. Go and tell your grandpa to make up the fires, keep the place warm for our new baby.'

Albie bent down to kiss her cheek. 'That's the spirit! I knew you wouldn't let them Joneses beat you.'

As Morgan helped Non into the seat, she felt exhilarated. Ruby stood in the road and gazed up at her. 'You're doing the right thing, girl,' she said.

'Me and Albie and Grandpa will be waiting here to welcome you home.'

Non felt alive for the first time since she'd given birth to her baby. She was going to get him back, and while she was at it tell George Jones a few home truths.

The shabby streets soon gave way to the spacious squares and gardens of Bloomsbury, and Non felt her heart flutter with fear. George Jones had money and power; she had only her love for her child. Would it be enough?

'Don't you go creeping round the back, now,' Morgan said. 'Look, I'll come with you. We'll march right up to the front door and push our way in if we got to.'

Non nodded, too nervous to speak. She let Morgan help her down from the trap and then followed him up to the large entrance to the imposing house.

A manservant opened the door and looked down at them with his mouth open, but Morgan was not about to observe the niceties. He pushed past him into the grand hallway. 'Mr Jones!' he called. 'Mr Jones, come out here, see if your bullying ways will work with me!'

All at once, the hall seemed full of people. Prudence Jones was fanning her face with her hand and George Jones came out of the drawing room with the baby in his arms. Some of the servants appeared and stared open-mouthed at Non.

'I've come to take my son home,' she said quietly, 'and if you refuse me I'll stand on your doorstep and scream until your precious neighbours complain.'

'There will be no need for that.' Non spun round

as Caradoc came into the hall and stood at her side. 'I went to your house last night to find you, but Albie's grandfather told me you weren't there. I thought you'd had enough of me and my family and gone back to Swansea.'

'Well I've not and I want my baby,' Non said. 'You're not taking him away from me.'

'I've no intention of taking him away from you, Non.' Caradoc turned to his father. 'Give me my son,' he said in a hard voice.

Reluctantly, George gave him the baby, and Non saw Caradoc's expression soften as he looked into the face of his son.

'He's so tiny,' Caradoc moved closer to Non, 'and so very perfect.'

Non was dimly aware that people were moving away; the servants returned to their duties and Prudence went into the drawing room, still fanning her face with her hand. Morgan took a step towards Non, but Caradoc waved him away. 'You've no need to worry about Non or the baby,' he said. 'I'll be looking after them from now on.'

'If that's what Non wants then it's all right by me,' Morgan said. 'Is it, Non?'

She nodded, looking from Caradoc to his father, knowing somehow that this moment was going to be a turning point in her life. 'Go home, Morgan, and take my feelings of deep friendship with you.'

Morgan hesitated a moment, and then quietly let himself out of the door.

'I love you, Non.' Caradoc put his arm around her shoulders. 'I've loved you ever since I met you and I allowed silly pride to spoil things between us. But when I was at death's door I realized what was important to me—not money or property or being the leader of the cattle drove. Without you, Non, none of it was worth a light.'

His arm tightened around her shoulder. Non looked up at him and, seeing the light of love in his eyes, felt a lump rise to her throat. She knew he loved her, he'd always told her so, but what about marriage, had he changed his mind?

He brushed her cheek with his lips. 'I know you've got your medicines to make, a career to forge, and I would never stop you from doing what's important.'

She tried to speak but he pressed his mouth against hers, silencing her words.

'You needn't say anything. I know you won't desert your friends: Ruby, Albie and the old man, they all depend on you. We'll stay in London if you like, or if you decide to go home to Swansea, Ruby can run the shop for you. We can always come and visit, as many times as you like.'

Non looked up into his eyes. 'What are you offering me, Caradoc? Speak plainly.'

'I'm asking you to marry me, you silly girl.' He put his arms around her with their baby cradled between them. 'We'll get married in Swansea, have a really grand affair, let everyone we know come to the celebrations, how about that?'

Non felt tears run down her cheeks; she was too full of love to think of an answer. After a moment, Caradoc led her towards the door.

'No, son, don't go like this.' George Jones stepped forward. 'I've been hard and thoughtless. I've tried to railroad you all—Georgie; you, Caradoc; and most of all, Miss Jenkins—just to get my own way.' He held out his hand to Non. 'Can you ever forgive my cavalier treatment of you?'

Non hesitated. Could George Jones ever change? For Caradoc's sake, she must give him the benefit of the doubt. 'Well, Mr Jones, my son is going to need a grandfather, isn't he?'

'In that case, you'd better stay here until proper arrangements are made for your journey home.' His voice was thick with tears. He clasped her hand tightly. 'You're a daughter-in-law any man would be proud of.'

'Go along, settle Aunt Prudence down before she has an apoplexy,' Caradoc said, 'and stop being so ruddy sentimental.'

And then they were alone in the hall. Non looked up at Caradoc over the silky crown of her baby's hair. 'I want to call him Rowan,' she said softly, tears in her eyes.

'Rowan is a fine name,' Caradoc said, 'and I pray our son will be as sturdy as the tree he's named after.'

Non kissed the top of the baby's head and sighed. 'I know we have plans to make for the future, but for now I want to take my baby home. Ruby will look after me until we've decided what we're going to do.'

Outside, an unexpected sun was shining, so Non didn't immediately see the crowd of people standing in the street. A great cheer went up and Non bit her lip as she recognized some of her customers.

'You're an angel, Non Jenkins!' a voice called out. She looked across the crowd and saw Albie standing on a railing, waving wildly at her.

'Looks like I'll be the one taking a back seat in this marriage,' Caradoc said in delight. 'Are you sure you want to marry a mere cattle drover?'

'I've never been more sure of anything in my life.'

He bent forward and kissed her lips in full view of all the onlookers, and to Non it was as though he'd reached into the sky and handed her the sun, the moon and all the stars.